MW00533820

ROYAL ELITE BOOK ONE

DEVIANT KING

ROYAL ELITE

SCHOOL

RINA KENT

To all the fighters,
It's easy to lie down, but it takes courage to step up and fight.

AUTHOR NOTE

Hello reader friend,

If you haven't read my books before, you might not know this, but I write darker stories that can be upsetting and disturbing. My books and main characters aren't for the faint of heart.

Deviant King is a dark high school bully romance, mature new adult, and contains dubious situations that some readers might find offensive.
If you're looking for a hero, Aiden is NOT it. If you, however, have been itching for a villain, then by all means, welcome to Aiden King's world

To remain true to the characters, the vocabulary, grammar, and spelling of Deviant King is written in British English.

This book is part of a trilogy and is NOT standalone.

Don't forget to Sign up to Rina Kent's Newsletter for news about future releases and an exclusive gift.

The villain isn't supposed to be king.

I have a simple plan.

Finish Royal Elite School and get into my dream university.

One glance from the school's king blows my plan up in smoke.

One glance and he suffocates my air.

One glance and he issues his death sentence.

His first words spiral my life into irreparable chaos.

"I will destroy you."

Everything about Aiden King is black.

Black mind.

Black heart.

Black soul.

I should've remained quiet and endured the time I had left.

I didn't.

I made the irrevocable mistake of provoking the king on his throne.

The devil in his hell.

And now, I'll pay the price.

Being hated by Aiden King is dangerous.

But being wanted by him is lethal.

PLAYLIST

Grip—Bastille & Seeb

Hipnotised—Coldplay

Shiver—Coldplay

Power—Bastille

Avalanche—Cemetery Sun

Destroy Yourself—Dangerkids

Dangerous Night—Thirty Seconds to Mars

Fire—The Faim

Beautiful Drama—The Faim

State of Mind—The Faim

Collide—Normandie

Moth—Normandie

Believe—Normandie

Lethargy—Bastille

Doom Days—Bastille

Good Grief—Bastille

Bury Me Low—8 Graves

RIP—8 Graves

A Rush of Blood to the Head—Coldplay

Warning Sign—Coldplay

Swallowed in the Sea—Coldplay

Square One—Coldplay

42—Coldplay

You can find the playlist on Spotify.

ROYAL ELITE BOOK ONE

DEVIANT KING

ONE

They say it doesn't take long for your life to be flipped upside down.

A moment.

A second.

And it's all over.

I should've known. If I had, I would've done things differently.

Maybe I would've walked the other way.

Maybe my tale wouldn't have ended the way it did.

But the thing about 'maybes'? They're useless.

I wave at my aunt as I stand on the old, Victorian-era pavement. She waves back from the window of her silver Audi with a blinding smile.

Aunt Blair's red hair never lost its fiery, natural colour, hanging in perfect waves to her shoulders. She has high cheekbones and a tall, slender, model-like figure that makes my awkward, sixteen-year-old body look like a potato in comparison.

I strive to be her when I grow up. Not only in the looks department—although I'll never pull off the red hair, but also the hard work and the personality. She's a partner with her husband in their overflowing business. Their small company, Quinn Engineering, grows tenfold larger each day, and I couldn't be more proud of them.

"Show them what you got, Elsie!" She honks.

"Aunt." My face flames as I search sideways, spying for anyone who might have heard. "Elsa. Just Elsa at school."

"But I like my Elsie." She pouts in an anime-cute way. Her phone rings in a standard, professional melody. Her eyebrows furrow as she checks the call before silencing it. "You'll be okay, hon?"

I nod. "You didn't have to drive me."

"I wouldn't miss my Elsie's first day in this huge effing place for the world." She motions around. "Freaking Royal Elite School! Can you believe it?"

"I wouldn't have been here without you and Uncle."

"Aw stop it. We might have pulled a few strings, but if you didn't have the grades, you wouldn't be here."

And money. She forgets to mention that it costs a fortune and several organs sold on the black market to get me here amongst the elite.

Still, the weight that's been perching on my chest loosens a little at her contagious enthusiasm. "Teamwork."

"Teamwork!" She opens her car door and whooshes outside to clasp me in a mama bear hug.

I try to ignore the level of weird my future schoolmates must think of me and wrap my arms around Aunt. The smell of cocoa lotion and Nina Ricci's perfume envelops me in a safe cocoon.

When she pulls back, her cobalt blue eyes shine with unshed tears.

"Aunt…?"

"I'm just so proud of you, hon. Look at you all grown up and so much like…" She trails off and wipes under her eye with the side of her forefinger.

She doesn't have to say it for me to catch the meaning.

I look so much like my mum. While Aunt took after my ginger-haired grandfather, Mum took after my blonde grandmother.

Or that's what I'm told.

The ache that never died resurfaces like a demon from the dark, murky water.

Time heals everything is a big fat lie.

Eight years later, I still feel the loss to my bones.

It still aches.

It still hurts.

It still brings frightening nightmares.

"Gah, I'm being so sappy on my baby's first day at school." Aunt Blair gives me another quick hug. "Don't forget your meds and *no* junk food. Go get them, hon."

I wait until she gets into her car and shouts something at a slacking driver in front of her. Aunt has no filter when it comes to her precious time. That's why I feel guilty when she insisted on driving me.

Once her car speeds into the distance, I resist the urge to call and tell her to come back.

Now, I'm truly on my own.

No matter how old I am, the feeling of being stranded isn't something anyone forgets.

I stare at the massive building in front of me.

The old architecture springs an eerie, imposing feeling. Ten tall towers adorn the perimeters of the school's main building. Three-storey high, the school sits on a large piece of land surrounded by an enormous garden that's better suited for a palace instead of an educational establishment.

Royal Elite School is basically its name.

Located in the outskirts of London, the school was founded by King Henry IV at the beginning of the 14th century to provide education for scholars that later served in his court. After that, every king used it to cultivate his best subjects.

The school was later owned by aristocratic families and influential figures. They have the harshest and most closed-off entrance rates in the country. To this day, Royal Elite School—or RES—accepts only one per cent of the intelligent and filthy rich elite. Kids here inherit high IQ's alongside their parents' massive bank accounts.

Most prime ministers, parliament members, and business tycoons graduated from this school.

The high-privileged education can give me a sure push into

Cambridge. Aunt Blair and Uncle Jaxon studied there, and they're my role models in everything.

My dream is theirs. Teamwork.

This is my chance to escape all the rumours in my old school and start anew.

A fresh page.

A new chapter.

A blank book.

I stare down at my uniform that my aunt pressed to perfection and the adorable black ballerina flats—a present from Uncle Jaxon. The blue skirt is tight at my waist and flares down to a little above my knees where my thigh-high stockings accentuate my tall legs.

My white button-down shirt is tucked into the skirt's high-waist. A dark blue ribbon snakes around my neck like a dainty tie. I also wear the obligatory school jacket on which the school's golden symbol is engraved; a shield, a lion, and a crown.

My white-ish blonde hair falls in a fluffy ponytail down my back. I went out of my way by applying a bit of makeup. The mascara enhances my eyelashes and brings out my baby blue eyes. I even put on Aunt's Nina Ricci perfume.

Today is the day that determines my life for the next three years. Hell, it'll determine my life afterwards if—*when*—I get into Cambridge, so I needed to do everything right.

As I stride through the school's huge, stony arch, I try to mimic the other students' confidence. It's hard when I already feel like an outsider. Students here wear their pristine uniforms as if they're made from gold-soaked cloth. The aura of high, mighty, and a bit snobby drifts from every chatter and measured step.

Ninety per cent of Royal Elite School attended Royal Elite Junior prior to this. They chat amongst each other like old friends reuniting after the summer while I stand out as a loner.

Again.

An itch starts under my skin and spreads along my hands.

My breathing deepens and my steps turn forceful as memories filter back in.

Poor thing.

Did you hear what happened to her parents?

Heard she's a charity case by her aunt and uncle.

I shake those voices away and forge through. This time, I'm determined to blend in. No one here knows about my past, and unless they specifically search me, they wouldn't.

Elsa Quinn is a new person.

By the entrance, I spot a student who's avoiding the crowd by sneaking her way along the side pathway leading to the huge double doors. I notice her because I was also contemplating the same path.

While I'd love to fit in, crowds cause that familiar itch to rise under my skin.

The loner's skirt is bigger. She's on the thick side and has the roundest, cutest features I've seen on a girl my age. With her huge rounded eyes, plump lips and braided long brown hair, she almost looks like a child.

And she's the first presence in this school that doesn't give me the 'untouchable' vibe.

I catch up to her and match her fast-walking pace. "Morning."

Her head snaps my way, but she soon stares at her feet and tightens her grip on the strap of her messenger bag.

"I'm sorry." I offer my most welcoming smile. "I didn't mean to startle you."

Perhaps she's one of the new kids here, too, and feels intimidated.

"You shouldn't be talking to me," she whispers under her breath. Even her voice is cute.

"Why not?"

She stares at me for the first time with eyes so green, they nearly sparkle like a tropical sea. "Wow. You have beautiful eyes."

"T-thanks." Her lips curve into a tentative smile as if she shouldn't be doing the smiling thing. She kicks imaginary rocks as she speaks. "You're too pretty, you shouldn't be talking to the school's outcast."

"Outcast?" I echo, incredulous. "There's no such thing as an outcast. If I want to talk to you, I will."

She troubles her bottom lip and I swear, I'm itching to pinch her adorable cheeks.

"Are you new here, too?" I ask, instead of acting like a creep on the first meeting.

She shakes her head. "I studied in REJ."

"REJ?"

"Royal Elite Junior."

"Oh."

Considering how she wasn't in a horde of people, I assumed she's new. Perhaps her friends haven't arrived yet.

"Do you want me to show you around?" she asks in a tentative, small voice.

Aunt, Uncle, and I came for a tour during the summer, but I won't refuse a chance to bond with my first potential friend.

"Sure." I interlink my arm with hers. "What's your name?"

"Kimberly. You?"

"Elsa—and in my defence, I was born way before the Disney film came out."

She chirps a little laughter. "Your parents must have psychic powers."

"Aunt said Mum named me after a Swedish nurse who did lots of saving in both World Wars and was nicknamed the 'Angel of Siberia'. You know, Siberia, Elsa, and then Frozen, the ice princess? So maybe Mum did have psychic powers. Pretty lame. I know."

"No. It's so cool." Her shyness slowly withers away as we walk together. Now that I have her, I don't feel as alone or dejected.

My grin widens as Kimberly shows me around elegant, huge classes. The locker rooms. The pool—that I avoided. The principal's office that she jokes we shall never visit in a Shakespearian-like tone.

My three years in RES will be marvellous. I can almost feel it.

Once we reach the enormous, bright green football pitch, another type of giddiness takes me over. Not only because I'm such a nerd fan of Premier League and a die-hard Arsenal fan like Uncle, but also because of the long track surrounding the pitch.

This school definitely has better equipment than my last and I can continue running as usual. Hopefully, my heart condition won't start acting up again.

A crowd of RES's students gathers near the wiring that surrounds the pitch. Eager murmurs and excited gleams float in the air and it tastes like Christmas or a kid's first visit to the amusement park. Everyone seems to be naturally drawn to this place and they keep multiplying by the second.

"Elites."

"They're here."

"I say it's a championship year."

"For sure."

"Have you seen how that little shit became even more illegal? I'd so do him."

"Shut it. He doesn't know you exist."

While everyone chatters happily, Kimberly stands at the far end of the wiring, near the wall to the exit. Her easy, albeit timid smile withers away and her fair skin whitens some more.

I join her and follow her gaze.

On the pitch, the football team players pass the ball amongst each other with their heads or shoulders. They weren't playing or even in the team's jerseys. The school's uniform for the girls is pretty, but it's dead gorgeous for the boys, especially if they have fit bodies like these athletes.

They wear pressed dark blue trousers, white shirts and fitted jackets like ours. The only difference is that the boys have red ties with the school's symbol.

The crowd's attention strays to the four boys standing off to the side, half-playing with the team and half-chatting amongst each other.

It doesn't take a genius to figure out they're in a league of their own.

Kimberly's gaze remains on the tallest boy who's throwing a ball in the air and laughing like a young film star in the making. He has a classical, golden boy handsomeness. Slicked blond hair, sharp jawline, tanned skin, and a blinding smile, even from this distance.

However, the expression on Kimberly's face isn't of admiration or excitement like everyone present. If anything, it's of... dread?

"Who are they?" I ask, curiosity getting the better of me.

"They're the elite of the elite." Her voice trembles, genuinely, it *trembles*. "If you want to have a peaceful life in RES, you have to be on their good side."

"That's ridiculous." Kids can't own a school. "Who's the golden boy?"

"Xander Knight and he's trouble," she blurts fast as if her butt is on fire. "I like you, Elsa, and I mean it when I say, *stay away*."

His put together type doesn't interest me, anyway. I throw another look at him for a double-take.

The hairs on the back of my neck stand like needles when I meet the smokiest, most chilling eyes I've ever seen.

I hadn't noticed him earlier because he was half hidden by Xander and his ball. He's almost the same height as Xander, but with more developed shoulders. His uniform is missing the tie and he looks ruggedly handsome. Inky black hair runs long and slick in the middle, but it's buzzed on the sides. His nose holds an aristocratic vibe although it appears a bit crooked like it was hurt before. That little imperfection adds more mystery and intrigue to him.

Something in my chest moves. I don't know what it is, but it just moves.

It's like a prisoner has been lurking in the corners of my chest and now decided it wanted to be set free.

Even if I want to break eye contact, I can't.

He stares at me with a slightly tilted head and a silent, manic interest as if he's meeting an old friend.

Or foe.

"Shit! Shit!" Kimberly grabs me by the jacket and pulls me in the direction of the exit.

"What…?" I'm incredulous, and a bit hazy from breaking eye contact with that boy.

"Just walk, Elsa," she hisses as her quick footsteps pad along the pavement.

"Why are you taking me away?"

"King," she mumbles under her breath. "Aiden freaking King."

"And… who's that?"

"He's as much of a King as his last name. Heir of King Enterprises and of this damn school. His and the others' parents own this place and you don't want shit with them."

"Okay."

I don't want shit with him either. He's too attractive for that. Though I can't place whatever got into me when I locked gazes with him.

Boys don't interest me. I'm too nerdy for that and my studies always came above any boy drama.

That won't change now.

Especially since my Cambridge dream is within reach.

Then why am I itching for another glimpse at those metallic eyes?

"Oh. Damn!" Kimberly curses again. "They're coming this way."

I glance over my shoulder and sure enough, Aiden and Xander stride towards us and the rest of the football team follow like a gang in a mafia film. All laughter disappears and even the bystander's chatter halts abruptly and a tomb-like silence conquers the air.

The crowd parts for them like the red sea did for Moses.

"Run!" Kimberly whisper-yells, her nails digging into my wrist until I'm sure she'll draw blood.

"Why would I run?"

Due to my struggles with Kimberly, they reach us in no time and block our epic failure run to the exit.

Up close, Aiden's eyelashes are thick and as inky as his hair. A small, beauty mole sits at the edge of his deep, smoky eyes.

He stares down at me with a cold, foggy edge that matches the colour of his eyes.

Call it instinct, but something tells me I should be scared of him.

Like that prisoned thing from earlier, something claws at the corners of my chest, screaming at me to run and never look back.

That's ridiculous. I don't know Aiden, why should I run?

"Isn't it Berly?" Xander asks Kimberly in a detached tone before his lips curve into a cruel smirk. "You look even nerdier this year."

Everyone around us bursts into laughter, throwing fat-shaming remarks her way. My cheeks tint in red on Kim's behalf, but it's not due to embarrassment.

My blood boils to smash Xander's golden boy looks to the ground.

I open my mouth to say something, but I'm cut off when Kim lowers her head, lips trembling, and sprints past Xander to the exit.

He follows her with a smirk tilting his lips.

I should've seen what'll happen next coming.

I don't.

A strong hand wraps around my throat and pushes me against the wall. My back hits the brick and pain shoots down my spine and tightens the pit of my stomach.

I always thought myself brave, but nothing, absolutely *nothing* could've prepared me for this sudden, aggressive attack from a complete stranger.

The grey eyes I thought were beautiful seconds ago glare into my soul with murderous intent. The dark shadow on his face terrifies me more than his grip on my throat.

His other hand clutches my jaw, and my lips tremble at the thought that he'll snap my neck.

"W-What are you doing?"

He leans forward so his mouth hovers inches away from mine and growls. "I will destroy you."

Those words seal my fate.

TWO

Two years later,

Senior year. Last year before Cambridge.

Can I skip the entire thing and somehow still end up in Cambridge?

According to the obligatory grades' system, that's impossible.

The Mini Cooper swerves in the school's car park so hard, the tires screech in protest.

I gasp. "Kim!"

She grins at me as if she didn't almost run us into a pole. "What? Silver almost got the spot and I'm not letting that bitch walk all over me anymore."

My lips pull in a smile. I'm so proud of how far Kim has come during this summer. She went on a camping trip for self-spirituality and came back as this confident, smiley girl.

If only I could let go of my inner chaos as successfully as her.

She stares at her face in the rearview mirror. "How do I look?"

Another thing about Kim's trip? She lost more than twenty pounds and returned with this model-like body. Even her face has thinned, giving her cheekbones an alluring edge. Although I do miss her chubby cheeks. The mint-green coloured highlights make her appear like a fairy. She wore her skirt short, too short. Like a gust of wind can show her underwear, short.

I release my seatbelt. "You were always pretty, Kim."

"Only to you, Ellie." She rolls her eyes. "And my dad, but you guys don't count."

"Hey," I scowl. "Rude."

She sticks out her tongue. Determination sparking in her deep green eyes. "Today, I'll show all those suckers what I'm made of. I'll walk with my head held high like you."

I can't help the awkward smile breaking free. Kim thinks I'm that courageous, but she doesn't know the entire truth.

Silver bangs on Kim's window, her nostrils flaring. "You fat bitch!"

Two of her minions follow after her like she's their mama duck. They're all huffing and puffing, but I doubt it has anything to do with the weather.

Silver Queens is every bit the cliché of a mean girl. Blonde. Tall. Slender. Her mother is a member of the parliament. Her father is a minister. She also belongs to the school's best students. Aka, the top ten per cent.

She has it all and makes sure everyone in Royal Elite School—or RES—knows it.

Kim lowers her window, grins at Silver, and flips her middle finger. "Fuck you, bitch."

Silver and her minions' jaws drop so hard, so fast, they turn speechless.

I'm speechless, too.

My best friend doesn't curse and she certainly doesn't flip people off—or bullies, to be more specific.

Kim didn't only change in appearance. Nuh-uh. The world needs whatever self-confidence training she had.

"Let's go, Ellie." Kim opens her door, pushing the dumb-founded mean girls back.

I take my backpack and exit, too. I hold my head high as I stare down at Silver.

"What are you looking at, Frozen?" Silver snarls.

Of course.

The beloved nickname at RES.

But it's not because of the Disney film. No.

Since the first day I walked into RES, I've been instantly marked as an outcast.

Kim and I were the butt-end of every fat and nerd joke. While Kim—the old Kim—hid in the garden behind the school until everyone went to class, I walked the hallway with my head held high.

Aunt and Uncle didn't raise me to be stepped on. I kept to myself, but I never let them touch my dignity.

Apparently, I have an epic resting bitch face. Thus the nickname.

"Oh, I'm sorry." I keep my expression neutral as I meet Silver's malicious eyes. "You're not important enough for me to stare at."

I interlace my arm with Kim and walk into the school's huge doors. The ten towers appear eerie like they belong to a horror film, not a prestigious old architecture.

But then again, that's how I categorised RES since that first day.

My hands turn clammy and my body tightens as if I'm off to battle.

Kim smiles, but it's forced and makes her nose twitch in anxiousness.

"We've got this," I say more to myself than to her.

One more year in this hell.

One more year until Cambridge.

Kim's head bobs up and down, causing her mint-coloured strands to bounce.

"If we die," I joke. "I want to go in full Shakesperian mode. Tragedy."

She laughs, the sound is throaty. "For thy love of thee!"

We break into a fit of laughter as we head down the vast, main hallway. The school's golden logo, Crest-Lion-Crown decorates the entrance hall and the announcement board.

The moment we cross the entrance area and step into the hallways filled with other students, the real nightmare starts.

"Hey, Frozen. Did you freeze any beaches this summer?"

"Where's your fat friend?"

"Is she stuffing her pregnant belly with carbs?"

Kim's grip tightens on my arm. I can't believe they don't even recognise her.

Truth be told, I had to look at her twice after the summer camp to make sure it was her.

"Are you still swallowing cocks, Teacher Slut?"

I bite my lower lip against the rolling wave of anger. That particular rumour makes me want to hit someone.

Two years ago, after the entire class went out, I dropped my pen in biology. When I dropped down on my knees to pick it up, my hair got caught in the table—cliché, I know. Mr Silvester, the biology teacher, helped me out by untangling my hair.

Apparently, one of the dickheads here saw that moment and spread the rumour that I was giving our biology teacher a blow-job before he fucked me in class. Right before the exam—that I had a perfect score on.

Since then, I've been labelled a teacher slut.

Whenever I get a perfect score, it means I slept with the teacher.

But of course, no one talks about how Levi King, the oldest of the two kings, slept with a teacher. For real. They were caught in the act by the principal himself.

Nope. He gets a pass. The teacher gets thrown out of the educational system and she had to flee the country, basically.

Oh, and his guardian, the mighty Jonathan King, CEO of King Enterprises, got an official apology from RES.

Levi King got out of it unscathed. In fact, he became more popular, more loved, more admired.

Why? Because his last name is King.

And the Kings hold more power than the actual queen of this country.

Levi King was idolised for fucking the teacher.

I'm called a teacher slut for unfound rumours.

Kim's grip turns deadly even though she's holding onto her courageous mode.

I'm used to this rubbish and name-calling in the hallways. Kim isn't. I want to protect her from all these bastards.

Protect yourself first, Elsa.

Kim and I try to ignore them by talking about my running competition this weekend or the start of the Premier League season.

We release a collected breath when we finally arrive at our class.

At least, the wankers keep their distance when the teachers are around. But the thing about bullies? They work under the surface in front of adults.

RES is a prestigious, posh school, so the students need to keep up a certain image.

The rich are scarier than any normal criminal.

They have all the money and influence to allow them to twist anything around. They're never labelled criminals. No. They're labelled as elites.

Kim stops abruptly two steps into the classroom, and I run into her rigid back.

Her breathing becomes audible.

My own breathing picks up pace, and the hairs on the back of my neck stand on high alert.

Since that entrance day, there's been this baffling level of awareness that won't leave me the hell alone.

Every fibre of my being is honed for the inevitable confrontation.

For that crash and burn.

I suck in several deep breaths and begin the usual chant.

I'm loved. Aunt, Uncle, and Kim love me. I won't break. Not today.

I need to remind myself of those facts to remain strong and not let him get to me.

That's what the devil's reduced me to.

My gaze finally strays ahead, following Kim's field of vision.

Xander Knight. Cole Nash. Ronan Astor. Aiden King.

The four horsemen of RES. They earned the title for their impressive team play on the football team.

I call them the four arseholes.

And they're all here in our class.

No wonder Kim froze. We've barely escaped their wrath without being in the same class.

As in breathing the same air all year long. And not just any year, senior year.

Maybe I need to speak to Aunt and Uncle about my plans for Cambridge.

Cambridge, who?

The four are laughing and jesting. Xander is throwing the ball at Ronan, and the latter catches it with an *Oomph*.

Cole, the new captain of the football team after Levi King graduated last year, holds a book in his hand and laughs quietly at the other two.

My gaze strays to the main devil.

The hell ruler.

The black king.

You'd think the summer would somehow erase him from my consciousness and nightmares.

It didn't.

Aiden is the only one sitting. His legs stretch in front of him, crossed at the ankles. His fingers are interlaced across his stomach making him appear every bit the King his last name suggests

A ruler on his throne.

A devil in his hell.

Over the summer, I thankfully hadn't seen him, he's bulked up—due to the football camp, no doubt. His uniform's jacket stretches over well-defined shoulders. The dark blue trousers tighten around his muscular thighs and even his legs have become taller. I'm sure the coach would be so proud of his star player wanker.

His dark hair is between being tousled and slicked. Under the dim classroom light, his dark grey eyes appear black. Everything about him is.

Black mind.

Black heart.

Black soul.

I should've listened to Kim that day when she said those little bastards owned the school. Their parents are the biggest shareholders. Everyone in RES, including some teachers, fall to their knees for them.

All of them are sons of ministers or lords.

All except for Aiden.

His father owns those ministers and the rest of the UK's politicians.

Jonathan King leads the most successful conglomerate, not only in this country, but also worldwide. If he sponsors a politician, they're sure to win.

If he brings someone down, they're sure to vanish and never return.

That's the only reason I haven't reported the bullying or mentioned it to Aunt and Uncle.

Quinn Engineering is a small fish and their contract with a subsidiary of King Enterprises is the reason they're flourishing. Losing their company would devastate them.

If I stir up any trouble with Aiden, I have no idea what the devil will do. After all, he's the heir to his father's kingdom.

Aunt and Uncle saved me ten years ago, and I'd rather die than hurt them in any way.

Ronan notices us first. He's the typical teenage boy with messy brown hair and eyes. All he cares about is partying and shagging his way through school. Kim and I are probably the only moving things with a skirt he hasn't fucked.

That's probably why he licks his lips suggestively while he looks us up and down. Then he stops abruptly and nudges Xander.

The latter pauses tossing the ball to Cole and freezes. Literally. His easy-going smile falls, the dimples disappear, and his demeanour changes.

Kim's new appearance shocked him.

In his bloody face.

Aiden's eyes are on me. The murderous energy is in the air without me having to look at him.

Xander stares at Kim with contempt. "What have you done, Berly?"

Kim's hand starts shaking. He made her life a living hell like Aiden made mine. The only difference is that her bullying has been going on since the previous school. She doesn't talk about it, but considering that she knew these arseholes her entire life, I'm sure it's been going on for even longer than that.

"Ignore him," I lean in so only she can hear me. "They get off on a reaction. Don't show it."

"You think you're all pretty now?" He strides forward with a barely tucked-in menace.

Kim shrinks into me, biting her lower lip. Even with her courage resolution, I can't really blame her.

Xander is an intimidating arsehole both because of his stupid football build and his influence as a minister's son.

Besides, he's humiliating her in front of a class full of kids who always hated her.

"Once a nobody, always a nobody, *Kimberly*." He snarls her name.

Her bottom lip trembles, which means she's about to cry. The arsehole always makes her cry.

"Xander, p-please," she whispers.

He slams his hand on the wall, and Kim flinches. "You don't say my fucking name."

"That's enough." I level him with a hard glare.

"Stay out of it, Frozen." He's speaking to me, but his entire attention is on Kim and her bowed head.

I'm about to pull her into a seat when Silver barges through the door, carrying a coffee cup. Her minions follow after, flipping their hair and making a show of their entrance.

Great.

Silver hits my shoulder and spills her cup of coffee on Kim's front.

I gasp as Kim's white shirt, jacket, and even the skirt soak in caramel coffee.

Kim closes her eyes and a tear rolls down her cheek.

The rest of the class snickers.

"What the hell do you think you're doing, Silver?" I'm about to lunge at her, but Kim digs her nails into my arm, stopping me in my tracks.

"Oops." Silver holds the empty cup. "Go change, Berly. While you're at it, lose the whorish skirt. It doesn't suit your fat hips."

Her minions chuckle and everyone in the class follows suit.

Everyone except for me and the four horsemen.

My gaze snaps to Aiden. He's twirling the ball on a finger, but he's not watching the scene.

He's watching me.

Despite my resolution to not get stuck in his games, I meet his glare with one of my own.

For a moment, it's as if only the two of us are in the class.

He's surrounded by his murderous demons while I seethe for what his minions do.

Since that first time he announced he'd destroy me in front of the entire school, I've become RES's outcast.

He doesn't even have to do anything. He just sits like a king on his throne and watches what his loyal subjects do.

The bullying and the rumours that I slept with professors for my grades never fazed me because I know who I am.

Who Aunt and Uncle raised me to be.

Every day is a battle in this war Aiden created.

Sometimes, I get weak and hide in the library or cry by myself in the bathroom.

However, I never show weakness in front of him.

Not when I'm almost sure he gets off on it.

He's usually sitting there, relaxed, watching intently as his minions turn my life into hell.

Only there's nothing relaxed about his expression. I swear if demons can spill from someone's eyes, they'd be crowding his space.

When he plays football or when he's in class, Aiden is every bit the golden boy.

Excellent grades.

Elites' ace striker.

Contagious smile.

But with me?

Aiden King is one dark fucker.

He only gives me murderous glares as if my mere existence offends him. As if I'm the reason for the world's endless wars and famine.

That arsehole ruined my fresh start in this school.

My dream.

My new page.

I hate him.

Kim releases me and runs out of the classroom. Xander starts after her with wide strides.

I attempt to follow, but Silver blocks my way with a plastic smile. "She doesn't need a maid, Frozen."

"Get out of my way," I grind out. When she doesn't move, I push her and throw over my shoulder to no one in particular. "Oh, and if you have to bring someone down to feel so good about yourselves, then I feel sorry for you."

I don't wait for a reply as I run down the hallway.

It's a trip to the back garden where Kim usually hides—or finds peace, as she calls it.

After a minute of full-speed running, my heart's palpitations skyrocket into an irregular rhythm.

I stop at the corner of the third tower to catch my breath. My palm clutches my heart as sweat breaks over my brows.

Breathe in. Blow out.

Inhale. Exhale.

In.

Out.

My nails dig into my chest over RES's logo as I exit the building and head to the back garden.

With every step I take into the cut grass, a weight crushes my chest. My breathing becomes irregular, too.

A sliver of panic lodges deep within. My hands tingle and that familiar urge to scrub them clean takes over my senses.

I can't think past the sensation that my hands are dirty. They need to be scrubbed clean.

The pain in my chest is like tiny needles, tirelessly prickling my heart, even when I walk as slow as possible.

My heart condition can't relapse.

It simply *can't*.

Being able to run again didn't come easily after the surgery. There were Nazi-style rehabilitations and a complete change in my lifestyle.

The nightmare can't be back.

I *need* to run.

If I don't purge my energy and stress into running, I'll go crazy.

Kim and Xander's silhouettes appear in the small cabin house on the outskirts of the garden. She's crying and yelling, but I'm not close enough to hear what she's saying.

That and my ears are buzzing so loud, I can barely hear my own breathing.

This is bad.

I blink twice and breathe through my nose then my mouth.

Xander pushes into Kim, imprisoning her against the edge of the cabin. Her back hits the wooden pole and her eyes widen.

It could be because I'm disoriented.

It could be that this is the straw that broke the camel's back.

Or it simply could be that I've finally had enough.

I'm done with these arseholes ruining mine and Kim's life.

I pull out my phone and record a video. Xander grips her by the hips pulling her into him. Although I want to cut off his dick for putting his hand on my best friend, I know that will bring nothing. The video, however, will.

I can see Xander Knight's fall in sight. Either he leaves Kim alone or I'll blackmail him with sexual harassment. RES might be under his father's command, but the press isn't.

They'd be delighted to hear how sick and entitled a minister's son actually is.

I'm in the mood to ruin his future like he's been actively ruining her life.

Once I have enough footage of him manhandling her, I stop the video and smile in triumph. Even my heart problem fades away.

I start towards the cabin to stop Xander.

A shadow blocks my way.

I cease to breathe when I stare up at my nightmare.

THREE

Aiden hates me.

He loathes me.

I can imagine him playing my death in the back of his mind.

Why?

I don't know and I never asked.

Because I have a rule: Never try to understand bullies.

They're entitled arseholes who use their power to humiliate others, what's there to understand about them?

But as I stare up at Aiden's punishing eyes, my earlier thoughts shrink behind my trembling, defective heart.

He scares me.

Call it instinct or an intuition, but something terrifying lurks behind that easy-going smile and football star image.

"What did you just do?" His voice is calm and quiet with a slight huskiness.

An outsider would find it welcoming, but I know it's one of his multiple façades.

The voice the devil would use to lure his victims.

I lift up my chin, even though my hand clutching the phone trembles. "I don't know what you're talking about."

He extends his palm in front of me. "Give it."

I start to bypass him. Aiden sidesteps in front of me. He's stupid tall. Stupid broad. Stupid everything.

He blocks my vision of Kim and Xander.

But he's not done.

Aiden advances into my space. He's so close that I can make out that small beauty mole at the corner of his right eye.

I instinctively step back with every stride he takes forward. My throat dries, and I hate how I shrink in front of his attack.

He's just too damn tall and has this unreadable mask on his face. The only available image of Aiden is the one he shows to the outside world. Aside from that, he's… nothing.

A dark secret.

A deep hole.

An endless abyss.

My back hits a tree trunk, and I wince. When I attempt to walk past him, his arm shoots up and slams on the tree by the side of my head.

I'm imprisoned, just like the first damn day I met him.

Since then, Aiden has never gotten this close. He's the 'King' after all. All he has to do is issue a decree and the entire kingdom would bow. People do his dirty work for him—including bullying.

He still smells of body wash and something entirely his. It's strange how certain things never leave our memories.

He extends his hand again. "Give it, Frozen."

Frozen.

I'm just that nickname to him. It's another form of bullying and intimidation.

But I've already decided that I'm done with being a victim to Aiden's unjust war. I'm tired of being the one who always breaks eye contact first and hurries in the opposite direction.

We should give back.

Kim's words play in my mind.

If it were the old me, I would've done everything in my might to avoid confrontation with Aiden and stay as far away from his vicinity as possible.

I've always tucked my ghosts between my defective heart and my ribcage, but he needs to learn that the world doesn't revolve around his stupid last name.

I fold my arms over my chest and jut out my chin. "No."

He narrows his left eye. "Who do you think you are, Frozen?"

"Just a human being who deserves to be left in peace."

He cocks his head to the side, watching me with his demon eyes. "Not all human beings are in peace. Why should you be?"

"Are you freaking serious?"

"Give me the phone. I won't repeat myself another time."

"No." I mimic his tone. "I won't repeat myself another time."

He does something unexpected then.

Something I would've never seen coming.

His fingers wrap around my wrist that's clutching the phone.

Something in my stomach twists in a painful, strange kind of way.

Aiden *never* touches me.

The last time was two years ago when he wrapped his hand around my throat.

His touch is still… the same.

Calloused. Rough. Smothering.

He's not cutting off my breathing like the other time, but the air around me crackles and then ceases to exist altogether.

He reaches towards the phone, but I'm out of my stupor before he manages to snatch it.

We struggle for a few seconds. Or more like I struggle to block him. He's like a bull going after the red cloth.

An unstoppable, murderous bull.

Panting, I yank the phone close and hug it to my chest.

Aiden doesn't waver and shoots for it.

Why the hell had I thought the arsehole had boundaries?

Trying to block him with one hand, I loosen my ribbon enough to have an opening then tuck the phone in my bra.

I smile in triumph, tipping my chin at him.

Aiden's smoky eyes glint with something unreadable. "You had to screw up."

"What?"

"You really think that will stop me?"

Aiden dives straight to my shirt and undoes the first button. I'm so shocked that I stare with parted lips without reacting. It's not until he gets to the second button that I push at his chest.

"W-what the hell are you doing?" I shriek.

He pauses, tilting his head to the side with that manic expression. "Are you going to give me the phone?"

"N-no."

He continues his ministrations with the buttons of my shirt. My throat closes and I feel myself about to start hyperventilating. I push him, but his hold is steel. Impenetrable, hard steel.

"S-stop!!"

There's a strange rush flowing through my veins and tightening my muscles. I have no idea how to explain it except that Aiden needs to get his freaking hands off me.

I push at his chest again, but he already has the three first button opened so the edge of my bra is visible.

My lips part when I realise what else is in full view.

My surgery scar.

For years, I did everything in my power to make sure no one saw it. I never wore low-cut shirts. I bought one-piece swimsuits that hid my chest. I don't even like showing it to my aunt. Kim probably saw it twice and even then, only by accident.

And now, Aiden is staring at it.

No. He's not only staring. He's devouring it with his gaze as if it's some sort of wonder.

He stops unbuttoning my shirt, but he hasn't removed his fingers from the fourth button. In fact, he undoes it so the shirt is open to underneath my bra and he has a full view of the diagonal scar at the top of my left breast.

Ugly.

Long.

Faded.

The reason I started hiding it is because of the pitiful looks people gave me. Even Aunt Blair gives me that look sometimes.

However, Aiden's expression is anything but pity.

I didn't expect such emotion to exist in his black soul, but I thought there would at least be a softening of his devilish heart.

I couldn't be more wrong.

His eyes were murderous before, but now he seems like he wishes he had a knife to slice my scar open and rip out my heart.

Twigs crush underneath nearby footsteps.

I shake myself out of my stupor, push him away, and turn around to re-button my shirt. My breathing shortens despite my attempts to regulate it.

Behind me, I can feel his unwanted heat near my back. One step closer and he'd be breathing down my neck—or probably chopping it off.

"Mate." Xander's cool voice sounds from behind me. "You caught yourself an ice princess?"

"Actually, the ice princess is for you. She has something of yours."

Once my shirt is buttoned—with the phone still tucked in my bra—I whirl around. Getting on my tippy toes, I peek around Xander but there's no sign of Kim.

Xander appears victorious like he just did something to be proud of.

If he hurt Kim in any way, I'll ruin his face and pluck out those stupid dimples.

"Something of mine?" Xander's gaze bounces from me to his arsehole friend.

"She recorded you." Aiden doesn't spare me a glance. "I'm sure she's thinking of using it against you on social media and the press to ruin yours and your father's future. That sort of thing."

I couldn't keep my jaw from dropping even if I tried to. Aiden figured out my plan to a T.

Am I that obvious?

Xander bursts into laughter like he actually finds all of this funny. A cruel smirk tugs Aiden's lips as if this is some inside joke.

"All right, Frozen." Xander faces me, his laughter

disappearing. "It's so cute that you think you can hurt me and all. Now that you've had your fun, give me the video."

Barely-concealed fury erupts into hot, scorching flames. It could be because I saw this same arsehole harassing Kim or because of how Aiden touched me like he had every right to.

I widen my stance, glaring up at Xander. "You've ruined Kim's life for freaking years for no reason. It's time someone puts a stop to your spoiled, rich arse. I don't care if you're the minister's son or if you're bloody royalty. If you don't stay away from her, you'll regret it."

Silence.

Long, thick, fog-like silence.

Xander studies me with a raised eyebrow while Aiden remains poker-faced. If he weren't so close, I would've thought he hadn't heard me.

The more they remain reaction-less, the harder my pulse pounds in my throat. It's a miracle I'm not fidgeting.

"The phone is in her bra." Aiden breaks the silence with a levelled tone. "You want me to get it, or will you?"

"I don't know." Xander ponders. "Let's toss a coin."

"How about you hold her for me?" Aiden's gaze strays to my breasts.

I instinctively cross my arms over my chest.

Xander doesn't say a word. He yanks both my arms behind my back. He's so arrogant that he locks both my wrists in one hand. My chest pushes forward for Aiden's eyes.

Dark, metal eyes.

Demon eyes.

I try to struggle, but Xander tightens his hold until it's almost impossible to move, let alone fight.

"What do you think you're doing?" I hiss, voice plagued with tremors.

Aiden's punishing gaze meets mine.

There's so much in there.

So much hate.

So much cruelty.

So much… evil.

He doesn't break eye contact as he rips the ribbon from around my throat. I gasp as the cloth falls to the ground.

"I will scream!" I yell with strain even though I know no one would hear me out here.

"We love screams," Xander whispers in my ear. "Scream, Frozen."

The corner of Aiden's lips curves in a smirk as if he's agreeing.

We love screams.

I think I'm going to be sick.

How could I not think of that option when I put myself into this situation? I should have known nothing good would come out of a confrontation with Aiden and Xander. Their brand of unhinged doesn't care about moral lines or societal standards.

They were raised to think they were above everyone else.

If they got into trouble, their parents' influence got them out of it unscathed. Like in Levi King's case, the school apologised for something he had done.

Their moral lines are screwed up and blurred. Hell, they might not even exist at all.

How could I so foolishly assume that they have the same moral line as mine?

Stupid, stupid me.

If I want to get out of this with minimum damage, then I need to lower myself to their level and try to see this from their warped perspective.

They're bullies which means they get off on their victim's struggle.

I swallow my pride and quit trying to squirm free.

Aiden tilts his head to the side with a slight twitch in his left eye. I recognise the first gesture as contemplation, but I'm not sure what the twitching means. Is it anger? Annoyance? Something else?

Damn him and how hard it is to read him.

Aiden steps closer so his chest almost grazes mine. "You're a proud little thing, aren't you, Frozen?"

I'm taken aback by the change of subject. I thought this was about the phone?

"You don't give a fuck about anyone. Always walking around here with that head of yours somewhere above and beyond like no one here deserves your time." He pulls a stray blonde strand of my hair and twirls it in his fingers, watching it with manic interest. "So… Frozen."

My breathing catches the more he twirls the strand. I don't know if he'll pull me by it or rip it out of my skull psycho style.

A dark, claustrophobic sensation grips the centre of my chest.

I'd be lying if I said I wasn't scared. Even when I stayed out of his way, I always noticed the hidden dark tendencies behind Aiden's metallic eyes.

He tucks the strand behind my ear. To a passerby, it'd seem like a doting, caring gesture, but from Aiden, it's the calm before the storm.

The sound of airplanes overhead, right before the bombing.

The slight movement of the ground, right before the earthquake.

"Tell me, Frozen. What pushes your buttons? What are you afraid of, hmm?"

You!

I swallow down the scream, tipping my chin up, and meeting the devil's eyes.

He squeezes my jaw between his thumb and forefinger. "Tell. Me."

When I keep my right to remain silent, something flashes in Aiden's face. It's fast and fleeting and disappears as soon as it's there.

He releases me with a softness that startles me. No, not startle. It's something much more potent.

I don't like Aiden's kind side.

It's deceptive.

Destructive.

Deadly.

"Last chance before I find the answer myself."

Yeah, good luck with pulling the answer out of my head, monster.

Something shines in his eyes. People's eyes shine with excitement and happiness. Aiden's spark with unhinged sadism.

He reaches for me, and before I can do anything, he rips my shirt open. Buttons fly everywhere like abandoned pebbles.

My heart lunges in my chest and shame sinks to the bottom of my stomach. Unshed tears fill my eyes, and I realise right then that I'm not fit for this game.

I'm a coward and cowards lose before the game even starts.

But I'm smart enough to cut my losses short.

I swallow my tears and my stupid pride. "F-fine. I'll give you the phone."

The smirk on Aiden's lips seals my doomed fate.

"Oh, no. That was before. You had your chance. Now, I've changed my mind."

FOUR

I thought I knew fear.

My parents' death brought me raw, inexplicable fear.

So much fear that I buried it all in a black, inaccessible box.

As I stare at Aiden's impassive face, I realise that I know nothing about fear.

Or if I did, then I forgot it.

Because Aiden, an eighteen-year-old, is giving me another definition of fear.

I've never really known Aiden King until this moment when he has me at his complete mercy—or the lack thereof.

Pride and dignity were the only things that got me through the past two years from hell.

But now, as I stand with my hands locked behind my back and my shirt ripped open, that pride is crumbling apart like it was cartoonish.

An illusion.

A lie.

"Aiden…" His name gets stuck in my throat like smoke.

He's like smoke.

Suffocating, slippery, and undecipherable.

"Stop this." My voice drops, softening, pleading with any human part in him.

But I should've known better.

There's no humanity in a monster.

His steel gaze darts my way, and I cease to breathe.

They say the eyes are the window to the soul, but for Aiden, there's… nothing.

It's empty in there.

A dark, bottomless hole.

"What are you willing to do to have me stop?" His voice is calm. Too calm. It's terrifying.

"Let's take the phone, King." Xander's voice holds an uncertainty that matches my jumbled insides. Even though his grip remains steel-like.

"No." Aiden doesn't break eye contact. He's like a dog with a bone. There's no stopping him until he gets what he wants.

"Frozen here will give me what I want so I'll let her go, right?"

I shake my head once, holding onto the last thread of dignity I have left.

Xander presses on my wrists harder as if communicating something. What, I don't know.

The sadistic spark from earlier returns as Aiden watches me intently. "What do you say, Frozen?"

He reaches for the lace of my bra, his fingers tracing along the lace. My back stiffens, and I shrink into Xander as if he's my defence against his friend.

In all honesty, he may be the only defence I have.

Aiden gets bolder, hooking his finger against the cloth. His skin brushes along the valley of my breasts, leaving a trail of something so foreign, it's horrifying.

He's not even reaching for the phone. No. He watches me with that poker face the more his fingers lazily trace along the curve of my breasts, stopping at my scar.

His endgame seems to be making me uncomfortable in my own skin.

It's working.

It's freaking working, damn it.

Xander tugs on my wrist again as if pushing me to end this.

"Fine!" I seethe. "What the hell do you want?"

Aiden steps back but doesn't break eye contact. I don't want to back off first, but staring into those hollow eyes is exhausting.

It's like being trapped in a void and screaming, but the only sound you're able to hear is the echo.

"Everyone calls me King."

"And?" I ask, not knowing what he's getting at.

"You don't."

"That's because you have a first name, why the hell would I call you by your last?"

"Who gave you the right to call me by my first name?"

"Huh?"

"Call me King." His face lights up with malice.

He's enjoying this. The bastard is enjoying seeing me helpless.

I thought Aiden was crazy before, but it turns out he's a fucking psycho.

"Call you King?" I repeat, incredulous.

"It's not rocket science. Say, *please let me go, King* and I might."

I wiggle against Xander's hold, hating how my breasts bounce with the move. "I don't care who you are, *Aiden*, and you too, arsehole." I throw over my shoulder at Xander who's... playing on his phone? Seriously? I jut my chin at Aiden. "If you do anything to me, I'll report you for sexual harassment and ruin your entire future."

"Damn, Frozen. You're truly fucked now." Xander whistles. "You *really* shouldn't have threatened him."

"I thought you were smart." Aiden tsks. "But I guess you have your stupid moments, too."

Before I can ponder on that, he yanks me from his friend's hold. I cry out as I collide against his hard chest. His rough fingers dig into my bra. He retrieves my phone and throws it behind me. To Xander I suppose. Then he grabs both my wrists behind my back, locking them in one bruising hand.

"I'm out of here," Xander says in an absent-minded tone. "Don't take long."

His casual footsteps disappear into the distance.

I never thought I would want Xander to stay, but I'm ready to beg him to. He might be cruel, but he doesn't have an empty gaze like the one Aiden is watching me with.

"You have the phone."

"So?"

"So let me go." I stare at his shirt, not wanting to meet his gaze.

"That would be a no."

His fingers are back to my bra again, but instead of tracing like earlier, his thumb and forefinger latch onto my pebbled nipple through the cloth and he pinches.

A sound claws its way up my throat, but I clamp my lips shut around it. A strange heat invades my body and I hate it.

I hate the tormenting sensation.

I hate *him*.

I try to struggle, but that only pushes my half-naked breasts forward, making them bounce in his hands.

"Are you putting on a show for me?" He smirks.

"Screw you."

He pinches hard again, and pressure builds behind my eyes.

"Try again."

"What do you want from me, damn it?"

He pinches again, and I bite my lower lip so hard that I taste blood. I'm all flushed, sweaty, and sticky. It kills me that I'm allowing him to have this effect on me.

"So now you want to know what I want?" He tsks, lazily brushing his thumb on my hard nipple.

"Just tell me."

"What makes you think I want to tell you now? Maybe I changed my mind. Maybe I like you this way."

My chest heaves up and down in an erratic rhythm. He's not even looking at me. All his attention is on my breasts and… the scar. He doesn't break eye contact from it like he's a child who's found a new favourite toy.

He watches intently with that slight furrow in his thick

brows. His suffocating interest makes me feel even more exposed than when he ripped my shirt open.

"I'll do it," I blurt. "Tell me what you want and I'll do it."

His smokey eyes finally slide up to mine as he tilts his head.

It's a dangerous tactic, but it's the only way to swipe his attention from my scar.

"Apologise," he says with a casualty that negates his blackening eyes and the torturous swipe of his thumb on my nipple.

"Apologise for what?"

"For threatening me."

Hot fury whooshes through my veins like a fast-spreading fire.

Enough.

I'm not taking his entitled shit anymore.

"You're the one who's supposed to apologise to me! You ruined my life for two years for no reason and you're now holding me against my will."

"Hmm, for no reason." He repeats with a casualty that kills me. "Is that what you think?"

Nope. No. I'm not breaking my rule. I won't try to understand bullies.

Not now.

Not ever.

I wiggle against him, stomping my feet and groaning with pent up frustration.

"You might want to stop, Frozen."

"Screw. You," I grunt, willing all my strength to get me out of his hold.

"Keep struggling, and you'll have to take care of this." He pushes his hips into me. Something pokes against the softness of my belly.

My eyes widen, and I go completely still.

He's... hard.

His usual bored expression is gone. The star, perfect player is gone, too.

Instead, there's this dark spark of sadism.

He gets off on my struggle. No. Scratch that. He gets off on seeing me helpless.

The arsehole is turned on by my weakness.

Is he… a full-blown sociopath?

"You're sick," The words leave my mouth in a haunted whisper.

He lifts a shoulder. "Could be."

His fingers snake into my bra and circle a nipple. I thought it was torturous over the cloth, but having his skin against mine is complete hell.

I can feel the pulse of his nerves—or mine—and it's making me hyper-aware of everything.

Of the pine scent around us. Of the rustle in the trees. The humidity in the air. And his sheer asphyxiating presence.

I screw my lids shut, not wanting to feel whatever sensation that's crawling up my spine.

His touch is bruising, uncomfortable even, but there's a flash of something going through me that I can't identify.

No one has ever touched me this way before, and I hate that Aiden King is the first to invade my body.

"Do you like me hard for you?" he asks in a nonchalant, almost amused tone.

"Of course not. Are you crazy?"

"Then why aren't you giving me what I want? Because the more you resist, the harder I'll get."

"Go fuck yourself, Aiden." I stare at him straight in the eyes. "I won't let you break me."

It's false bravado.

I'm scared of this monster. After what he did today, I honestly don't know how far he'd go.

However, after my parents' death, I vowed to never apologise for something I haven't done.

Aiden fucking King won't make me go back to that helpless child I was.

"Don't put ideas in my head." He runs the pad of his thumb over my nipple. "It's already crowded with so many fantasies about you."

So many fantasies about me?

Aiden has freaking fantasies about me?

"Are you going to tell me what scares you, Frozen?" It's a taunt, his mocking way to put me in my place.

"Nothing scares me."

"I call bullshit on that. Everyone has something that scares them." He sounds thoughtful. "What's yours?"

I lift my chin. "I told you. Nothing."

"You're a terrible liar, but I'll play the game. If you won't tell me, I'll find out myself."

His fingers leave my nipple, but before I can release the breath I've been holding, he trails his hand down and over my bare stomach.

I suck in a crackling breath at how gentle, almost soothing, his touch is. It's the complete opposite of the devil look in his impenetrable eyes.

His fingers play with the waistband of my skirt. "Are you a virgin, Frozen?"

My stomach plummets with so many feelings I can't keep up with. I look away from him and stare at a tree so hard as if willing it to go up in flames and end this nightmare.

It's not prudeness that fills me. It's not even shame.

This arsehole actually terrifies me and I hate myself for it. I also hate the tingles erupting at the bottom of my belly.

What in the ever loving hell are they supposed to mean? He's violating me and I'm freaking tingling?

"No?" He sounds almost disapproving. "Who did you give it up to? The biology teacher? Some loser in your previous public school?"

I meet his demon eyes again. "That's none of your business."

"Did you like it when he plunged inside you?" he continues as if he didn't hear what I just said. "Or did it hurt? I bet you were too tight, huh? Did he tear you in one go or did he take it slow? I bet the sorry fuck worshipped you like some Goddess, didn't he? But you're not a Goddess, you're Frozen. I bet he didn't know you have an icy heart when he was giving you foreplay and taking it easy on you. Did you bleed all over his dick or on the sheets? Did he get you off or did you have to fake it? Or maybe —"

"Shut up!" My face burns at the crudeness of his explicit words.

What type of person has so many questions about how someone lost their virginity?

Worse. Why did his expression darken with every question as if he's... pissed off?

Aiden's hand plunges inside my skirt and he slaps my thighs apart.

I cry out, my heart shrivels into a black hole. "A-Aiden, what are you doing?"

"For the last time, it's King." His face is completely blank except for the slight smirk. "You said you'll report me for sexual harassment."

"W-what... ?"

"It's your lucky day. I'm making the report come true."

"You... can't be serious?" My voice cracks.

"Have I ever joked with you, Frozen?"

I struggle against him, my heartbeat increases with every second that I can't budge away. "Aiden! Stop it."

"Wrong name." He hums, his finger teasing the hem of my boy shorts.

My throat closes the more his fingers invade the inner part of my thighs. The more I try to close my legs, the harder he slaps my thighs apart.

My walls crumble and I can feel myself losing and crashing to pieces by him.

I suck a breath into my lungs and try to level my tone. Uncle Jaxon always told me that the best negotiating method is to be confident. Even if it's only the fake type. If I show weakness, Aiden will only lunge towards it like a shark to blood.

My best bet is to be calm—no matter how hard that is.

"King!" I blurt. "Are you happy now?"

He smiles with approval. "Not really, but you're learning."

"So?"

"So what?"

"I called you by your stupid last name, what else are you waiting for? Hail to the king?"

He chuckles. "Let's save that for another day."

As if there will ever be another day with this bastard. However, I smile. "Fine. Now, screw off."

"You know…" he trails off. "You really play stupid moves."

"What?"

"When your opponent charges for the attack, you're supposed to stay low, not crash with him head first. You're the only one who'll get hurt."

Whatever the hell that means.

"I was ready to let you go, but you pissed me off, so I changed my mind."

I watch his poker face closely. Aside from the slight twitching in his left eye, he looks peaceful to me.

Not pissed off at all.

But then again, what the hell did I know about Aiden's body language? He's like a fort.

Impossible to climb, to peer over, or to destroy.

"Then change it back," I mumble.

"That's not how it works."

"Let me go and I won't tell anyone," I say in my most neutral tone.

"Is that so?" His fingers draw small circles inside my thighs, and I clench my fists against the sensation.

I bite back the discomfort and the freaking tingling. "Yes. I only want to finish this year in peace."

"What makes you think I want you to have any peace, Frozen?" He grips my sex harshly. "You were born to suffer."

I cry out at the intrusive gesture. A zap bolts straight from where he's gripping me to my entire body.

Aiden is watching me with those sadistic eyes. Only now, the glint is becoming darker. Hazier. Stronger.

He loves having this effect on me. He's getting high on it.

Like a drug addict who can't get enough, he seems ready for more.

The harder I refuse, the more drastic his methods become.

It started with demanding my phone then he wanted me to call him by his last name then he wanted me to apologise.

Whenever I say 'no', his assault becomes relentless.

Ruthless.

Remorseless.

I'm provoking a monster.

A full-blown monster.

During my years of struggle against bullies, I learnt to never give them what they want. If I acknowledge their bullying or show them I give a damn about what they did, it'd give them the incentive to push harder.

Aiden is darker than the usual bully, but he's still a bully all the same.

Only he doesn't want those apologies or for me to beg or even the damn phone. He wants my struggle.

He wants my helplessness.

My weakness.

"I'm sorry," I blurt and try to mean it.

He pauses his ministrations for a second, but he doesn't release my sex. His gaze meets mine and his left eye twitches before he presses his thumb on my clitoris above the cloth.

My legs shake and I briefly close my eyes, willing the feeling to go the fuck away. I shouldn't be affected by whatever this monster is doing.

"Why did you say that?" he asks.

"You told me to apologise."

"You don't mean it." He leans closer and whispers in hot breaths against my ear, his voice amused. "Did you seriously think I'd fall for that, sweetheart?"

Sweetheart?

Sweet-fucking-heart?

It takes everything in me not to let my anger seethe to the surface. I want to push him so badly, but I know it'll only give him the upper hand.

Aiden's type gets off on hysterics. It's their driving force.

I level my tone. "I apologised as you asked."

"Apology denied." He muses. "You of all people don't get to play games with me."

You of all people? What the hell is that supposed to mean?

"You said you'd let me go. This isn't fair."

"Who said anything about fair, hmm?"

How am I supposed to win if he keeps changing the rules?

An idea flashes in my head. It's something I learnt from old Chinese war books.

When cornered, use your opponent's attack mechanism.

"What do you want, Aiden?" I soften my tone. "Tell me."

There must be something he wants. If he asked me the question then he must already have an answer of his own.

"Let me guess." He smiles without humour. "You'll make it happen?"

"If you let me go." It's a dangerous game and he might decide to not play fair again.

"You never cry." He observes me, sliding his thumb back and forth over my clit.

I clamp my lips against the sound trying to claw its way through. I want him to stop, but I also want something else.

What, I don't know.

"Why do you never cry, Frozen?" he asks with an almost gentle tone.

I want to tell him I do cry, just not in front of him or any of his bully minions, but I keep that information to myself.

If I get worked up around him, it's game over.

"These eyes should be filled with fucking tears."

"Aiden, seriously, what the hell is your problem?"

"Cry and I'll let you go." He deadpans. "You have to be convincing, though."

My lips part. Is he serious?

"I won't cry."

He tightens his grip on my sex, and I whimper. Pain shoots through my core along with something else I don't want to think about.

"Hmm. I'll be generous and give you the right for two moves. Either cry or we can stand here all day and I'll see how far I can take your sexual assault report."

I look over his shoulder, desperately trying to find anyone. But I should've known better. Kim purposefully chooses this place because no one wanders this far in the back garden.

When I stare back at Aiden, he's watching me with a strange mixture of emotions. Interest? Curiosity? Hate? I don't know what it is, but I need this freaking psychopath as far away from me as possible.

If crying will push him away then so be it.

"Do you need me to count to three?" he asks.

"Tears don't come on demand." I can't help but snap. I'm too angry and flustered to just cry.

"Let me help." Still gripping my core, he uses my bound hands to push me back until my breasts thrust in his face.

He glares at the scar as if it's a person he loathes.

"This should've killed you." His warm breath tickles against my skin and goosebumps erupt in its wake. "You should've died, Frozen."

My nose tingles and pressure builds behind my eyes.

With a few words, he thrust me back to my child-self. To the fear. The helplessness. The unknown.

He's right. That heart surgery almost killed me. But that's not the reason behind my unshed tears.

It's the memories surrounding the surgery—or the lack thereof.

The reason I hate the scar so much isn't because of the surgery or the non-aesthetic appearance.

It's because the scar is a reminder that everything before it is blank.

All I have left are nightmares and phobias and a distant reminder that I once had parents.

The scar represents that missing part of me.

Before I can try to seal those emotions into their dark box, Aiden bites on the flesh of my breast. I cry out as his teeth sink into the skin and then he sucks and bites along the scar with such animosity that leaves me breathless.

And terrified.

It's like he wants to bite the skin off.

Unleash those memories.

The nightmares.

The smoke and the flames.

And the blood… so much fucking blood.

"Aiden, s-stop."

He doesn't.

He continues feasting on my skin like he's a cannibal.

Everything will be out.

All of it.

This can't be happening.

"Stop!" My lips tremble as tears fall down my cheeks.

Aiden lifts his head. He stares at my face, at my tears, and the expression of hate that must be written all over my face.

His features are expressionless.

Closed.

Impassive.

"Good girl."

He finally lets me go. The space between my legs feels kind

of strange when he removes his hand. My shoulders ache from how he locked my wrists behind my back.

I expected him to step back and leave me be.

But Aiden never acts like you expect him to.

His upper body leans over and he darts his tongue out.

Aiden licks the tears falling down my right cheek. My skin turns hot and cold at the same time.

He moves to the left cheek, taking his time in tasting my tears.

When he pulls back, he doesn't appear as shocked as I feel.

However, his devil mask slips.

I get my first glimpse at the real Aiden.

The one he hides behind the smiles. The true form.

If the smirk on his face and the manic look in his eyes are any indication, then the fucking psycho enjoyed licking my tears.

A phone rings, startling me out of my stupor.

He checks it and sighs like someone is ruining his fun.

He gives me one last, unreadable look. "Be smart and stop making stupid moves."

More tears continue falling down my cheeks as I watch his stupid tall frame disappear behind the trees.

I turn in the opposite direction and run.

FIVE

Running in the rain steals my breath.

Ruins it.

Smashes it.

Nearly eradicates it.

When I arrive home, my soaked clothes are stuck to my skin. My shoes are slouching. My toes are cold and stiff.

Erratic strands of my hair stick to my temples and forehead, dripping all over me.

I stand in our small garden, catching my breath, and press a shaky palm to my chest.

My heart's palpitations grow uneven and out of beat as if protesting. I close my eyes and tip my head back, letting the rain beat down on me.

Soak me.

Rinse me.

The droplets pound on my closed lids almost like a soothing caress.

I've always loved the rain.

The rain camouflaged everything.

No one saw the tears. No one noticed the shame or the humiliation.

It was just me, the clouds, and the pouring water.

But that's the thing about the rain, isn't it? It's only a camouflage, a temporary solution.

It can only rinse the outside. It can't seep under my skin and wash away my shaky insides.

Wiping away my memories isn't an option either.

It's been barely an hour since Aiden had his hands on me—all over me.

I can still feel it.

His breath.

His nearness.

His psychotic eyes.

I lock the encounter deep in the darkness of my head and trudge to the entrance. I need to change before I catch a cold.

Our house sits in a cosy upper-middle class neighbourhood. It's two-storey and with more rooms than we need. The three of us did everything to make it as homey as possible. We planted an orange tree. A few roses. Uncle and I made sure to take care of the gardening ourselves—but lately he doesn't have time to.

My movements are numb as I hit the code and step inside.

The interior design has been carefully picked by Aunt Blair. Despite being minimalist, it's classy and modern. The lounge area has dark blue and beige sofas. The bookshelves are also dark blue with a touch of strength that doesn't only represent Uncle Jaxon's alpha character, but also Aunt Blair's.

Not bothering to open the tall, french windows, I drag my numb feet upstairs.

Aunt and Uncle wouldn't be around until late at night. The more their company grows, the less I see of them.

Sometimes, they pull all-nighters—whether in their company's office or their home one.

Sometimes, one of them returns to spend the night, but most of the time, they don't.

I'm going to be eighteen soon and I've always acted responsibly, so I stay alone just fine.

Deep down, I know they don't like leaving me alone—especially Aunt Blair. When I'm by myself or with Kim, she calls a thousand times—even with the safe neighbourhood and the alarm system.

God. I can't believe I ditched school.

I just couldn't sit in the same class as Aiden and pretend I was fine.

For two years, I took pride in walking the halls with my head held high no matter what the minions said or did to me. Today was too raw.

Too deviant.

Just too much.

The steel will I thought I had crumbled in a matter of minutes.

I always heard about people's breaking points, but I was too delusional to think I didn't have one.

I discovered the hard way that I do.

A breath leaves me as I step into my room.

My sanctuary.

I always joked with Aunt and Uncle, calling it my kingdom.

The decor is cosy with a mixture of pastel pink and black. I have my own library stacked with psychological and Chinese war books organised alphabetically. CD's hang from the ceiling like a curtain separating my bed from my desk.

The wall across the bed has two huge posters of my favourite bands; Coldplay and Bastille.

I let my backpack drop on the floor and press play on my Ipad. *Hipnotised* by Coldplay fills the space.

Tears barge into my eyes as I strip from my soaked clothes and step into the bathroom.

My hand itches. The need to scrub the filth off it fills me with an obsessiveness.

I stop at the sink and wash, scrub and rub my hands together until they become bright red.

When I lift my eyes to the mirror, my lips part.

It's me. The witchy, white-blonde hair. The baby blue eyes. But at the same time, it isn't.

There's a void in there.

A... numbness.

I'm about to move to the shower when something else stops me. My scar.

Several angry red marks surround it. Did the psycho leave freaking hickeys around my scar?

What in the ever living hell was going on in his defective brain?

I rip my gaze away from the mirror and take the longest, most scalding shower in history.

When I step back into the room, the song has changed to *Good Grief* by Bastille. I let the music drift around me as I climb into bed, still in a towel, and close my eyes.

I fight the tears and lose.

I startle awake.

My hair sticks to the side of my face with sweat.

Heat smothers my body and my breasts tighten against the towel.

That's not all.

Oh. God.

My hand rests between my legs and I'm... wet.

I jerk my hand free as if I was caught stealing.

I don't even remember the dream, so what the hell is this reaction supposed to mean?

My surroundings come back into focus. The soft light from the lamp. The music I left on. The chorus from *Grip* by Bastille strikes deep inside me. Something about the devil having him by the arm and pulling him into the night.

The neon red numbers on the nightstand read seven pm.

I slide from the bed, willing my body temperature to go back to normal.

With a deep breath, I put on my pyjamas shorts and a T-shirt, gather my hair in a bun, and sit at my desk.

My first day at senior year started with a disaster, but nothing will take Cambridge away from me.

I retrieve my books and tasks organised in Eizinhower's method and dive into it.

For thirty minutes, my mind is tuned to studying. Then, I start drifting.

The pen grazes my bottom lip as my thoughts spiral into directions they shouldn't.

Even when I want to forget, my body has a memory of its own. My body still remembers how Aiden held me. How he was hard because I struggled.

My eyes still remember that dark, bottomless emptiness and disregard.

If I didn't cry, what would he have done?

A shudder goes through me at the thought.

In old Chinese war books, it's said that the best way to understand someone is to see things from their perspective. To think as they do.

There's no way in hell I'm doing that with Aiden.

Depraved bullies don't deserve to be understood.

After being singled out as an outcast, I thought that one day, karma would bite bastards like Aiden in the arse and he'd stop tormenting my existence in RES.

I was only fooling myself.

Aiden might be a psycho, but he's a smart one. He knows when to push buttons and when to step back.

He took me by surprise today.

Ha, understatement of the freaking century there.

He rattled me.

He shook my world.

He made me doubt myself.

Since he kept his distance for two years, I never thought he'd get close. *That* close.

I'm still all too confused about what I felt. What I *feel*. And whatever dream—or nightmare—I just had.

I know for sure that he took something he had no right to take and that I fucking hate him for it.

But more than him, I hate myself for letting him take it.

A knock sounds on the door. I startle, biting the pen and my lip.

Ow.

I smother my expression. "Come in."

Aunt and Uncle walk inside, both of them still wearing their work suits.

When Aunt Blair leans in for a hug, I stand up and remain in her embrace for a bit too long. Beneath the cherry perfume, she has Mum's scent. Something that resembles cotton candies and summer.

I don't know why I'm thinking about that right now when I don't even remember my mum.

Today, I miss her.

I miss the life that I don't remember.

Reluctantly, I pull away from Aunt and hug Uncle Jaxon. He plants a kiss at the top of my head.

Uncle is classically handsome with brownish blonde hair and cobalt blue eyes.

Although his build is above average, he has a beer belly.

"I called and you didn't pick up." Aunt studies my face in that scrutinising way that brings her clients to their knees.

It's like she's detecting the lie before I even say it.

"Sorry, I forgot it."

"I called the school," she says. "They said you went home?"

"I…" Darn. I didn't think that far when I left. "I didn't feel so good."

Uncle Jaxon looms over me, his forehead creasing. "Are you having palpitations, pumpkin?"

"No." I force a smile and hope to hell they believe it. "I just had a headache and wanted to come home and rest. Sorry I didn't call you."

"We were so worried about you, honey." Aunt smooths my hair back. "I came home to check on you earlier, but you were asleep."

"I told you she would be fine." Uncle chimed in. "Where did you forget your phone?"

"At… school."

Real classy, Elsa. I'm shooting one freaking lie after the other.

It hurts to lie to them, but I'd rather die than put Aunt and Uncle's company in jeopardy.

Their names and Aiden fucking King's name shouldn't exist in the same sentence.

Aunt continues scrutinising me and checking me up and down like she's expecting me to collapse any second. "A headache out of nowhere is suspicious. Maybe we should visit Dr Albert."

"It's just a headache, Blair," Uncle says on my behalf.

"Headaches are symptoms for the nastiest diseases, Jaxon." She scolds.

"One of them is simple fatigue."

"I'm fine, really," I chime in, not wanting them to argue. "I'm just going to study for a bit and have an early night."

"Dinner first, pumpkin. And we should play a chess game." Uncle hooks me under his arm and drags me out of the room. He asks about my first day and tells me a joke about a worker of theirs. He almost fainted when he got a phone call that his wife was in labour.

Uncle Jaxon has a way of lightening up the mood, and I smile along.

Aunt follows, but she's not amused. She keeps watching me intently as if trying to see through me.

Once we arrive at the kitchen, I smile. "Aunt, do you have time for some yoga? It helps with headaches."

"Hell yeah." She chuckles then her smile dies. "I'm sorry I haven't had much time for our girls' time, hon."

I shake my head and say in a mocking tone, "Nah, it's for the best. Too much girls' time would distract me from Cambridge."

Aunt busies herself behind the counter and I slide to an

empty stool. Uncle comes behind me and massages my shoulders. "I'm going to coach you so well for Cambridge, pumpkin."

Aunt rolls her eyes. "This isn't a Premier League game, Jaxon."

"Ignore her." Uncle leans in to whisper, "I've got tickets for Arsenal's game next week. Guess who's asking you on a date?"

My chest flutters with excitement. I hate our school's football team, or more specifically, I hate the arseholes who play in it, but I love the game. Uncle converted me to the dark side and turned me into a Gunner—Arsenal's diehard fan.

"You better not be asking her to abandon her studies to go to some stupid game."

"Of course not," Uncle and I say at the same time, then he snorts and I can't help but laugh, too.

Aunt folds her arms and taps her foot on the floor.

Uncle and I busy ourselves with retrieving vegetables from the refrigerator while trying to suppress our laughter.

"Teamwork," Uncle and I murmur to each other.

For the moment, just this moment, I forget what happened today.

Or I try to, anyway.

In the morning, Aunt drives me to school on her way to work.

I kept recalling yesterday for the entire night and contemplated not showing up today. But then, I had a serious angry session with myself.

No one—Aiden included—will break me.

My early childhood didn't and he certainly fucking wouldn't.

I just have to be smart about dealing with him. Like avoiding the shit out of him and go back to glaring from afar.

I wave at my aunt and stride into the school with my head held high like usual.

The taunts begin, but I don't let them rattle me.

A little voice in my head whispers at them.

Run along, kids, your little pranks are nothing compared to Aiden's depravity.

Despite my pep talk this morning that gave me much needed courage, a tremor shoots down my limbs the closer I approach the class.

I'll see him again. I'll see those demon eyes.

Those sadistic smirks.

That dark soul.

Son of a bitch. How the hell am I supposed to survive an entire year with him in the same class?

To make matters worse, Kim is nowhere to be found. Since I don't have a phone anymore, I called her from the landline earlier but she didn't pick up.

I still have some time before the first class, so I head to her spot in the garden.

My pace falters near the tree where Aiden trapped me yesterday.

A strange awareness grips me by the throat. My body's memory acts up again.

I can feel his hands all over me.

I can smell him amongst the trees.

I can see that soulless look in his eyes.

A strong wave of hate takes over me, but that's not the only thing.

Something else, something completely immoral grips me, too.

Get out of my head, damn you!

My brows scrunch when I arrive at the cabin and find no trace of Kim.

Like me, Kim never skips. If she did, something serious must've happened.

That wanker Xander better not have hurt her or I'll go all mama bear on his arse.

I turn around and my head collides against a strong chest.

"Are you here for more, sweetheart?"

SIX

He needs to stop calling me sweetheart or I'll get a voodoo doll with his face on it and stab it to death.

Better yet, I'll cut it limb from limb.

I step back to an arm's length. If I keep enough distance, he won't be able to catch me.

There's no way in hell I'll let him trap me like he did yesterday.

This time, I'll either scream or run.

Yup. Sounds like a plan.

I gulp, but it lodges in my throat like an external object. No pep talk or courage could erase the memories from yesterday.

No pep talk could convince the nerves tingling with suffocating fear that I'll be fine.

My limbs are screaming at me to run.

Hide.

Never look back.

I don't.

Running away from someone who gets off on vulnerability isn't the smartest thing to do.

He'd chase me. Hell. I'm sure the psycho would enjoy it, too.

Who'll come out victorious?

Yeah. Not me.

So instead of flight, I choose to fight.

I lift my chin, calling all the courage I have left.

But the moment I meet his gaze, most of that courage falters.

The thing about Aiden? He's so well-put-together.

Perfect face.

Perfect body.

Perfect style.

He doesn't even wear the tie on most days, and it still looks like the school's uniform was tailored for his firm, muscular body.

His entire appearance is another asset he uses to intimidate.

To charm.

To screw everyone over.

I even fell for that charm the first day I met him. From afar, he looked like a God. Up close, he's nothing more than a monster.

Since he choked me in front of the entire school and announced he'd destroy me, I realised that his entire look is a façade.

The only thing I see is the void in his steel eyes.

The hate.

The black rage.

I don't understand how no one else notices it. Either they're too far gone under his spell or they simply don't care.

That's what it means to be king, isn't it? He can be corrupt all he wants. Hell, he can order a war that will slaughter half the nation and starve the other half, and the ones who remain alive will still chant 'Long live the king.'

It's not out of love. No. It's out of fear.

People naturally gravitate towards power and in RES, Aiden is *IT*.

Last year, his older cousin, Levi King, ruled and now that he graduated, RES belongs to the youngest of the two kings.

"You ran away from school yesterday," he says matter-of-factly.

"I didn't run away. I had a family emergency." I would've patted myself if I could. That lie came out perfect.

Shoving a hand in his pocket, he studies me up and down. His gaze lingers on my left breast as if he's trying to burn a hole through my shirt.

It takes everything in me not to cross my arms over my chest.

His attention finally slides back to my face. "I think you're lying, Frozen. I think you were pushed to your limits so you took the easy way out."

"Guess what, Aiden? I don't care what you think."

"You should. What I think will have a direct impact on your life, sweetheart."

"Stop calling me that," I hiss. "I'm not your sweetheart."

"You are whatever the fuck I say you are, *sweetheart*."

Is it possible to curse someone into a dark, bottomless pit of hell? I'm not above using black magic. I just need him to bloody disappear. The earth will be a tad more peaceful.

I seal my temper as I turn around to leave.

He won't get to me. He *won't*.

A strong hand clutches my arm and swings me back so hard, I land flush against his hard chest.

He grips me with brute, bruising force.

"Did I say you can go?"

I struggle against him. "I don't know if you noticed, but I'm not one of your subjects, *your majesty*. I don't follow your orders."

"There's a start to everything."

He releases me but only so he can wrap both his arms around my waist and rests his hands at the small of my back like we're some freaking lovers.

This close, my air fills with his scent and his body heat mingles with mine.

I'm not short, but he still has height and broadness on me. Deep down, I know that seize is just an intimidation factor.

I push at his chest, wiggling sideways and backwards, trying to unlink his hands.

He doesn't even move to stop me. All he does is keep his steel-like hold.

"Ugh." I pant. "Let me go."

"Why should I, hmm?"

"Why shouldn't you?" I counter back.

"I love it when you struggle." His eyes gleam with that

now-familiar sadism as he reaches up and pinches my cheek. "You should see the tint of red on this."

I go limp against him. My arms fall lifeless on either side of me, and I even school my expression into a neutral one.

If he loves my struggle, then he won't be getting it anymore.

"Are you done?"

His left eye twitches.

Obviously, the sick bastard doesn't like not getting what he wants and I beat him at his own game.

"I'm going to give you a valuable piece of advice. You already know what I'm capable of." His voice is calm. The dangerous type of calm. "Don't push me."

"You're the one who's pushing me!" I can't believe this bastard. "You're lucky I haven't reported you for what happened yesterday."

"Lucky?" He laughs with a humourless edge, and it's stupid that even the lines of his face stretch in beautiful angles.

Someone pour acid on his features.

"I don't know if you're trying to be adorable or if you're *that* naïve."

"What is that supposed to mean?"

"You think you can hurt me, hmm?"

He clutches my chin with his thumb and forefinger, angling my head back so he can invade my face with his intrusive gaze.

My heart palpitates harder and faster.

No matter how many tactics I come up with, no matter how much I like to think I have control over this situation… I don't.

And my heart recognises the danger.

The void.

The black hole.

My rigid spine also recognises the tingle of fear.

The need to run and hide.

The need to never be found.

A side of me I fought to keep buried is rising, crawling, and resurrecting to the surface.

You're my masterpiece, Elsa.

I briefly close my eyes against that haunting voice from the past. When I open them again, the eerie voice disappears but Aiden's steel expression remains.

Damn him and how easily he can poke open that part of me.

I kept it buried for more than ten years, but he's slowly letting it loose in a matter of two days.

"Maybe I can." My voice sounds a lot calmer than I feel. "What do you even know about me?"

"A lot more than you think." He squeezes my jaw so hard, I wince.

"I swear to God, either let me go or —"

"Or what?" His features spark with the promise of a challenge. "You can't do fuck to me. Let me put it this way, if I murder you, Coach will burn the corpse and the principal will scatter the remains. If I commit a crime, the school board will flip it around so it seems as if I'm the victim. You might have your head in the sand like little miss Ostrich, so here's a quick reminder, I'm king here."

His words sting because they're true. As long as he has the King's name, his father doesn't even have to interfere for everything to blow over.

The injustice flares inside me and blurs my vision with unshed tears.

Nope.

I won't give him the satisfaction of seeing me cry again.

"But if you feel entitled to." The corner of his lips lifts in a smirk. "If you think you can take me, then, by all means, show me what you got, sweetheart. I'm curious to see who will believe that I touched you without your consent. I can have any pussy I want, what's so special about yours?"

"That you can't have it."

I regret the words as soon as they're out. I can't believe I just dangled a freaking steak in front of a predator.

"Frozen." He muses.

My lips thin in a trembling line and I nearly fidget in his hold, waiting for his next blow.

Any moment now, he'll —

Aiden releases me and steps back.

Wait.

He… he's letting me go?

I cautiously watch his expression like a deer caught in the headlights.

He schools his features into that poker face.

For some reason, I expect him to laugh in my face and grab me again.

I'm happy he's letting me go, I am. But I can't help the tinge of annoyance at not being able to read him.

He places a hand in his pocket, appearing casual, almost nonchalant. "Show me the mark."

"What?"

"You're not an idiot so don't act like one and show me the mark I left yesterday."

"You're out of your mind."

My limbs are shaking but I turn around to run. I need to escape his space.

His presence.

His damn face.

"If you take one more step. I'll chase you, sweetheart. And this time…" he trails off, his voice turning suffocating like smoke. "I won't stop."

I gulp audibly and stop in my tracks.

A part of me doesn't want to believe he'd go that far, but who am I kidding?

Aiden won't stop until he gets what he wants.

With my heartbeat in a knot, I face him. "Why are you doing this, Aiden?"

"Why do you think?"

"Because you can?"

"Because I can, huh? Interesting." He pauses. "You are so… frozen, did you know that?"

"Your minions wouldn't stop reminding me of that fact, thank you very much."

"You're missing the entire point."

"What point?"

"If you're missing it, why should I tell you?"

I open my mouth to say something when he cuts me off. "Take off your shirt."

My fists ball on each side of me.

"If you don't, I will. How many ripped shirts do you want to collect?"

"You're sick."

"Do you honestly believe that's an insult to me?"

I clamp my lips in a line.

"Last chance. Take off your shirt."

"No."

We watch each other for one second.

Two.

Three —

He starts in my direction. All blood drains from my face and a tremor shoots down my spine.

It's real.

That look. That determination.

This time he won't stop.

"Fine!" I blurt, stepping back. "I'll do it."

He stops, but his poker face remains in place. He appears calm and casual, but if I take one step, I've no doubt that he'll chase me like a starved wolf.

Think, Elsa, think!

A crazy idea explodes in my mind.

"Do it for me," I say in a neutral, almost uninterested tone.

Aiden's left eye twitches.

I'm sure my suggestion has taken him by surprise. He

thought I'd either cower to his threat or he'd do it by force. I'm sure the sick bastard hoped for the second option.

The fact that I'm offering him to do it without the whole violence factor ought to throw him off balance.

Those who give two options don't expect a third. The third option rattles them, and that's exactly what I'm betting on.

He narrows his eyes, "You're trying to play a game again."

"I'm just giving you what you want."

"Are you now?" His tone turns stone cold.

"Yes."

"You'll regret that." He approaches me and reaches for my ribbon.

I place both palms on his stupid broad shoulders and dig my fingers in his uniform's jacket.

He pauses at my first button and searches my face.

Touching him was never a part of the deal, and he must be wondering why I'm doing it willingly.

I don't know if he hates or loves it, but I don't give him or myself time to think about it.

I lift my knee and hit him in the crotch. Hard. As hard as I can.

His face contorts and his hands shoot out for me, but I duck and run past him.

A huge grin pulls on my face.

I just kneed Aiden fucking King in the balls!

SEVEN

I kicked Aiden in the balls.

I kicked Aiden fucking King in the balls.

My feet skid to a halt at the threshold of the classroom. I'm panting.

My hands are sweaty.

The wave of adrenaline vanishes from my system, leaving a tremor in my limbs.

My shoulders shake with suppressed laughter. If I didn't worry that my classmates would start calling me a lunatic, I would've laughed so loud right now.

I want to run, jump, and bump fists with myself.

It's a strange type of freedom that I haven't felt in like... ever.

I was always quiet and introverted, but right now? I feel like I can punch the moon and kick the stars.

With a deep breath, I push my shoulders back and stride into the classroom with my head held high.

Some snickers and 'Frozen' remarks get thrown in my direction, but they're like white-noise.

These little minions can give me their freaking best and it wouldn't matter.

I just kicked their king. In the nuts.

I'm smiling inwardly when my gaze falls on the other three demons.

Cole is sitting at his desk, reading his physics book. Xander sits on the top of the desk arguing with Ronan who's standing.

The rest of the class are either trying to get in on the conversation or they're watching.

The sad part is, I think they're doing it subconsciously. They're drawn to everything the four horsemen represent.

Power.

Charm.

Wealth.

Ronan is Death because he's an impenetrable rock in the midfield.

Cole is Famine; silent but deadly when he attacks.

Xander is War; all he knows is how to wreak havoc.

And he did something to Kim. Because even now, she's not here.

Kim was never late to school.

It could be my false sense of courage or the remains of adrenaline still buzzing through my veins, but I don't stop to think about it.

I grip my backpack's strap and stride towards the trio.

"I'm telling you, mate." Ronan taps his index finger on the table in front of Xander. "She came to the party because of me."

"Everyone came because of you," Cole says. "You threw the party, remember?"

"*La ferme*, Captain! That's not the point." Ronan continues speaking to Xander. "Face it, she was there for me."

"If it helps your ego, sure thing." Xander laughs. "Can you pass me what you smoked last night?"

Ronan frowns. "Why?"

"That shit is good if it makes you believe things that don't exist."

"Screw you, Knight." Ronan lunges at him.

In that exact moment, Cole's neutral gaze meets mine. He clears his throat and the other two who are still bickering grow silent.

"Frozen?" Ronan jerks back as if he's been punched. "Am I seeing things or is Frozen actually in front of us?"

He searches behind me and all around me then he grins. "Are you here to confess your love to me? I knew you always had a crush on me, but sorry, I only take confessions in the afternoon. Rules are rules."

I ignore him and face Xander. "Where is she?"

Xander hops down from the desk. "Where's who?"

"Kim," I grind out.

"Oh," Xander's brows draw in feigned concern as he searches underneath the desk. "Captain, have you seen a little Kimberly around here? No? How about you, Ro? Search your pocket, maybe she hid in there."

Ronan makes a show of stuffing his hands in his pocket. "Nope, not here." He smirks fishing out a condom packet. "But I found this."

My lips thin in disgust.

"*Quoi?*" Ronan asks. "Always safe."

"I'm not here for your games," I tell no one in particular.

"Then what are you here for?" Xander asks.

"Kim. Where is she?"

"If you don't know where your friend is, how am I supposed to know, Frozen?"

I step closer, still clutching my backpack's strap. "I know you did something to her yesterday."

He smiles like a maniac. "Do you have proof?"

My nails dig into my palm until I almost draw blood.

"Hold up." Ronan steps between us. "What happened? What proof? Someone fill me in."

Cole shakes his head at him.

"What? I feel left out." Ronan kicks his friend's leg. "First, King flipped his shit at practice yesterday, then Knight does some fuckery behind our backs, and now, Frozen is speaking to us. You've got to admit that there's nothing normal about this."

Only one sentence remains playing like a loop in my head.

King flipped his shit at practice yesterday.

What the hell is that supposed to mean? Aiden is an exemplary player and student. He doesn't just *flip his shit*.

Does this have to do with what he did yesterday?

"Someone fill me in." Ronan stares between his two friends. "Someone? Anyone?"

"Stay away from Kim," I tell Xander with as much venom as I can manage.

"Or what? You'll stop me?"

I'm about to reply when, unfortunately—or fortunately, it depends on how you see it—the teacher comes into the class. Everyone takes a seat and I find an empty one near the back.

My gaze meets Xander's playful one. He sits in the row beside me, throws me my phone, and smirks.

I shudder. Arsehole.

"Oh, look. Kimberly isn't in class." The boastful tone he uses grates at me.

"Mr Knight." The teacher, Mrs Stone, calls. "Class started, I'd appreciate it if you pay attention."

"You've got all my attention, Mrs Stone." He gives her a dimpled smile and opens his notebook.

Mrs Stone starts enumerating the class's curriculum. I retrieve my pen and notebook and start scribbling notes.

Our English Literature teacher is probably the oldest in the school and will probably retire soon. Her grey hair is tied in a conservative bun and her glasses are held by those golden straps that no one uses anymore.

The door opens. The entire class falls silent. Even Mrs Stone stops talking.

I pause mid-scribble and lift my head.

A flushed Kim peeks from the door, her hair in disarray.

Snickers and laughs erupt in the class.

"You're ten minutes late, Ms Reed," Mrs Stone scolds.

"I… um…" Kim stumbles upon her own words.

I wince, feeling her discomfort under my skin. She always hated being put in the spotlight.

"What's the matter, Berly, did you lose your tongue along with the fat?" Someone taunts from the side.

Mrs Stone shoots him a glare. "Another word and that'll be detention for you, Mr Robbins."

His face turns ashen, and I want to get up and hug Mrs Stone. She's probably the only teacher who doesn't turn a blind eye on the bullying. At least from insignificant people like Robbins. I doubt she'd do anything if one of the 'Elites' were involved.

A shadow appears behind Kim's fidgeting body.

I stop breathing.

It's like the earth has opened and is now sucking me into its depths to be buried alive.

Aiden places both his hands on Kim's shoulders.

He has his filthy hands on my friend's fucking shoulders.

Not to be dramatic, but I think I'm going to throw up.

His gaze meets mine and something sparks in it. A corner of his lips lifts in a cruel, psychotic smirk.

That's it.

I'm going to kill him.

I'm going to sacrifice my entire future to save the world from his evil.

The smirk falls as fast as it showed. Still gripping Kim by the shoulders, he flashes Mrs Stone his golden boy's smile. "I'm sorry. Kimberly wasn't feeling well so I had to take her to the nurse."

Is he for real?

I'm mortified when Mrs Stone's expression shifts from scolding to acceptance. "Are you all right, Ms Reed?"

Kim nods without saying a word.

"That was nice of you, Mr King." Mrs Stone offers him a smile. "Both of you take a seat."

My jaw is probably dropping to the floor. I can't believe this.

The dark hole from earlier expands until I can hardly breathe.

He must've done something to Kim, and now, he's making everyone believe he was helping her.

I search his face for any signs.

He's smiling, mask firmly in place, appearing every bit of the golden boy everyone envies.

The girls want him. The boys want to be him.

But none of them sees that emptiness inside him.

The void.

The... nothingness.

They only know this Aiden. The one he puts on for show. The image he projects their way. They're too blinded by his fake light to see the shadows.

But isn't that better? Isn't the lie better than the truth?

After all, the truth destroys before setting anyone free.

My heart hammers with each step he takes. This time, it's not fear for me.

It's for what he's done to Kim.

I knew that kicking him would come back to bite me, but I never thought it would be this fast.

Or this lethal.

I never thought he'd go after Kim.

My lips tremble as I try to meet my best friend's gaze and make sure she's okay. Her head is bowed. Curtains of her mint-coloured hair camouflage her expression from me and the world.

Aiden stops beside me. I catch a glimpse of his hand slipping in his pocket before I concentrate on my notebook, gripping the pencil so hard, it almost breaks.

His body looms over mine like a grim reaper and his eyes burn holes at the top of my head.

A part of me wants to look up and glare back. Like I've done for the past two years.

But back then, I didn't have the slightest clue of what he was capable of.

Now, I do.

After what seems like forever, he saunters to the vacant seat behind me. The seat I was saving for Kim.

She fidgets beside the only empty seat in the class. In front of Xander.

The latter gives her a taunting look as if daring her to sit.

"Ms Reed?" Mrs Stone's impatient tone calls. "Is something the matter?"

"No," Kim whispers.

"Then please take a seat so we can continue the class."

Kim slides into her seat slowly as if afraid there's a bomb waiting there.

Cole flashes a look behind him to Kim and Ronan winks at me from in front of me.

We're surrounded by the enemy.

EIGHT

I try.

I really try to concentrate during class.

It's impossible.

For one, Kim seems out of it, barely taking any notes. And it's worrying me shitless.

For two, RES's football team's forward line surrounds us like a pack of wolves with the big bad wolf right behind me.

Aiden hasn't said a word, but he doesn't have to.

His presence can't be mistaken even if he remains silent. I can feel his eyes digging a hole in the back of my head and feasting on my brain.

Mrs Stone starts talking about a preparatory test. I concentrate on her for the first time since the class started.

"You'll perform a known script and add your special touch to it. The more creative you are, the more bonus points you will get."

I love bonus points. It's my perfect chance to build up my record for Cambridge.

"Can we pick who we perform with?" A girl at the front of the class asks.

"Partners will be chosen at random," Mrs Stone says. "Swapping partners is prohibited."

"Can we go solo?"

"Absolutely not," Mrs Stone says. "This is to teach you team spirit."

Some whine softly while others snicker.

I spend the rest of the class trying to take as many notes as possible to occupy my mind.

But one can't erase how Aiden looms like the devil in the corner, waiting to steal my soul.

As soon as the class ends, Kim shoves her things in her bag and takes off out the door.

I'm about to follow her when my pen falls, rolling on the floor.

A tall frame bends over and picks up the pen.

I cease breathing when Aiden stands to his full height. His focus is on me as he twirls the pen between his index and middle finger.

That pen can go to hell for all I care. Call me a coward, but I can't handle another face-off with Aiden right now.

Besides, Kim is my priority.

Without sparing Aiden a glance, I bolt out of the classroom while it's still full of people.

New resolution: never get myself trapped alone in the same place as Aiden.

That's my best bet to survive.

It takes me a few minutes to find Kim. She's lurking by the corner of our next class, earbuds in, and her gaze lost somewhere out of reach.

I run to her and clutch her shoulder. "Kim! I was so worried about you. Why didn't you call me back?"

Her face is pale as if she's seen a ghost while she removes the earbuds. "Ellie…"

"What? What is it? Did Aiden do something?"

"Aiden?" Her brows furrow. "What does he have to do with anything?"

"Uh… Kim? You came to class with that arsehole."

"He found me in front of the nurse's office and told me to walk to class with him."

My blood boils. "Did he hurt you? Force you?"

"What the hell? Why would he do that?" Kim plays with the straps of her backpack. "He asked nicely. Almost…"

"Almost what?"

Something nostalgic flashes in her eyes. "Friendly."

"Whoa. Kim. Are you hearing yourself? Aiden isn't friendly. He can't be friendly." *He's a fucking psycho!*

Please don't tell me he's playing with Kim's mind, too. Is this a 'fuck you' to me? Or am I being too dramatic?

But then again, Aiden is the type who calculates his moves before making any.

Kim scrunches her brows, lips tightening. "Why are you so tense?"

"I'm sorry," I smooth my voice. "It's just that I'm worried about you, okay? Aiden has never been friendly to you so why would he start now?"

"King was never mean to me either. We go way back, you know." Her lips tremble.

Way back?

I know Kim studied at Royal Elite Junior with the rest of the horsemen, but I've never gotten the impression that she was friends with them before.

I mean, Xander bullies her at any chance he gets. Why would the others be friends with her?

Especially Aiden.

"Why were you at the nurse anyway?" I ask.

"Just a headache." She smiles, but it doesn't reach her eyes. "I went to pick you up but your uncle said you already left."

"Sorry about that. Aunt picked me up and I forgot my phone at school."

She's silent for a second, chewing on her bottom lip.

She'll eventually tell me whatever happened. For now, I rub her shoulder and speak in a light tone. "Senior year, senior resolutions, right?"

"What resolutions?"

"You know, we'll nail this year, too."

She stares at me, appearing lost. "How? How can we do that? Because your empty optimism never brought us anything."

"Kim…?"

She doesn't seem to have heard me and continues in rapid-fire. "We can't stop them. We can only stay under the water while it's being poured on us and pray they don't miss so we don't have to endure it again. We can only bow and let them strike, hoping this will be the last."

"Kim!" I shake her. "Don't say shit like that again. We weren't born to be stomped on. Do you hear me?"

"I'm not all strong and put together like you, Ellie." Tears shine in her eyes. "I can't freeze the world out as you do. It hurts. All of it hurts. I'm tired, okay? I'm just so fucking tired of this shit. It was ten years ago. Ten fucking years. Yes, I fucked up, but I'm only human. I deserve a second chance."

I remain rooted in place as Kim wipes her eyes and storms around me to enter the class.

She… snapped.

Kim isn't the type who snaps. She's so kind and quiet and… bullied.

What happened to make her snap? And what the hell did she mean by saying that she deserved a second chance?

A second chance from whom?

Maybe I don't know my best friend as much as I thought I did.

Something prickles at the back of my neck and my stomach tightens with strange awareness.

I turn around only to be captured by the smoky eyes of the devil king.

And he's smirking.

For the rest of the day, we're so preoccupied in our classes that I can't find a chance to talk to Kim.

I'm fidgeting, my legs won't stop bouncing, and I keep biting the cap of my pencils.

There's also the fact that the pack of four horsemen surrounded us in every class. Every. Freaking. Class. Aiden always sat behind me like a looming threat.

If anyone took the seats on either side of me and Kim, all they had to do was stand there and anyone who occupied that seat scrambled away.

Aiden didn't make a move to talk to me or even acknowledge my existence since the smirk he flashed earlier.

His silence is scarier than his words. I can react to his words. How can I react to... nothing?

In the span of a day, he made my head about ready to explode.

When Kim bolts out of class, I run after her.

I spend five minutes searching for her around the school's perimeter. She's not at the cabin or the library.

My head hangs as I step into the school's ninth tower—where we have our last class.

My head collides against something hard.

Ow.

Xander stands right at the entrance, blocking it.

He's staring ahead, fists clenching.

I follow his field of vision, and something dies in my heart.

Kim is crying against Aiden's chest and he's rubbing her back.

NINE

There are a few things no one wants to imagine.

Your parents having sex.

Your pet's death.

The end of the world.

Kim crying in Aiden's embrace is one of the things I never wanted to imagine.

My best friend is seeking comfort in the one person who's been actively ruining my life.

A sense of betrayal hits the bottom of my stomach and shoots straight to my chest.

The logical part of me recognises this as Aiden's form of revenge. He knows that Kim is the only one I have in RES and he's using that against me.

That part also knows that he's an opportunistic psycho.

But I can't suppress that other part. It's tiny and barely noticeable, but it's there.

The anger. The bitterness.

For what, I don't know.

Xander storms in their direction, a fist clenching at his side.

He might be nicknamed War, but he's not violent. Xander Knight is the type who kills you with kindness and with that dimpled smile.

Playful, albeit hateful.

This might as well be the first time I see him exhibit any sign of violence.

The hall is filled with countless onlookers—including the president of the school's photography club who's taking pictures of Kim in Aiden's embrace.

Whatever happens now will be broadcasted all over RES in a matter of hours.

Wait.

Is this what Aiden wants? He planned this entire show, didn't he?

Xander stops in front of both of them. His face is stone cold and his rigid shoulders strain against the uniform's jacket.

His glare falls on Aiden's hand around Kim's back.

I find myself glaring at it, too.

I want to break that hand.

I want to burn it and feed it to dogs.

Neither Aiden nor Xander say a word. They stare at each other, having a conversation without words.

Conquest and War complement each other, but right now, they look on the verge of destroying one another.

Xander looks two seconds away from blowing up while Aiden wears that infuriating poker face.

Everyone else falls silent, barely breathing as if they're waiting for a bomb to drop.

Xander hooks his fingers in Kim's jacket and yanks her back. Her teary eyes widen when she meets Xander's murderous gaze.

I run towards her, but before I reach them, Xander lets her go and she sprints in the opposite direction.

I should've followed her. Instead, I stop in front of Aiden. He's watching me with keen interest even though Xander is almost throwing daggers into his face.

Aiden leans in to whisper so only I can hear him, "I'm still waiting for you to show me the mark."

"You did all of this for that?" I hiss.

Poker face.

"I don't even have words for you," I whisper-yell.

"Say no, sweetheart." His hot breaths send shivers along my skin. "I dare you."

"After school," I deadpan. "Meet me after school."

Aiden raises an eyebrow as if wondering where I want to go with this. I don't know either, but I need to stop him somehow.

From here to then, I'll figure something out.

I leave him and a tense Xander.

Cole and Ronan, who missed the show, saunter out of the cafeteria.

"I'm telling you, Nash," Ronan speaks animatedly to a calm Cole. "I'm having those bunny cake hookers for my birthday."

Cole raises an eyebrow. "I thought that was last year's fantasy?"

"Captain Levi killed my vibe last year." Ronan hits his chest, laughing with mischief. "He won't stop me this year."

"Well, I'm your captain this year and I'm telling you that there won't be any hookers."

"*Mais non!*" Ronan's face falls with dramatic disdain. "I thought we were friends, fucker."

"The jury is still out on that."

"That's it. You're crossed from my friends' list. Best of luck finding where to party because I'm banning you from my house and…"

Their chatter dies away as they reach the other two.

The reason I focused on their conversation was to distract myself from the unwanted attention at my back.

And it's not from the gawking students.

No.

The back of my neck prickles and goosebumps cover my skin due to that annoying awareness.

That unbreakable connection.

It's like he's invading every part of me and engraving himself under my skin.

I find Kim hiding beneath the staircase in the corner. Her

eyes are bloodshot and swollen, and her hands shake as she grips her backpack tighter.

Her hair is in disarray, the mint-coloured strands appear like a lab experiment gone wrong.

"Kim…?" I approach her slowly like she's an injured animal.

A part of me wants to shout at her and demand why she let Aiden hug her.

It's like I don't know her after she returned from her summer camp. Kim didn't only change physically, it's like she's been building a wall around her.

My chest aches. She's slipping from between my fingers and I don't know how to keep her or talk to her.

Her dark green eyes meet mine. They're filled with so many emotions, but the most prominent of all is sorrow.

Deep sorrow.

She throws herself at me, and I can't help but wrap my arms around her. A sob tears from her throat as she buries her face in my chest.

I feel like a horrible friend for not detecting her breaking point and not being there for her.

This is probably why she cried in Aiden's embrace. She only wanted comfort.

Like a shark to the blood, Aiden must've smelled it and stepped in like a white knight.

If he planned to rattle me by using her, then it worked.

"Kim… you're my best friend and I love you, but you have to tell me what's going on."

She steps back and wipes her eyes with the heel of her palms. "Have you ever wondered if you could be the villain in someone's story?"

"The villain? You? You're the kindest person I know." I laugh but she isn't laughing along.

"Sometimes villains look so innocent, Ellie." Her gaze is lost in the distance. "Actual villains don't know they're villains because they think everything they do is right."

"What do you mean?"

"I did something unforgivable and I'm paying for it." She releases a strangled breath. "I just have to find a way to survive this year."

"Kim." I clutch her shoulders. "You did nothing wrong, okay? Don't believe whatever rubbish Aiden told you. They're the bullies, not you."

"Should we egg their cars?" She smiles through her tears. "Better idea, we can steal their jerseys or do some voodoo at the pitch so they'd lose their upcoming game."

I mirror her smile, feeling loose now that she is. "That'll bring me down to their level and I refuse to stoop so low."

"Ugh, you're like an old lady." She jokes. "Stop being a mature bitch."

"I'd rather be mature instead of a bully."

"You know…" she trails off, meeting my gaze. "Aiden wasn't always like this."

"Nope. Not hearing it. I don't care what he was like."

That rule about not attempting to understand bullies? I take it to heart.

"Maybe you should care, Ellie. Don't you ever wonder why he picked you? Why does he never bother anyone but you?"

"So what do you suggest? I dig around his life? Find his traumatic past and *fix* him because he's such a good person on the inside with a heart of gold?" I sigh. "That only happens in your romance novels and Korean soap operas, Kim."

"Rude!" She hits my arm. "Don't go insulting my romance novels and for the thousandth time, they're called K-dramas."

"Yeah, sure. K-dramas."

"Exactly." She feigns a curtsy. "So tell me, did something happen with King?"

"Why would you say that?"

"You seem more aggressive about him than usual. I mean, you just said an entire paragraph about him when you used to refuse to even say his name."

Something in my chest shrinks. I want to tell Kim all about yesterday, but I'm such a coward.

I don't want Kim to judge me for being weak. She always calls me strong and hardened, but I crumbled with a single push yesterday. I'm ashamed to even look her in the eyes, let alone tell her what happened.

"I'm just angry that he hugged you."

"Why?"

"What do you mean, why? He's being his manipulative self."

"How do you know that when you refuse to get to know him?"

I purse my lips.

"Come on, Ellie, don't they tell you in your Chinese war books to keep your enemies closer than your friends? You can't defeat him if you know nothing about him."

I want to protest, but she's right. I know nothing about Aiden and that puts me at a disadvantage.

Whenever Kim offered to tell me what she knows about him from the years they grew up together, I always shot her attempts down.

Aiden is that itch that makes me all uncomfortable and aware. The mere mention of his name smashes my mood and pulls at my sanity strings.

I did everything to erase him, but the king can't be erased, can he? Even if he's not there, his name floats all over RES. Hell, even at home, Aunt and Uncle always talk about King Enterprises.

He's like a ghost haunting me wherever I go.

Maybe I've been looking at things wrong. Maybe erasing him isn't the solution.

If I choose to get to know him, it's not to understand him. It's only a tactic so I'd know how to counter him.

"You know Xander," I tell Kim. "It did you nothing, though."

"*Knew* Xander. Past tense. He's been a stranger for years." She releases a pained sigh. "Besides, I don't intend to fight him. You, on the other hand, seem bent on challenging King."

"I'm only defending myself and…" I clutch her hand, my throat suddenly dry. "Our friendship. I hate that he's getting between us, Kim."

"My relationship with King isn't like that."

Relationship?

Before I can question her, the last class's hour dings.

"Your track training," Kim says.

I give her a quick hug. "I'll see you later?"

She doesn't take any sports classes.

A grin breaks on her face. "We'll binge Lucifer?"

"Absolutely."

In the locker room, I finish changing my clothes in record time before the other girls arrive.

I'm always the first or the last and usually in the far corner so none of them catches a glimpse of my scar.

A scar that's now surrounded by hickeys.

I wait in the hallway for Coach. Some of the girls are chatting amongst each other.

Since the first day when Aiden deemed me as an outcast, the track team doesn't really like me.

I remain in my zone and they stay in theirs.

I retrieve my phone and open social media.

It's only to know what I'm up against, I tell myself.

Nothing more.

I find Aiden_King on Instagram only because he's been following me for about a year. I never thought much of it at the time and I always ignored the itch to go through his profile.

He has a few hundreds of thousands followers. Hundreds of freaking thousands. Geez. It's not like he's a celebrity or something.

His caption is *Go Elites.*

His feed is filled with pictures of the game. He has full shots of the entire team. Most of his pictures are with Elites' forward line. Xander, Cole, and Ronan.

He has pics in parties while they drown alcohol. In other pictures, they have girls squeezed between them.

In older pictures, they have Levi King with them. Aiden's older cousin and Elites' previous captain and a current player for Arsenal. I know him because I've been following him so closely since the beginning of this season.

He added so much balance to Arsenal's midfield.

At the end of last year, Levi led Elites to win the schools' championship. Aiden commemorated the moment with a picture of the forward line carrying Levi on their shoulders. A brunette stands beside Aiden laughing so happily and genuinely.

Even Aiden appears… happy? No. Not happy. More like euphoric.

It must be some sort of a power, right? Even through his Instagram, he shows that perfect golden boy and star image.

It's easy for the world to believe he's living the best life and loving it.

The more I scroll, the more it feels like a mask. A method to hide something. What, I don't know.

Then, a break of pattern catches my attention. Now and then, between rows of happy go lucky pictures, he'd post a black and white shot that doesn't have his face on it. One has his dark silhouette from behind. Another shows a ball with his name on it. A few others have the chessboard.

He doesn't have captions on those pictures, and if he does, they're short and strange.

Mood.

Urges.

Long Live the Queen.

Play the player, not the game.

Stop & Stare.

Ruin before you're ruined.

I find myself hunting for every picture of that type. Unlike the other pictures, these seem like a true window to Aiden.

He posted the last black and white picture last night. It's a shot of a glass chessboard. Right in the middle, the black king piece stands tall while the white queen falls at his feet.

The caption is, *Sick*.

All the commenters—mostly females—gush and wish him to get better soon.

I don't think he meant sick in the physical term. He's screwed up in the head as I told him.

As *I* told him?

I shake my head. That can't be true.

"Come on, Girls. Go! Go! Go!"

Coach Nessrine's voice startles me. I close the phone, throw it in my bag and head out to practice.

The thing I hate the most about track practice in RES is that we run around the football pitch where the football team is practising.

Nope. I won't let them ruin running for me.

Coach gives us instructions on today's practice. As I stretch, my gaze drifts to the pitch.

I find him without even trying to. Being hyper-aware of him makes him stand out of the crowd even if I don't want him to.

Aiden wears the royal blue jersey and shorts like he's some model. The uniform sticks to his body like a second skin outlining his developed chest and his toned thighs and legs. He calls for the ball and when it reaches him, his eyes spark with that challenging streak. He doesn't take long to cut through the defence.

Conquest.

He stops at nothing to get to the goal.

I hate the bastard, but with his level of talent, he can be scouted into one of the Premier League's top teams. That is if he wasn't already. Maybe, like his cousin, RES won't allow him to leave until he graduates.

Elites are divided into two teams, playing against each other. Cole and Aiden are on the team who wears the blue uniform. Xander and Ronan are on the team with neon T-shirts.

Aiden and Xander are the team's strikers, but now, Xander is playing defence. A position he doesn't usually play.

What? I might have been listening when Kim told me about the home games she watched last year.

Aiden goes for the ball, leaving a few of his opponents behind. Just when he's gaining momentum towards the net, Xander tackles him with brute force. Aiden hits the ground with a thud.

A few gasps escape from the girls around me. Even our coach stops and stares.

The audience who gathered to watch the practice fall silent, their mouths hanging open.

That's the effect Aiden has on people. Even though RES's known for academics, they've been obsessed with football these past few years. They're dreaming about another championship after the one last year.

Xander doesn't even reach down to help Aiden. Cole and Ronan do. Coach Larson, a middle-aged man with a bald head and bushy brows, hits Xander with a paper bat on his shoulder.

If he's affected, he doesn't show it. All he does is cut a poker-faced Aiden a deadly glare.

"Wow. Knight is tense," one of the girls whispers from behind me.

"I know, right?" Another replies. "He's like out for blood."

So I'm not the only one who noticed that.

It's the first time I've seen Aiden and Xander at each other's throat.

The captain, Cole, and the coach speak to Xander on the sidelines.

Judging from Coach Larson's reddening cheeks, he doesn't look so happy.

I snort. Of course, he wouldn't be. I'm sure he's barely stopping himself from murdering Xander for touching his star. Aiden is the ace striker, and strikers always get full credit, no matter how many good assists they get.

Still warming up, I search for Aiden. He stands near the

bench, gripping a bottle of sports drink, but his attention isn't on the drink or on Xander or on Ronan who's talking to him.

It's on me.

I freeze in the middle of stretching my hand behind my back. The position thrusts my breasts against my tracksuit. Aiden's gaze trails down to the curve of my breasts slowly. Too slowly. It's painful.

My throat closes. I feel like pumping air out of my lungs, gasping, and begging for breath.

When his metallic eyes slide back to mine, they're full of undisclosed hunger.

Raw.

Furious.

I can't breathe even if I want to. I feel like if I take one breath, he'll jump me.

For two years, I got used to murderous glares from him. What's up with this one?

I can take his hateful looks. Hell, I want us to go back to the hateful looks' stage. At least back then, I wasn't rattled out of my mind.

But this look? This hunger? This one I can't take.

I break eye contact first. He can play whatever game he wants on his own.

The practice goes well for the most part. It's after the fourth loop that exhaustion starts to settle in.

I take more pauses for water than necessary. My record keeps slowing down.

Now and then, when I look into the football pitch, I find Aiden's destabilising eyes on me.

God damn him.

After practice, Coach calls me into her office as the other girls head into the shower.

Coach Nessrine has olive skin and dark blue eyes that give her an exotic look.

"Everything okay, Quinn?" Her brows furrow. "Your numbers

weren't optimal by the end. Have you been practising during the summer?"

"I have." I swallow. "I'll work hard. I promise."

"Is it your heart condition?" she asks.

When I told Aunt Blair I want to run, she refused. Uncle and I did everything to coax her. She only agreed with her terms. One of them being that my coach knows about my heart condition and to always call her if anything comes up.

I can't be removed from the team's line up. Running is what keeps me alive.

"No. It's only because of the season's changes."

Coach Nessrine nods, but she doesn't seem convinced. We spend another twenty minutes strategising our next competition before I head to the showers.

The last of the girls leave the locker room. I release a relieved breath as I shimmy out of my clothes and step into the shower.

My head tips back as water cascades over me. I pretend it's the rain soaking me and washing away all impurities.

Once I'm done, I scrub my hands clean and wrap a towel around my torso while stepping out of the shower.

A small rustle comes from the other side. Must be Coach who came to lock up.

I round the corner and freeze.

Aiden stands in the middle of the locker room.

TEN

Aiden is in the locker room.

The girls' locker room.

For a second, I'm too stunned to do anything except stare.

He leans against the locker. His arms and ankles crossed and a dark spark dances in his cloudy gaze.

He's watching me with an unnerving focus like he's a ravenous predator salivating after his prey.

His attention slides down my body and I follow his gaze. Water still drips from my loose hair, creating rivulets down my skin. The towel barely hides the top of my breasts and stops at the middle of my thighs.

I cross my arms over my chest.

Standing in front of Aiden in nothing but a towel is about the worst situation I can be in.

Tipping my chin, I point at the door. "Get out or I'll call for Coach."

He continues measuring me up and down, not bothering to hide the sick desire from his features. "You said to meet you after school."

"I meant outside, not in the locker room."

He lifts a shoulder, his gaze finally sliding up to mine. "You didn't specify the place. This is as good as any."

"Get out. I'll meet you outside."

"Why not here?"

"Are you freaking kidding me?"

"No."

"Damn it, Aiden. I can't just talk when I'm only wearing a towel."

His lips curve into a sadistic smile. "What's the matter, sweetheart? Are you shy?"

"Of you? Not a chance."

"Hmm." He tilts his head to the side. "Then are you afraid of temptation?"

"More like I want your attention nowhere near me."

"Here's the problem, Frozen." He pushes off the locker and stalks towards me in cool, predatory strides.

Don't step back.

Don't you dare step back.

I can't believe I have to remind myself to be strong and not allow Aiden to hurt me.

Then I remember that I kicked him in the balls and he might be here to take revenge.

A tremor shoots down my spine and my feet move back.

With every step back, he pushes forward like a hurricane.

Looming.

Unstoppable.

Dangerous.

Everything heightens.

My breathing becomes quicker and shallower. The droplets of water still coating my skin drip between the valley of my breasts, creating razor-sharp friction. My hold on the towel turns into a death grip.

My back hits the wall, and I startle, barely stopping a yelp from escaping.

Damn him and damn me for allowing him to affect me.

When I attempt to sidestep him, he plants a hand on the wall beside my head, caging me in.

He invades my personal space until all I can smell is his clean, straight-from-the-shower scent. He's changed into the school's uniform but didn't bother with the jacket.

He's only wearing a crisp white shirt that wraps around his narrow waist and is tucked haphazardly into the band of his trousers.

Then I realise I'm looking at his trousers and snap my attention back to his face.

Huge mistake.

This close, we're almost breathing the same air. I can see the small mole at the corner of his right eye and the hollowness in said eyes.

His free hand reaches for my hair and he twirls a blonde strand between his fingers. "You didn't ask for my attention but you're getting it anyway, Frozen. All I could think about since yesterday was touching you again. I keep wondering how you'd feel with my hands fisted in your hair and my dick shoved deep down your throat."

My lips tremble, falling open.

"Or how you'd feel beneath me as I fuck you until you pass out," he continues in that casual tone. "Or how you'd taste when I tongue-fuck you or how —"

"Stop…" I meant it as a warning but it comes out as a helpless whimper.

An overwhelming, strange sensation takes over my body because of his crude words.

I wish it's embarrassment or anger, but it's far from it.

The bottom of my stomach tightens and heat pours all over my skin. My nipples pucker and strain against the towel until it's slightly painful.

Aiden watches me with a tilted head as if he's searching for something.

He always takes whatever he likes without asking for permission. Hell, he loves not having permission. It's weird that he's going as far as gauging my reaction.

"Are you wet, Frozen?"

It takes everything in me to jut my chin out. "No."

"You're not, hmm?" He releases my hair and drags his thumb at the bottom of my lip. "So you're telling me that if I reach under the towel, you won't soak my fingers?"

I clamp my lips shut around whatever voice that's been clawing its way through.

"Maybe I should check, huh? Just to make sure."

Keeping a hand around the towel, I plant the other on his chest. The word 'stop' hangs on the corner of my tongue, but knowing he'd probably take it as a challenge and continue, I swallow it back inside.

Instead, I say, "The only way you'll be able to do that is if you knock me unconscious."

"That's both necrophilia and cheating. Neither interests me. When I bring you to orgasm, I want your face flushed red and your screams cutting through the air."

"You really are sick."

"And you're really beginning to sound repetitive."

His gaze drops to my naked shoulders and the hint of my scar surrounded by the hickeys he left.

"Aiden... don't..." I warn. My nails dig into my palm as if my grip on the towel is my lifeline.

"I asked you nicely this morning." His dark eyes meet mine. "But maybe you don't like nice, sweetheart. Maybe deep down, you like the opposite of nice."

"I like being left alone."

"Is that what you believe?" His thumb traces down my cheek and swipes harshly along my bottom lip as if he's attempting to wipe something off.

I can't even fight him away because that will mean leaving my towel and my body at his mercy—or the lack thereof.

"Do you know what I think? I think a part of you likes the opposite of nice, but because you're such a good girl, you're out to destroy that part. You're scared about what it could mean about you. How can you like something so deprived when you're such a perfect human being? You're scared of yourself, sweetheart."

"You're delusional."

"Am I?" He releases my face and his fingers drop down to my collarbone. Every contact of his skin against mine is like a scorching fire.

And like any fire, ashes is the only thing he'll leave behind.

"Leave me the hell alone," I hiss.

"I told you. I can't."

He yanks the towel down, exposing the scar and my pale breasts.

It's a miracle that I keep the towel fastened around my middle. Or maybe I only keep it because he allows it.

He wraps his thumb and forefinger around my nipple and squeezes hard.

A zapping sensation shoots straight to my core and I close my eyes with shame.

"Your nipples are so hard." He squeezes some more until a whimper leaves my lips. "See? They're all tight and sensitive so maybe they like the opposite of nice, too."

I purse my lips together, scared that an alien sound would come out.

"Fuck." His metallic eyes fill with wonder.

He continues pinching and twirling my nipple, but it's not his focus. His entire attention is on the angry red marks he left around my scar.

Biting down the sensations going through my body, I stare, incredulous. "Do you get off on causing people pain?"

His gaze reluctantly leaves my chest to meet my eyes. A sheen of indifference covers his features, sealing whatever interest sparked earlier. "Are you in pain?"

"No, but I'm uncomfortable. Spare me your attention."

"Why?" He pinches my nipple hard.

My lips tremble as I try to gather my wits around me. "You're toxic. And oh, you ruined my life for two years."

He leans over, lips ghosting on the shell of my ear sending chills to the bottom of my stomach as he whispers, "Not enough."

"What have I done to you?" My voice trembles around the words.

"You exist."

Tears rim my eyes at his words.

Somewhere deep inside, I agree with Kim. Aiden doesn't bully anyone else in school—not even her. He doesn't go out of his way to trap others as he does me.

"Why me?" I shout. "Why the fuck is it my life you decided to ruin? Was it a toss of a coin? Did you wake up that day and decided it would be me?"

His hand wraps around my neck and he squeezes. It's tight enough to make me beg for air and show that he's the one in control.

That he can in any second squeeze the life out of me.

"Do you think I was destroying you?" he asks with a dark voice. "You've seen nothing, Frozen."

I try to push at his chest, but he reaches his free hand to my nipple and pinches it while squeezing my neck harder.

I can't breathe.

I can't freaking breathe.

My lungs choke on non-existent air as I thrash and claw at his hand and arms.

My eyes bulge, feeling every nerve ending tingling. Lightheadedness grips me and everything turns hazy.

"The more you fight, the harder I squeeze." He swipes his tongue along my parted bottom lip and whispers against my mouth, "You're smart, aren't you, sweetheart?"

My hands tremble as I drop them to either side of me.

He loosens his hand the slightest bit to allow some air in. I gulp it greedily, my lungs and eyes burning with oxygen.

"Good girl," he twirls his thumb over my nipple as I tremble with tiny bursts of breath.

"You could've stayed away, Frozen." His voice is dark and chilling like a moonless night. "But you had to start the war."

What…?

"Elsa?" Coach Nessrine calls from the door.

Her footsteps come closer with each passing second.

My face heats and panic grips me by the gut. If she finds me with Aiden, I can kiss my clean, perfect record goodbye. I will endanger Cambridge and everything I've worked for.

Aiden releases me and strides to the window. He throws me one last indecipherable look before he jumps down and disappears.

I release a shaky breath as I pull the towel up my body. My legs are trembling and barely holding me upright.

Coach Nessrine comes into view. "Is everything all right?"

"Yeah," I whisper.

Not really.

Not at all.

ELEVEN

Aunt Blair and I switch from a side plank to a meditation position.

Eyes closed, we just feel.

The sound of the birds chirping in the trees fills my ears like soothing music. The humid air sticks to my cheeks and ruffles my hair back.

For as long as I remember, Aunt and I have shared this moment of inner peace.

The only difference is that I can't focus right now.

The confrontation I had with Aiden in the locker room yesterday keeps replaying in the back of my mind like a recurring nightmare.

My skin prickles with unease.

Or is it unease?

My body didn't forget how close he got. How he touched me like he had every right to.

Since my return to school this year, everything has been spiralling out of control. The inner peace I've been doing my best to protect is being chipped, chewed, and thrown out. Or maybe it's been crumbling for the past two years while I've been doing my best to be strong.

Or the ten years before that.

Damn Aiden to the darkest pits of hell.

He's stirring a part I've been keeping under wraps from everyone. Hell, I've been shielding myself from that part, too.

Haunted memories.

Excruciating pain.

Dead eyes.

Every time I stare into his smoky gaze, I see a hint of the darkness I left behind. I'll be damned if I let him or anyone else force me to remember that nightmare.

"Elsie?"

My eyes snap open to find Aunt sitting cross-legged in front of me. She's staring at my clenched fists with furrowed brows.

"The idea is to relax." She's smiling but concern is etched on her creased brow. No wrinkles whatsoever.

Aunt is an ageless beauty, basically.

Her face hasn't changed an inch since that day she took my small hand in hers and promised me a new life.

People believe in guardian angels, I believe in Aunt Blair and Uncle Jaxon.

"Sorry," I smile back and take the bottle of mineral water she offers. "I've been thinking about a test."

I do have a maths' test, but that's not what's occupying me right now.

Ugh. I hate lying to my aunt.

She pushes my bangs off of my forehead and behind my ear. Aunt and I are in yoga trousers. She's wearing a sports bra while I'm in a sleeveless top. She shifted her mat so we're facing each other instead of the green scenery of our back garden.

"You know we're proud of you no matter what you do, right? It doesn't have to be Cambridge if you don't want to." Her smile is warm but also pained.

Sometimes, I wonder if she sees my mother in my face. I'm becoming more and more a carbon copy of her.

"Blasphemy," I laugh. "Don't let Uncle Jaxon hear you say the words 'no Cambridge'. Besides, I want Cambridge, Aunt. It's my dream."

She rolls her wedding band. "Don't tell Jaxon and we'll eat ice cream while watching a cheesy chick flick until we pass out."

"Deal."

We roll our mats, close the door against the garden's chilly air and go inside.

Aunt lied about letting me eat as much ice cream as I want. She barely let me have two spoonfuls before her parent side took over. Ice cream isn't good for my healthy food dosage.

We scroll through Netflix for ten minutes before we decide to re-watch Pride and Prejudice for the thousandth time.

The book is still better. Just saying.

Aunt answers her emails as we snuggle on the couch with popcorn—mine doesn't have salt because… healthy.

Since Aunt came home today, Uncle will probably pull an all-nighter. Lately, they've been up to their necks in a new project. My heart squeezes knowing that I'll be seeing less and less of them.

"You can work from your office, Aunt," I offer.

"Nonsense." She pulls me in so I'm leaning against her shoulder. "It's girls' night."

We're about half an hour in when I ask, "Aunt?"

"Hmm?" She glances at me then back at her phone.

"Have we lived in London before? I mean, my parents and I?"

She raises her head from her phone slowly, too slowly. "No. You were born and brought up in Birmingham."

That's also what I know. Since that accident, my memories have been wiped clean, but I remember Birmingham. The copper air. The suffocating, grey atmosphere and the smell of a lake.

"Why would you think you lived in London?" Aunt has abandoned her phone and is staring at me with an unreadable expression.

"Nothing. I just wondered if we came to visit you at the time?"

"Your uncle and I studied at Cambridge at the time. We didn't live in London until we started our business."

"Yeah." I smile awkwardly. "I'm just flipping things."

Aunt faces me. The look on her face is still unreadable, but it brings back a distant memory when her nose scrunches and she asks me the same question she did when I woke up in the hospital. "Do you remember anything?"

I shake my head.

"Do you want me to call Dr Khan?"

My shrink.

Since I was seven, my life has been shackled by two doctors. The heart doctor and the shrink.

"No, Aunt. It's nothing."

"You know that normal people talk to shrinks, right? It's relieving and healthy." She laughs. "Hell, I tell him more than I tell you or Jaxon."

"I'll think about it."

A lie.

I'd rather not step into Dr Khan's office again. I dislike having my brain probed.

Aunt ignores her phone for the rest of the film. Once we reach the end, I call it a night to revise my notes before sleep.

As I change into my PJ's, I pause buttoning the top and stare at the hickeys Aiden left on my flesh.

In the past, whenever I looked at the scar, I'd have haunting flashbacks about the incident when I lost my parents.

Now, I don't.

The flashback is still haunting, but it's filled with deep grey eyes gnawing into my soul as he bit the skin and left his mark in an intrusive, intimate way.

I think a part of you likes this but because you're such a good girl, you're out to destroy that part.

I button the rest with jerky hands. I'm angry at myself, no, I'm furious. How the hell can I remember his words, let alone give them weight?

I meant it earlier. I didn't want his attention, but on the flip, damning side, he's having mine.

The fact that I'm starting to be invested in him creeps me out of my skin.

While a psycho, Aiden is a human being, and I can't help wondering why he does everything he does.

Everyone has a motive, don't they? No matter how much I've tried to shove Aiden into the black category, I'm only fooling myself.

I crawl into my bed, play *Power* by Bastille, and check my phone.

Kim sent me a message saying she'll be driving her baby brother and therefore she won't be able to pick me up tomorrow.

She sends a cute picture of Kirian clinging to her leg. Although Kim is a brunette, her brother has the most golden blonde hair.

Kim: Babysitting. Save me.

Elsa: *heart emoji* I'll have that cute little elf.

We chat for a while before I head to Instagram. On RES's official page, I find a picture of me taken by the school's photography club. They had a perfect shot while I ran in practice. It's from behind, but my name and the school's logo are clear.

The tag reads. *Great minds in excellent bodies.*

RES has changed their policies over the years. Now, they're constantly promoting that they're not only about academics, but also sports.

Right after my picture, I find another one with more comments and likes. It's about the football team, so no surprise there.

The photography club managed to snag a perfect shot of Aiden during practice when he was about to shoot and score. One of his hands flings back in symmetry with his left foot like he's about to take flight.

It could be because he's a leftie, but that posture is too... unearthly. Damn that perfect, aesthetic posture.

I zoom in to erase everyone in the pitch except for him.

After a few seconds of staring like a creep, I exit Instagram altogether and cover my head in exasperation.

I'm turning into something I hate because of the bastard.

My phone dings, and I lunge for it expecting it to be Kim.

Aiden.

Wait. Aiden?

Of course. He had my phone for a whole day after all. If he can crack the code, he can save his number.

I'm tempted to toss my phone and crack it to pieces, but curiosity gets the better of me.

I swipe the screen to read the text.

Aiden: Asleep?

I contemplate sending him a 'fuck you', but decide to ignore him instead. I seriously don't know what he's thinking by texting me.

It's not like we're old friends or even acquaintances.

Another text comes in.

Aiden: I'm not.

Obviously.

My phone dings again.

Aiden: I'm picturing you naked, screaming my name while I pound into your tight little pussy.

A tingle warms its way down my body and between my legs.

Aiden: If you don't reply, I'll keep telling you about my fantasies.

I purse my lips. He won't get to me.

Aiden: I'm thinking about your pouty lips around my dick as I face-fuck you while you stare up at me with teary blue eyes.

The explicit image draws a shudder from my spine.

Aiden: I miss your full tits and how perfectly they fit in my palms. Are your nipples sore?

My nipples harden against the soft cloth of my PJ's and I cross an arm around them as if he can see them.

Aiden: I know you're not asleep, sweetheart. Last chance. You'll regret it if you don't reply.

When I remain silent, he sends another one.

Aiden: As you wish.

He stops sending texts. I wait for five minutes, but

nothing comes out. My hands tremble as I put the phone on the nightstand.

Why did he stop texting?

Nope. I'm not allowing him to get under my skin.

In the morning, I wake up with my hand between my legs.

Again.

Shit.

I don't usually remember my dreams, but I recall glimpses of this one. Dark grey eyes. Tears in my eyes and something thick in my mouth.

I take the longest, coldest shower I ever had and stumble downstairs.

"... maybe she's remembering."

I halt near the corner of the stairs at Aunt Blair's worried voice.

"You're overthinking." Uncle's sounds muffled due to something he must be eating.

So he did come home last night.

"Maybe we should try Dr Khan's recommendations." My aunt again. "She'll be eighteen soon."

Dr Khan's recommendations?

And what does my age have to do with anything?

Dread lodges at the pit of my stomach. I don't like where this conversation is going.

"Stop overthinking, Blair." Uncle scolds. "I'll go see if she's up. She'll be late for school."

Aunt mumbles something, but I don't hear it. I make a deliberate sound of my feet flapping against the floor as I round the corner with a big smile on my face. "Morning!"

I kiss Uncle on the cheek and let Aunt kiss mine. I drop my backpack on the chair and dig into the jam and butter. Special jam without much sugar and special non-animal butter.

My life is based on healthy food.

Appetite escapes me, but I force down tiny bites. If Aunt Blair notices I'm not eating, she'll freak.

"Is Kim late?" Aunt asks.

"No, she has to pick up Kir this morning. I'll take a taxi."

"Nonsense. I'll drive you, pumpkin," Uncle says.

"No. You drive recklessly." Aunt smiles. "I will."

The bell rings. Must be Mrs Robinson next door. She loves baking and giving her muffins to neighbours. Although Aunt doesn't let me eat them.

I take the chance to distract Aunt from my barely eaten sandwich. "I'll open!"

Uncle gives me a look. "I will do it. Finish your breakfast, pumpkin."

Busted.

"Why don't you wear your hair down?" Aunt asks, smoothing my ponytail.

I take a sip of the orange juice. "It's a hassle."

Truth is, I never liked my hair down.

"Pumpkin?" Uncle's voice sounds bemused as he appears at the threshold. "A friend came for you."

"A friend?" Did Kim change her mind?

But then again, Uncle Jaxon doesn't call Kim a 'friend'.

My *friend* appears and I choke on the orange juice.

Aiden fucking King is standing in our dining room.

TWELVE

I don't believe in extraterrestrial beings but at the moment, I would rather have an alien standing in my dining room instead of Aiden fucking King.

I'm too stunned to react. The toast is suspended mid-air with my jaw almost dropping to the floor.

Aiden saunters to the middle of my dining room with confident, nonchalant steps.

People feel awkward—or at least reserved—when entering a place for the first time.

Not Aiden.

His gleaming eyes fix mine with so much ease like all this is an everyday occurrence.

The school's jacket stretches over his defined shoulder muscles giving him an older edge than his eighteen years. His inky hair is slicked back to perfection and he's even wearing the tie, today. His pressed trousers and elegant, designer shoes complete his shiny appearance.

Aiden only looked this way at the end of the year ceremony when he had to give speeches. He doesn't dress to impress, but today, he most definitely is.

It's a subtle reminder that he's not only a student at RES but also the future heir of the school.

He's not only Aiden, but he's also Aiden King.

The air turns stuffier and tighter with his presence.

I'm shocked, Uncle appears confused and Aunt grips the

glass of orange juice so tight, her knuckles turn white. She stares at Aiden as if she's seeing a ghost.

Uncle clears his throat. "I didn't know Elsa had other friends aside from Kim."

Way to go, Uncle. Might as well tell him that this family exists because their biggest contractor is King Enterprises.

Aiden pouts—the bastard actually *pouts*—and stalks towards me. "I'm hurt, sweetheart. I didn't know you were hiding me from your parents."

In a few subtle words, he made Aunt and Uncle believe we're in a relationship. He said it so casually, no one would peg him as a liar.

Those aliens might as well kidnap me in their spaceships and throw me on their planets.

Uncle's brows furrow and Aunt stares at me hard. Something twists in my chest. It feels as if I betrayed her.

"It's not like that," I whisper past the lump in my throat, but Aunt doesn't seem to be hearing me.

"You didn't tell us you knew Aiden, pumpkin," Uncle says in a more cheerful tone.

"It's my fault." Aiden faces my uncle with the most sincere, solemn expression I have seen on him. Even his accent becomes posher. "Due to your company's contract with my father's company, Elsa was worried about implicating our parents. I respect her wishes, but I also want to show her off as my girl."

Elsa?

My girl?

Am I in a freaking nightmare right now?

I want to shove his perfect face in a sink full of water and hold him there until no more breaths come out.

My chest squeezes at the image.

It's so familiar and… disturbing.

My widened eyes snap back to Aiden.

Subconsciously, people are ashamed about lying and their

brains express that in the form of tells. A rub of the nape. A twitch of the eye. A twist of the lips.

Not Aiden.

He feels none of that shame and therefore, his lies come out in a smooth, intricate web.

If the relaxation of Uncle's shoulders is any sign, he believes him.

"Is that true?" Aunt Blair faces me, still gripping the orange juice glass tight.

"It's…" My hands ball into fists in my lap, but before I can continue, Aiden is by my side.

He touches my cheek with his knuckles, and they heat like a pit of flames.

Damn him. How can he touch me in front of Aunt and Uncle?

"See? I told you not to worry last night. Didn't you say Mr and Mrs Quinn are open-minded and will always back your decisions?" He places a subtle hand on my shoulder as he turns his attention to Aunt and Uncle. "I heard a lot about your work ethics from my father. I'm happy to find out that your familial ethics are just as excellent."

Knock Out.

Complete knockout.

I don't even have a case anymore.

Aiden didn't only make them think that our 'relationship' is in the closet because I respected and loved them, but he also brought up their work.

Their God.

The reason both of them breathe.

Even I don't compare. Quinn Engineering is their biological child and I'm the adopted child. They love me, but I always come second.

How did Aiden know that?

How far did he dig to come up with this bit of information?

Uncle's easy smile makes an appearance. "Mr King talks about us?"

"All the time, Sir. Your recent project had been the talk of the last BOD's meeting. King Enterprises can only move forward with strong assets like Quinn Engineering. Some would argue that small companies mean nothing in the great scheme of things, but it's small companies that fuel the production and build the pyramid to the top. King Enterprises was also a small company at one point."

Perfect posh accent.

Perfect manners.

Perfect everything.

"Indeed, son." Uncle's chest puffs. "King Enterprises has a bright future with you as an heir."

He's calling him Son.

Fucking *Son*.

But then again, it shouldn't be a surprise that Uncle is impressed. He always loathed how big companies looked down their noses at smaller ones, but here is an heir of the biggest company of all telling him exactly what he believes in.

"I can only try, Sir. I'm only at the beginning of the path, but I hope to work as hard as you and everyone else."

I know they're rehearsed words that he must've said a thousand times before, but with the sincerity mask he's wearing, even I am close to being fooled.

Aiden is a parasite.

No.

He's the devil who can flow in someone's bloodstream and tell him exactly what he likes to hear without appearing sleazy or an obvious manipulator.

But before you know it, he'd be telling you what to do and how to do it.

By then, you'd have no control over your actions.

"You didn't have to hide it from us, pumpkin." Uncle beams

at me, already under Aiden's spell. "We're not that strict with you, are we?"

If I begin screaming right now that Aiden is lying and that we should burn and bury his corpse in the back garden, Aunt and Uncle will probably take me back to Dr Khan and ask him to admit me to that hospital I hated when I was a kid.

"That's because Elsie never had a boyfriend." Aunt is softening, too, but unlike Uncle, something is holding her back.

Aiden raises one perfect eyebrow at the needless information Aunt just shared.

His lips move in a tiny smirk only meant for me as he squeezes my shoulder hard. I suppress a wince. He quickly masks his sadism to resume his perfect disguise. "I'm honoured to be her first."

Aunt touches her collarbone, a habit she does whenever she's uncertain. "We'll talk about this, Elsa. For now, you should go to school."

She packs my sandwich in a container and places it in my backpack.

"Come on." Aiden clutches me by the arm like a doting boyfriend. "We'll be late."

While I'm thinking about ways to get away with murder, Aiden offers Aunt and Uncle his golden boy smile.

"It was nice to finally meet you, Mr and Mrs Quinn."

"Please, call us Jaxon and Blair, Son." Uncle glances at me. "Make sure to bring him over."

Over my dead body.

"I'll certainly visit." One more blinding smile. "Elsa tells me you're an Arsenal fan."

"Why, indeed. A gunner at heart."

"Me, too. In fact, it runs in the family. My cousin, Levi King, plays for the team. The president is my father's old friend. If you want to attend a game, let me know and I'll get you a special pass."

Uncle might as well have been star struck. "That would be brilliant. Go, Gunners."

"Go, Gunners," Aiden fist-bumps him.

Uncle is the one to usher us out. I'm contemplating running upstairs to my room, hit rewind and pretend this morning never happened.

Or better yet, I'll wait for Aiden at the door with an axe.

He parked his car in front of the house. A bright red Ferrari. Of course. An arsehole like him would drive a fast Italian car.

Aunt remains at the threshold of the house. Her folded arms and unreadable expression are the complete opposite of Uncle's enthusiasm.

Aiden guides me to the passenger seat with his hand on the small of my back. I try not to squirm in the black leather seats and hold my backpack close to my chest like a shield.

Once we're seated, Aiden throws one last pleasantry at Uncle before he hits the button. The engine's strong vibrations startle me and I grip the backpack tighter.

The car revs in the wide streets. I suppress a gasp at the strength of this thing. I can't even help clenching my thighs together.

"You like the power, sweetheart?" Aiden watches me intently as I fight the strange rush of excitement.

All the thrill fades away when I recall that I'm riding with the devil. "Pull over."

"We're not there yet."

I face him with an incredulous look. "You really think I'd let you drive me to school?"

"I told you yesterday that you'd regret ignoring me."

"You honestly believe I would reply to your crude texts?"

He lifts a shoulder. "But for future reference, I dislike being ignored."

"I don't care about what you dislike, Aiden." My voice rises.

The stunt he just pulled and Aunt's disappointed face makes me sick to my stomach.

"You should or..." He reaches over and clutches my hand in his. "I will continue dropping in unannounced and make your adoptive parents fall in love with me." He lifts my hand to his lips and brushes a kiss to my knuckles.

To an outsider, the gesture would look gentle, almost chaste. But this is Aiden fucking King. The malice in his eyes twists me in knots.

"The look on your face when I stepped into your house was priceless, sweetheart. I should've caught it on camera."

I jerk my hand free. My automatic reaction would be to scream and make him drop me off, but things don't roll that way with Aiden.

He gets off on anger and strong emotions. Since I'm almost sure he's a psycho, and therefore lacks feelings, he uses them to antagonise others.

If I give into his trap, I'll never find a way out.

I just saw first hand how he manipulated Aunt and Uncle, who've known me for my entire life, into thinking I was hiding a love affair from them.

The only way to escape his intricate manipulation web is to be level-headed.

I square my shoulders as I face him. My voice is calm. "I don't know what your obsession is with me, but it's not going to work."

He squints an eye. "Let me worry about that, sweetheart."

"I'm not your sweetheart, Aiden. I'm just a girl you bully and I hate to say this, but I prefer the days you had your minions bully me over this unwanted attention. I don't want you anywhere near me or my family. It's one more year and everyone will go their own way, so let's pretend these last couple of days never happened."

"Pretending was never my thing."

"Oh, please. You just pulled off a Broadway-level performance about how much you care about me when we both know you don't."

"I do care about you, sweetheart. Maybe not in the conventional term, but I never stopped caring about you. It's becoming tiresome and fucking irritating." His dark eyes shoot a path into my soul. "The time has come to do something about it."

THIRTEEN

The time has come to do something about it.

The car ride has been silent since Aiden said those words.

I'm at a loss for words.

Trying to find a crack in Aiden's wall is like hitting thick steel; it's hard, painful, and maddening.

As the car cuts the distance with high speed, a crazy idea barges into my head.

Maybe I've been using the wrong method to find that crack. Not only does strength have the opposite effect on Aiden, but he's also getting the upper hand whenever I display it.

If I try to be logical and push all my prejudice aside, the crack might be as simple as... me.

Aiden King never shows interest in anyone except for his horsemen and football.

Unlike Xander and Ronan, he doesn't have girls hanging onto his arm—and it's not from the lack of trying. He seems to tune girls out—aside from Silver. I don't know what's his story with her, but she's the only girl that gets to ride in his Ferrari.

What? It's not my fault who I see when Kim and I go home.

Anyway, even with Silver, he usually has a nonchalant behaviour and his infuriating poker face.

The fact that he's directing all his energy towards me is disturbing, but if I see past the surface and my discomfort, his interest in me might as well be the only chip in his armour that he allows the world—or at least me—to see.

I can use that.

I can pretend to be his toy so I could disarm and then crush him.

Now, I have to decide if I'm strong enough to play his games in order to escape him.

Considering how easily he figures out when I manipulate him, it'd be nearly impossible to fool him.

It's a challenge to ride with him in the same car let alone to fake I have a genuine interest in him.

But then again, one can't play with the devil in his hell and pray not to burn.

Aiden is a deviant. A dangerous deviant.

And deep down? I do have some interest in the way he's wired. If he was in one of the Chinese war books I love, Aiden would be the tactic no general can predict.

I want to know why he's been keeping his distance for two years, letting his minions treat me like shit, but now decides he'll get close.

I feel like I'll never find peace unless I unveil the truth.

You're still avoiding the truth about your parents. Where's your peace in that, hypocrite?

The car rolls to a stop in front of an antique-looking coffee shop. I blink, coming out of my haze.

I glance at the secluded location. Although it has an ancient feel, the coffee shop isn't on the main street. Only a few houses are nearby. This isn't a poor neighbourhood per se, but it isn't high end either.

"Why have we stopped here?" I face Aiden, but he's already out of the car. He reaches my side and opens the door.

I gawk at him.

Did he just open the door for me?

Do devils do that?

Wait. Maybe he has a storage house around the corner to

which he lures his victims and kills them in cold blood before he dissolves them with acid.

"Are you going to sit there all day?" He raises an eyebrow. "Would you rather I carry you inside, sweetheart?"

"We have school."

"If you checked the school's website, you would've seen the notice that Mr Bently will be absent today."

I fish for my phone in my jacket's pocket. Sure enough, on the students' portal, it's announced that our first class is cancelled.

I stare up at him. "You tricked me."

"Hmm, did I?"

"You knew we don't have class, but you ushered me out as if we'd be late."

"We were going to be late."

"For what?"

"You didn't have breakfast so I'm buying you."

"What makes you think I want to go anywhere with you?"

His poker face slips and the chilling, cold void takes its place. "I could've kidnapped you to a place where no one would find you. I'm being nice here, Frozen. I'm giving you a choice to have breakfast with me in a place full of people so you're more comfortable."

I finger the strap of my backpack with sweaty fingers. Although fear is locking my shoulder blades, I can now see past it to what Aiden is actually saying.

Kidnapping me is his first choice and nature. He wants to rob me of my will, he wants the thrill of seeing me at his mercy.

However, he's forcing himself to make me comfortable.

Why?

I know for certain that he doesn't care about the moral line or my comfort.

This must be another game.

Another mindfuck.

"You realise that this isn't a choice, right?" I ask.

"Hmm. How so?"

"A choice is supposed to lead in different directions. Yours only leads back to you."

A wolfish grin breaks on his stupidly handsome face. "It only leads back to me, huh?"

God. His way of repeating my words is infuriating and makes me want to slap him.

I swallow the urge down because now, I realise it's his way to get a rise out of me.

"You're manipulating me, Aiden." I lift my chin. "I don't like it when people manipulate me."

"I'm manipulating you, huh?" He leans over, blocking the hint of the sun and the entire world with his frame. His voice drops to a whisper. "How does it feel to be manipulated, sweetheart?"

I swallow against the warmth rising up my throat. He can do it a thousand times, and I still wouldn't get used to being this close to him.

His fresh scent.

His tousled jet black hair.

The small mole at the corner of his eye.

I find myself staring at that longer than I like to admit.

Winning a staring competition with Aiden has always been impossible. The bottom of my stomach always does this stupid shit as if something is slicing, cutting, and ripping it open from the inside.

Hate. This must be how extreme hate feels like.

It consumes and destroys you from the inside like a stage five cancer.

He pulls back as fast as he leaned down. I release a breath I didn't realise I was holding.

"Kidnapping or breakfast in a coffee shop." He deadpans. "What's your move?"

No. It's *his* move. Even when he provides options, he makes sure the outcome works in his favour.

This level of cunning can belong to the criminally insane, but Aiden isn't just insane. He's highly intelligent and he knows it.

Hell, he's so assertive about it that it's disturbing.

If he weren't wealthy and young, what type of monster would he be?

Probably the century's most notorious serial killer.

I hold the backpack to my chest like a shield and step out of the car. If I'm starting my dance with the devil, I might as well do it now.

Aiden offers me his golden boy smile as he locks his car.

I hate that smile.

It's the fake one he gives to everyone else. I already had a glimpse of what he truly is, so he might as well stop the pretence around me.

Judging from the granite walls and the ancient feel the outside gives, I expected the coffee shop to be antique.

My expectations are smashed when we step inside.

The walls are covered in a pastel green wallpaper and the tables are in a smooth brownish colour. A few black and white motivational quotes hang from the ceilings.

The decor is soothing and the atmosphere is… cosy, to say the least.

A few patrons are scattered about, but Aiden doesn't take any of the available tables. He places a hand at the small of my back. A weird awareness coils beneath my skin, and I flinch at the contact.

He guides me up hidden stairs with pastel green and white steps. There's only a man facing the huge glass window.

He appears in his mid-forties, wears a crisp white shirt and reads from a newspaper while sipping from his coffee.

Aiden leads me to one of the tables with a cushion.

I slide inside, expecting Aiden to sit across from me.

And surprise, he doesn't meet expectations.

He plants himself right beside me. The distance between us is so minuscule, I can feel his body heat and smell his clean, toxic scent.

Damn his scent.

I purse my lips against the protest itching to be set free. If I tell him to change positions, he'll do the exact opposite. Hell, he'll go above and beyond to make my skin crawl.

He places his elbow on the table and leans his head against his palm as he watches me with a smirk.

"What?" I snap.

"You're so expressive, it's adorable."

"And you're not."

"I can live with not being adorable."

"I meant you're not expressive. The star image doesn't count. I know it's a mask."

"You know it's a mask, huh?"

"Would you stop repeating what I say?"

"Do you know how euphoric it feels to get under your skin, Frozen?"

"How the hell would I know that?"

"Exactly." He chuckles, reaching a hand to pinch my cheek. "You should see how red these get. Do I affect you that much?"

I wiggle away from his touch. "More like you infuriate me."

"You can lie to me all you want, sweetheart. But do you think it's a good idea to lie to yourself?"

"Maybe we all lie to ourselves." I mirror his gesture and lean on my palm. It's a way to disarm him, make him believe that he's getting to me. "You, too, have a mask all the time."

"A mask, huh?"

"What? You'll deny that you show the world a calculated image of who you want them to believe you are?"

"It comes with the family name." He winks. "I can't be a sobbing, emotional mess if I'm going to be a leader."

I focus on him. Like really focus on him. Not the arsehole Aiden, the school's king, or Elites' ace striker, but the other Aiden. The Aiden King. Heir to King Enterprises.

If he's so mature at this age and knows exactly how to behave and what to do for his leadership position, he must've had a lot of pressure growing up.

Sociopaths are made.

My spine jerks at that idea.

Was he... abused? Not that it excuses what he did—and continues to do—to me, but that could put some pieces of the puzzle together.

I take a sip from the water. "Was your father hard on you?"

"I wasn't abused by either of my parents if that's what you're thinking about."

Damn. I wasn't smooth enough in bringing out my assumptions.

There's no helping it now that it's out in the open.

"If it wasn't your father, then were you abused by someone else?"

He stares at me. Hard. The energy radiating off him becomes foggy and suffocating.

If his eyes were his hands, he would've choked the life out of me by now.

A waitress stands at our table, interrupting the moment.

"Mineral water, please," I say.

"Boiled eggs. Bacon. Large protein shake." Aiden lists without looking at the menu. "And a vegetarian breakfast menu with zero fatty acids."

My lips part. I was going to ask if they have any non-fatty acid breakfast menus since most restaurants don't.

The waitress scribbles our order, nods, and leaves.

I face Aiden. "How did you know that I only eat that type of food?"

"Your aunt was packing a vegetarian lunch and there was a special brand of biscuits with no fatty acid on your breakfast table." He glances at me. "Besides, you only eat your lunchboxes at school."

"You've been watching me at school?"

He ignores my question and tilts his head. "Why don't you ask the cafeteria for your type of food?"

I shrug. "I don't like eating at the cafeteria."

"Why not?"

"It's where the bullying gets worse."

He hums as if he never thought about that.

Dickhead.

My fingers play with the straws on the table. "Why did you really bring me here, Aiden?"

He grins. "I told you. Breakfast."

"You want me to believe that you don't have an ulterior motive?"

"I only want to feed you." He pinches my right cheek. "Stop overthinking."

I pull away from his touch. "It's kind of hard when you were my bully for years."

If he thinks I'll ignore the elephant in the room, then he has another thing coming.

"I did nothing to you, Frozen."

"Do you seriously believe that?"

"Believe what?"

"That you did nothing!" My voice raises. "You signed my death certificate that first day. You must've known they'd target me."

"And why would I know that?"

"The entire freaking school bows down to you. Did you honestly think they'd leave me in peace after you so eloquently announced that you'd destroy me?"

He grins with that sadistic edge. "It's not my fault I'm so loved."

"You're not even sorry for it, are you?"

"No."

Something squeezes in my chest. I don't know why I thought he'd show a bit of remorse.

There's no remorse in an unfeeling monster.

I stand and throw the napkin at his chest. "Thank you for the clarifications. Have a shitty day."

He clutches my wrist and pulls me down so fast, so hard, I yelp as I fall back down on something warm.

His lap.

I'm sitting on his lap.

My heartbeat picks up at being this close. So close that we breathe the same air. So close that I feel every ripple in his strong, hard thighs underneath me. So close that I can almost hear the pulse in my ears.

His face is a few inches away from mine that our noses nearly touch. His arm wraps around my waist in a steely, almost painful hold, and his eyes zero in on my lips as he speaks, "Did I say you can leave?"

It takes everything in me to ignore his proximity. I concentrate on his face despite the urge to look at his lips.

"I'm trying to understand, Aiden, I really am, but it's impossible. You made my life hell for two years and now you want to get close to me without as much as an apology? Do you think I'll forget about all that torment just because of your majesty's presence?"

He continues feasting on my lips with his gaze. "Do you think you have a choice, sweetheart?"

"Every time I look at you, I remember when I was locked in the showers for five hours until Kim found me. I remember someone stealing my track clothes and feigning a headache to not practice that day. I remember being tripped in the cafeteria the first day I stepped in there and having pasta and juice all over my clothes, face, and hair. I remember being called a Teacher Slut and accused of sleeping with them. I remember being hated for being me!"

I'm panting after my outburst, my heart almost leaping out of my throat. I never thought there'd be a day I'd give Aiden a piece of my mind.

"I'm sorry." He doesn't even miss a beat.

"You don't mean that."

His nonchalant, fake apology hurts more than the lack of it.

"You said you wanted an apology, not that I should mean it. Besides…" His fingers skim down my throat and to my pulse point before he wraps his hand around my neck. The gesture is gentle, almost caring if it weren't for the immediate danger of suffocation like the other time. "You wronged me first."

"What?"

The waitress returns with our orders. She stands a small distance away, watching us with unfazed attention. I scramble away from Aiden's lap, my cheeks flaring.

Aiden lets me go with a smirk.

For God's sake, can't he see we're in our school uniforms? There's a rule somewhere about not sullying RES's top-notch reputation.

After the waitress leaves, I dig into the low carb muffins and tomato omelette.

I've been starving since the morning. If he's buying, I'm eating. Food has nothing to do with my animosity with the devil.

Said devil doesn't touch his food and watches me silently like a creep.

I lift my head and give him a questioning look.

He removes his jacket, places it on the edge of the chair and rolls the cuffs of his shirt to near his elbows, revealing strong veiny arms and… tattoos.

He has tattoos at the underside of his forearm.

It's a simple two black arrows pointing in opposing directions. I lean closer to watch the direction of the tattoos.

That's when I notice it.

Near his elbow, there's a faded scar at which one of the arrows points.

His movements are meticulous as he cuts his eggs and takes a bite.

I motion at the tattoo. "Is there a meaning?"

His dark eyes meet mine and I'm transfixed by their depth. It's like someone pushed him into an impenetrable fog and he's unable to get out. "Some scars are better left hidden."

"Like what?" I ask slowly.

"Like your scar. You hide it so well, don't you, Frozen?"

I stab my omelette and cut eye contact.

"Ah. So you like talking about me, but when the subject turns to little miss Frozen, it becomes a red line. Do you realise how double standard that is?"

"Stop twisting everything to fit you."

"The answer is no."

"Do you get off on it?"

"On what?"

"On being this infuriatingly in control."

"Perhaps."

My lips twist. "Has there ever been something out of your control before?"

"Twice." He hums. "And you're the third."

I pause drinking from my orange juice, my voice slow. "How?"

"Be mine."

I choke on my juice, droplets splattering from my nose and all over the table.

Aiden chuckles, offering me a napkin. "Jesus. I didn't ask for your firstborn."

"This is worse." I stare at him as I wipe the mess on my face. "You're not serious, are you?"

"Have I ever joked with you?"

"You know that my answer will be no, right?"

"No is a start, sweetheart."

I gulp.

"Besides…" He places a hand on my thigh, his fingers trailing up. "Your mouth is a liar. I'm taking my answer from something that doesn't lie."

FOURTEEN

Aiden's body pushes into mine.

It's subtle as if he's just leaning in to tell me a secret, but there's nothing secretive about the way he's gripping me.

In a fruitless attempt to get away from him, my back hits the wall. Aiden grabs both my wrists in a death grip against the cold wallpaper. He manoeuvres my legs so they're lying on his hard thighs.

With this position, it's impossible to fight him off. Every time I try to squirm free, he digs his fingers into my wrists until I wince in pain. Damn him and his brute strength.

I curse my stupidity for locking myself between him and the wall. Why the hell do I always find myself trapped with him?

He plants his large palm on my thigh in the small space between my skirt and my stockings. A wave of that strange awareness shoots down my spine. My skin heats and prickles with the tension crackling in the air.

My body's reaction to him isn't funny anymore. How the hell does he push those buttons?

"Aiden," I hiss through my teeth.

"Hmm, sweetheart?" His intense eyes never leave my face as his fingers flex on my thigh, teasing, and threatening to go up.

"We're in public."

"And I'm supposed to care about that?"

Of course, he wouldn't care.

Blood rushes in my veins at the possibility of being caught while Aiden is touching me. The older man is facing the window and he's far enough that he can't hear us, but if he deviates his head, or decides to leave, he'll see everything.

"Say yes to my offer and I wouldn't have to search for your body's yes."

"I can't just be yours."

"Why not?"

"I hate you, that's why."

"Hmmm."

Despite the humming, his tone is flat as he grips my thigh tighter.

"Aiden," I grind my teeth, my vision bouncing between him and the old man.

"Let's play that choice game you love so much."

"I don't love your games."

He tilts his head to the side, watching me intently as his fingers draw circles on my inner thigh. "I think you do love them, but you just don't love admitting it."

I shake my head frantically.

"Be mine or I'll finger you so hard, so fast, that man will be calling for help when you come all over my fingers."

My thighs clench, lips parting open.

My face must be as red as the blood rushing to it, but Aiden's expression remains unaffected.

How can he stay like that after the crude words he said? How can he start a riot in my body with mere words?

"Is that a yes, Frozen?"

"No," The word falls from my lips in a murmur.

"Hmmm." His fingers slide up my thigh. "I didn't realise you were an exhibitionist, sweetheart. Does it turn you on to know we can be caught any minute? That man can turn around now." He strokes my inner thigh, his thumb hovering over the edge of my underwear. "Or now."

I kick my feet, trying to push him, but he only tightens his grip on me.

I close my eyes against the intrusive sensation. Every fibre of my logic is willing me to hate this, to consider it a violation, but... is it a violation if I want him to reach up? Is it a violation if his dirty words are causing an uncontrollable throb between my legs?

He leans in so his hot breaths brush against my throat. Goosebumps break over my skin as he murmurs in a low, husky voice, "Say yes."

"Aiden..." I trail off not knowing what I want to tell him. Is it to stop? To keep going?

"That's not the word. I need you to say yes."

"Why?" I don't even recognise my breathy voice.

"Say the word, Elsa." He's still speaking against my throat, and I tilt to the side as if giving him better access. To do what, I don't know.

"You know, I could've threatened your family's company. I know King Enterprises is their biggest contractor and they'd struggle and eventually go bankrupt with the amount of debt they currently owe to the bank. I have information that'll keep Kimberly gravitating towards me and away from you. The only reason I didn't destroy your life yet is because I've been saving it to the right moment. If I choose to, I'll threaten everything you love and you'll have no choice but to fall at my feet."

With every word he says, my eyes blur with tears.

I want to believe he wouldn't be able to do what he said, that they're all empty threats.

But this is Aiden. He never promised something he didn't follow up with.

This is his way to show me how weak I am in comparison to his strength.

But I don't crumble and swallow my tears. He won't be seeing my weakness.

"Then why aren't you doing all that?" I ask.

"I'm offering you the chance to make the first move."

"Why is that so important to you?"

"I'm testing a theory." His fingers splay on the hem of my boy shorts, eliciting a zap of pleasure from the bottom of my stomach.

"What theory?" My voice is choked.

"That you like being forced to make any move. The rush turns you on, doesn't it?"

God. He's insane.

"No…" It's my weakest 'no' of yet.

The double assault of his breaths against my throat and his fingers at the edge of my most sensitive part awakens a deep-seated throb. My thighs clench around his hand as if inviting him to the place that aches the most.

"No one in RES will come near you if you're mine. You'll spend a dream senior year."

Damn him and his smooth ways. Just like with Aunt and Uncle, he's telling me what I want to hear.

"I don't want the dream year," I hardly manage the words.

"Then what do you want, sweetheart?"

In some place in my mind, I know this is wrong. He is one million times wrong.

Wrong or right, my body doesn't understand that. It's enchanted to Aiden whether I like it or not. He's turning my body against me.

Dickhead.

Sweat breaks on my forehead and my skin pulses as if begging to be touched by him.

"You won't get anything out of me."

"You should play smarter, not stronger." Aiden's lips brush against my throat, sending a violent chill down my back. "Admit your deepest darkest desires, Elsa."

I don't know if it's because of his lips or the low-throaty, almost husky tone he said my name with, but I'm a goner.

A full-body shudder goes through me like I'm being pulled under a soundless, crashing wave.

I can't even fight the pull anymore.

Aiden's fingers trace the rim of my boy shorts, slowly slipping underneath. I whimper then hide my head in his shoulder to suppress the sound. I almost forgot that we aren't alone.

The man's presence is supposed to turn me off, but it has the complete opposite effect.

I'm burning and Aiden is my hell.

He cups me through my underwear. I sink my teeth in my lower lip to suppress the needy sounds clawing its way out.

"You're fucking soaked," Aiden growls against the side of my neck.

I arch my back as his thumb swipes up and down my folds through the cloth.

"What's turning you on, sweetheart?" His lips find my ear and a small voice that resembles a moan leaves my throat. "Is it the public setting? The risk of getting caught? Or is it the fact that you're completely under my mercy?"

All of that.

But that's not all, is it?

The main reason is… him.

I don't think I would've had all these overpowering, crushing sensations if it were someone else.

His finger slips beneath my underwear and thrusts inside me. I bite his hard shoulder over the shirt.

Oh. God.

Is it supposed to feel so intimate and deep?

He thrusts another finger and I arch against him, my entire weight held by his.

"Aiden…" It's supposed to be a warning, a protest, but it comes out as I moan.

"Admit it, Frozen."

I shake my head, feeling a lump grow bigger and suffocating at the back of my throat.

He reaches his free hand up my stomach, stops to flick a hard, throbbing nipple over my shirt, before he wraps his fingers around my throat. He scissors his fingers inside me as he tightens his thumb at my neck's pulse point.

"Would you rather admit it when you're screaming my name?" he whispers in dark, hot words.

I bite my lower lip, staring at him with frantic, lust-filled eyes.

"Fight it all you like, but if I want you to scream, you'll fucking scream, Elsa."

His thumb rubs up and down my clitoris in slow circular movements as he thrusts his fingers inside me.

The triple assault against my clit, my walls and my neck and his hot breath brings me to the edge.

A wave builds inside me, doubling and magnifying until a chill of terror engulfs me.

What the hell is happening to me?

Aiden parts his fingers at my throat so his lips can find the pulse point. He sucks hard.

Everything spirals out of control.

I moan against his shoulder as that wave nearly hits the shore. I grind against his hand.

Just one more friction.

Just one touch.

The feeling is so, *so* close, and I never needed something as much as I need this foreign wave to hit me.

Aiden stops.

He slips his fingers from my stimulated nerves, withdraws his hand from under my skirt and releases my throat.

Emptiness engulfs me as he slides back against the cushion, giving me back the personal space he violated a few seconds ago.

I blink a few times.

Humiliation and frustration eat at my insides like burning acid.

Humiliation because I almost gave the arsehole my first sexual experience with another person in a damn coffee shop.

Frustration because he stopped. As if he didn't touch me in the first place.

I don't know who I should hate more. Myself or him.

I expect him to mock me and this time, I'd freaking deserve it. For a moment, I moaned. For a moment, I ground against him. For a moment, I *wanted* the depravity the arsehole offered.

Someone kill me.

Aiden keeps the unnerving eye contact as if he's dissecting my soul, ripping it, and dancing in its remains.

Then he does something that shocks the freaking bejeesus out of me.

He brings his glistening index and middle fingers to his face—the same fingers that almost brought me to the edge—and sucks them into his mouth.

He flicks his tongue along the fingers and does a slow show of licking them clean.

Why is that so… *hot?*

Even if I want to look away, I can't. My thighs tighten around my throbbing core and I feel like I'll explode right here, right now.

After one last lick, he removes his fingers and flicks his tongue around his bottom lip.

I find myself transfixed by that bottom lip. That tongue.

I'm angling towards him against my better judgement.

"Do you realise how long I fantasised about your taste, sweetheart?" he grunts deep in his throat.

Unable to utter a word, I shake my head.

"I fantasised about locking you in a dark classroom, pushing you on a table, pulling your legs over my shoulders, and sucking you until you screamed. I fantasised about kidnapping you from the track practice, pinning you against the tree in the back, and fucking you until you passed out."

"Aiden… stop…"

His dirty talk provokes a part of me I never thought existed.

His crude words will be the end of me.

It'll be my damnation.

My descent into hell.

Not if I can stop it.

I place a trembling hand on his chest and I startle at the maddening heartbeat beneath the hot, hard muscles.

He appears so composed and in control that I never thought his pulse would be this... erratic. It's almost as out of control as my own heartbeat.

"I can't stop my fantasies, sweetheart." He wraps his hand around mine that's on his heart—his black, black heart. "But I won't tell you the rest of them, do you know why?"

I shake my head once.

He yanks my hand away from his chest as if I burn him. "Because you're not ready for those. I'll tell you this, though." He leans in to whisper in hot words. "You taste better than any fucking fantasy."

FIFTEEN

A few days pass.

No matter how much I want things to go back to normal, they don't.

Since that day in the coffee shop, Aiden hasn't stopped texting me every night and morning.

The first strings of texts came that same night while I was watching Nat Geo with Uncle Jaxon.

Aiden: What did you have for dinner?

Aiden: We had pasta, but you were all I tasted on my tongue. I can't stop thinking about my fingers inside your soaked walls as you whimpered. Pity I didn't get to taste you properly and thrust my tongue inside that tight, little pussy.

Aiden: Next time, sweetheart.

I barely mumbled my goodnights to Uncle as I fled to my room.

He's been sending those types of crude texts every night, and sometimes in the mornings.

I called him a psycho a few times. Insane at other times. But that only made him religious about his texts.

Dickhead.

Kim and I sit in the back garden for lunch. We're both eating salad and watching the tall pine trees in the distance as she talks about her latest Korean soap opera with great details.

"Did you notice anything weird?" I ask when she finishes her retellings.

"Like what?" She chews on a mouthful of cucumber.

"Like no one calls you names anymore? Even Adam, the biggest bully of all bullies, passed you by this morning without a word."

She grins, her mint-coloured hair flying in the wind. "My new look is shocking the hell out of them."

As much as I love her new confidence, I don't think that's the case. Her new look didn't stop Silver and her minions from bullying her at the start of school.

"Don't you find it weird that all of this changed since Aiden comforted you in front of the entire school?"

If their king showed interest in her, they'd be signing off on their death certificates if they bothered her.

That's Aiden. Those on his good side live in heaven, but the rest rot in hell.

"Well, yeah." Her expression changes into something unreadable before she waggles her brows. "Maybe you should get comforted by him, too, so RES will get off your case, too."

"Kim!" I hit her shoulder.

"What? Use them while you can, Ellie."

"Is that what you've been doing with Aiden? *Using* him?"

She lifts her shoulder.

Kim isn't the type of person who uses people. God. It's as if I don't know my best friend anymore.

"You do realise that Aiden King isn't the type to be used, right?" I stab a fork at the bottom of my container. "He'll read through your manipulations in no time."

"Maybe we're using each other." She drops the container at her side and crunches a red apple.

Maybe we're using each other?

What the hell is that supposed to mean?

"King played such an excellent game on Saturday. You should've seen the goal he scored." Kim gushes. "Thirty metres away, can you believe that?"

I pause playing with my food. "You went to Elites' game?"

"Uh, yeah? I told you I was going out on Saturday."

"I thought it was to have dinner with your family." My lips twist. "I also thought you quit going to their games."

"I felt like going." She shrugs. "And I'm so glad I did, King was a freaking star. So bright and dazzling. I can't believe he doesn't play in the Premier League like his cousin already."

"Kim." My throat dries as I stare at her with what must look like a horrified expression. "Do you hear yourself? You're idolising Aiden fucking King right now."

"What? He plays like a God. You can't deny that."

Yes, I can. That's why I refuse to focus on him while he plays.

"Xander played like shit, though." Kim's pink-painted lips twist. "Fucking psycho almost got a red card for tackling an opponent so hard, he almost knocked his teeth out. But Kirian still wouldn't shut up about him, can you believe that little shit?"

Kim's little brother idolises Xander, and that always ticked her off.

"He's just a kid."

"He's my baby brother, not his. Fucking arsehole."

Then she launches into a full report on the game. It's her usual thing, but this time, I notice the impressed tone whenever she talks about Aiden. Or maybe the impressed tone has always been there and I was too deaf to hear it.

I'm going to be sick to my stomach.

Just when I'm about to stop her, a shadow looms over us.

My head snaps up to find Ronan grinning down at us like an idiot.

"What do you want?" I snap.

"Relax, Frozen." He slides beside a stunned Kim, smiling with unmistakable charm. "I come here in peace."

Peace? He's got to be freaking kidding me.

I search behind him and around the trees, expecting the devil to come out and play.

Nothing can convince me that this isn't another one of Aiden's depraved games.

I fold my arms over my chest. "Since when do you talk to us, Ronan?"

"Since Kim is a fan." He grins at her, placing a stray strand behind her ear. "How come you never showed it before, *chérie*? You don't have to be a closet fan."

"I'm not." She smiles, appearing to relax. "I love Elites' team play. Cole is the perfect captain. Aiden is the ace striker and you're one of the best midfielders in the school's championships."

"Correction. I'm not one of the best. I'm the best, Kimmy."

"The freaking best!"

They go on a long string of football conversation about the few games Elites played this season and last year's championship.

Ronan Astor and Kim are bonding.

Gag. Someone kill me.

I slam the lid of my container shut with a force that gets their attention. "Are you done?"

"*Bah alors*, Frozen. Anyone ever told you to chill?"

"I'll be perfectly *chill* when you're as far away from us as possible."

Kim frowns. "That's rude, Ellie."

Rude? Doesn't she realise he's playing a game? A game Aiden must've put him up to it.

"No wonder he's possessed," Ronan mutters before he smiles at Kim, completely erasing me. "How about you stop being a closet fan and come over to one of my parties?"

Kim's eyes almost bug out. "Who? Me?"

"I'll win the drinking competition for your sake, Kimmy."

"You will?" She almost shouts.

"I do anything for our fans." He winks, brushes his knuckles over her hand before he stands and glances at me. "You can come, too, if you lose the frozen act."

He throws a dismissive hand and leaves.

I continue aiming daggers at his back even as he disappears between the trees.

"Did you hear that? He invited us to one of his parties."

"So what?"

"It's Ronan Astor's party, Ellie! I've always dreamt about attending one. I can't believe he invited us."

"Kim!" I grip her shoulders. "We agreed to never mingle with them, remember? We belong to different worlds and have different standards."

"It's just a party, Ellie. It's senior year, we can at least go to a party." The spark in her eyes doesn't disappear. If anything, she looks about to explode from excitement.

That's when I see it. The eagerness. The child-like thrill.

Kim wants this. She always had this dreamy look in her eyes whenever she talked about the football game or when we overheard other students talk about Ronan's parties.

Unlike me, she wants to see that other crowd—Aiden and his pack of wolves' crowd.

Maybe she's been holding back because of the bullying. Maybe it's because of me.

Either way, the new Kim isn't afraid to go after what she likes. If anything, she runs straight to it.

Nothing I do or say will change her mind about the party.

I have to take care of the source of the problem.

A certain arsehole who's been manipulating her throughout her new change.

We go back to school for our next class. Kim wouldn't stop talking about the party even when I try to change the subject. I preferred the Korean soap operas retellings.

Near the class, Aiden crosses our path, coming in from the opposite direction. He stops near the door and Kim stops, too.

"Morning, Reed." Aiden offers her a smile that somehow reaches his smokey eyes.

My chest squeezes in an uncomfortable, almost painful way.

"Morning, King." Kim smiles back.

"You were amazing in the last game. We need more fans like you."

"Go Elites!" Kim grins. "We're so getting the championship this year."

"Hell yeah, Kimmy!" Ronan cheers from behind us, draping an arm around Kim's shoulder and leading her inside.

I hurry after them when a large-as-life presence pushes me back against the wall.

The students' chatter disappears and my back snaps upright as I stare up at Aiden's soulless eyes.

All the smiles he offered Kim disappear, leaving the actual demon Aiden is.

Looking up at him, I can't help recalling his skin against mine. His finger sliding inside me. His lips biting my neck —

Nope. He's not getting under my skin.

"Are you going to be mine?" he asks so low that the tenor of his voice vibrates on my skin.

Every day since that damned breakfast, he corners me somewhere and asks that same question.

I jut my chin out and give him the same answer I tell him every day, "No."

"Hmm." His fingers dig at the back of my scalp beneath my hair as he grips my nape and pins me in place.

There's no escaping him even if I tried.

He's freaking everywhere like the asphyxiating smoke in his eyes.

If I want to protect my sanity, I need to play my cards smartly.

If this were a football game, this is that time when the team is losing and the coach has to make decisive choices. He can lunge for offence and leave a void at the back that will cost him dearly in case of a counter-attack. Or he can hold his formation, draw in the adversary, and then attack when the other party least expects it.

I always preferred the second option.

Since I met Aiden, I had been the team that accepted defeat before the game even started. It's like in the world cup when all

English people have no hopes for the national team to go any-where before it even started.

The forfeiting strategy was fine when Aiden just claimed his victory and moved along. Now that he's pushing me, it's time for a change of tactics.

Since the beginning of this school year, I used the all in at-tack, which obviously doesn't work on Aiden. Not only is he a stronger, bigger—and a meaner—opponent, but he also gets off on my useless struggle. It's time I go for the second option.

Lure. Wait. Attack.

Gah. I'm beginning to think like him.

But then again, one needs to be a monster to stop a monster.

He leans closer so his breath tickles along my lower lip. My breath catches. He's always so close enough to kiss me, but he never does.

"Careful, sweetheart." He pulls at a fistful of my hair. "You're pushing me."

"You pushed me first," I grit out. "At least now you know how it feels to be pushed."

"That's nothing." His lips hover over my ear before he darts his tongue and licks the shell. "I promise you won't like it when I push back."

I bite back the chill at his words and proximity and meet his gaze. "Aren't you doing it already? What the hell is your game with Kim?"

He tilts his head to the side, his lips curving in a smirk. "Be mine and there won't be a game."

"Goddamn it, Aiden. You can't play unfair like this."

"Who said anything about fair?" His hand climbs to my throat and his thumb fingers the pulse point.

He's obsessed with that.

"I told you I'll threaten everything you love. Reed is only the beginning. It's time you make a move, sweetheart."

He pulls my cheek. "But don't take too long. Patience has never been my strength."

He releases me, leaving me breathless and boneless against the wall as he saunters inside the classroom. I hear him call Kim's name.

And I know, I just know that Aiden's strike will hit so deep.

He caught me by the arm that hurts the most.

When I peek into the class and find Kim laughing with him and Ronan, my heart squeezes and my chest aches.

A finger taps my shoulder. I startle, facing the intruder.

Xander's gleamy blue eyes stare down at me. "I have an offer to make."

SIXTEEN

For a week, I managed to avoid Aiden and Xander.

It might have to do with the weekend. I studied as much as I could, but whenever I was left to my thoughts, it was chaos.

I keep watching the steps of my house, expecting Aiden to show up unannounced like he did the other time.

He doesn't corner me like he used to, but he's spending more time with Kim. His 'Morning, Reed' has morphed into conversations, and I don't know how to scream that he's manipulating her without sounding crazy.

He knows all the buttons to push and all the things to say to sound proper, and loveable even.

Kim believes him just like Aunt and Uncle did.

No one knows him the way I do. No one saw the void behind his eyes or has heard his low threats.

If I scream bloody murder, I'll just appear insane.

I wish Aiden and I could go back to the stage where glares had been our only language. When I battled with how long I could keep eye contact before forfeiting.

Who am I kidding?

We can never go back to that stage after what Aiden has done to me.

After he touched me.

Invaded me.

Tasted me.

I've been having fragmented dreams about his hands, his face, and his scent. God. His scent would never leave my memories.

And his lips.

I dream about them doing depraved things to me.

If my subconscious thinks about it, what does that make me?

As if Aiden's drama isn't enough, Xander has been hunting me after every class about 'his offer'. I shot him down every time, refusing to even hear it.

Xander is Aiden's best friend. If they think I'm naive enough to fall for their games, then they have another thing coming.

I blow a long breath as I trudge through the school's hallway during lunch break. I don't usually hide from the bullying in the main entrance, but today is just a wrong day.

It started with a nightmare about blood, black eyes, and drowning in murky water. The seven year-old version of me has been screaming 'Da!' over and over again.

Seeing myself in that nightmare has been surreal. I've forgotten about how I looked; a dirty, blonde monster ball.

Since I moved to London with Aunt and Uncle, I didn't have one single memory of my life with my parents in Birmingham.

No photo albums.

No mind images.

No... nothing.

Everything was burnt with the house. The only reason I survived that day was because I wasn't inside.

Nightmares are the only episodes that tie me to that dark past. I thought I was slowly escaping them, but today proved me wrong.

Maybe I should go back to Dr Khan. He was able to stop the nightmares a long time ago.

I'll leave Dr Khan as a last resort to not worry Aunt and Uncle.

I retrieve my phone from my pocket to text Kim. Instead, I find the two texts Aiden sent at six in the freaking morning.

Aiden: I dreamt about pounding your tight pussy until you screamed my name. I'm kind of contemplating slipping into your room and fucking you like in the dream.

Aiden: Oh, and morning, sweetheart.

Damn the bastard. I'm starting to get used to his texts. Hell, I'm starting to look forward to them, wondering what kind of depravity he'll send this time.

And I might've spent a few minutes watching from my room's window, expecting him to barge inside like the devil.

What? I can't put anything past Aiden King.

He didn't show up.

Not only that, but in school, he pretends as if those texts never happened. When I passed him by this morning while he was listening to Ronan's animated speech, he barely spared me a glance.

Why does he get to be all unaffected when I'm boiling from the inside out?

I shake my head and text Kim. She took the lunch break to pick up Kirian.

Elsa: Are you done?

Kimberly: Mum isn't available so I'm driving Kir home. I'll be there in a few. Xo.

Elsa: Kiss his adorable cheeks for me.

Kim sends a selfie while she gives Kirian an open-mouthed kiss while he tries to shove her away.

I smile, zooming in to watch his innocent, boyish features.

I have information that'll keep Kimberly gravitating towards me and away from you.

Aiden's words stab me in the stomach and bring a taste of nausea to the back of my throat.

It's working. His threat is working.

My plan to lure, wait, then attack hasn't even taken off since he didn't take the damn bait.

I was so stupid to believe someone like Aiden would take the bait. He's the one who got me hook, line, and sinker.

All I keep thinking about are his threats and what he's capable of.

A presence looms behind me.

I startle, coming to a screeching halt. My phone falls, but Xander catches it.

Whoa. Nice reflexes.

He glances at my phone, face closing for a second too long, before he hands it back with a mischievous gleam in his eyes. "Got you, Frozen."

The golden shade of Xander's blonde hair is impossible to have even with chemicals. It's so bright and shiny. Add his co-balt blue eyes and he's the epitome cliché of a golden boy. Unlike Aiden, I haven't noticed him manipulating people, but then again, what do I know about Xander Knight except that he actively makes Kim's life hell?

He's wearing his uniform with meticulous care. Even the cuffs of his shirt are rolled over the jacket neatly as if someone dresses him up. Which wouldn't be surprising considering that he's a minister's son.

He leans against the wall, subtly blocking my way. "Why are you running away from me?"

"Why are you chasing me?" I shoot back.

"I told you. I have an offer for you."

"Not interested." I sidestep him and walk on my way.

"The bullying will stop," he calls from behind me ever so casually.

I halt and slowly turn around. Xander is smirking as if knowing he got me.

I lift my chin. "How do you intend to do that?"

"I'm a star on the football team. If anyone sees you with me, it'll be enough to stop it all."

I finger the straps of my backpack. He's right about that.

Just like Aiden stopped all the bullying for Kim by holding her, he can stop it for me, too, but only at the cost of 'being his'.

I'm not naive to think that Xander is giving me the golden ticket without consequences.

The higher the offer, the higher the cost.

"What do I have to do in return?"

His gaze slides over me from head to toe.

I fold my arms over my chest. "In your damn dreams."

He laughs, the sound long and genuine. "Sorry, love. You're pretty but you're not my type. I'd rather not be frozen to death."

So he's not after sex. Well, well.

My interest peaks and I face him fully. "Then what do you want from me?"

"Be my pretend girlfriend."

My jaw almost drops to the floor. "What?"

"You know, not a real girlfriend, just a pretence in front of everyone."

"I know what a pretend girlfriend means. I'm asking why you want me to act like yours."

"It'll stop the bullying." He grins. "Isn't that what you want?"

I narrow my eyes. "What's in it for you?"

"Why do you care? You get to spend your senior year in peace."

"You seriously expect me to just give in without knowing what I'll lose?"

He holds a hand to his heart. "I promise that you'll lose nothing."

"No. Tell me about your reasons."

Being in the dark is a sure way to lose before even starting.

He remains silent, scowling at me, to intimidate me no doubt.

I meet him glare for glare. "If you don't tell me, I'm not signing up to this."

His shoulders turn rigid as he says in a monotone tone, "I'm teaching someone a lesson."

"Who...?"

It hits me then.

Xander was beyond pissed off when Aiden held Kim the other week. He's been unnecessarily aggressive with him during practice, too. And I noticed that they stand together only when Ronan and Cole are with them.

"You're doing this to spite Aiden?" I whisper-yell then inch closer to him when a classmate gives us the stink eye while passing by.

Or more like she gives me the stink eye. She's one of Xander's endless admirers.

Another reminder of what I'll deal with if I agree to become his pretend girlfriend.

Xander raises an eyebrow. "You have a problem with that?"

"Not really, but…" I inch closer. "You're overestimating Aiden's temporary obsession with me. He doesn't care about me."

He cares about belittling me, dominating me, and having me bend at his will.

He only cares about breaking me.

"Why do you think no one asked you out these past two years?" Xander lifts an eyebrow.

"W-what?"

"Other girls have boyfriends, but you don't. Ever wonder why?"

"Other girls aren't bullied," I grit out. "They aren't called Teacher Sluts."

"That's the point." He snaps his fingers and points at me. "Who do you think started the rumour that you sucked off the biology teacher? That you're a Teacher Slut? And the other about you having a contagious disease?" He counts on his fingers. "King and King and… oh, King."

I'm too stunned to speak. My mouth opens then closes like a dying fish.

All these years, I thought Aiden just stayed in the background. I thought the bullying started only because he expressed hatred towards me in front of the whole school that day and therefore, they acted upon loyalty to him.

Turns out he staged it all and let his minions do the rest.

Minimum effort. Similar results.

The bastard.

My blood whooshes with a hot, red feeling.

"Why?" I don't even recognise my haunted voice.

"It's his way to eliminate competition."

"Why would he want to eliminate competition?"

"Beats me." He lifts a shoulder. "I've known King for his entire life, and I've never seen him as transfixed by someone as he is with you."

Aiden said it, didn't he? His care isn't normal, labellable, or conventional.

But then again, why do I have to pay for his unconventional ways?

Anger sweeps over me like a black, bottomless ocean.

Somewhere in my brain, I realise that I shouldn't make snap decisions while I'm angry, but I couldn't care less.

"Deal," I tell Xander. "I'll be your pretend girlfriend."

There's no better way to have revenge on Aiden than to 'date' his best friend.

And I know why Xander approached me.

He likes the idea that Aiden has spent years successfully 'eliminating' all competition, just so I'd end up in Xander's arms.

It's such a dick move, but I like Xander a little bit for it.

I like anyone who rebels against the entitled, psycho king.

Xander's lips stretch into a wolfish grin as he offers me his arm. "Let's make our first appearance, love."

I reluctantly slip my arm in his.

This isn't my character.

Hell, I don't even like to lie, let alone be someone's pretend girlfriend.

But if Aiden's using my best friend against me, the only way to strike him is to use his best friend back.

Eye for an eye.

Blood for blood.

He started the war. I'm just keeping up.

My feet falter in front of the cafeteria. There's a reason I don't eat here, and it's not the food.

It's like a high-end restaurant, but for high school kids. Even the staff appear like butlers straight out of the palace.

During the lunch break, RES's entire student body gathers

here. If something happens in this place, it'll be engraved in everyone's memories.

It'll be posted on social media.

It'll be the talk of the entire school.

Last week, Silver spilt juice on a freshman—she spills beverages a lot—and it became the talk of the week. The incident reached me even though I don't eat here.

"Relax." Xander's cool voice wrenches me from my thoughts. His face is all grins and smiles.

Easy for him to say. He's a popular star and the son of a minister.

Attention is his middle name. Hell, he might even thrive on it.

I can end all this now, but my need for revenge simmers beneath the surface like an untamed animal.

This time, I'll be the one who inflicts pain.

Whoa. That's a scary thought.

I'm not that person. I don't need to inflict pain. All I need is justice.

Yes. *Justice.*

With a deep breath, Xander and I walk into the cafeteria. Chatter and utensils clicking fills the air. Some students laugh at one another, others are in heated conversations, and a few loners sit in the back.

My heartbeat increases with every step I take. Beads of sweat cover my temples and a tremor shoots through my limbs.

Once we're in the centre of the cafeteria, the chit chat withers away and almost everyone's attention zeroes in on us.

Some jab their friends while others murmur in hushed tones.

Being in the limelight stiffens my shoulder blades.

My heart flips when I make out where Xander is guiding me.

The centre table.

The football team's table.

The table at which Aiden sits. He's nodding at something Cole says while nonchalantly moving his fork around his half-full plate.

He's wearing the team's blue jacket with the school's logo. The first few buttons of his shirt are undone, hinting at his tanned skin and hard muscles.

Ronan is half-sitting on his chair, speaking enthusiastically while the rest of the team snickers. All except for Aiden who's watching with a poker face.

Cole's laugh falls as he notices us.

His eyes stray from me to Xander and then straight to Aiden. He doesn't need to alert him, though.

As if having a sixth sense, Aiden pauses picking at his food and lifts his head. His smoky gaze falls on me, and for a second, he appears to be taken aback as if he doesn't know what I'm doing here.

Then his eyes dart to where I'm clutching Xander by the arm. It's at a time like this that I wish Aiden had an expressive face.

His poker mask is strapped tight around his features as he drops his fork with a clank and stands.

He calmly, too calmly, wipes his mouth with a napkin before setting it down.

My heart nearly leaps out of my throat as he stalks towards us with sure, confident steps.

I want to believe that Aiden wouldn't humiliate me in public now that I'm with Xander, but I can't put anything past him.

The smirk on Xander's face isn't helping. "He's pissed off."

"How do you know that?" I whisper back.

He appears completely detached to me.

"The twitch in his left eye." Xander grins. "He can control anything but that."

Xander removes my arm from his but just so he'd wrap it around my shoulder.

He smells of sandalwood.

That's the last thought I have before Aiden slams his fist in Xander's face.

SEVENTEEN

I stare in stunned silence as Xander's body jerks back and slams against a table.

A few girls shriek. Other students gasp.

I'm in the shocked category.

My back hits the edge of a table and I grip the hard wood for balance.

Aiden has never been the violent type. He said it the other day, didn't he? That he'd rather play smarter, not stronger.

So why is he punching his best friend?

Before Xander can recover, Aiden lunges at him with a slamming punch.

It's the first time I see him this way.

Violent.

Animalistic.

Out of control.

It's like a different Aiden altogether.

Xander releases mocking laughter before he shoves Aiden and jabs a punch at his face. Blood explodes from Aiden's lower lip.

I swallow. Should I interfere? Do something? Say something?

But it's not like they're fighting because of me—although I might have played a part.

Aside from the sound of punches, the cafeteria is completely silent. None of the other students utters a word. Hell, I doubt they're able to breathe properly. It's understandable.

Aiden and Xander have been close for as long as anyone remembers. No one would've imagined that they'd turn against each other.

This fight might as well be the event of the year.

Cole and Ronan are the first—and the only ones—who dare to approach them.

Cole tries to grip Aiden, but he's like a bull. He shoves him away and lunges back at Xander. At the captain's sign, the rest of the football team joins. It takes a few of them to stop Aiden and Xander from killing one another.

Two teachers and Coach Larson quicken their pace inside, followed by... Kim.

She called the teachers?

Coach appears pissed off as he orders the football team to drag Aiden and Xander to a disciplinary office.

Uncontrolled murmurs erupt between the students. Even the two teachers appear stunned that Aiden and Xander fought.

RES isn't the type of school for fights. This place is full of elites and academically accomplished people. Rank, grades, and money are the only things that matter in RES.

Violence has never been something the board had to worry about. Especially not from the two stars of the football team.

On his way out, Aiden brushes past me. My skin electrifies at the harsh contact. I shrink into the table, the wood digging at my back as his hard, metallic gaze falls on me.

The corner of his left eye twitches as he stops in front of me. Hot, intrusive breaths trickle the side of my face as he whispers, "You'll pay."

Aiden and Xander don't come back to class for the second period.

The incident at the cafeteria becomes everyone's favourite subject of gossip.

I keep getting funny glares, but no one has dared to speak to me.

Everyone's theory is that Aiden and Xander will get disciplinary actions that might include temporary suspension from the team.

I find it hard to believe that Coach Larson will allow RES to take his two star players, but the board is strict about any act of violence.

My mind goes rampant with ideas shooting all over the place. True, I wanted revenge and to inflict pain as Aiden had inflicted upon me, but I'm not that person. It doesn't feel good to hurt others.

Even if they're monsters.

It's impossible to concentrate during class. I keep watching the entrance, expecting Aiden and Xander to return. The day ends and neither of them does.

Kim and I leave the classroom together, but neither of us is talking. She's been throwing me glares since lunchtime, and I've been too out of my skin to focus on her moodiness.

When we're in the car park, Silver and her two minions cut into our path.

Oh, come on.

She's the last person I need to talk to on this shitty day.

She taps her designer shoes on the ground, staring me down like I'm her maid.

"Who the hell do you think you are, Frozen? You're a nobody, so stop trying to become somebody."

I grit my teeth, but I choose to ignore her.

Never give bullies what they want.

"You should go back to your frozen castle," one of Silver's minions calls at my back.

"Shut it before she gives you a snowstorm." Kim snarls at them.

I pull her by the arm towards her Mini. "They're not worth it."

"Well, I guess I'll clean up your mess," Silver says from behind me in a calm, smug voice that pisses me off.

I don't want to hear what she has to say, but I also won't run towards the car and show her my flight mode.

No one in hell will see my flight mode.

"Since King is tense, I'll have to give him a visit and loosen him up," Silver continues.

I drop into the passenger seat and slam the door shut harder than I intended.

My breathing is harsh and uneven and my ears ring as if someone slapped me.

Loosen him up.

Who cares who loosens him the hell up?

I'm glad Kim pulls out the car in silence. My temper flares when Silver gives me a smug smile and waves her phone on which 'King' flashes.

He's calling her.

Aiden is calling her.

The entire ride home is spent in unnerving silence.

Despite the weight perching on my chest, I hate the strained air between Kim and I.

I finger the strap of my backpack. "What's wrong, Kim?"

She cuts me a stern look before she focuses back on the road. "I should be asking you that. After years of brushing off guys, you're suddenly interested in Xander?"

I blink. "I'm not interested in Xander."

"So you just held his arm for show? You walked into the cafeteria for the first time in years with Xander for show, too?" Her lips tremble. "Wait. Did you... did you have feelings for him all this time?"

"Absolutely not."

"Then, what is it? You know he bullied me for years! I'm sure it's written in some friendship code that you don't date your best friend's bully."

I stare at her reddened cheeks, incredulous. Being the rational party right now is so freaking hard. "And does that friendship code say that you shouldn't hug your best friend's bully and cry in his chest? Does it allow you to act all friendly around him when it clearly makes me uncomfortable?"

Kim's lips part as she hits the brakes, stopping the car on the side of the road. A driver yells and honks, but she ignores him and taps the steering wheel maniacally. "So this is what it's all about? You're taking revenge because of that?"

"I'm not taking revenge."

"Then what?" Her eyes rim with tears. "It's Xan, Ellie. You can't be with him... *please?*"

"I'm not with him. It's a pretence and a game to stop the bullying. Didn't you tell me to use them while I can?"

"Oh."

Silence takes claim in the car. I stare from the window at kindergarten kids crossing the street.

"King and I aren't what you think." Kim's voice softens.

"Can't you see he's getting between us, Kim?" My voice is defeated.

"I won't allow that. I'm not an idiot, once I get the information I need, I'll step away from him."

"What information?"

She goes back to tapping the steering wheel. "I'll tell you when I'm sure. The point is, I promise to never hurt you, Ellie. You saw me when I was invisible, and I'll never forget that."

I face her, tears blurring my vision. "And I would never hurt you, Kim. You're the best thing that happened to me since I got into this godforsaken school."

Kim lunges at me in a bear hug. I wrap my arms around her, inhaling her soft, floral perfume. I didn't know I needed a hug until she offered it.

When she pulls away, her eyes shift sideways before they meet mine. "Why did Xander ask you to be his pretend girlfriend?"

"I'm not sure, but I think it's his revenge for Aiden hugging you the other week and all the attention he's been giving you since."

Her lips part and she bites back a smile. "Really?"

"Why do you sound happy?"

"I'm not!" She clamps her mouth shut.

"You totally are!" I jab a finger into her side.

She squirms and huffs, throwing a dismissive hand. "You and King, huh?"

My chest tugs at the mention of his name. "Me and King what?"

"Come on, Ellie. The ever so calm King started his first fight for you."

I shake my head. "He just has some issues with Xander."

"Yup. He had issues with Xander touching *you*. I've never seen him lose control, not even when his mother died."

"You were there when his mother died?"

I know Mrs King is no more, but I never actually wondered how her absence can play in Aiden's life.

How could I not have wondered about it before? People's psychological issues always start with their parents. The world's most notorious psychopathic killers usually had mum issues.

"Of course," Kim says. "We're neighbours, you know."

Right. I forget that sometimes.

"How old were you then?" I ask.

"We were maybe seven? I was anyway. She died of illness but…"

"But what?"

Kim lowers her voice as if telling me a top-secret. "Rumour has it that her actual cause of death is suicide, but King Enterprises disguised it as illness."

"Why?"

Kim shrugs. "I don't know, but it could be because of stocks and stuff."

"Was she suicidal?"

"I don't think so? Aunt Alicia was so sweet and caring. I

remember that she loved Aiden and was overprotective of him—something Uncle Jonathan didn't appreciate. Poor Aiden wasn't even there during her death."

I lean forward in my seat. "What do you mean?"

"He went into a summer camp, and when he returned, his mum was dead. I still remember the hollow look in his eyes at the funeral. It still gives me chills… brr. You know, he didn't cry that day. He stood beside his father in complete silence during the entire ceremony."

Something tightens at the pit of my stomach. Losing his mother at such a young age while he was away must've been devastating. I don't even remember my parents, but sometimes, I still feel the loss as if it happened yesterday.

Kim drives me home and we spend the rest of the evening studying then binge watch a few episodes of Lucifer until Aunt returns.

A while later, Kim leaves to help Kirian with his homework. She always pretends that he's a pain, but she can't spend an entire day without thinking about him.

Kim's father is a diplomat who spends most of his time in Brussels and is rarely home. Her mother is a renowned artist who's usually locked in her studio, so Kim has become a grown-up since Kirian was born eight years ago.

She's not only his eldest sister, but she's also his mother and father and best friend. She always said that she doesn't want him to feel the emptiness she felt while growing up.

Aunt and I prepare dinner together. I barely listen to her and tell her about my day at school.

I'm distracted out of my mind.

"Is there something on your phone?" Aunt asks with a suspicious tone when I check it for the millionth time in the past hour.

I force a smile. "No, nothing."

Absolute desert.

Aiden didn't send any of his night texts.

I'll loosen him up.

Silver's voice wraps a noose around my neck. My fingers itch and my hands feel dirty even though I just washed them.

I put them underneath the water in the sink then pull back when I notice Aunt watching me.

She knows I only get obsessive about washing my hands when I'm anxious.

"I'm heading to the grocery store," I blurt to dissipate her attention.

"What for?"

"I ran out of tampons," I say the first thing that comes into mind.

"But you're not on your period, honey?"

"I'll be in a few days. You know I like being prepared." I'm already heading to the door.

"Elsie."

"Yeah?" I throw over my shoulder.

Aunt Blair waves a bill. "You forgot the money."

"Right." I offer an awkward smile and take the bill from her.

"And wear a sweater. It's chilly outside."

"Yes, Aunt," I call from the doorway.

"Hurry back."

Shoving my feet into flats, I throw a thin sweater over my black cotton dress on which is written 'Comfy at Home'. It's similar to an oversized T-shirt that stops at my knees.

The moment I'm out of the house, the first drops of rain hit my nose and lashes. I could've gone back for the umbrella, but I don't.

Instead, I let my legs take reign.

I run down the empty, lit streets as hard and as fast as I can. The night's chill slaps me across the face and the rain soaks me in seconds.

But it isn't enough.

There's a weight on my chest.

It's suffocating.

It's robbing me from any clean air.

Every breath I take feels dirty and impure.

I feel dirty and impure.

The only thing able to cleanse me is running and the rain.

Only… it doesn't.

Images of Silver *loosening up* Aiden keep playing at the back of my mind like some porn.

That must be why he's too busy to text me.

I close my eyes and try to purge the images out of my head.

Silver and Aiden are made for each other.

I don't care about them and their after school activities.

But why ask me to be his if he already has someone to tend to his whims?

Dickhead.

Once I arrive at the grocery store, I buy some tampons and an umbrella. I would rather run back in the rain, but Aunt will give me grief about it.

Not to mention that my heart feels kind of funny. I won't push it for no reason.

I'm around the corner to our house, carrying the grocery bag in one hand and the umbrella in the other when I notice a black Mercedes with tinted windows. I think it's been there since the grocery store.

Panic grips my chest and I run the rest of the way home. I opt for the back entrance since it's the closest.

The moment I round the corner, a strong hand clamps around my mouth. I shriek, the umbrella and the bag fall from my hands.

My scream is drowned by the hand on my mouth.

I'm hauled forward. I trip and my cheek smashes against the hood of a car. I recognise his smell before his hot breath whispers in my ear.

"Time to pay, sweetheart."

EIGHTEEN

"A-Aiden?"

My heart lunges in my chest, beating sporadically against the hood of the car.

His car.

The dim light coming from around the corner doesn't allow me much vision, but I *feel* him.

It's impossible not to when I smell his clean, unmistakable scent mingling with the rain.

The bottom of my stomach hurts with that strange awareness I always had for him.

That damn awareness is like an incurable disease refusing to leave my body.

I try to lift my head and look at him, but he smashes my cheek back down against the wet hood.

"What are you doing —"

He grabs a fistful of my hair harshly. "Shut the fuck up, Elsa."

I whimper around the pain ripping at my skull and the uncomfortable position he's forcing me into. The car's cold, wet metal digs into my stomach the more I try to move.

When I open my mouth to say something, he pulls me up by my hair so I'm staring at his dark eyes.

His plain black T-shirt is soaked, sticking to his muscles like a second skin. The rain forms rivulets down his hard face, his strong jawline and the bump on his lips due to his fight with Xander.

He appears angry.

No. Lethal.

It could be because of the dark or the rain or the desolate streets, but a chill of terror spreads over my skin.

This is Aiden's true form. The soulless, unfeeling psycho.

"Shh, not a fucking word." His left eye twitches. "You don't want to test me right now."

My lips tremble and it's not because of the cold or the rain.

"Aunt is just upstairs." I try to threaten. "She'll come down for me."

His lips brush my ear as he whispers in a cruel voice, "Then why aren't you screaming?"

Before I can think about that, he bites the shell of my ear. Hard. So hard that I think he's after my flesh.

I shriek, but his hand clamps around my mouth, turning it into a muffled, haunted sound.

The type victims make when they're kidnapped in the middle of the night.

"Do you like blood on your hands?" he asks with a dark, chilling tone.

My back snaps at the image.

Blood on my hands.

In my hair.

In my —

"If I killed Xan today, it would've been all because of you."

I mumble against his hand, but he only pulls me harder by my hair. "Do you know that I feel murderous when someone touches you? Is that why you pulled that fucking stunt?"

I shake my head, tears rimming my eyes and mixing with the pouring rain.

God. He's a psycho. A sick sonofabitch.

Then why am I not fighting?

Fucking fight, Elsa. You're a fighter.

My limbs remain locked in place no matter how much I beg them to move.

"Answer me."

I mumble an unintelligible sound. He's blocking my mouth, how the hell am I supposed to answer?

"Scream or fight and I'll fuck you raw against the car until the entire neighbourhood learns my name. Understood?"

I swallow, nodding once.

He removes his hand from my mouth, but he pins me to the hood of the car with a strong hand around my nape.

"You're using Kim against me," I pant, my voice hoarse and raw. "Is it such a surprise that I'd decide to use your friend against you?"

"Hmm. Maybe I should get rid of all said friends."

My ears ring at his dispassionate tone. He's… serious. They're not his friends in the way Kim is to me. If they pose any threats to his plans, they become disposable.

Absolutely nothing.

His complete disregard for human emotions is scary.

No. It's terrifying.

What's more horrifying is the fact that someone of his calibre has this sick fixation on me.

"You started those rumours about me." *Shut up. Shut up, don't provoke him.* No matter how much I reprimand myself, the words won't stop spilling like venom from my throat. "It's because of you I'm labelled a slut. It's because of you no one approaches me."

"And no one will." He's at my face, so close that we breathe each other's air. "Do you know why, sweetheart?"

"Why?" I murmur.

"Because you were always mine. You just didn't know it yet."

He yanks my dress up and air slaps my bare thighs, causing goosebumps to erupt all over my skin. I clamp my eyes shut as he pulls my boy shorts down, leaving me naked and exposed to the rain and his merciless gaze.

"If you were going to take what you wanted anyway, why did you ask me to be yours? Was it a mindfuck? A play? Did it turn you on to see me hanging onto false hope, thinking I had a say in anything you do to me?" I choke on the words. My voice is so emotional, so angry, that I feel it crackling down like thunder with the raindrops.

"I told you. That was your chance to make the first move, but I was right. You don't want nice. You want me to take your will, don't you?"

"Get off me, you sick bastard."

"You're sick with me, sweetheart. You're so wet, I can smell you in the fucking air."

He thrusts a finger inside me and my ears heat with shame when he finds no resistance.

No pressure.

No nothing.

His finger finds refuge inside my tight walls as if that's where it always belonged.

Like he had a claim on me since the very first time we met.

"Being dominated by me turns you on." He thrusts another finger inside, causing me to whimper. "Being at my mercy makes you fucking soaked."

I shake my head against the metal, but with his death grip on my neck, I barely move.

"You don't have to admit it now, but you will…" He thrusts savagely into my pussy. "Eventually."

My eyes roll to the back of my head and I clamp a hand on my mouth to stop a loud moan from coming out.

Aiden doesn't stop. He pounds his fingers inside me hard and fast as if he's fucking me with his cock. I arch off the hood with each merciless thrust.

I'm gasping, panting and mewling. The worst part is that I have no control over it.

Even with the rain, the public place, and the fact that Aunt can peek from the kitchen balcony any second, I can't stop.

Hell, it's making me hotter. So hot that the rain nearly evaporates on my skin.

He's possessing me and transforming me into this foreign, scary version.

"You won't let any other man touch you. Is that clear?"

I'm too consumed by his devilish fingers to pay attention to his words.

Something brutal and destructive builds at the bottom of my stomach, clashing and smashing with his rhythm.

I can feel that wave. It's just within reach. I've brought myself to orgasm before, but I always held back last minute, afraid of the intensity it brings.

Now, I can't stop it even if I want to.

You like your will taken, don't you?

His words draw a fierce sensation in my inner walls.

God. What's wrong with me?

"Say yes," he orders, flicking my clit.

The moan escapes from between my lips no matter how much I try to confine it.

He tightens his grip on my neck. "Say yes or I'll stop."

His rhythm drops in intensity as if proving a point.

I whimper, eyes bulging.

No. He can't stop. Not this time, too. I'm there. Almost there.

"I... I..."

"Fucking *say* it." He pumps harder into me, causing stars to form behind my lids.

"Yes!" I scream as the sharp power hits me.

I open my mouth to say something, but it remains in an 'O' and no words come out.

He stole my ability to speak

To breathe.

To think.

The fierce wave doesn't let me go. Not really. Not even when he removes his fingers from inside me.

He stuffs his fingers—that still glisten of me—at my mouth.

"Open."

I shake my head, parting my lips to protest, but he uses the chance to stuff both his fingers in my mouth.

"Do you taste yourself on me, sweetheart, hmm?" He gets past my lips and strokes his fingers on my tongue.

My mouth waters, but I want to shake my head in mortification. The clenching of my core answers before I can utter a word.

"Suck."

I do, tentatively, just so I don't drool like a dog.

Tasting myself on him is a strange, out of body experience. But I don't stop.

I can't.

It's like my tongue wants to express something after the sensation he just brought me.

Aiden pops his fingers out as suddenly as he thrust them in, leaving me dazed and still slumped against the car, breathing harshly and unevenly.

Then he does something that shocks the living bejesus out of me.

He drops a gentle kiss on my nose.

His eyes are still dark, but they're a lot clearer when he says, "Good girl."

For the rest of the week, neither Aiden nor Xander shows up at school.

They were both suspended.

According to the gossip, Coach has them in a private camp until the end of their suspension as his form of discipline.

No coach would want his two star players at each others' throat. Especially not in the senior year.

Me? I'm just happy I get space from Aiden.

After unravelling all over his fingers during that rainy night, I need more than space.

I need a continent between us.

How could I give in to him? Climax even?

He's a sick monster. He'll only hurt me.

Destroy me, even.

So why the hell can't I stop thinking about that night?

Aiden still sends the usual dirty texts about what he's thinking about doing to me once he returns. They get cruder and more taboo by the day. I never read them in front of Aunt and Uncle.

The bastard is ruining me and I have no way to stop it.

Since Aunt and Uncle work over the weekend, I decide to sleepover at Kim's on Sunday. We have a maths' test in a few days, so we spend some time studying.

Kim's house is on the upper-class side. Their neighbourhood screams of wealth and it's filled with aristocrats and new money. I stand in Kim's bedroom and stare out the balcony. Xander's house is across from hers. I can't begin to imagine what it feels like to be neighbours with your bully.

Aiden's house is down the street. It's huge and imposing and… lifeless. No one comes in or out.

Aiden must still be at his camp.

Not that I care.

Yellow by Coldplay blasts from my phone and Kim hums along with it as she fishes into her closet.

We just put Kirian to bed after we goofed around with mac and cheese. Kim's mother is in her studio and is not to be disturbed when she's chasing after her next masterpiece.

Kir seemed pretty happy with just Kim and me for his Sunday dates.

"What are you doing?" I finally focus on her and all the outfits she's tossing on the bed.

"Ronan is throwing a party this weekend. He just texted me."

Since when does Ronan text her?

"You're really going to Ronan's party?"

"It's senior year, Ellie. We won't live it twice." She grins, posing with a faux plume scarf around her neck. "Come on, pick something."

"Pass. I'm not interested in those parties."

"Stop being Frozen and let's go."

"No."

"One of these days, I'm going to convince you."

"Never, Satan."

I'm about to change into my PJ's when my phone vibrates.

My pulse nearly erupts when I see Aiden's name.

Aiden: Let's meet.

I can almost imagine his bossy tone if I heard him say those words. I guess this confirms that he's back from the camp.

Aiden: I miss you.

Something squeezes so hard in my chest, it's painful.

How can he say words like that so easily? How can he rattle me just as easily?

Aiden: I know you miss me, too. You don't have to say it.

Arrogant bastard.

And no, I don't freaking miss him.

Who misses their tormentor?

Their bully?

Their nightmare?

Aiden: So? Are you coming to meet me or should I improvise?

No idea what that means, but it can't be good for me.

Elsa: Don't you dare.

He doesn't reply.

Goddamn the psycho and damn me for showing that I care.

My gaze strays to Kim. If he's out of camp, then he must be going to Ronan's party, right?

"Kim." I throw my phone on the bed and walk to her. "Don't go and I'll watch a Korean soap opera with you."

She laughs, pulling out two dresses. "We can do that when I return."

Damn it.

"Xander is back from camp," I blurt. "You don't want to run into him at the party, right?"

"Xander can go fuck himself." Her lips twist in defiance. "I won't let him ruin my life anymore."

Well, shit.

It looks like I have to party tonight.

NINETEEN

As Kim and I walk out from her car to Ronan Astor's huge house, I try telling myself that I'm only here because of Kim.

There's no way in shit I'm leaving her alone at a party where Xander Knight is present.

Deep down?

I'm at the edge of myself with that damned awareness slicing and clawing at the bottom of my stomach.

This is the first time I'm seeing Aiden after he pushed me against the hood of his car in the rain.

After he wrenched an explosive orgasm out of me where anyone could've seen us.

Could've seen *me*.

What would've happened if Aunt looked out? If Uncle returned home? If one of the neighbours passed by?

Getting all tangled with Aiden is provoking parts I never wanted provoked.

Because at that moment? All I thought about was chasing the sensation he was pulling out of me.

God. I hate him.

Kim's eyes sparkle with excitement as we walk through the front door of Ronan's mansion. Loud music thumps from the walls even before we get in. A butler who looks straight out of Downton Abbey, all complete with the uniform and the tight smile welcomes us in.

Ronan is a lord's son, but the butlers and servers at a teenager's party are too much.

I smile, imagining him forcing his parents' staff to serve at his endless parties.

Almost everyone from RES is here. It's weird to see them out of their uniforms, laughing, drinking, and grinding against each other to a hit pop song.

This is a normal Sunday night to them. Kim and I are about the only ones who avoid them. For two years, I never felt like I was missing out on the whole teenage scene.

However, Kim always talked about such parties with a certain sadness that knotted my heart. Unlike me, she longed for the normal teenage life. She wants to go to college with one last hurrah.

I won't kill her wishes just because these scenes aren't for me. That's what best friends do, right? They abandon their comfort zones for their friends.

Kim lent me skinny jeans and a black tank top that keeps falling off my right shoulder. Since Kim lost weight, her new size is a bit too tight on me and I feel like combusting in the trousers. I kept my face make-up-less and pulled my hair into a loose ponytail at the top of my head.

Kim opted for a hot pink dress that hugs her petite frame and hints at her cleavage. She's even wearing heels and has her hair loose.

We're going all out.

Her words, not mine.

Dangerous Night by Thirty Seconds to Mars fills the space as Kim snatches a drink from a butler's tray.

I face her. "Are you nervous? We can go home if you like."

"Nope!" She laughs. "We agreed to not run away anymore, remember?"

"It's fine to run away sometimes. You know, for self-preservation."

She chugs half of the drink. "How do you do that?"

"Do what?"

"Act so strong, Ellie! I wish I had your cool head."

I lift my shoulder. "I'm not really that cool, Kim. I don't show it."

"Show it?"

I catch a dark figure in my peripheral vision and the blood in my veins turns to ice.

Blood.

So much blood.

Steel blood runs in your veins. You will not disgrace it.

The haunting voice booms in my head like a demon's. The tips of my fingers tingle and turn icy.

An urge to scrub them clean takes over me like a drug addict burning for a fix.

A weird sensation crawls down my spine as I feel eyes on me. Blank, lifeless eyes. They're watching.

They're coming to get me.

They'll eat me.

Run, Elsa!

NOW!

"Elsa?"

My gaze snaps to Kim who's waving a hand in front of my face.

"Huh?"

"You just zoned out." Her brows furrow. "Is everything okay?"

"Yeah." I force a smile. "I just need the restroom. I'll be right back."

I bolt out of there before she can say another word. With one of the butlers' help, I find a restroom. The burn under my skin becomes like hellfire, about to consume me whole.

It only cools once I pour water and scrub it clean over and over again.

I watch my surroundings the entire time as if expecting someone to jump me from the walls. Or worse, the mirrors.

I stare at my spooked reflection. My pupils are round as saucers and my white-ish hair looks like a witch's.

"It's nothing." I force a smile out of my trembling lips. "You're going to be okay."

After smoothing my expression and cleaning my hands, I step out of the bathroom.

I'm lost in my thoughts when I walk back into the lounge area where music thumps and everyone dances like they're in a club.

I barge into a hard wall—or a person.

Ow. Strong hands clutch me before I fall back on my butt.

"Sorry," I mumble. "I didn't see you."

"Obviously." The laughter draws my attention to the tall, broad and very familiar face.

Levi King.

The previous captain of Elites and the current gem of Arsenal's midfield.

I'm caught in a near-fangirl moment at seeing a Gunner in real life. I mean, I did go to games with Uncle Jaxon, but this is the closest I've gotten to a player.

"Have you seen my dickhead cousin?" Levi's inquisitive eyes roam over my shoulder.

His cousin. Right. Aiden is one year younger than him and his cousin. Jonathan King is his guardian.

I visibly shake myself. I can't believe I was almost too caught in the fangirl mode to forget who Levi actually is.

"Wait a second." He studies me close—too close—that I smell his expensive aftershave.

While Aiden has the whole dark vibe to a T, Levi has pale blue eyes that flick to clear grey in the dim light. His sandy blonde hair is tousled and messed up like he couldn't care less about combing it when he rolled out of bed.

He's wearing Elites' royal blue jacket over a white T-shirt and dark jeans.

"It's you." He grins. "Frozen."

"Elsa is fine, thanks," I say with sarcasm.

He laughs. "Elsa, right. I didn't know your real name."

Of course, he didn't. Kings don't know all their peasants, do they?

"What are you doing at Ronan's party?" he asks. "Wait. Did Aiden drag you here?"

I'm honestly not surprised that he thinks that.

"He did, didn't he?" He searches me up and down as if Aiden will materialise from underneath my skin. "And where is he now?"

"Don't know. Don't care."

"Huh. He must be playing a chess game against himself like a freak."

"Wait. He does that?" That's so weird. I thought I was the only one who does that.

"Stage five freak. I'm telling you." He winks.

Well, Levi isn't exactly like the image I painted in my head. After everything I had heard about screwing the teacher and being Elites' captain, and the king of RES, I expected an older, more bastard version than Aiden.

Instead, he's more... welcoming?

Would I appear like a creep if I ask for his autograph? Uncle Jaxon would be so happy.

Just when I'm contemplating the idea, the music comes to an abrupt halt. Ronan jumps to the top of a table in the middle of the lounge area where the football team surrounds him.

"Listen up, bitches." He uses a beer bottle as a microphone. "We're here today to celebrate our win against New Castle. One to nil. Championship, here we fucking come."

Everyone hoots and cheers, "Go Elites!"

Even Levi smiles, shaking his head.

"It hasn't been easy to win without our two strikers." Ronan's tone and expression turn to sorrowful before he grins. "But yours truly can transform into a striker any day, bitches! King and Knight, who?"

"Fuck you, Astor," Xander mumbles from beside him and everyone else laughs.

"*La ferme*, Knight. Don't kill my vibe." Ronan goes back to grinning. "Anyway, let's ignore Knight's bitter arse. We have a special guest tonight. Our own Premier League star. Let's welcome our previous captain, Levi King!"

"He had to do it," Levi mutters under his breath. "Fucker."

The rest of the football team cheers and hits the table like crazy.

Ronan points at Levi and shouts. "Come here, Captain!"

"Captain, captain, captain…" The rest chant, led by Ronan and Cole.

Levi grunts and starts to leave, but stops and looks down at me. "Remember what I told you about Aiden being a stage five freak?"

I nod once.

"He's also a stage five creeper. It's better if you stay away from him." He winks. "For your sake, not his."

And then he's gone.

I stare at his back, incredulous, as the football team members clasp him in bro hugs.

What on earth does he mean by 'for your sake, not his'?

"First of all," Levi says in a joking tone, glaring down at Ronan. "I'm only here to get my dickhead cousin, so fuck you for the speech setup, Astor."

"Come on, Captain." Ronan waves him off. "Some encouraging words for the championship."

"If you don't get it again this year…" Levi trails off. "You'll be punished, captain style."

They all grunt, except for Ronan who jumps up. "Nah, you're not our captain anymore." He grins, clasping Cole by the shoulder. "Nash is."

Levi raises an eyebrow. "And who do you think gave Nash that captain position."

They all break out in a dispute, except for Cole who watches them with a smile, shaking his head.

Levi put Cole as captain? It's weird that he didn't pick Aiden, considering that he's his cousin.

"Ellie!"

I rip my attention from the football team to Kim who's grinning as she holds onto a brunette's elbow.

"This is Astrid." Kim beams. "Astrid Clifford, you know, the one I told you I sat with during last year's games."

I smile at Astrid and her glowing aura. She's rocking simple overall shorts and fishnet stockings. It's cute in a girly kind of way.

It's not the first time I've seen her. Her rocky relationship with Levi had been the talk of RES last year. I even caught Aiden hanging out around her.

Actually, Astrid and Silver are the only two girls Aiden has associated himself with.

Not that I've been watching him or anything.

"Astrid, this is my best friend, Elsa."

"Elsa." Astrid rolls my name off her tongue with a discreet smile.

"What?" I ask.

"Nothing." She laughs, waving her hand. "I just heard so much about you and the only names I got were Frozen and Ice Princess. I'm glad to know your real name."

I wince.

"Oh, sorry. I didn't mean to offend you." She clasps my hand. "I'm really glad to finally meet Aiden's obsession."

"Wait. What?" My lips part open.

"He used to watch you all the time."

She's about to say something when her gaze strays to where Levi stands with the football team.

An electric current passes between them and I find myself caught in the way they watch each other.

It's like they're the only two people in the room.

The longing and the passion are so tangible, I almost taste it on my tongue. My chest squeezes for no apparent reason.

"Come here, princess," Levi shouts.

"Yes, my queen." Ronan yells. "Let's have a drinking competition for old times' sake."

"In your fucking dreams," Levi growls at him.

"I'm in." Astrid laughs then looks at me and Kim. "Let's go."

Kim takes her hand, but I shake my head. "It's not my scene, but thanks for offering."

Out of the corner of my eye, Kim gives me a reprimanding look as she follows Astrid to the middle of the party. Ronan is already preparing the drinks with the help of his teammates.

Time to search for a hole where I can hide for the rest of the party—and watch Kim.

She's on her second—or third shot. We're definitely not driving back to her house.

A taxi it is.

My gaze gets lost in the crowd as if I'm searching for something.

Or someone.

Nope. I'm absolutely not searching for *him*.

I head to the reception-style table to pick something to eat.

Here's to hoping it's not all junk food.

I collide against a hard chest. Ow. Seriously, what's with colliding into people today?

Only this time… it's different.

A strong arm surrounds my waist with ease. I feel his warmth and smell his familiar, head-turning scent before seeing him. My heart does that slight jump that turns my insides upside down.

I step back, but I can't go far since he's gripping me tight by the waist. When I lift my head, I'm greeted by the smokiest, most turbulent eyes. Something unreadable forms a sheen in his gaze.

A week.

It's been less than a week since I saw him, but it feels like forever.

That strong jaw, the straight nose, and the jet black hair seem like a far, distant memory.

Only... they're not.

Aiden is dashing in the school's uniform, but he's irresistible in simple jeans and a black T-shirt. He carries the nonchalant vibe so well, it's almost unfair.

My gaze locks on the cut near the corner of his mouth. I shouldn't be feeling guilty considering that I've done nothing wrong, but I still do. It doesn't delight me to see him hurt.

I'm *not* that person.

The chaos of the drinking competition, the music, and the chants cease to exist.

It's only me and him now.

Me and my tormenter.

I reach up and touch the pad of my forefinger to the cut on his lip. "Does it hurt?"

He yanks my hand free and holds it prisoner in his.

"You're getting good at lying, sweetheart." His eyes gleam, but they're not playful. They're downright sinister. "You got me for a second there."

"What?"

"You don't have to pretend that you care about me."

He thought I was pretending? Screw him.

And screw me for actually having that lapse of judgement.

I lift my chin. "I don't care about you."

"Is that so?"

"Not at all, Aiden. You're nothing to me."

"Nothing, huh?"

"Absolutely nothing."

I don't get a warning.

Aiden's lips crash to mine in an animalistic frenzy. I don't get to think or breathe.

All I can do is... feel.

Still holding me by the waist, his other hand grabs my nape in a possessive hold.

Aiden doesn't kiss me, he claims me. His teeth nibble on my bottom lip before he thrusts his tongue inside my mouth.

It's a clashing of tongues and teeth and lips.

It's suffocating and liberating.

I can't breathe.

But who needs breathing?

My fingers dig into the hard ridge of his chest, fisting into the T-shirt for balance.

Aiden lifts me and sits me on some surface. I wrap my legs around his waist while he continues ravaging my mouth. My head turns dizzy, hazy, and begins floating.

Aiden's presence doesn't only fill my air, but it conquers it.

Smashes it.

Breaks it apart.

His hand sneaks under my T-shirt at that place where my top meets my jeans. I hiss in a breath when his rough, calloused hand meets my softer skin.

Aiden pulls away, and air assaults my lungs. I'm disoriented when he smirks in a lazy, sinister way.

"Nothing, huh?" he motions behind him.

That's when I realise we're in public.

I just let Aiden kiss the shit out of me in front of the entire school.

My cheeks heat and I freeze as if that will make me disappear.

No chatter comes from behind us, so I'm sure everyone's attention is on us.

Can the earth swallow me, please?

While still tangled around him, Aiden lifts me up and carries me out. I hide my head in the crook of his neck, not daring to make eye contact with anyone.

Aiden leans into my ear and whispers, "It's time you become completely mine."

TWENTY

Aiden doesn't stop when murmurs break whenever we walk.

He doesn't stop when his teammates howl behind us.

His steps are confident and sure while his fingers continue drawing circles down my back.

I want to think it's an endearing touch, but that's not how Aiden works, is it? He doesn't do endearing. Possessiveness suits him better.

The entire school just watched us tonguing each other and all I can think about is the meaning behind the tiny circles.

Truth is, I couldn't care less about the audience.

All my senses are filled with Aiden. His height. His muscles that might as well be made from granite. The effortless and sure way he holds me.

His strength always had me in knots. There's something about the way he carries me that's all… male.

And his scent. His damn, clean, addictive scent.

With my head hidden in the crook of his neck, I can't resist the urge to inhale him in and safeguard his scent to memory.

A door clicks then closes and Aiden stops. It's my cue to lift my head. I release a breath when I make out a simple, non-characteristic room that must be for guests. There's a medium-sized bed, a nightstand and a cupboard. Floral wallpaper covers the walls.

It reminds me of… home.

Not my home with Aunt and Uncle, but my actual home in Birmingham.

That's such a disturbing thought.

I don't remember home and I don't want to.

My attention drifts back to Aiden who's been watching me intently.

Since the beginning of this year, he's been having this slight draw in his thick brows. It's like he's cracking a mathematical problem or a cyber code.

The brief show of humanity disappears and the poker face takes over.

It's then I realise that I've been holding him like a vice.

Worse. We're alone in a room and he's blocking the only exit.

I attempt to scramble down his body, but his lethal hold tightens around my midsection.

"Ow. That hurts!" I push at his chest.

"Then stay still."

"Ugh. Let me go, Aiden!"

"Why? You came here for me, didn't you?"

The arrogance of this bastard. "You wish, arsehole."

"Then who did you come for, hmm?" His eyes spark, and it pisses me off.

He pisses me off.

And apparently, I'm vindictive as hell because I give him a taunting smile. "Who do you think? I came for my boyfriend Xander."

His eyes darken, but he smiles in a chilling, horror film kind of way. "Repeat that."

I gulp, and the sound crackles in the burning tension in the air.

"Go ahead, sweetheart. I dare you to say that again."

I shouldn't.

Considering the murderous energy swirling around him, I should cut my losses short and shut up.

I must be out of my mind because I say, "My boyfriend Xander. He must be looking —"

It happens so fast, I barely register it.

Aiden throws me on the bed and crawls atop of me. My breath hitches when I make out the crazed look in his eyes. It's as if someone turned the switch on.

I turned the switch on.

I lie beneath his looming body. His shoulders strain against the cloth of his T-shirt and he's breathing heavily as if he's coming down from a run.

I clench my thighs together not wanting him to see the overwhelming effect he has on me.

Because at this moment when he's all threatening and scary, I don't see the danger.

I should see the danger.

Instead, I'm searching behind that danger, thirsting to dig my claws in him and rip open the poker face to peek behind it.

I'm almost sure I'll find a monster, but I still want to see it anyway.

I still want to see what he's made of. *Why* he's made this way.

His hand reaches for my face. I swallow as he traces a sensual finger down my cheek. It's meant to be soft, but all I see is the darkness lurking beneath the surface.

I crave it. I want him to unleash it.

If he's sick and I want his sickness, what does it make me?

"Seems that night in the rain did you no good." His voice is too calm as he pinches my cheek. "I told you, sweetheart. You're already mine, so stop acting otherwise."

"I'm not yours."

"Being mine is a fact, not an option. I don't give a fuck if you embrace it or fight it in front of me." He nuzzles his nose over my cheek. "But I'm done giving you freedom. You don't get to act like you don't belong to me."

"Or what?"

He shakes his head. "You don't want to know that."

"Why the hell not?"

"Be mine and you become the queen on my board." He pauses and flicks his tongue to lick my lower lip. "Fight and you'll remain a pawn."

Something bubbles to my throat and I can't swallow past it. He's fuming.

No. He's enraged.

To another person, this version of Aiden would appear normal, soft even, but Aiden is the type who hides his anger beneath layers of calmness.

To say I'm not scared would be a lie, but I got past the blinding fear stage. Now, I'm able to see past the fear to his obsession with me. The way he seems so physically intent to possess me. I see the spark.

The want.

My want.

The way I react to him is beginning to scare me more than how he reacts to me.

As if all my senses aren't filled with him already, Aiden squeezes my jaw so I'm glued to the grey storms in his eyes. They're turbulent, beautiful, and downright terrifying.

Now, I know why storms are named after people.

"Which one will you be?" He drawls. "Queen or pawn?"

"None."

"None, huh?"

"I'm not a chess piece on your board, Aiden. I'm human with human needs."

His lips tug with a smirk. "Human needs. Hmm. We can work on that."

I hit his shoulder. "That's not what I mean."

But then his lips claim mine.

When I open with a stunned gasp, he growls into my mouth and devours me. If the earlier kiss was head-turning, this one is animalistic and out of control. Aiden threads his fingers into my hair, tugging the strands loose, and brutalises my mouth.

The kiss is savage.

No.

It's barbaric like he never kissed before.

Like he's only discovering what it feels like to kiss.

It's like he wasn't kissing me earlier. Like he was holding back.

I'm in that phase where there's no air and no other thoughts but him and his lips. His firm, yet soft lips.

His brutalising lips.

His body crashes into mine. All his hard lines mould into my soft curves. My hands find refuge on both his sides and I moan into his mouth.

Aiden breaks away, breathing harshly, and grunts against the corner of my mouth.

I had expected him to let go of his anger with the kiss, but it's worse. His rage is a living, breathing being right now and he doesn't even bother to mask it.

"If anyone dares to look at you, let alone touch what's mine, I'll fucking murder them. Is that clear?"

My lips part, unable to breathe properly, let alone speak.

"Is that clear?" He grits out.

"I'm not your thing, Aiden." Damn him to the pits of hell. What does he think I am? An object?

He chuckles, the sound is dark and domineering. "Oh, but you are and if you still doubt it…" His lips graze my ear as he whispers in a dark tone, "I'll fuck you so hard, so deep, you'll be begging for me to never leave your tight pussy again."

I clench my thighs at the image he painted inside my head. I try to chase it, but it won't go away.

Am I defective? Wrong in the head?

Otherwise, how can I react so strongly to his crude words?

Aiden yanks down my jeans before I can form clear thoughts of what's going on.

"Remove the T-Shirt," he orders as my jeans reach my knees.

"Aiden…" It's that breathy voice again.

The needy, damn voice I shouldn't be using in front of Aiden.

"If I do it, I'll rip the thing off." His darkened gaze meets mine in a challenge for dominance or a challenge to make him do it. I don't know.

A part of me is tempted to let him, but the other part just pulls the shirt over my head and throws it somewhere beside me. I'm lying in front of Aiden in my white bra and underwear.

I should be feeling embarrassed considering that he's the first to see me this way, but I'm not.

If anything, I'm meeting his challenging gaze with one of my own.

Because he's not done. He'll never be done taking things from me. If I give him one, he takes ten.

His heated gaze travels up and down my half-naked body like whips of fire. I try to ignore it and fail miserably.

"Remove the bra," he orders, meeting my gaze.

This time, I don't move.

"Last chance, Elsa." His lips curve into a smirk.

No matter how much I like the sound of my name out of his mouth, I don't let it sway me.

Instead, I glare at him. Like we're back to that time where we had glaring battles from afar.

I miss those times.

At least back then, he was simply an arsehole.

Now, he's an arsehole who knows all the buttons to push in my body.

Aiden reaches to my back and yanks the bra free.

His eyes fill with overwhelming lust. My head turns away. I might not be embarrassed about my body, but the scar is another story.

The scar is my disgrace.

The key to my Pandora's Box.

Aiden crawls atop of me, supporting himself on his palms and places kisses along my scar. Shock reverberates beneath my skin and tears fill my eyes.

"Stop that!" I don't like the vulnerability.

Of all people, Aiden doesn't get to see me bare, both body and soul.

"Too bad you don't call the shots tonight." He grins before his mouth goes back to worshipping my scar, his stubble tickling against the skin.

I try to push him. His index and thumb latch around a nipple and squeezes. Hard. I cry out as a zap of intense pleasure and pain pools between my thighs.

Aiden lifts his head with a smirk. "You like that, don't you?"

I want to shake my head, to tell him to screw off, but my expression must appear dazed.

Aiden pinches my nipple again, and I hiss. Then he massages it, giving me a hazy pleasurable feeling. Before I can fall into it, he pinches again. He does it over and over. Just when I'm falling into the pleasurable feeling, he pinches.

I become delirious and drunk on the ecstasy he wrenches out of me.

He bites the other nipple into his hot mouth. My back arches as he surrounds the hard pebble with his lips and then nibbles slightly. "I love these." His warm breaths send shivers along my skin. "Don't you love what I do to them?"

I make some sound I can't pinpoint.

"Do you want me to bite?"

I'm breathing heavily, my nipples are assaulted and sensitive, but I can't say no.

I can't say yes either.

I can't say anything.

Maybe Aiden is right. Maybe I like him to dominate me.

His eyes darken as if reading my thoughts. He doesn't wait for an answer. He bites, hard.

Pain zips down my spine and a strange sensation tightens the bottom of my stomach. He massages my throbbing nipple with his tongue, and I whimper. He bites again and again.

I'm a writhing, crying mess beneath him, but I can't tell him to stop.

I don't want to.

I haven't felt such an onslaught of emotions in my life before and I'm craving it.

I'm craving more.

Is crazy contagious? Because I'm starting to feel as depraved as Aiden.

Just like with his fingers, the soothing massaging is just a build up before he tortures me with his bites again.

He does the same to the swell of my breasts and the soft skin of my stomach before travelling down.

"Should I ask, sweetheart?" His voice is husky and filled with the deep lust that's coursing through my veins.

His fingers curve into the hem of my underwear before bringing it down my legs.

I shudder when cold air hits my sensitive, wet folds.

Aiden sniffs the air and grins.

I see the devil in his eyes, and the first thought is… I want that devil.

How can I want a devil?

"I can smell your arousal." He growls. "What am I going to do with you now?"

TWENTY-ONE

Aiden grips each of my thighs, spreads them wide, and lowers himself between them.

For long seconds, he just studies me. I'm glad I always keep it shaved down there. I can't get a clear look at him, but I can *feel* him.

His harsh breaths. The heavy rise and fall of his shoulders. His brute strength gripping both my thighs to keep me spread-eagled for his eyes.

He's only watching me, but that's enough for a primal sensation to hit me.

It's like he's burning and melting me with his gaze.

"Aiden..."

I don't know why I call his name. All I know is that I can't bear the suffocating tension.

"Hmm. You're wet." He releases a thigh to trace a thumb up my folds. "Were you wet since I kissed you? Or after I threw you on the bed?"

"I... I don't know."

"I love kissing you."

So do I.

Damn me, so do I.

"Your lips were made for me, sweetheart." He pauses. "Everything about you was made for me."

He places a chaste kiss on my folds. The contact is so intimate, so... crude that a shudder crawls down my spine.

"Did someone eat your pussy before? Did you let them?" There's an edge to his tone as if he doesn't want to hear the answer.

His mere words are enough to paint a dirty picture in my head. Aiden's mouth on my most intimate part.

I want that picture.

If I don't get that picture, I'll probably dream about it and wake up with my hand between my legs.

He flicks a thumb against my clit. "Answer me."

I suppress a moan. "N-no."

He freezes, and I do too. What have I done?

Was this some sort of a test and I screwed it up?

"And no one will in the future." He thrusts a finger inside me, making me arch off the bed. "Your pussy will only know my fingers, my tongue, and my cock. Is that clear?"

I nod. I would've nodded to anything at the moment because I'm busy telling my body not to grind against his finger and not to recall how that same finger brought me to the throes of plea-sure not so long ago.

"I won't take it easy on you." Aiden's voice and eyes darken. "You don't get to tap out. You don't get to tell me to stop. You don't get *anything*."

My lips part as goosebumps erupt all over my skin.

"I need you to understand that." His grip on my thigh tight-ens as if he's restraining himself. "I won't stop."

This would be one of those times where it'd be wiser to flee and never return. Aiden is going out of his way to give me a chance to stop now before he's all in. Any normal human would take the chance.

Obviously, I'm not normal.

"I understand."

Two words. Two simple words. And I'm done for.

Aiden lunges at me like a madman. He removes his finger, and before I can protest, his tongue swipes from the bottom of my slit to the top.

Oh. God.

My head rolls back and my back arches off the bed. He does it again. I cry out at the intrusive, enthralling sensation.

An unfamiliar tightness grips my stomach. My chest squeezes so hard, I'm genuinely scared something is wrong with my defective heart.

The fact that a single touch can cause this raw reaction is scary. Thrilling, but scary all the same.

Something within me unlocks.

It's a detonation. An awakening.

I'm thrashing, mewling, and gripping the bedsheets as if they're lifelines. What in the ever living hell is he doing?

He nibbles on my clit before he thrusts his tongue inside me, fucking me like it's his cock.

"Aiden... Oh, my God, Aiden!!"

He stops, his head peeking from between my thighs with a shit-eating grin on his face. "I love the idea of being your God."

Then his tongue plunges inside me again.

I'm a goner.

I'm a victim of him and his wicked tongue.

He fucks me with it like he's worshipping me and punishing me at the same time. His pace is relentless, unapologetic, and so out of freaking control.

There's nothing predictable about what he'll do next or how far he'll go.

I can't help falling into his well-crafted web like a dumb fly.

I can't resist it.

I can't resist *him*.

His thumb and forefinger flick my clit and all the building comes crashing down. I fall apart with a wordless scream. The fierce sensation is like being wrenched into a storm.

I ride the hurricane, not wanting to find a landing.

When I do come down, I expect to find Aiden staring at me with a smug gleam.

He's not.

He continues eating me out. His tongue licks up and down my wetness without as much as a pause. My skin is sensitive and every lap of his mouth springs both pleasure and pain.

"Stop…"

I grip a handful of his jet black hair and try to push at him, but he thrusts his tongue in and out of me. This time, he adds a finger. I writhe against the bed, my eyes rolling to the back of my head.

"Please…" I'm pushing and pulling him at the same time. The assault of endless sensations kills me slowly like death by a thousand cuts.

"This time, scream." He rasps, eyes hazy with lust before he pounds both his finger and his tongue inside me.

Another shattering orgasm sweeps over me. My scream cracks into a sob. I'm a crying, screaming mess. My voice turns hoarse. My nipples throb in pain both from his earlier assault and the over-stimulation of my sex. My head is dizzy and I can barely open my eyes.

Aiden isn't stopping.

"Please, please, please…" I'm crying and gripping his shoulder. "No more, I beg you."

I expect him to brush me off and hit me with another orgasm.

Aiden's head glances from between my thighs and he does a slow show of licking his moist lips.

No. He's not licking his lips. He's licking *me* off his lips.

Why is that so hot?

Aiden crawls atop me and kisses me with abandon and animalistic need. He grabs my face and plunges his tongue against mine. My sensitive core pulses at tasting myself on him.

"Do you like your taste?" he whispers against my lips. "I sure as fuck do."

My cheeks flame.

"Let me see if you'll still taste the same after one more orgasm."

I grip his bicep. "Don't. Please."

I don't think I can take any other stimulation.

He swipes his tongue along my bottom lip. "What will I get in return?"

"My appreciation?" I give a weak smile.

He shakes his head. "You have to step up your game."

I place a hesitant hand on his T-shirt, rise up and capture his lips in a tentative kiss. He groans before he deepens the kiss, leaving me breathless and boneless.

When I break apart, he smirks. "Still not enough."

If I can keep the attention on him, he'll leave me alone, right?

I push him back so he's sitting on his haunches and I'm in a similar position in front of him. "Take off your T-shirt."

He raises an eyebrow as if he doesn't know where I'm taking this. "Why would I do that?"

"Just do it."

He chuckles as he pulls the back of his T-shirt over his head and throws it behind him.

I try not to gawk and fail miserably. If he looked good with his uniform and jersey on, then he's looking absolutely delectable with nothing on.

The hard ridges of his muscles aren't only cut, but they're also defined like he spent time sharpening every ab. He has a few beauty moles at his side like the one at the corner of his eye.

One of the arrow tattoos seems to be pointing straight at his heart.

I reach a hesitant hand to where his heart lies. My palm burns at the contact and my own heart nearly topples over at the skyrocketing beat in his.

The regular, healthy beat.

Not wanting to be caught feeling his heartbeat like a creep, I caress his hardened nipple feeling mine tighten and throb as if he's touching it.

"I'm almost sure you don't know how to be a cock tease." His voice is rough, deep, and chilling. "But you are."

"W-what?"

He snatches my hand from his nipple and flattens it against the thick bulge in his jeans. "Do you feel what your little teasing does to me?"

My eyes widen and my pulse drums in an irregular rhythm.

Before I can react, Aiden unzips his jeans and yanks them with his boxer briefs away, freeing his rock-hard cock.

Holy. Shit.

The only dicks I've seen in my life were from porn—I was curious, don't judge. I always had the idea that the real thing isn't as aesthetically pleasing—or big.

Well, I'm proved wrong because Aiden should get his crotch painted. Or photographed.

Or anywhere that's not near me, basically.

That thing isn't supposed to be within human reach.

Aiden watches me watch his cock with that dark look. "Have you wrapped those lips around a dick before?"

I gulp, shaking my head.

As if possible, Aiden's erection hardens more.

"Fuck." His eyes shine with a sheen of possessiveness that strikes deep within me.

My body leaps to attention, and I keep licking my lips even though I don't mean to.

He pushes me so I'm lying on my back and he's on top of me, his knees rest on either side of my face.

"You'll let me fuck that mouth, sweetheart?"

My frantic eyes bounce between him and his dick.

"Or do you want me to fuck your pussy?"

Oh, God. He'll break me if I let him inside me.

With one last gulp, I slightly part my lips.

That's all the permission Aiden needs.

He plunges inside my mouth in one go. "*Fuck.*"

I try to take him in as much as possible, but he hits the back of my throat. My gag reflex shoots and tears spring to my eyes.

Aiden pulls out almost completely. I don't get a chance to catch my breath before he slams in again.

He's hard and rough and out of control.

"Do you know how much I fantasised about you taking me all in like a good little girl?" He rasps, grabbing a handful of my hair to angle my head and hit deeper. "Do you know how fucking beautiful you look stuffed with my cock?"

I make unintelligible sounds as I try to lick him and somehow slow him down.

It works since he rolls his hips and caresses my hair with rough fingers. "I should've done this before. You should've been mine before."

I'm too full of his taste and the effects he has on my body to pay attention to what he says.

Since he likes what I'm doing, I continue with more energy. My tongue swipes up and down, and I cup his balls.

Aiden allows me to take my freedom even though he still has his grip on my hair.

Then, he picks up his pace thrusting in and out of my mouth before he curses as his shoulders stiffen. I watch mesmerised as he grunts and spills down my throat. I angle my head and try to swallow it all—despite the position.

Cum streams down the corners of my mouth. Aiden watches me with a mixture of awe and manic interest. That streak of possessiveness shines in his eyes as he follows the cum. He wipes it with his thumb and smears it on my lips.

"Open."

I do. I just… do.

He thrusts his thumb into my mouth, smearing his taste over my tongue.

"This mouth is fucking mine," he growls before pulling me into him and slamming his lips to mine.

I'm still hazy from the double orgasm and his orgasm. I kiss him sloppily at first, then open-mouthed and hungrily, matching his pace.

We spend a few minutes tangled around each other, kissing and exploring each other's mouths.

Aiden keeps a possessive hand at my hip the entire time.

He pulls away from my mouth to stroke a strand of hair behind my ear. "Sober up, sweetheart. I'm just starting with you."

"W-What?"

"Give me a minute and I'll fuck you so hard, you'll scream the whole house down."

My body throbs at the image, but I grip his bicep, shaking my head.

He narrows his eyes. "Why not?"

"I'm so sensitive. I don't think I can't take any more stimulation."

He grins like the devil. "It'll only make it more heightened when you come."

"Aiden. No."

"What did I say when we were getting started?"

I bite my lower lip and remain quiet.

He wraps a fistful of my hair around his hand. "What. Did. I. Say?"

"That I don't get to tap out."

"And what are you doing right now?"

"Aiden…"

"What are you doing right now, Elsa?"

"I didn't think it'd be this intense, okay?" I blurt.

"And is that supposed to be my problem?"

I know that when he said he wouldn't stop, he meant it. I'm just fighting a losing war, but I don't even want to fight. I'm putting on a façade. A belief that I don't want this. I just… like it when he takes what he wants.

That's too immoral, isn't it?

He smirks down at me. "You're doing it on purpose, aren't you?"

"I really am sensitive." I clench my thighs together, already feeling his growing bulge.

"But you still want to go on."

It's not a question. It's an observation.

"You're being a little tease, aren't you, sweetheart?" He plays with my throbbing nipple causing my lids to shut. "You're saying no just to have me dominate you into it."

I moan. "I… do?"

"Oh yeah… you do. Deep down, you want me to fuck you, but this is your twisted version of playing hard to get. Did you do it with the one you lost your virginity to?"

"N-no. Only you."

His fingers stop skimming over my nipples. I crack my eyes open to find him watching me with that slightly furrowed brow.

"Why?" he asks.

"Why what?"

"Why do you do that only with me?"

I only know you intimately, dickhead.

I shrug instead.

"I meant it earlier. I won't stop."

I always liked his brutal honesty. Aiden is a no filter type of person. His erection grows thicker and my thighs tighten at the promise.

"You won't even pretend that you will?" I ask.

"Do you want me to lie to you?" His head tilts to the side as he studies me. "Would it make you feel better?"

"It's not that. It's…"

He holds my hands in his and draws circles on the palm. "I don't know what I'm capable of when it comes to you. I want to think I have boundaries." His dark eyes skim over my face. "But I don't."

My spine snaps upright.

This is the part where I run and ask for help, isn't it?

But the truth is, I also don't know what I'm capable of when it comes to Aiden either.

I never thought I'd be invested in him to the point of craving him, but he has a way of engraving himself under my skin.

"Do I scare you, Elsa?" He's watching me with that manic interest as he lays my palm on his hard abdomen.

"No," I say softly.

"Some things never change." He chuckles. "You're still such a horrible liar."

"It's not a lie," I scold.

His stormy eyes plunge in mine. "I know when you lie, sweetheart."

"How?"

"You have a tell." He taps my nose, his expression playful. "Your nose twitches the slightest bit. You should school it."

Is that what he did with all his tells? Did he *school* them?

"If I do, wouldn't it be hard for you to tell if I'm lying?"

"I don't need a tell to know whether you're lying or telling the truth."

"How?" I must appear confused as hell because he laughs.

"Try telling me something and I'll say whether it's true or false."

"I came here alone."

"Lie. I saw you with Reed. Try something I don't know."

"It isn't fun if I play alone. How about one for one?" This is my only way to learn more about him and there's no way I'm missing it.

I shiver. He drapes a sheet and his arms around me, enveloping me in a tight embrace. I'm half lying on top of him with his legs cocooning mine. It's strange how natural it feels to be in his hold.

"You go first," he says.

"I'm adopted."

His eyes shine with something unrecognisable as he says, "Truth. But I already know that."

"Fine. Your turn."

"I wish I were adopted."

I study him closely, and his face doesn't change. "Truth."

"False." He grins. "I like who I am."

"Do you?" I don't know why I think he's lying.

Logically, he has no reason to hate being King Enterprises'

heir, but deep down, I think he... doesn't. Not in the way everyone expects him to, anyway.

"Is it questions now?" He raises an eyebrow. "I like questions better and I get to ask first."

"Why?"

"Because you already asked yours."

I roll my eyes. Give it to Aiden to twist everything to his liking. "Whatever."

He appears thoughtful for a second. "Why were you adopted?"

I should've expected the question, but that doesn't make the answer any easier.

"I'm originally from Birmingham. I've been told there was a fire. I lost both my parents in it, and Aunt had custody of me and eventually adopted me."

There's none of the pity I usually get on Aiden's face. If anything, he seems calculative. "You've been told. As in you don't remember."

It's amazing how nothing escapes him. What's stranger is that I want to bare it all to him.

Aiden is dangerous, and could—would—use this against me, but at the moment, I don't care.

"No. I don't," I say. "I only have fragments and little pieces. That time feels like a giant, black puzzle. Every piece is so similar, I can't even start to gather it together. The sad thing is that I don't even remember my parents' faces and I'm absolutely fine with not remembering them. I'm such a horrible daughter."

"Or it could be that your brain made a wise choice." His voice drifts. "Sometimes, parents aren't what they're supposed to be."

I want to ask him what he means by that, but his expression is closed. I doubt I'll get anything no matter how much I push.

So, instead of poking his wound, I ask the question that's been haunting me for years.

"Why did you decide you hated me the first time you saw me?"

I'm not going to sugarcoat it for Aiden. He was—still is—my bully. He ruined my life in RES. My body and mind might be unapologetically drawn to him, but that will never change what he did to me.

He stares down at me, but he's not really seeing me. His grey eyes turn into a raging storm.

"You were a ghost."

TWENTY-TWO

A ghost?

I was a ghost?

My head tilts back against Aiden's chest as I study his features, searching to see if he's joking or screwing with my head.

I should've known better since he doesn't joke. At least not in this sense. His jaw is tightened and his thick lashes frame a darkened look.

"What is that supposed to mean?" I try to appear calm, but my pulse rises with every second until I'm afraid he can hear it.

"You're not ready for what it means, Frozen."

The fact that he's using that damned nickname can only mean that he's putting me at a distance.

Aiden isn't exactly the closed-off type. He's not ashamed to admit to all the fuckery in his head.

However, I'm not foolish to believe that he'd bare his soul to me that easily. He keeps a fraction of himself hidden behind the walls of his fortress.

Maybe I can't escape his chessboard after all. One has to be in the battalion so they can take down the king.

"I don't like it when you call me that," I say, wiggling away from his hold.

"Call you what?"

"Frozen. I'm not *frozen*."

"Hmm, but you are." He pats his chest. "You're so frozen, it kind of stings."

"What is that supposed to mean?"

Aiden flips me underneath him and rips the sheet from around me. Shivers break all over my arms as the air hits my skin.

His ferocious gaze dips to my nakedness as if he's seeing it for the first time.

My heart hammers so loud, it's painful.

There's something about the way he watches me.

A possessiveness.

An obsession.

A… madness.

I hate how my body reacts to this unhinged side of him. Aren't all girls supposed to be attracted to the white knight? Prince charming? Why the hell am I gravitating towards the villain?

I ignore the pool of heat gathering between my thighs, pull at the sheet, and drape it around my torso.

Aiden's stormy eyes pierce through my soul as his fingers tug on the sheet. "Don't cover yourself from me."

"We're talking." I hold the piece of cloth with all my might. "You can't just shut me off for sex."

"Watch me." He rips the corner of the sheet.

I gasp and roll away from underneath him, taking the sheet with me. Aiden wrestles me back. I push at him. Lust, hate, the need to win rush through my limbs. I love fighting Aiden. Judging from the wetness coating my thighs, maybe I love it a bit too much.

It doesn't help that Aiden's eyes are gleaming with too much pleasure. He loves the fight, too.

We wrestle for minutes or hours, I don't know. My lungs are heaving and I'm sweating. Nothing changes in Aiden's posture except for that spark in his eyes. Either he has impressive stamina or I'm just not that strong.

I pull myself on four and try to crawl away from his caveman clutches. He grips me by the ankle and yanks me back. I lie flat on my stomach, almost my entire back is bared.

Aiden crawls atop of me, his slick hard chest covers my back and he imprisons both my wrists above my head on the mattress.

He's panting in my ear, his breaths making my eyes flutter closed. Being dominated by him pulls on my unhidden strings.

An urge.

A need.

A deprivation.

"Do you still want to fight, sweetheart?" he murmurs in my ear, his voice dropping to a chilling range. "Or would you rather I make you scream?"

He rolls his hips and a thick, hard bulge settles against the crack of my arse.

I don't know if he's hard because we fought or at the promise that he'll make me scream.

Or both.

He's sick. Absolutely, utterly sick.

Apparently, I'm sick, too, because my core is slick with arousal.

"You're an arsehole."

His hot breaths tickle my earlobe as he bites down. "Don't tempt me into fucking yours, sweetheart."

I gasp then go rigid when his fingers spread my arse cheeks.

What... is he doing?

He presses a calloused thumb against my back hole. "Hmm, this looks virgin to me."

"A-Aiden... stop."

"Don't worry, I won't fuck you here... yet." He pushes the tip of his thumb, and I stiffen. "But when it's time, you'll let me, won't you?"

He can't talk about fucking my arse when I don't even know what it feels to have proper sex.

"Or would you rather I take it, too?" He runs his erection up and down my slick folds while teasing my other hole.

Holy...

Why does this feel so... good?

Not only his touch, but also his entire presence at my back. The way he touches me feels like he knew my body for decades.

Like he *owned* my body for decades.

There's something about his absolute confidence that reduces me to a mere marionette in his hands.

"I'll own every one of your holes... eventually." His finger leaves my arse to slide down to my soaked folds. "But I'm starting here. I'll fuck the memory of anyone else out of you."

The onslaught of his words is like having his tongue licking me in that delirious, maddening pace.

He nibbles on my earlobe, sending tiny bolts of pleasure across my spine. "You'll let me own every inch of you, won't you, sweetheart?"

My nerve endings are so stimulated, I can't breathe straight, let alone think or speak.

A deep moan is the only sound that escapes me.

"Fuck." He flips me so my back hits the mattress.

His stormy eyes study my face intently as if some mystical language is written all over my features.

A language that he's the only one to speak.

"Stop me," he murmurs in a strained voice.

"S-stop you?"

"Do it."

How am I supposed to stop him? Besides... "Didn't you say I'm not allowed to tap out or stop you?"

"This is the only time I give you the first move. Tell me to leave and I will." He rolls his hips, sending a shiver of pleasure down my abdomen as his hand wraps around my throat. "I'll let you live your last year in RES in peace. I'll kill the fantasy. I'll end it all."

My mouth trembles.

That's what I want, isn't it? I'll spend my last year in peace and Aiden will leave me alone.

Aiden will leave me alone.

My heart pounds, but it's hard to concentrate with his erection stabbing at the bottom of my stomach.

"Are you playing a mind game?" I snap. "Is this the part where you laugh in my face and tell me I've been pranked?"

"This is the part where you lost your only chance to escape me." He squeezes my neck. "You're well and truly fucked, sweetheart."

His lips crash against mine in an all-consuming, mind-crippling kiss.

A part inside me dies; the part that yearned for freedom, for the chance to escape Aiden. But the other part? That one fills me with an odd sense of relief.

A chill of terror crawls down my spine.

This isn't me.

I'm not this person.

How could I be so… defective? So immoral?

I press a hand on Aiden's chest in a fruitless attempt to push him away.

He doesn't budge.

If anything, he crushes me beneath him. His torso flattens my breasts, his fingers squeeze my neck, and his knees immobilize my thighs.

I can't escape even if I want to.

He's had me completely at his mercy.

He can crush me, ruin me, and no one will know.

My mouth falls into a gasp as his erection nuzzles between my thighs. I'm thankful Aunt had me on the shot for a while now.

Stop.

I scream in my mind, not knowing whether it's at Aiden or at my own body.

Aiden doesn't get my virginity. I hate him. I despise him. He ruined my life.

Then why am I not saying it aloud?

Speak, Elsa. Freaking speak.

Even if I do, will he listen? Will Aiden respect my will?

A loud bang on the door interrupts my chain of thoughts.

Wait. What?

Aiden wrenches his lips from mine with an animal-like growl. "Fuck off."

"Emergency!" Ronan's voice comes from the other side.

"You better be fucking dying or I'll kill you myself." Aiden grunts and pushes off me.

"Come out, fucker."

Aiden's eyes darken as he pulls on his boxer briefs.

I reach for the tangled sheet and wrap it around my torso. I'm panting, skin sweaty and on fire as I blindly search for my scattered clothes on the floor.

Aiden cuts me a glare when I touch my bra. "Don't even think about dressing."

I let go of the piece of clothing as if I'm a kid who's been caught stealing from the jar.

The moment the door closes behind him, I almost curse myself. Who does he think he is to boss me around?

Besides, this is my chance to stop this.

Whatever *this* is.

My fingers are numb. No, not numb. They're too stimulated that they feel numb.

Standing on wobbly feet, I quickly put on my clothes, trying to ignore the potent smell of sex in the air.

And his smell.

Damn his smell.

I feel like I'd be a ninety-year-old lady and will still remember the way he smells.

Aiden returns when I'm pulling my hair into a ponytail.

He narrows his eyes on my clothed body. "You're lucky we're done for today."

We... are?

"Is your cousin taking you?" I ask, fighting the sense of disappointment hitting me out of nowhere.

"My cousin?"

"Levi King. I saw him earlier."

"You saw him earlier," he repeats with clear menace.

"Yeah. He said he's here to get you."

"Lev says lots of shit." He raises an eyebrow. "Do you honestly think he can tell me what to do?"

No. It was stupid to even consider it.

Also, he calls him Lev. That's the only time I hear him give someone a nickname. Hell, it's rare to even hear him call anyone by their given names. Even his friends are last names to him.

"If it's not Levi, then what is it?"

He narrows his eyes before he schools his expression. "Kimberly passed out."

Aiden drives us and Xander sits in the passenger seat, staring at us through the rearview mirror now and again.

I cradle Kim's head on my lap while she snores softly.

If it weren't for the suffocating silence, it would've been funny that her snoring is the only sound in the car.

I have no idea how to dissipate the silence—or tension—between Aiden and Xander, so I just focus on stroking Kim's hair out of her face.

She swats my hand away as if I'm a fly. The smell of tequila permeates the air. She's so going to regret the hangover come tomorrow.

Ronan's house is only a ten minute drive from Kim's and I'm so thankful for the short distance. Aiden parks in Kim's driveway.

"I could've driven," Xander says in a bored tone. "I live here anyway."

Aiden's expression is stoic. "You're not allowed near her when I'm not around."

I'm not sure which 'her' Aiden means, and something twists in my chest at the thought that he could mean Kim.

They were childhood friends and practically raised together. Same schools. Same hobbies. Even their parents belong to the same circle. Maybe Aiden has a bond with her. He did hug her while she cried.

"You mean my *girlfriend?*" Xander turns around and winks at me. "You want me to drive you home, babe?"

Aiden grips the steering wheel so hard, I'm surprised it doesn't crush to pieces.

When he smiles at Xander, it's almost manic. "Do you have a fucking death wish, Knight?"

"Do you, King?" Xander's expression hardens until his jaw ticks.

I swallow past the lump in my throat. Despite the bruises from last week, they still look like they're on the verge of cutting each other from limb to limb.

There's no football team to stop them from killing each other this time.

"Hey," I try to sound nonchalant as I open the backseat's door. "Can one of you help me get Kim out of the car?"

Xander breaks the murderous war of glares and steps out of the car. He pulls her from my lap with ease. I catch a whiff of alcohol from him, but it's not as strong as the tequila on Kim.

He lifts her in his arms bridal-style with so much ease like she's a rag doll.

Her eyes crack open the slightest bit and she groans, head falling against his chest. Then, seeming a bit awake, she checks him out and pulls at his hair.

"You!" She slurs. "All because of you!"

"Kim." I follow them.

"*Elliiie.*" She grins, and it's surprisingly charming considering that she's drunk. "Let's commit *muuurder!*"

I smile. "Not a good idea, Kim."

"*Noope*! Best *ideaaa*," she slurs as her fingers lazily plunge in Xander's hair, almost... stroking it? "*Xaaan*, am I pretty?"

"No." He doesn't even hesitate.

Her eyes shine with tears. "Are you ever going to forgive me?"

"No."

"*Fuuuuck. Youuu.*"

Xander halts and I do, too, to avoid slamming into his back. Some staring contest erupts between him and Kim. Her eyes fill with unshed tears while his darken under the garden's dim light.

A strong hand wraps around my arm and pulls me back, closing my connection with whatever is going on between those two.

Kim falls limp again and Xander punches in the code to their house.

Wait. He knows the code?

"It's the last room on the second floor," I tell him.

"I know that," he says over his shoulder.

Okay. That's not weird at all.

I'm sure Kim's mother won't come out from her workshop or even if she does, she wouldn't care much. She's very... open.

Once Xander disappears inside, I meet Aiden's narrowed gaze. His posture is rigid at best. What is he angry at me for?

"What?"

"Close your doors and windows. All of it."

"Uh, the house has an alarm system. We'll be fine."

"All of it," he grits out. "Don't make me repeat myself."

The hot and cold is giving me whiplash.

Even if he's pissed off at Xander, he has no right to unleash his anger on me when I haven't done anything wrong.

I hate it when people use a weaker opponent as the punching bag of their emotions.

A whip comes down my back and another and another. I scream so loud, my ears pop.

I flinch at the random vision. What in the ever living hell was that all about?

"Elsa?"

My gaze flicks to Aiden who's clutching me by the shoulders as I almost topple over.

Wait. Did I just… lose time?

Aiden's inquisitive eyes search into my soul. "What happened just now?"

"Nothing."

"I don't lie to you so give me the same respect in return and don't fucking lie to me."

"The same respect?" I wiggle free. "You and the word respect shouldn't even be in the same sentence."

"What happened to you just now?"

"I don't want to tell you."

How dare he demand that when he freaking triggered that vision?

"Either tell me or I'll extract it out of you." He grips my jaw. "I'll find out anyway, the method is up to you."

Screw him and his mind games.

All I want is to curl into a ball in a dark, small corner.

Just when I'm about to give him a piece of my mind, the front door opens and Xander comes out with a deep frown etched between his brows.

I take Aiden's momentary distraction, run inside the house, and lock it.

I remain behind the door and peek through the lounge area's tall windows. Xander has crossed over to his house. Aiden remains where I left him, staring at the door.

Ten seconds pass.

Twenty.

Thirty.

Sixty.

His poker face is on as he follows Xander.

My phone vibrates in my back pocket and I jump.

Aiden: A queen or a pawn.

Aiden: You don't want me to make the move for you.

With a groan, I power off my phone and tuck it back in my pocket.

Screw him and his mindfuckery.

My eyes flutter closed and then open when that vision assaults me.

Only, it wasn't a vision, was it? It was a memory.

Something that happened in my life.

TWENTY-THREE

"Remind me to never drink again." Kim groans from behind the wheel of her car.

She cursed me all ways to Sunday when I woke her up this morning. She only appears a bit human because I gave her Advil and Kirian helped me in preparing her hot soup for breakfast.

If it weren't for Kir's school, she might've never left the house.

Her hair is in a messy bun atop her head and her uniform is barely in order.

I'm not in any better shape either.

Sleep has eluded me most of the night—I chased it away by drinking a gallon of coffee.

The thought of a nightmare terrified me. I don't sleep after visions as Dr Khan calls them.

Visions.

As if I'm psychic or something.

They were memories, not visions.

To chase them away, I studied, re-read the Art of War by Sun Tzu and I might have spied on Xander's house from Kim's balcony.

Aiden spent the night there—since his car remained in the driveway. I hoped Xander's parents were home to prevent any murder plots between Elites' strikers.

I dozed off after dawn, and when I woke up, Aiden's car wasn't there.

"I look like shit, don't I?" Kim asks.

"Not worse than me." I sigh, then face her. "What actually happened last night?"

"Aside from drinking?" She hits her head. "I don't remember much."

"When Xander carried you last night, you apologised and asked for his forgiveness. What is that supposed to mean?"

She throws me a terrified look. "X-Xander carried me?"

"All the way to your room."

"And you let him?"

"To my defence, I couldn't carry you inside."

"Shit." Her eyes almost bulge as she glances at me. "What else did I do?"

I hold up my fingers and count. "You pulled Xander's hair, asked him if you were pretty, then you asked if he forgives you, then you cursed him."

She groans, head bowing. "Someone kill me. Let's go home. I can't physically be at school today. I'll stuff you with ice cream and not tell a word about it to your aunt."

"I don't think it was that bad." I laugh. "At least you didn't get kissed in front of the whole school."

Kim hits the brakes so hard, I would've tumbled forward if I hadn't the seatbelt on.

"Kim!"

"You…" She swallows, giving me a frantic look. "Y-you were kissed by Xander?"

"Xander? No. Aiden."

"Aiden?"

I lift a shoulder, feeling subconscious.

Her eyes widen, but it's not in a judgemental way. "Wow… I don't know how to comment on that."

"I'm still not wrapping my head around it either." And all the things we did in private.

I climaxed. Twice.

I hide my head in my hands, groaning. "It was in front of

the whole school, Kim. I don't know what the hell am I going to do about that."

"Do you… like him?" she asks almost hesitantly.

Do I?

Aiden destabilizes me. From the beginning, he has never looked at my surface. He dug his nails deeper and brought out sides of me I didn't even know existed. He toys at forbidden lines that rattle me to the bones.

I crave his sickness. I'm becoming attuned to his darkness and intensity.

But do I like him?

It takes a level of trust to like a person, and I can safely say that I don't trust Aiden.

Or maybe I don't trust myself around him.

"No." I groan. "I don't know."

Kim makes an affirmative sound as if she knows what that means. "But you liked the kiss?"

"I… don't know. Maybe? I was kissed in my previous school but it wasn't all that consuming, you know?" I pause, peeking at her through my lashes. "You're not going to judge me?"

"Hell to the no." She faces me and leans over to half-hug me. "I'm always on your side, Ellie. You need some adventure in your life and consuming kisses sound like one hell of a start."

I didn't know I needed her approval until she voiced it. I squeeze her arm, silently telling her how grateful I am.

"Just…" Kim's features sober up. "Be careful, okay?"

"What do you mean?"

"I just don't want you to see you hurt."

Her words douse her earlier enthusiasm. I nod because she just told me the truth I needed to hear. That's why Kim is my best friend. She can be both happy for me and see the negative side of things, too.

When we arrive at the school's car park, we're stopped by the bitch queen and her minions.

Seriously. Silver is the last person I need today.

"Isn't it Frozen and her fat friend?" One of Silver's minions says. Her name is Veronica if I remember correctly. Her uniform is so tight, she almost combusts in it.

I attempt to sidestep them, but the other minion, Summer, clutches my arm. "We're talking to you, Teacher Slut."

"And I'm not." I wiggle free. Kim remains on my other side, and I'm proud of the way she lifts her chin.

Silver finally steps in front of me. She's a few inches taller and she uses every inch to look down on me with that condescending air.

"Stay away from King, you little bitch."

I plaster a smile on my face. "Why don't you ask him to stay away from me? He's the one who's been chasing me."

I had expected that to shut her off and wipe that smug look from her face, but it only deepens.

"You're nothing but a fling, Frozen. Do you know why?" She pauses after asking her rhetorical question. "King has always been mine. There's nothing you can do that'll change it."

My blood boils despite the calm façade I keep. My hand fists by my side, and Kim clutches my arm.

Silver throws me one last glance. "A king needs a queen, peasant."

Her minions snicker before they push past me and Kim to the entrance. It takes everything in me not to pull them back by their hair and drag them to the floor.

But I'm not that person, am I?

I don't fantasise about hurting others.

So why do I feel like demons are swirling all around me?

"Never mind her." Kim strokes my arm. "She's just being a usual bitch."

My lips curl in what I hope looks like a reassuring smile as we walk into the school.

"They're staring," Kim whispers.

That's when I notice that everyone is ogling me. Some even

take a sneaky picture here and another one there. When I make eye contact, they pretend to be occupied with their phones.

I don't have to wonder for long. The more Kim and I walk down the hall, the louder the whispers become.

"Is she really King's girlfriend?"

"Wasn't she with Knight the other day?"

"Really? King has a girlfriend?"

"Have you seen Instagram?"

"I've seen it live at the party."

"Girlfriend...

"... girlfriend..."

Reality hits me like one of my unwanted visions.

Aiden did it on purpose.

The arsehole kissed me in front of the entire school to stake a claim that Xander didn't.

Aiden must've known that everyone would be talking about it the next day.

Hell. He *planned* for everyone to talk about it.

I'm going to *kill* him.

Kim nudges me while we round a quieter corner. Her eyes are almost bulging out of their sockets. "Oh my gosh, Ellie."

"What now?" My voice is filled with dread.

She shows me her phone. More specifically, Aiden's Instagram profile and his last post.

Someone took a picture of us at an optimal angle while Aiden sat me on the table and ravaged my mouth. My legs and arms are wrapped around him and his body is moulded into mine.

The caption: *Mine*.

"No, he didn't," I whisper, not knowing if I'm mortified or just plain shocked.

"Oh yes, he did." Kim grins and fans herself. "Consuming is the understatement of the century, Ellie. He looks like he was eating you alive."

"We'll be late for class." I cut off her stupid grin and head in the direction of our first hour.

Kim falls in step with me. "No wonder Bitch Queen felt threatened and showed her claws. King never had a girlfriend and he sure as hell never posted a picture kissing someone."

Huh. That feels... good.

In your face, Silver.

As soon as we enter the class, I halt. The chatter of the four horsemen ripples in the air. Of course. They're all here.

Aiden leans back against his chair, his legs crossed in front of him and his fingers interlace across his abs. His entire attention is on me as if he's been waiting for my entrance. The clouds of his eyes are gleaming with both triumph and a darkness so pitch black, it knots my stomach.

He got what he wanted.

The whole school thinks I'm his girlfriend. Once again, he took the decision from me, and this time, I'm freaking pissed off.

It might also have to do with what Silver said. The confident way she said it with grates on my nerves.

And because it hurts, I need to inflict it back.

I walk to Aiden with wide steps. Ronan grins like an idiot. Xander looks through the window, appearing lost somewhere. Cole who's been talking to Aiden stops speaking when I stand in front of Aiden's desk.

I plant my palm on it and lower myself to meet him point-blank. He arches an eyebrow as if challenging me.

Game on, dickhead.

I say in a clear voice for the whole class to hear, "I'm *not* yours."

TWENTY-FOUR

When I told Aiden I'm not his, I expected anger.

Hell, I expected his mean side.

Because that's what bullies do, don't they? When pushed, they push back.

Instead of letting go and showing his true self, his lips curve into a mocking smile. "That's not what you were saying when you came all over my face. Twice."

My jaw nearly hits the floor.

No.

He didn't just say that.

Kim gasps from beside me and murmurs break all over the class. No one has the audacity to speak up in front of Aiden.

Ronan is the only one who laughs, nodding, "I second that. I heard the screams."

Fuck my life.

Aiden opens his mouth again, but I silence him with a hand against his lips. Whatever he has to say will ruin me more than he already did.

If he appeared triumphant before, he looks absolutely smug now. He raises his brows in a silent dare, challenging me to deny it.

The bell rings and Mrs Stone comes into class. I let go of Aiden and plop into the seat in front of him because it's the only one available. My movements are flustered as I retrieve my notebook and pens.

Warm breaths tickle my ear before Aiden's smooth voice whispers, "Try denying that you're mine again and I'll fuck you in front of the lot of them to prove it."

My eyes widen as I grip my pencil tighter. He disappears from my back all too soon as Mrs Stone continues her lecture.

I'm struggling to school my features and chase away whatever picture Aiden just painted in my head.

Damn him and his dirty mouth.

The space between my legs heat, and I rub them to chase the sensation away.

It doesn't work.

On the contrary, the friction becomes unbearable, almost like when Aiden had his mouth on me, his teeth grazing the sensitive skin, his tongue and fingers thrusting in and out of me while —

"Miss Quinn?"

I startle at Mrs Stone's voice and my cheeks feel on fire.

"Are you all right?" Mrs Stone's voice sounds from above me.

"What?"

"You look flushed. Do you need medical care?"

"I'm fine." I grip my pencil tighter, wishing the earth would open up and swallow me.

When she leaves, a low gravelly voice murmurs, "Certain memories coming back to you?"

"Shut up," I hiss.

I don't have to look behind me to see Aiden's smug grin.

After the two morning classes, I gather my books, wave at Kim, and head to the locker room, opting to skip lunch.

Aunt told me to buy my special food from the grocery store, but I forgot this morning.

A tall frame steps in front of me before I round the corner to the locker room. I hate how my heart flutters upon seeing him. I hate how perfect he looks in the team's jacket and how his long legs make him appear like a model.

I hate everything about him from the slight sway in his dark hair to the kissable lips to the sharp jawline that no eighteen years old should have.

"I hate you," I tell him with all the pent up frustration I've been feeling this morning.

"I think you don't, sweetheart, but you wish you did." He reaches for me and pinches my cheek. "You're adorable as fuck when you're all flushed."

He strokes a strand of hair behind my ear. The gesture is so caring and gentle, it almost crumbles my defences.

Then I remember that he's a sociopath and he could be doing this just so I'd let my guard down in front of him.

"Why do you never wear your hair down?" His fingers massage my skull like he's fascinated with it.

"I just don't like it."

He tilts his head to the side. "Why?"

I don't know myself.

And his caring act won't distract me from his demonic soul.

I wiggle away from his hold. "What were you thinking about earlier?"

He goes back to stroking my hair like he can't stop himself from doing it. "Earlier?"

"In class!"

"When Mrs Stone caught you fantasising?"

My cheeks heat and I turn away. "That's not true."

"Liar." His voice drips with a seductive drawl. "You were reliving last night, weren't you? Was it the part where I had my tongue inside your hot, wet pussy while you screamed my name and —"

"Aiden!" I place a hand in front of his mouth. Mortification tugs at my stomach as I search around to see if anyone heard.

He removes my hand but doesn't release it as he cocks his head to the side. "Why are you embarrassed about that?"

"Are you serious? Of course, I'd be embarrassed."

"I fantasised about you all night, do you see me embarrassed about it?"

"You're a different species." I doubt he even knows what embarrassment means.

"Don't."

"Don't what?"

"Don't turn this into a you versus me argument."

"Then what is it about? Enlighten me."

"Own your sexuality, Elsa." He grips my hand in a possessive hold. "You sure as fuck have an abundance of it and I don't plan to let it go to waste."

"Stop being so crude. I'm supposed to focus in class."

"So you were thinking about it." He smirks. "Are you wet?"

"No."

"Come on," he pushes. "Admit it."

"What if I am?" I cross my arms, all the pent up frustration rising to the surface. "What are you going to do about it? Fuck me at school and risk having both of us expelled? Oh, wait. Your father owns the school, so it doesn't matter if you get caught. You can even get away with murder, right? I'll be the one to be thrown out after they make it look like I seduced his majesty Aiden King. After all, you're king and I'm a fucking nobody."

It's only after my outburst that I realise how fantastic it feels to throw his words back at him. He used them to belittle me and put me in my place before, but now they're smashed straight in his face.

I lift my chin, daring him to say anything.

His left eye twitches, but his expression remains unreadable. "Watch that mouth."

"Or what?"

"Or I will fuck it."

"Screw you, Aiden. Okay? You don't get to push my buttons the entire time and only expect yes, your majesty. At your order, your majesty. What do you want next, your majesty? Should I lie down and spread my legs for you? Would you get me out of your system if I let you fuck me?"

I pant after my outburst.

I don't even know what the hell is wrong with me, but I'm so pissed off about Silver's words and his casual attitude. He'll always get what he wants and eventually, he'll get bored of me and leave.

I want him to leave now because I can feel my walls crumbling, and if I let him inside, he'll just destroy me like he said the first time we met.

He'll be the storm that only leaves havoc in its wake.

I'd rather take the bullying rather than lose myself to him. "No."

I gawk. "No?"

"Spreading your legs won't get you out of my system. I love owning your body, but that's not the only thing I'm interested in."

"Then what else do you want?"

His voice drops in a haunting whisper. "Every. Fucking. Thing."

My mouth parts open, but no words come out.

Ronan saves me when he slams into Aiden's back. The latter holds his position as a grinning Ronan circles his shoulder with an arm.

"Yo, King! Time for lunch."

Aiden cuts him a glare, but his voice is calm. "You've had a death wish since yesterday."

"Oops, bad timing?" His inquisitive eyes bounce from me to Aiden.

The latter continues to glare at him. "Leave."

"I'm wounded, mate." He massages his chest. "Words like that trigger my abandonment issues."

My eyes widen as I swallow. "You have abandonment issues?"

He nods, staring at Aiden from under his lashes. "And he keeps reminding me of them. *Connard*."

"Hey!" I nudge Aiden. "That can scar him."

He just watches me with amusement like he's enjoying the show.

"I'm already taking therapy," Ronan continues.

"Shut the fuck up or the only therapy you'll take is for your broken nose."

"Not the nose, King." Ronan hides his nose. "This shit is aristocratic."

"Not when I'm done with it."

"Wait." I stare between them with a dumbfounded expression. "You were joking?"

"You looked fucking adorable." Aiden smiles.

"Uh.. go back." Ronan stares at Aiden as if he grew an additional head. "Did you just say 'adorable'?"

Aiden's poker face returns.

"No, no, no… don't close off. Come on, King." He retrieves his phone. "Say it again, I need to get it on camera."

Aiden stares at Ronan's camera and mouths. "Fuck. You."

Ronan flips him off as he tucks his phone in his pocket. Then he leans in to whisper. "I'll give you one hundred if you record footage of when he says shit like that."

"What?"

"Five hundred."

I continue staring at him, too shocked to say anything.

"Okay, final offer. Nash and Knight will also pay five hundred each. That's one point five thousand."

Aiden barges between us, cutting off Ronan's one-sided negotiation.

"Don't you have some place to go to?" Aiden asks.

"*Mais non.* I'm good right here." Ronan gives a Cheshire cat-like grin.

"Come eat with us, Ellie."

"*Ellie?*" Aiden snaps.

"What? Kimmy calls you that, doesn't she?"

"Don't you call me Frozen?"

He lifts a shoulder. "I like Ellie better. Come on, let's eat."

"Pass." I turn to leave.

A strong hand wraps around my arm and Aiden all but drags me to his side. "You'll eat."

He keeps a possessive arm around my waist as the three of us walk to the cafeteria.

If he thinks that he won this round, then he has another thing coming. The cafeteria doesn't have my food and I won't eat like I said.

My phone vibrates. I reach into my jacket.

Uncle J: I don't think we'll make it to the game this weekend. I'm buried with work. So sorry, Pumpkin.

My chest squeezes, but I manage to reply.

Elsa: It's okay. I have to study anyway. You'll miss me when I'm in Cambridge *fireworks emoji*

Uncle J: Don't make me all emotional now. You'll beat our records. Teamwork.

Elsa: Teamwork!

I'm not feeling the words as I type them.

Uncle J: Lock up tonight. We might come home late. There are vegetables in the fridge and your aunt says no ice cream.

Uncle J: We love you, Pumpkin.

Another lonely night.

Elsa: No problem! Take care of yourselves. I love you guys, too *heart emoji*

When I shove the phone back in my pocket, I feel eyes on me. I lift my head and Aiden is watching me intently with a tilted head. Did he read the texts?

Ronan is speculating about the next game's line-up, but Aiden isn't paying him the slightest attention. His thumb grazes the small of my back. A shiver blooms over my skin at the intimacy of the gesture.

Why do people say that physical contact doesn't matter? Why do they assume that emotions grow in some alien place?

Physical touch *always* plays a part.

I know better because Aiden's touch has been screwing me over since that day he broke the invisible 'no-touching' rule.

We head straight to the football team's table—of course. Aiden removes his hand so he can sit me beside him.

Xander grins at me, both his dimples on display. It seems genuine enough, so I return a tentative smile.

Aiden cuts us a glare so harsh, I decide to focus on my backpack. Xander's grin just widens. Aiden places both hands on my shoulders. "From today onwards, Elsa will be eating with us."

Hell no.

I move to stand up, but he leans over to whisper, "Stay still or I'll tell them how many times I took you last night."

"You didn't *take* me," I hiss so only he can hear.

He raises an eyebrow. "They don't know that."

I bite my lower lip to stop myself from screaming.

Why does he have this ability to royally piss me off?

None of the team members says anything about the new eating arrangement. I don't expect them to. He's King after all. His word is a royal decree.

Ronan waggles his eyebrows. "Welcome aboard, Ellie."

"I'm hurt, Frozen." Xander scoots closer. "Aren't we a couple?"

Aiden's grip on my shoulders tightens, but I don't have to look back to see his pissed off face.

I don't know why Xander keeps provoking Aiden. He must know how much of a crazed devil he can be.

"Hey, Knight…" Aiden's voice drifts in clear menace. "If you say things like that again, I'll be saying things you won't like."

The dimples disappear from Xander's face and he narrows his eyes before throwing his fork on his pasta plate. "Fuck you, King."

"Wait. What things?" Ronan stares between them. "Seriously, I'm tired of being left in the dark. Why doesn't anyone tell me anything around here?"

"Because you have a big mouth?" Cole says.

"No, I don't."

"Yeah, you do." Everyone at the table agrees.

Ronan launches into a long argument about all the secrets he kept for them—by spilling them.

It's amusing to watch him being a bit of a drama queen with Xander provoking him and Cole trying to shut him up.

With one last squeeze to my shoulder, Aiden strides to where they serve the food.

"Are you sure you want to be with a stage five-creeper like him?" Xander slides to my side, grinning, and appearing unaffected by Aiden's threat. "I'm always here if you change your mind."

He starts to inch closer, but Cole steps between us. He gives Xander a knowing look. Some sort of a secret conversation goes on between them. Xander rolls his eyes and focuses back on his food.

"Stop provoking King, Knight." One of the football team's players, the goalkeeper, says. "We're going to screw up the championship if our ace strikers continue being at each other's throats."

A few of his teammates give me a condescending look as if I'm the source of this entire chaos.

"Why are you looking at me that way?" I square my shoulders. "I didn't ask for either of their attention. If you can keep your ace striker the hell away from me, I'd appreciate it."

Silence falls on the table except for Xander who grins, showcasing his dimples. "No wonder she's the best friend."

"You think anyone can tell King anything?" Ronan shakes his head with a sly smile. "I mean, you're the one he called adorable."

"He… did?" the goalkeeper asks.

"I swear to God, I'm not shitting you. I still have the creeps, for real!" Ronan says. "Come on, Ellie. Record it for us next time."

I can't help but suppress a smile.

The football players who used to give me harsh stares are now watching me with… awe?

Cole clears his throat. "Knock it off, Ro."

"Naw, come on, Captain. Don't kill the fun." Ronan stands on his chair. "I'm opening the auction with five hundred. Who'll add?"

They each start adding numbers like in a real auction.

Huh.

The rich kids sure do it differently.

Cole shakes his head and opens a book. *The Anatomy of Evil.*

Hmm. Who knew a football player would be interested in such books? I'm stereotyping, though.

"Aren't you going to eat?" Cole asks without paying me much attention. "You can have mine."

"She doesn't eat that." Aiden's voice sounds from behind me, and I hate the chills that shoot down my spine because of his presence.

He pushes Cole aside and sits beside me, holding out two plates. One has pasta. The tray he slides in front of me has salad and non-gluten pasta.

"Where did you get this from?" I look up at him. "The cafeteria doesn't have this type of food."

"They do now."

They do now.

Just like that, he makes it happen.

I don't want to be impressed that he brought me my first special meal at school, but I am. This is the most thoughtful thing anyone but my aunt and uncle has done for me. He remembered and he made it happen.

I peek at him from beneath my eyelashes.

Being on Aiden King's good side is heaven. His bad side is complete hell.

It's time to choose on which side to fall.

TWENTY-FIVE

Aunt and Uncle barely come home for the entire week. They usually change their clothes, fill the fridge with food, and then they're off again.

I hate the house when neither of them is here—especially when it goes on for consecutive nights like this.

It's frigid and… cold.

Kim spent a few nights with me—and Kir. We studied, binge-watched the last season of Lucifer, and we goofed around to Coldplay.

Although she has more electic taste in music than me, we agree on Coldplay.

For the past week, I somehow managed to convince Kim to sit with me at the football team's table.

I was both shocked and proud of her when she sat at the same table as Xander and pretended he didn't even exist.

"You sure you can't stay? It's Friday night." I ask from the doorway as she sits on the steps to tie her shoes.

"I'd love to, but I can't let Kir down."

"I know." Her dad returned from his endless diplomatic trips and her mother is finally out of the studio. They promised Kirian a family dinner a few months ago, and this is their only chance to make it happen.

"My house is usually dead so I understand what it feels like when it's alive." I sigh. "Have fun. Text me pictures of Kir."

"You bet." Her lips twists. "I hope those two will be parents for fucking once and not disappoint him."

"Kim…"

"Doesn't matter. Kir has me." She throws a dismissive hand as she stands and faces me with a strange expression. "You know you can talk to me about the whole King thing, right?"

I hate how my chest flips at the mere mention of his name.

"The whole King thing?"

"You know, the part about coming all over his face? Twice?"

My cheeks heat and I wish I could hide in a hole. "Here I thought you'd forgotten about that."

"Hell no." She chuckles, nudging me. "I was waiting for you to fess up."

"I'm just…" I hang my head against the wall. "I don't know. He's so intense and I feel like if I give in to him, I'll never find a way out. Not to mention that he's distracting me. Cambridge is just around the corner and there's no way in hell I'm letting anything take it away from me, especially not some boy drama, but…"

"But?"

"But I feel a sick type of relief whenever he comes to find me, corners me, and takes away the decision. Isn't that crazy?"

"All the best things usually are." She grins.

I jab her shoulders playfully. "You're not helping."

"Ellie, you're my best friend and I love you, but you're too… safe." Kim's voice shifts to the grownup tone she uses with her little brother. "You've been living your life so much by the rules, it's like you're a thirty year-old woman wrapped in an eighteen year-old body."

I should be offended, but I'm not.

"That's not true," I tell her.

"Not true?" She gives me an 'Are you shitting me' look. "You didn't touch the ice cream even though your aunt isn't here. I'm sure a bite or two won't kill you, but you don't even want to consider going against your aunt's wishes."

"Those types of food rot the body."

"Do you hear yourself? You sound just like your aunt—and that's not a compliment."

"Kim!"

"I mean, look at your interests."

"What about them?"

"You picked up yoga because of your aunt. You like football because of your uncle. Hell, you're going to Cambridge because they're alumni."

I cross my arms. "Aunt and Uncle saved me from the alternative of foster homes. They gave me a safe, healthy upbringing. If it weren't for the heart surgery they paid for, I would've died. There's nothing wrong with wanting them to be happy."

"Sure. You're totally right." Kim leans against the wall. "But have you thought that maybe you're living your aunt and uncle's lives, not yours? Maybe that's why you're so inexplicably drawn to King."

"What? How?"

"You've always lived by the rules. He doesn't. He's free in ways you aren't. Maybe that's why you're attracted to him."

Kim's words strike so deeply, I visibly flinch.

"You know, in the summer camp, this Buddhist priest chap told us an interesting tidbit," she continues.

"What?"

"Souls are attracted to each other."

After saying goodbye, I stand rooted at the entrance, her last words playing like an echo in my head.

Souls are attracted to each other.

Aiden's soul is black, so what does that make mine?

I'm about to head inside when I catch movement. A black car is parked across from the house right under the streetlamp. The windows are tinted so I can't see inside.

The car has been there for the entire day before I went to school and after I returned.

An ominous feeling creeps down my spine. It's like I've seen that car before.

Where?

I bolt the door and activate the alarm system.

The house feels so calm, eery and... cold.

I sit down for dinner, but I'm not really hungry. I eat anyway so Aunt won't feel upset if she finds the boxes as she left them.

Have you thought that maybe you're living your aunt and uncle's lives, not yours? Kim's words return and I shoo them away.

I need to eat because my heart is acting up again. I know I should visit Dr Albert soon, but I need to participate in the track competition first.

The other time, Dr Albert mentioned another surgery. Not only will I kiss track running goodbye, but I might lose precious months that I should use to prepare for college.

I intend to live this year to the fullest, and then when it's time for the surgery, I will have it.

While I'm eating, I play chess against myself, knocking the black king a few times.

See, I love playing chess. Kim was wrong, not all my interests are linked to Aunt and Uncle. Even if Uncle Jaxon first taught me chess.

After a few rounds, I push the board away and retrieve my phone to check the school's website.

Then I recall it's the weekend.

My finger hovers over Instagram. I don't even pretend to scroll in the feeds, I go straight to Aiden's profile.

He hasn't posted anything after that picture of us kissing. It's so unlike him considering that he posts at least once a day.

When I first saw the picture, I was too mortified to study it properly.

Now, I'm calmer.

Almost.

I zoom in and see how entangled we really are. The look of utter possessiveness and rogue claiming on his face. The look of abandonment on mine.

Some screw was loose at that time.

I scroll down to the comments. No girls gush all over him on this picture. Most are friendly teases from the football team.

Ronan wrote, *You better be sorry for stealing my show that night, King.*

I blush, remembering how he caught us.

My pulse spikes when I make out the last comment. It's only minutes ago and it's from Silver.

Side dish until the actual menu comes.

I stab my fork at the empty plate. What in the ever living hell is her problem? First, I'm a peasant then I'm a side dish?

And the bastard didn't even delete her comment.

I hit home and throw the phone on the table. With a few calming breaths, I take my plates and do the dishes as calmly as I can manage, not bothering with the washer. I almost break the utensils.

With the water still running, I grip the sink's edge with both hands as I breathe heavily. I always thought jealousy was for weak, insecure people, but apparently, I'm turning into one, too.

It's blinding and downright scary how much I want to hurt her for messing with what's mine.

But then again, Aiden isn't mine.

Not really.

So I'm being all pissed off about nothing. And that pisses me off more.

I finish the dishes and retreat to my room to study. It's the only logical thing in my life at the moment.

An hour or so later, I crawl into bed, trying not to think about how Aiden has been bringing my special food every day. How he made sure we're seen in the halls together so no one bullies me anymore. How he brings me water after practice. How he watches me with that concern when I'm running as if he knows my heart isn't doing so well.

I shouldn't appreciate the thoughtful gestures, but I do, and they're tumbling my defences worse than anything else.

Unable to resist, I check Instagram again. I scroll down to

Silver's comment, but it isn't there anymore. Not sure if she deleted it or if he did.

My phone vibrates with a text.

Aiden.

I sit up in bed, my heart somersaulting inside its cavity.

Aiden: Can't sleep. I'm thinking about you.

I should pretend to be asleep, but I just can't. I'm feeling so off tonight and I'm afraid that if I close my eyes, nightmares will barge in.

I type back.

Elsa: I can't sleep either.

Aiden: Why?

Elsa: I'm scared of going to sleep sometimes.

I regret that as soon as I hit send. He doesn't need to know that.

The three dots appear and disappear as if he's thinking about what to say.

Aiden: I don't like to sleep either.

I sit up straighter.

Elsa: Why?

Aiden: It's boring.

Elsa: *eye roll emoji* Really?

Aiden: Remember that ghost I told you about? It visits me often when I sleep.

Is the ghost his mother?

Before I can reply, he sends another text.

Aiden: How about we distract each other?

Elsa: I don't like the sound of that.

Aiden: Trust me. You will like it. Eventually.

Aiden: What are you wearing?

Elsa: Seriously? *facepalm emoji* we're playing this game?

Aiden: Tell me.

Elsa: Fine. PJs with little rabbits on them. Not sexy at all.

Aiden: Let me be the judge of that *wink emoji*

Aiden: Besides, everything is sexy on you.

I try not to blush, but I freaking do.

Aiden: Give me more. What are you wearing under the PJs?

I bite my lower lip as I type.

Elsa: Nothing.

Aiden: Fuck. Now, I want to be the rabbit PJs.

Elsa: And what will you do?

Aiden: Aside from rubbing against you until you come? I have to think of other options PJs have.

Heat blooms between my thighs, and my fingers tremble when I type.

Elsa: What if you were here with me? What would you do with the PJs?

Aiden: Is this a trick question?

Elsa: I want to know…

Aiden: First of all, I'll rip the thing off you, then I'll bite your nipple and suck on it until you beg me to stop. I'll finger fuck you until you come all over my hand, but I won't stop.

My hand slips under the waistband of my shorts and plunge into my slick folds.

Elsa: No?

Aiden: No. While you're coming down from the wave, I'll eat your pussy until you scream all over again. Then I'll release your hair and hold you with it while I fuck you until both of us pass out.

I rub up and down harder with every word in his texts. It's not my hand, it's Aiden's mouth that's driving me insane. His fingers inside me, his cock down my throat…

I come with a cry and muffle the sound into my pillow.

My cheeks are so hot, I think they'll explode.

I can't believe I just brought myself to orgasm thinking it was Aiden.

My phone vibrates one more time.

Aiden: Don't sleep.

Ashamed of what I just did—or what he made me do, I groan and stand up, abandoning my phone on the nightstand.

Opening the balcony's window, I let the chilling air fill my senses. The first droplets of rain hit my nose, and I close my eyes, tipping my head back to let it rinse me.

Cleanse me.

My nostrils fill with the scent of the earth after the rain and I inhale it in.

When I open my eyes, the black car is still there.

My lips tremble as I abandon the rain and crawl back into my bed.

Whimpers come from the basement.

My little feet follow the sound. I'm whimpering myself, but them whimpers from the basement are louder and more in pain.

Mmmmm.

Mmmm…

Mmmm —

I dart my eyes back expecting the boogieman to follow me down here. Ma says I should never be here because them monsters hide in places like these.

Ma looks like a monster sometimes when she's talking about him. The one who shall not be named.

Her eyes look black like them Da's friends.

Sometimes, she hugs and squeezes me till I think I'm joining the one who shall not be named.

"Elsa?"

Oh. No.

If Ma finds me, she'll squeeze me to death again. I don't like them monsters in her eyes because Da won't stop hitting her when she has them monsters.

Then his monsters and her monsters become the same.

Them whimpers turn into moans. I stop at the basement's door and peek through the opening of the key.

Them monsters took another person like the one who shall not be named.

This time, I have to help them. I have to stop them monsters in Ma and Da's eyes.

"Elsa!!" A blow smacks my back.

My head hits the door and something warm and red trickles down my temple.

I look back and see them monsters.

They're black.

They're murky.

They have hole eyes.

My lips tremble as I'm struck again.

Blow.

Blow.

Blow.

"You'll pay for that, Elsa."

I wake up with a start. Sweat trickles down my spine, sticking my PJ's to my back. I dart my eyes to the side and shriek.

A shadow looms over my bed.

TWENTY-SIX

The monster from my childhood stands over my bed like a shadow.

A boogieman.

He's finally coming for me.

Blood roars in my ears and my heartbeat catches on an irregular, sick rhythm.

Thump.

Th-thump…

Thump…

I screw my lids shut and cover my ears with both my hands. This is a dream. It's all in my head. The boogieman isn't real. The monster isn't real.

No matter how much I chant that, it doesn't stop the voices from filtering through my high-built fortress.

Murmurs.

Haunted moans.

Pained whimpers.

Heavy footsteps come closer and closer, suffocating me like a vice.

"Hush little baby, don't you cry…"

No. I place both hands on my ears, trying to suffocate the haunting sound.

I hate that song. I hate the way she sings it with that manic humming and them monsters in her eyes.

"…everything is going to be alright…"

NO!

"Mama's gonna buy you a little toy… and if that toy doesn't work, Mama will bring you another one…"

No, no, no…

"You'll never escape me, Elsa."

"You're my masterpiece, Elsa."

"Elsa."

"Elsa…"

"Elsa!"

They won't have me.

Not again.

Never again.

I hit at his chest with both fists. His arms surround me, making me nauseous. I swore I'd never let him put his hands on me anymore.

Not again.

Not this time.

"Maaa!" I screech.

She can help me. She has to help me. That's what mothers do, right? They save their children from them monsters.

"Ma, help —"

My voice and my breathing cut off.

I'm thrown into water. Dark, murky, bottomless water.

I gasp, but only water fills my throat, my lungs… all of me.

Thrashing, I try to surface, to find refuge from them monsters.

A hand holds my head underwater. It's suffocating. It fills my nostrils, my mouth, and my frantic eyes.

I can't breathe.

Please, Ma.

Please, Da.

P-please, help me.

Cold shocks my skin and my limbs turn numb.

I'm floating, drifting…

It's useless to fight it.

Maybe the one who shall not be named fought it, too. Maybe that's why his name isn't spoken anymore.

Maybe I'll be like him.

Through the foggy haze, someone calls my name with an edge to their voice.

He's calling my name.

I won't be like the one who shall not be named.

He knows my name.

"Can you see me behind them monsters?" I ask in my head.

"I do."

I don't think he does, but I hold on to that glimmer of a voice.

It's soothing.

So soothing.

Maybe them monsters are invisible to him.

He sees me like no one did before.

He sees ME.

"Elsa!"

Like being hauled from the depth of an ocean, I gasp and my eyes pop open.

My vision is blurry and all I see are dark shadows. My heartbeat doesn't calm, thinking I'm at that place again.

However, the arms surrounding me aren't scary. If anything, they're soothing. It's like an escape I couldn't find back then.

I blink the tears from my blurry vision. Furrowed dark features greet me. Strands of his dark hair fall on his forehead.

I blink once. Twice. He doesn't disappear.

"A-Aiden?" My voice is so hoarse, I barely manage to get the words out.

"It's okay." He strokes my back in tiny circles. "You're not alone. I'm here."

I don't know if it's because of his words or because of the nightmares I just had.

I don't care either.

My fingers curl into his T-shirt, my forehead falls against the hardness of his chest, and I let the tears loose.

Sobs wreck my chest, and I let it all out. I don't even know what I'm crying about.

They were only nightmares. They aren't real.

They *can't* be real.

I curl further into Aiden's lap and hold tighter onto him. He's real. His warmth and the strange sense of security I feel in his arms is real.

The nightmares aren't.

Aiden puts a hand under my bottom and pulls me onto him so I'm sitting on his lap. I wrap my legs around his waist, strangling him.

He doesn't complain.

He remains silent, stroking my back, my hair and the side of my arm.

I couldn't be more thankful for his calm, anchor-like presence. He's here, but he's not talking. He's letting me deal with it on my own.

The last time I had an episode like this, strangely, two years ago right after my first day in RES, Aunt and Uncle freaked.

And I mean, they literally freaked.

I thought Aunt was with the monster and I hit her. I screamed and cursed at her. I didn't stop until Uncle locked her out of the room.

When I regained my consciousness, Aunt wouldn't stop asking me what I saw. She had a horrified sick look on her face like she was going to throw up. In the morning, they took me to Dr Khan and I had therapy sessions for almost six months.

Since then, I've been avoiding nightmares, or at least, the strong crippling ones that seem so... real.

For two years, I never bothered Aunt and Uncle with my nightmares even when I needed a shoulder to cry on. Even when what I saw—what I felt—scared the hell out of me.

It's strange that Aiden, my tormentor and bully, fills the role no one did.

How can he be the shoulder I cry on?

Still gripping his T-shirt, I stare up at him. His brows are drawn together over the stormiest colour I've ever seen his eyes. His features are closed with deep concern.

My breath hitches.

Who thought there would be a day where Aiden King would be worried about me?

I should feel self-conscious for the ugly crying or hate the vulnerability I just showed him. Hell, my face must be chaos right now.

"Hey," I say over hiccoughs.

His hand doesn't stop caressing my back while his other hand lifts my chin. He searches my eyes as if looking for something.

Or someone.

"Do you feel better?" His voice is firm, but it's not harsh.

Some unshed tears rim in my eyes as I nod.

"Did I trigger that by coming through the balcony?" he asks carefully.

"I already had the nightmare when you came so I was triggered before."

"By what?"

"I don't know." My head hurts and I want nothing more than to sleep.

I push the idea away as fast as it came. What if the nightmare returns?

"Are your nightmares always triggered?" Aiden is still holding my jaw, making me stare into his unyielding eyes.

For some reason, they're not intruding as usual, they're just... curious. Caring even.

Maybe that's why I confide in him. "Yes. Dr Khan always tells me to stay away from anything that can serve as a trigger."

"Such as?" Aiden prompts.

"Candles. Basements. Dim, red light. Deep water such as pools, beaches, and lakes. Sleeping in the dark." I don't even know how Dr Khan got the list, maybe it's from the scraps of nightmares I've told him.

My lips part and I stumble to my feet. "The black car!"

Aiden follows me, staring at me as if I'm about to have the episode again.

"The black car," My voice breaks. "Is there still a black car parked across the street?"

"No."

"How do you know that?"

"I parked across the street and there was no black car there."

With snail movements, I slowly peel the curtains of the balcony back. Sure enough, Aiden's Ferrari is parked across the street, the lamp causes its red to shine.

No sign of a black car.

I sigh and fall back into a sitting position on the bed, pushing wild strands of hair behind my ears. My eyes feel puffy and swollen.

My nose is stuffed and I feel like hell. This isn't how I want Aiden to see me.

"What are you doing here, anyway?" I climb under the covers, trying to hide my chaotic look.

A sly grin lifts his lips as he sits beside me. "Why did you think I told you not to sleep?"

For some reason, that makes me smile back. "You climb onto people's balconies a lot?"

"Just yours. I usually prefer doors"

I bite my lip. "Wait. I had the alarm on."

"But you left the balcony's door open."

"Right." I was too consumed with the rain that I forgot to close it afterwards.

Some part of my brain thinks I should be mad at Aiden for sneaking into my room, but I'm not. Far from it. I don't know what would've happened if I had a strong episode while being on my own.

"Thank you." Fresh tears sting my eyes and I swallow them in.

Aiden kicks off his shoes and climbs in beside me. His broad frame and tall legs dwarf my bed.

I pull the sheet to my chin. "What are you doing?"

"Sleeping," he says ever so casually.

"You… you can't sleep here."

"Sure can."

"But —"

Words die in my throat when Aiden presses his lips to mine in a soft, quick kiss.

He pulls me into his chest, so my head lies against his bicep. My nostrils fill with his clean scent and I can't help inhaling deeper like an addict.

Strong arms surround me as he murmurs, "Just sleep, sweetheart."

I never sleep if I can help it after a nightmare because I'm scared it'll continue if I do.

But in Aiden's arms, I don't feel scared or paranoid. I don't even think about the double nightmares I had.

I feel… safe.

I curl my fingers into his shirt and place my ear over his soothing heartbeat—a normal heartbeat.

I close my eyes and surrender to the pull of sleep.

Safe.

TWENTY-SEVEN

No nightmares.

That's the first thought that crosses my sleepy consciousness as soon as I open my eyes.

Then, I take in the warmth. So, so much warmth.

Aiden spent the night here.

In my bed.

I stare at his sleeping face. His chin grazes my forehead and the slight stubble tickles my skin.

One of his arms surrounds my waist, his hand resting in the middle of my back. The other lies limp because I'm using his bicep as a pillow.

His leg cages both of mine like he's stopping me from escaping.

I have to crane my head to get a full view of his face. His lashes appear thicker and longer when his eyes are closed.

His features are serene as if he isn't feeling the weight of my head on his arm.

Who knew someone like Aiden would look so peaceful when asleep?

And who knew there would be a day where I'd sleep hugging him all night?

When he pulled me into him, I felt a sense of... belonging.

No. I shouldn't be feeling any belonging with Aiden when I still haven't figured him out yet.

He's the same person who choked me that day and told me

he'd destroy me. I can't start trusting him because he climbed onto my balcony and soothed my nightmares.

…right?

Feeling confused, I slowly peel his heavy arm from around my waist and inch towards the edge of the bed, scooping my phone on the way.

I stand and throw one last peek at the massive body sprawled in my bed. Tingles curl my toes and across my spine.

Nope, not going there.

I trudge to the bathroom and quietly close the door.

A gasp leaves my lips when I look at my face in the mirror. A mess is the understatement of the freaking century.

My eyes are bloodshot and puffy, it's a miracle they're still open. Strands of my blonde hair poke out of my head like antennas and tears have left streaks down my cheeks.

How did Aiden even look at me, let alone hold me to sleep? It's my own face and I'm disgusted with it.

I open the tap and splash water on my face. Weird. I don't have that urge to scrub my hands clean. It's usually the first thing I do after a nightmare.

After brushing my teeth and pulling my hair into a messy bun, I turn to leave the bathroom.

My phone buzzes on the counter.

Since it's almost seven in the morning, I don't have to guess who'd be checking in on me this early.

Aunt B: Morning, hon. It's the weekend so you sleep in, okay? We're still caught up so we might come back later tonight. I'll be checking the boxes so don't skip meals.

I stare at her text and contemplate what to reply.

Except that I don't want to reply right now. It's Saturday, so I'll pretend to sleep in like she told me to.

Don't you think you're living your aunt and uncle's lives, not yours?

I wish Kim never said those words because I can't stop replaying them.

Yesterday's nightmare reminded me of something I've always put on the backburner.

Like Aunt and Uncle's reactions to my nightmares.

Why would Aunt Blair ask questions? Why did Uncle Jaxon kick her out?

It's like they know more than they're letting on.

The nightmares aren't normal and they always follow the same pattern. In a basement. In water. In the dark.

They've been the same since I was seven.

Since my parents' death.

I grip the counter as tendrils of fear shoot through my spine.

For ten years, I always thought that the past should stay where it belonged.

Aunt and Uncle offered me a new life, and the only way to embrace it was to erase any life I had prior to that.

But then again, ignoring it doesn't mean it disappears.

With shaky fingers, I pull up google and type.

Fire in Birmingham ten years ago.

The first articles that come out are about a grand fire that happened in a copper factory.

Fifty people died on the spot, twenty in the hospital, and a dozen others followed after a few weeks.

It was a massive fire that shook the country and the government. The cause has been ruled as a negligent smoker and the case closed too soon.

I fall into a rabbit hole and study all the articles, comments, and even the interviews. A few workers said that Reggie, the one accused to have smoked inside the facility, never smoked inside. Not that Reggie can defend himself considering that he died on the spot.

I go back to the main search. It takes a few pages to find an article about a domestic fire.

My home.

No. My house. It feels weird to call it home.

The fire happened a week after the grand Birmingham fire.

My back leans against the counter as I read all the information I already know.

'*Stove Malfunction takes the life of a family. The only survivor is the daughter who had been outside by the lake.*'

The lake.

'*The fire burned the house inside out and straight to the basement. The detectives found it hard to gather evidence.*'

Basement.

'*The remains of Mr and Mrs Steel have been retrieved and identified.*'

Remains.

I don't know why I only keep seeing the technical details.

They say being burnt alive is the most painful death. I should feel something about the reminder that my parents died in so much pain.

However, I'm... disconnected. Probably because I don't really remember them. But is that an excuse?

'*The only witness is Ms Steel—a seven year-old girl. She has been under attentive mental and physical care. The doctor said that Ms Steel lost all recollection of what happened. After further investigation, the police closed the case as a gas malfunction.*'

I exit the article not wanting to read more. I don't remember having a lake near our house or even a basement. But Aunt and Uncle made it clear that they were never taking me back to Birmingham.

Not that I wanted to. At least in the past. Now, I don't know.

Am I ready to bury my head on the expense of having more nightmares?

I release a breath through my nose. I probably need to see Dr Khan again.

Once I exit the bathroom, I'm transfixed by Aiden's frame on my bed. He's still in the same position I left him in. His arm with the tattoo rests on the pillow as if I were still sleeping on it and his other arm is slumped on the bed as I left it.

Seems like he's a heavy sleeper.

At this time on Saturday, I usually do some yoga.

Not today.

I tiptoe, lift Aiden's arm and snuggle in the crook of his warm body. My head rests on his bicep. I'm becoming too addicted too fast to how it feels to be in his embrace.

I wrap my arm around his hard, defined midsection and push into him.

An unmistakable bulge stabs the bottom of my stomach.

I freeze.

This must be what's called morning wood.

I wonder if it can get harder while he sleeps. I run a hand in front of his face, but there's no response.

With hesitant movements, I rub my stomach against it.

Holy hell.

His dick becomes rock hard, tenting against his dark jeans.

Heat pools between my thighs and my skin warms. My nipples strain against the cotton of my PJ's.

I'm supposed to stop, but I *can't*.

When it comes to Aiden, there's this constant craving for more.

More contact.

More touch.

Just… *more*.

If I can't escape the beast or tame him, I can at least explore him.

My strokes become bolder as I pick up the pace. With each up and down, wetness coats the insides of my thighs. I suppress a moan with the back of my hand.

"You better be awake and well aware of what you're doing, sweetheart."

I freeze mid-rub, my ears heating.

Shit. Wasn't he supposed to be a heavy sleeper?

"Did I tell you to stop?" His husky, sleepy voice sends a throb straight to my core.

Aiden slowly peels his eyes open. I always hated his eyes. That grey colour reminds me of clouds, storms, and metal.

And ruining my life.

But telling myself that I hated them was only a deflection method, wasn't it? Because his eyes? They're fucking gorgeous.

Heartbreakingly so.

He threads his fingers into my hair and tugs the band free before bringing a strand of hair to his face and inhaling. "Hmm, you smell like temptation."

I offer an awkward smile. "Morning."

"Screw mornings."

I laugh. "Not a morning person?"

He's watching me intently in that inquisitive way before he narrows his eyes as his hand skims down from my waist to grip my hip. "Don't laugh in front of other people. Don't even smile in front of them."

"Why not?"

"Your smiles and laughs belong to me. I don't like it when others look at what's mine."

"Seriously?" I roll my eyes. "What's next? You'll lock me up in your cave and put a dozen babies in me?"

His lips quirk in amusement. "Can you handle it?"

"Handle what?"

"Me putting a dozen babies in you."

"Are you for real?"

"We should start now."

My mouth hangs open as I search for any signs that he's joking, but he has an impressive poker face.

It doesn't help that his erection is pressing into me and he's not even the least bit apologetic about it.

But then again, Aiden is never apologetic about anything.

I try to wiggle free. "Don't joke like that."

"Hmm, it's curious that I never joke with you, but you still think that I do." He flips me so I'm on my back and he's hovering over me. "For the record, I do want to hide you where no one will see you."

"Why?" That's such a stupid question.

He's just admitted to wanting to kidnap me, and all I care about is knowing why.

I'm beginning to think like the scientists at the behavioural unit. They don't care about the acts as long as they know the why behind those acts.

"The thought of any other man touching you drives me fucking crazy. Especially since I haven't staked my claim yet." Aiden's hand wraps around my throat and he caresses the pulse point. "It's time to change that."

TWENTY-EIGT

It's time to change that.

My muscles lock at his words.

Aiden hovers over me like a looming danger, a force not to be reckoned with.

The boy with metal eyes, harsh glares, and unhinged character got under my skin. And since he did that, he has the power to break me.

I will destroy you.

His first words to me are the defining point of our relationship. He can't just erase that with the few thoughtful things he did the past weeks or by holding me to sleep after my nightmare.

All of it could be another one of his mind games so I'll lower my guard.

Once he has my virginity, he'll drop me like a bad habit.

He'll crush me and walk on the remains.

Call it old-fashioned or naive, but I always wanted to save my first to someone I deeply care about.

Aiden isn't that person.

I place a hand at the centre of his broad chest. "I'm not ready."

He tilts his head to the side, supporting himself on tense hands on either side of my head. "What do you mean by you're not ready?"

"I... I need more time."

"More time for what?"

I need more time to understand myself and make sure that I'm doing the right thing.

You're too safe.

Kim's words slice through my brain like razor-sharp claws.

"I've been patient with you, Frozen."

I hate when he calls me that.

I fix him with a glare. "So that's what you wanted all along? You've been patient to get your dick wet?"

"If I wanted to get my dick wet, I would've fucked you and gotten you out of my system a long time ago."

Tears blur in my eyes and I loathe myself for ever feeling comfortable in his presence or thinking that there's another layer beneath the suffocating smoke.

"Then why haven't you? If you did, we would've gone our separate ways."

Why did you have to trick me into thinking that there could be more?

"I told you." His tone loses the nonchalance. "Sex isn't my endgame. And I've been patient to communicate that. You should know by now that I'm not a patient person, so don't push me."

I'm tempted to scream obscenities and push him off, but that will surely trigger his predatory side.

I'll have to be smart about handling this situation.

Seriously, I shouldn't be burning neurons to get him to act like a decent human being, but this is what I get for being involved with someone who disregards normal.

I force my body to relax and suck in a few calming breaths. "What have you been patient for?"

He lifts an eyebrow, apparently taken aback by my course of action. I like thwarting his plans. He's better to handle when he's taken off guard.

"For you to want me," he says with that air of casualty.

"Why is that important?"

"It just is."

"You don't care about the moral repercussions and you sure

as hell aren't scared about the criminal consequences, so why didn't you just take it? Why didn't you rape me that day?"

As soon as I say the word 'rape', I regret it. I don't want to put ideas in his screwed up head. But then again, he's a fucking lunatic, so he probably had worse ideas than that.

He arches an eyebrow. "Do you want to be raped by me?"

"What? No! Seriously? Is that your only deduction from what I said?"

"What am I supposed to deduce?" He lowers himself on his elbows so his chest grazes my breasts. "You just said that you wanted me to take from you."

"I *asked* why you didn't take from me, not that I wanted you to."

"Semantics."

"You're delusional."

His fingers find my hair, stroking it gently. Too gently. "You know, the more you say I'm delusional, the surer I am that you're the delusional one. You want to deny yourself? Fine. You want to think you're a politically correct person? Also fine. You can lie to yourself all you like, but you don't fucking lie to me. You don't rub yourself all over my dick then pretend you don't want me."

My lips tremble and I thin them into a line.

"I'm trying to get to you." His nose drops to my neck, and I suck in a cracked breath. "I'm really trying to be fucking nice here, but if you keep hiding in that ice castle, I'll have no choice but to conquer."

My fingers dig into his T-shirt, wanting to inflict pain. "Do I even have a choice in this?"

"You always have a choice with me. A queen or a pawn."

Of course. There's no in-between with him. "Either I become the most important piece or the most insignificant one. How... poetic."

He raises an eyebrow. "You play chess."

"How do you know that?"

"Those who don't play think that the king is the most

important piece because the game is over when he dies. They don't know that the king is useless without his queen."

Now, that is… poetic. Who knew someone like Aiden cared about the queen?

"We can play?" I ask tentatively. I'd take any option to dissipate the tension and get him off me.

"We have to take care of you first."

Of course, he wouldn't fall for that. Dickhead.

"Take care of what?"

"Have you heard about rape fantasy?"

My breathing catches in my throat. Fuck, fuck.

How the hell does he know about that? I mean, I read about it, I even so shamelessly searched it in the porn site bar. I felt sick to my stomach for the entire week after. How could I be interested in something that ruined women's lives?

How could I be so deprived to fantasise about it?

Maybe Aiden is my karma. Maybe I'm being punished for ever thinking about that.

A spark shines in his eyes. "You have heard about it."

"No," I murmur turning my head to the side. "You're the only one who's interested in these perverted things."

God. I'm such a hypocrite.

"You should look it up." He grabs my chin and makes me face him. "I think you'll find it useful."

"Useful how?"

A wolfish grin curves his lips. He knows he got my interest. Bastard.

"There are people who like the rush of adrenaline that comes with rough, out of control sex. So they like being forced into it."

"People like to be raped?" I thought it was just a fantasy, not practical… right?

"No. They like being forced to have sex. They usually plan it with their partners, so it's technically not rape."

"Is that the excuse you tell yourself?"

"I don't tell myself excuses. I'm completely assertive of who and what I am. I know I'm different, I just don't care." His finger traces down my cheek. "The excuse is for you since you seem to so desperately need it."

"I do not."

"Fuck, Elsa. Stop being so damn stubborn."

"Why don't you leave me alone?" I hate the tremors in my voice. "Why don't you let me go?"

A strange tightness grips my chest at the thought.

What if he really lets me go. What if he —

"I can't," His voice drops.

"Why not?"

"I don't have a choice."

Something sharp and heavy slices through my chest. Aiden always has a choice. Hell, he even makes it clear that all choices are to his benefit.

It doesn't make sense that he's the one without a choice.

"Are you playing another mind game?"

"Are you, Elsa? Because I was never supposed to like you this much. Hell. I wasn't supposed to think about you more than I think of myself."

I was never supposed to like you this much.

Did I hear that right? Did Aiden just admit to liking me?

I think it's right. I think… Aiden *likes* me.

And I believe him.

Unlike me, Aiden is assertive to a fault. He's not afraid of admitting what he wants.

He's free in ways you aren't. Maybe that's why you're attracted to him.

Kim's words hit me like an unexpected blow.

I waited for you to want me.

I'm not supposed to like you this much.

Those words dig black holes into my defences.

I let my hand travel up from his chest to the rippling tendons of his collarbone. Aiden grabs my hand in his stronger one.

He shakes his head once. "Not so fast."

"W-what? But why?" Shame at being rejected sinks at the bottom of my stomach.

Isn't this what he wanted?

"Kiss me," he says.

"Kiss you," I repeat, still confused out of my mind.

"This time, I want you to wrap your arms around my neck and kiss me first, Elsa."

He's so unfair. I should've known that he won't only take. I should've known that he'd eventually want me to give.

He's not interested in one battle, he wants to win the entire bloody war.

A small voice whispers that I'll regret this tomorrow, but I don't care about tomorrow right now.

I retrieve my hand from his and wrap both my arms around his neck.

Then I seal my lips to his.

TWENTY-NINE

My kiss is tentative. Experimental.

It's the first time I initiate a kiss. The first time I kiss Aiden without him basically forcing it on me.

At first, it's a slight press of my lips against his firm ones. Then, my tongue darts out and I lick his bottom lip over and over. Gaining more boldness, I pull myself up and slightly nibble on it before trailing soft kisses on the corner of his mouth.

The whole time, Aiden watches me with hooded eyes. Both his arms are taut as he leans his hands on the bed.

He's not touching me.

My bold phase shrinks a little. Maybe he changed his mind, maybe —

"Fuck this," Aiden groans as his lips crash to mine.

His kiss is the complete opposite of my gentle ones. Aiden kisses like a madman searching for his sanity. It's always out of control. My breathing ceases when he thrusts his tongue inside my mouth and devours me.

That's what Aiden does. He devours. He shreds me apart and strips me bare until he owns every part of me.

Now that he's taking charge, I feel like I can... let go.

Let go.

What a weird sensation.

I was never tempted to let go before. If anything, I did everything by the rules so I wouldn't have to let go.

Aiden's body is all over me. His legs barge between my

trembling thighs. His chest flattens my aching breasts. His hands are all over my hair, my cheeks, my face.

He's all over me.

His raw intensity seeps under my skin and shoots straight into my veins. It's contagious.

He's contagious.

Aiden wrenches his mouth from mine, and we both pant, breathing each other in.

I'm caught in his stormy gaze.

Since the beginning, he's always looked at me differently like we're connected.

Like he knows me better than anyone else.

And maybe, just maybe, I wanted to know him better than anyone, too.

He breaks eye contact to fling my pyjamas' top over my head. The cloth rubs against my hard, sensitive nipples, sending a chill of pleasure between my legs.

He palms one breast with a rough hand and grunts. "Did I tell you how much I love these?"

His fiery gaze never leaves mine as he sucks a nipple into his mouth and pulls at it with his teeth. He doesn't bite, but the threat is there.

My eyes droop and a moan spills from my throat.

Still teasing with his teeth, he pinches the other nipple. His stormy eyes stay transfixed on me as if he's challenging—or taunting me.

My fingers slide to his hair and I pull on the jet black strands. I don't know if it's to push or pull him.

And I don't get to decide.

Aiden wraps a firm hand around my throat and bites down on my nipple so hard, pain shoots across my spine and pleasure pools in my core. His tongue laps around it, soothing the ache before he does it again. I cry out, my back arching.

I can't move much because he's imprisoning me by his grip on my throat.

It's like falling down a cliff. There should be nothing pleasing about that because when I hit the bottom, I'll be dead. But right now? I don't think about the landing. I'm suspended in the act of falling. Beyond fear and self-imposed shackles, there's a thrill, excitement. The... unknown.

I'm becoming addicted to it.

Still biting down on my nipple, Aiden reaches the other hand to yank down my pyjamas' shorts. His fingers find my slick folds and he groans as he teases his way down.

My body feels like it's been lit on fire while still falling down that cliff. A thousand goosebumps cover my skin and seep into my bones.

"Aiden..."

He lifts his head. Lust and something else I can't put my finger on contort his face.

My fingers curl into his T-shirt and I attempt to pull it over his head. He clutches my fingers over his T-shirt, stopping me. Something crosses his handsome features. It's fast, and maybe if I weren't so much under his spell, I would've figured out its meaning.

The expression vanishes as fast as it came, and he yanks his T-shirt over his head.

He's an athlete so the six-packs shouldn't be a surprise, but the perfect proportions are a bit unfair. It's like he's shooting for a magazine.

Now that he's bending his arms, the arrow tattoos seem to be pointing straight at his heart.

Or mine.

When my gaze slides back to his, he's watching me with a hard expression like he's waiting for me to pounce.

I have no doubt that if I do fight, he'll fight back.

Depending on my choice, he'll make it as ugly or as pretty as he deems necessary.

A queen or a pawn.

My fingers trace up his hard sides and to his taut stomach. I don't know when touching him has become an addiction.

A pleasure.

A necessity.

What would it feel like to engrave myself under his skin?

That's… a scary thought.

Aiden yanks down his trousers along with his boxer briefs. He's as hard as the other time—if not more.

It'll hurt.

Why do I want it to hurt?

Without releasing my throat, he positions himself between my legs. His free hand cups my jaw. His stormy eyes forge a path straight into my soul. "You drive me fucking crazy."

"You drive me crazy, too. It isn't funny anymore."

Aiden is the cliff.

Unknown.

Unplanned.

Unpredictable.

He's my worst nightmare.

He's also the closest thing I've had to freedom.

Aiden squeezes my throat and slams inside me.

He tears me apart in one go.

I shriek against his mouth.

It hurts.

Holy shit.

It fucking *hurts*.

It's like being shred open from the inside by his size.

According to Aunt's romance novels, other virgins in this situation would wait to adjust. They'd feel the need for the man to go easy.

Me? I want it to go on.

The pain. I want the pain to stay.

My body arches into Aiden's. I grip his shoulders so tightly, my nails sink into the skin.

He freezes, eyes meeting mine, as he growls. "You're a virgin? How the fuck are you a virgin? Why —"

"D-don't stop." I cut him off, slowly rocking my hips. "Take it."

I want him to go hard on me because I need the pain, I don't know why, but I just do.

The pain means I'm alive. I'm living this moment.

Considering Aiden's rough nature, I expected him to accept the invitation.

Instead, he slowly rocks his hips forward, his thrusts are minimal as if he's waiting for me to adjust.

Then… he kisses me.

It's passionate but gentle. Our tongues dance in an erotic, slow dance. He releases my neck and he pulls me into him so I'm sitting on his lap. The new depth causes my knees to shake.

His thrusts become slow and deep and maddening.

I wanted the pain, but I got this euphoric feeling I didn't know I needed.

Aiden smashed the illusion I had. He broke it and tore it to the ground.

Something inside me cracks.

My fingers thread into his hair and I kiss him back with an intensity that matches his. I meet the gentle rock of his hips with mine.

For what seems like forever, we kiss, letting our bodies get accustomed to each other. We kiss like it's the last kiss we'll ever have.

Like a disaster will happen if we stop kissing.

I try urging him to go harder by pulling on his hair, but he tugs on my hair back as if silently communicating he won't follow my command.

Our limbs are so entangled that I don't know where he starts and I begin. A sheen of sweat covers our bodies and the smell of sex lingers in the air like an aphrodisiac.

Aiden thrusts faster and sharper. A whimper-like moan escapes my lips when he hits a sensitive spot inside.

Without breaking his rhythm, Aiden pushes me so I'm on my back. His hands slip under my thighs and he flings both my legs over his broad shoulders.

He wraps his hand around my throat whether to keep me in place or as a threat, I don't know.

And I don't have time to think about it.

He pounds into me with renewed energy. The new angle causes my walls to contract.

The headboard creaks with every wild thrust and rock of his pelvis against mine. My heart palpitations are so fast, I'm scared I'll have a heart attack.

It'll be worth it.

"You're so beautiful," He groans, his rhythm turning rougher and faster with every word he says. "You're maddening. You're addictive. You're fucking up everything."

I don't last.

Maybe it's because of his words, the feel of him inside me, or his hand around my throat.

Or all of the above.

A wave slashes through me and I scream as I fall down with no landing in sight.

This orgasm is nothing like the ones I had before. It's primal, raw, and so overwhelming that I can't breathe.

Aiden continues his overwhelming onslaught, chasing his own orgasm. He goes on and on.

And *on*.

I'm at that delirious state like the other time. I feel so sensitive and sore, but I don't want him to stop.

I crave the pain and the pleasure he brings.

I crave *him*.

His shoulders tense. I still, wanting to watch him fall over the edge as he did to me.

Aiden doesn't let me.

He reaches down to my clit and teases it before thrusting into me one final time. I come again with a hoarse cry.

"Fuck," he groans as warmth fills my insides.

Aiden remains inside me as he pulls me to him. My head rests on his chest, my ear against his heartbeat. His natural, but erratic heartbeat.

Thump.

Thump.

Thump.

I brush my lips against his skin and remain that way as my lids flutter closed.

Free.

Is this what freedom's supposed to be like?

THIRTY

Something warm envelops my skin almost like…

Water.

I startle awake, expecting to find myself in that murky, dark water from the nightmares.

My breathing returns to normal when I recognise my surroundings. I'm in my bathroom with its white tiles and pastel pink decor.

I'm also sitting in my half-full bathtub. Completely naked.

Warm water cascades from the tap, slowly submerging my breasts.

Aiden faces me, but is staring sideways, fussing with my shampoo in all his naked glory.

I bite my lower lip as I openly gawk at him. There's a primal quality to his beauty that drew my attention since the first time I met him.

His muscles flex with every move. The arrow tattoos slither with the rippling of his biceps. His cock is semi-hard, pointing in my direction. I wonder if it's always in that state because I've never seen it flaccid.

"You're finally awake, sleepyhead," he says without lifting his head.

I let my hand roam in the water. I can't believe Aiden is making me a bubble bath.

"How long have I been out?" I ask.

"About two hours."

"And what did you do during that entire time?"

"Watched you."

Watched you.

Damn him and how easily he can say things like that. If it were me, I would've never admitted it.

When I remain silent, he slides his metallic eyes up my body, and even though it's covered with bubbles, it's like he can see through them.

"I was also going through your Instagram."

I gulp. "You go through my Instagram?"

He tilts his head to the side. "Why do you think I followed you?"

I always thought it was some bullying method, not that he was actually taking the following factor seriously.

"By the way, you still didn't follow me back," he says as if it's something I forgot about.

"So why do you go through my Instagram?" I deflect.

He shrugs. "To see what you're up to."

"As in you're stalking me?"

He grins. "I prefer inquiring."

I splash water in his direction. "You're incurable."

"I'm curious…" he trails off. "Why do you never post your face?"

"What?"

"You have pictures of food, picturesque settings, your aunt and uncle, Reed and her brother, but there's never a full shot of you. The only pictures of you are taken from behind or the side. There isn't one picture where you look at the camera. It's almost as if you're scared of it."

I lift my shoulder. "Not all of us love the attention."

"Hmm. Why do I feel that's not your case?"

When I don't reply, he turns around to retrieve the shampoo bottle.

I gasp, the sound interrupting the cascading water.

Slash marks.

Aiden has two slashes down his back. They're faded into his tan skin, and that's probably why I haven't noticed them before.

What happened to you?

The question is at the tip of my tongue when Aiden faces me slowly. The darkness in his eyes cuts through me like a thousand needles.

It's like he's fighting with demons—and they're winning.

The expression disappears as fast as it appeared. His infuriating poker face erases any emotions.

"You must be sore." He moves behind the tub and out of view. "I read that warm baths help."

"Aiden…"

My voice catches in my throat, not knowing what to say. The scars appeared deep and old. They must've hurt like hell when he first got them.

Then it hits me.

Those marks must be the reason why Aiden is such a social anomaly. It must've been abuse. It looks so much like abuse.

Something inside me shifts and red, hot fury shoots through my veins. The need to hurt whoever did that to Aiden washes over me like a compulsion.

I want to kill them.

Aiden doesn't say anything, he just shampoos my hair. His fingers glide over my scalp, massaging it. I tilt my head back and sigh in contentment.

"Aiden," I speak more clearly this time. "Did your father…?"

"Jonathan King isn't a violent man." He sounds sarcastic. "He'll sue you for defamation if hears you saying such nonsense."

"Then who is it?"

"None of your business."

"Well, I'm making it my business."

"You're not ready."

"Try me."

"If I tell you, you'll have to tell me everything in return. And I mean every fucking thing, Elsa. Including your nightmares. If you're ready to bare your soul to me, then, by all means, start first, sweetheart."

I clamp my lips shut. Horror seeps into my bones at the thought of my nightmares and my childhood. I don't even like thinking about it, let alone talking about it.

I'm itching to know about his scars but not to the point of probing my own scars.

"That's what I thought." He spills water on my hair.

I close my eyes as the water and shampoo cascade down my face.

He managed to shut me up so easily.

His counterargument is fair enough. You talk, I talk. But I still can't help sulking.

Damn Aiden King.

We spend a few minutes silent as he finishes rinsing my hair.

"Why didn't you tell me you were a virgin?" he asks casually.

I pause, startled by the drastic change of subject. "I didn't tell you I wasn't."

"Is that so?"

"Yes. You assumed it yourself."

I crane my head to have a better look, but he grips me by the neck and keeps me facing ahead.

"Why were you a virgin?"

"Uh… what type of question is that?"

He carefully tucks the strands of hair on the side of my neck. His hands curl on my shoulders. "It's simple enough. Why did you wait this long?"

For the right person.

But I don't tell him that or he'd think he's the right person.

I lift a shoulder. "It's no big deal."

"You know." His tone is casual but the undertone isn't. "There will be no trust between us if you continue lying to me."

I crane my head back to glance at him. "Trust? You think I'd ever trust you?"

His lips tighten in a line, but he smiles. "Why not?"

"I don't know, Aiden. Maybe it has to do with the fact that you targeted me the first time you saw me. Or that my life has been a living hell for two years because of you? Take your pick."

One of his hands wraps around my nape. It's firm as if to keep me in place. "Then why did you give me your virginity?"

"I'm attracted to you," I whisper. "Even though I hate it, I just am, but that doesn't erase what you did the last two years. You keep pushing me. It's not like I have a choice in being attracted to you."

"Is that what you want? A choice?"

"What does it matter? You always get what you want." I huff. "Even when you give me a choice, it ends up playing in your favour."

Aiden is thoughtful for a bit. The scary, silent type of thoughtful. "I see."

He drops his hands.

A strange chill crawls up my spine despite the warm water.

Aiden's poker face is the last thing I see before he walks out of the door.

THIRTY-ONE

On Monday, Uncle, Aunt and I are having breakfast together when I say, "I want to see Dr Khan."

Two pairs of eyes snap from their tasks. Uncle pauses drinking his morning coffee and reading from his tablet. Aunt stops packing my lunch, her hands shaking around the container.

"Are you having nightmares again? What did you see?" Her tone is almost hysterical.

"Stop it, Blair." Uncle abandons his coffee and tablet on the table and rises to his feet. I face him as he clutches my shoulders and says in a cool voice, "Are you all right, pumpkin? Why didn't you call us when you had the nightmares?"

I can't help noticing the difference between Aunt and Uncle's reactions. Her eyes are shifty and she keeps opening and closing the container as if she's not aware of what she's doing. Whenever the topic of my nightmares resurfaces, Aunt never asked me if I was okay. Her first question was always 'what did you see?'

Uncle, on the other hand, always asked if I was fine.

It's weird.

In everything else, Aunt cares about my wellbeing more than Uncle. She's the one who acts like a Nazi to make sure I eat healthily.

Maybe she doesn't think that my mental state is part of my health.

Either way, I'm not in the mood to talk about my episode on Saturday.

I smile and hope it comes out convincing. "It's not about the nightmares. I just want to talk about the stress of exams."

Aunt's shoulders droop and she stops opening and closing the container.

Uncle's brows furrow. "You never had exams' stress before, pumpkin."

"Everyone is competitive at school and I keep thinking that maybe someone will push me out of the top ten per cent," The lies tumble from my mouth so easily.

Strange. I always hated lying to them, but not today.

Uncle nods. "I'll book an appointment."

"Thanks, Uncle."

Neither of them needs to know about my plans with Dr Khan. I'm changing tactics about the whole psychotherapy.

Uncle kisses the top of my head. "You know you can talk to us any time, pumpkin, right? You don't have to hide anything as you did with your relationship with Aiden King."

Just hearing his name slashes pain through my chest. Since he walked out of my house on Saturday morning, there has been no trace of him. He didn't call or send me his usual crude texts.

I've seen pictures of him on Instagram after the game on Saturday night. Elites won two to nil and Xander scored both. It's so rare for Aiden not to score at a game.

When I said what I said in the bathroom, I didn't expect he'd just walk away.

He's *not* the type to walk away.

I kept telling myself that he'll come back to pester me as usual. He'll barge into my life like he has every right to.

He didn't.

And that hurt more than I care to admit.

I nod absentmindedly at Uncle who goes back to his seat and resumes drinking his coffee. I sip from my juice. It tastes bitter and I want to spit it back up.

Aunt places the container in my bag and touches her collarbone. "Don't take this the wrong way, hon, but maybe you're stressing because you have a boyfriend?"

Uncle stares at her from above the rim of his cup.

"What? She never stressed before. It isn't a coincidence that she's starting to stress now that she has a boyfriend." She faces me, a warm glow on her face. "It's subconscious, Elsie. Your attention span will be unknowingly divided. You can't possibly give your studies one hundred per cent of your energy like you used to."

"Drop it, Blair," Uncle's voice is low with warning.

"No, she's right." I set my juice on the table. "I shouldn't let anything come before my studies."

"Right?" Aunt smiles with a victorious gleam as if she were waiting for someone to agree with her. "He's not good for you, anyway."

I perk up. "What do you mean?"

She gives an awkward laugh. "His last name is King. Their world is different from ours. It's better to end it now before you grow attached to him."

Too late.

Uncle sighs with exasperation, pinching his nose. "She has the right to make her own decisions."

"I just don't want her to get hurt or to sacrifice her future over some boy drama." Aunt shoots back.

My phone dings.

Kim: I'm here.

Thank God.

I stand up and sling my backpack over my shoulders. "Kim is here. I have to go."

"Take care, hon." Aunt smoothens my hair back. "Teamwork."

Uncle gives me a tight smile, apparently still angry with Aunt.

"Teamwork," I echo back, kiss them each on the cheek and head out.

Aunt and Uncle's voices rise as soon as I'm at the front door.

"She's not a child, stop treating her like one," Uncle says.

"I don't want her making mistakes, okay?"

"Mistakes? Come the fuck on, Blair. Are we going down that road?"

"She's my niece, okay? *Mine!* You wouldn't be in her life if it weren't for me so stop interfering, Jaxon."

"Eighteen is right around the corner. I can't wait to see what happens when the other shoe drops."

My feet falter at the last sentence. What the hell is that supposed to mean?

Kim texts again. I open the door and step into the windy air. My ponytail blows in front of my face.

"Morning, Ellie." She's smiling wide, appearing in a good mood.

"Hey, Kim."

Her smile drops. "What's wrong? You look like you've seen a ghost."

"I'm fine."

"Hell to the no." Her expression softens. "Tell me."

Where do I even start? I was ditched after giving up my virginity? My nightmares are becoming terrifying? Aunt and Uncle are fighting because of me?

Everything is tumbling over my head, and I can't seem to find a way out. I want to cry so hard, but that will ruin Kim's good mood.

Due to her own family and school drama, she rarely has a good mood. I don't want to ruin it for her.

"Menstrual cramps," I say. "I think I'm getting my period soon."

"Aww, that sucks!" Kim drives out of the driveway.

It isn't completely a lie, but it isn't menstrual cramps that hurt with every move. I'm still sore from Saturday.

I haven't been able to move without feeling Aiden inside me.

I try to listen to Kim talking about her family dinner, but my mind keeps drifting back to how Aiden left without a word.

At first, I was ashamed to be abandoned like that.

Then, I had another feeling that's more in tune with Aiden's character.

He only approached me for sex after all. Now that he got what he wanted, everything was over.

Good riddance.

If I can spend the rest of senior year in peace, then I'll consider my virginity a sacrifice.

The familiar pressure of tears builds behind my eyes.

I just wish he hadn't lied to me and made me feel like I meant something.

Fucker.

"By the way," Kim's voice cuts through my thoughts. "I heard Mum and Dad talk about something super weird yesterday."

"Yeah?"

Kim's attention remains on the road as she speaks, "Remember when I told you that Aiden's mother died of an accident?"

He's the last thing I want to talk about, but I can't help the curiosity. "What about her?"

"So Dad was saying that Alicia was suicidal, anyway, so her death wasn't a surprise. However, Mum said that Dad doesn't understand. Alicia wasn't suicidal, she only wanted to save her baby."

"She wanted to save her baby?" I echo.

"I know! Weird, right? Aiden is an only child and he was at a camp. What baby was she trying to save?" Kim's voice drops to a whisper-yell because she doesn't know how to whisper properly. "Unless she had a child outside of marriage. Maybe she was off to meet her lover and Uncle Jonathan sent a PI after her. There was a chase and she crashed."

"Whoa. You watch too many Korean soap operas, Kim."

"Most families' problems are because of secret births. Just saying."

Soon after we reach the school, Kim switches subject to our upcoming tests.

However, Alicia is all that occupies my thoughts.

I keep thinking about something I read in a psychological thesis the other day.

Most if not all mental issues start at childhood.

I dislike umbrella terms that gather mental health problems, but that one stuck with me. The more I think about it, the more it rings true.

A person is formed of jigsaw pieces and if you want to really know anyone, then start at the pieces that formed his childhood. They're the base. Everything else is built on that.

Uncle Jaxon, for example, had a healthy childhood. Lawyer parents. Steady income. Football team player. He grew up into a stable, ambitious adult. It's his parents' expectations that set him out to be competitive.

Aunt Blair and Mum had a poor background and a violent father when he's on the liquor. Unlike Mum, Aunt left Birmingham as soon as she was eighteen. She worked hard for a scholarship so she could leave all that rubbish behind. She never returned to Birmingham until the accident that took my parents' lives. Her poor background pushed her to strive for perfection. Anything less is an insult to her intelligence.

No matter how much of a perfectionist she is, a bit of her childhood seeps into her adult version. She's hotheaded and resorts to yelling when she doesn't get what she wants.

Even subconsciously, she's replicating the violence her father exerted on her.

It's an endless vicious cycle.

I'm sure that Aiden's behaviour has something if not everything to do with his childhood.

Starting with Alicia. She's beginning to sound more and more like a mystery.

Stop.

I want to bleach my head. Why am I even bothering with him anymore?

Still, as Kim and I walk the hallway, I can't help searching for the jet black hair and those metallic eyes.

We arrive at our class. Cole and Ronan are in deep conversation. Or more like, Ronan is in a one-man show while Cole reads from a book.

Upon seeing us, Ronan grins. *"Bonjour, mes demoiselles."*

Cole nods in acknowledgement.

I smile back as I slide into my seat and bring out my notebook and pencils.

"Wanna party at my place?" Ronan waggles his eyebrows at me, the insinuation of what happened at his last party clear.

"Holy hell." Kim's whisper-yell draws my attention.

I follow her field of vision and my heart stops beating.

Aiden walks into the classroom with Silver hanging off his arm.

THIRTY-TWO

The world stops spinning.

My grip tightens around my pencil so hard, I'm surprised it doesn't snap in two.

Silver has her hand around Aiden's bicep. She's chatting so happily as if they are in some cliche teen drama. He offers her his dazzling smile that he flashed me forty-eight hours ago.

Something inside me breaks.

I can hear the sound, loud and final.

I can feel the remnants shattering. Piece by piece, they gather at the dark corners of my chest.

Aiden's silver eyes meet mine, gleaming with mock condescension.

I can almost imagine what he would've told me if he spoke.

I took your virginity and now I'm back where I belong.

Silver has a smug expression. I try not to look at her, the shiny blonde hair cascading to her shoulders, or the uniform pressed to perfection.

A king needs a queen, peasant.

Pressure builds behind my eyes, but I refuse to let them see the effects they have on me.

I refuse to let him see me cry again. I was stupid enough to show weakness before. Not anymore.

For once, Ronan is speechless. He keeps staring between Aiden and Silver then me as if he's in some freak show.

Cole glares at Silver then at Aiden before throwing me a sympathetic look.

"You're okay?" Kim whispers from behind me.

I smile and for some reason, I think it comes out convincing. "Can I borrow your notebook?"

Kim appears confused for a second.

I plead with her using my eyes.

Come on, help me out, Kim.

"Uh, yeah, sure." She fishes into her bag and hands me her notebook.

I open it in front of me and compare our notes from the last class. My hand is still tight around the pencil and my shoulders are crowding with tension, but I manage to keep my expression as cool as possible.

I'm not going to cry.

The bitch queen stops beside my desk. Since I don't raise my head, my view is constricted to her hand clutching Aiden's arm. Her nails are French-manicured and she smells of Chanel. She always smells and looks classy, and although I never felt an inferiority complex before, it hits me like a hurricane now.

My eyes drop to Aiden's Nike shoes. The pressed trousers and a hint of his clean scent. It brings memories of how he held me against his chest.

It was all a game.

A stupid, little game.

"Aww, are you crying, Frozen?" Silver taunts.

Of course, she wouldn't leave me in peace.

Although I know I shouldn't stoop down to Silver's level and indulge her, I won't let her walk all over me.

I wipe under my eyes with my middle finger then flash it to her with a smile. "Oops, my tears froze."

Ronan snorts and Cole's lips curve into what resembles a smile.

Silver's cheeks tint in red as she leans closer as if to intimidate me. "Remember what I told you the last time, peasant?"

"Oh, I'm sorry. Your words aren't important enough for me to remember."

"Hashtag burn," Ronan coughs.

Kim snorts.

"You little—" Silver opens her mouth to say more, but Mrs Stone walks into class.

"You're nothing," she hisses at my ear. "Know your place."

Aiden guides her away without a look in my direction.

Not a word.

Usually, he'd sit on my desk and try to charm me with his golden boy grins. He'd say, "Morning, sweetheart. Did you dream of me last night?"

He'd poke and probe me until the teacher comes into class. He'd talk dirty in my ear and watch me with amusement as I squirm and fight not to blush.

At first, it was an infuriating routine, but then I've gotten used to it. Hell, I might have looked forward to it, wondering what he'd say.

Why did he do all that if he planned to take it away? Is this some sort of punishment? Another one of his mindfucks?

I try to focus during class, especially since we have an upcoming test, but I can't.

My attention keeps drifting back to Aiden and Silver. They're sitting next to each other at the back, downright flirting. He flashes her his golden boy smiles and she slips him notes every now and then.

I wonder what she's telling him.

Find me after school.

Fuck me after school.

Let's make fun of Elsa.

Damn them both to the darkest pit of hell.

I'm not going to cry.

I focus back on Mrs Stone's monologue about the importance of literature. I'm fuming and my feet keep bouncing underneath the table.

Honestly? I only have myself to blame. I'm the stupid fly who fell into his well-crafted web. I'm the moth who knew it'd burn but went to the fire anyway.

In a thesis done by a Norwegian doctor I don't remember his name, he highlighted the male species behaviour about a pursuit. He mentioned that men lose a considerable amount of their drive once they score the sex part of the deal. The general hypothesis is that subconsciously, men still have the caveman nature.

They live for the chase and once they have what they want, they just lose interest.

I hated that thesis when I first came across it. It was the epitome of sexism and general hypothesis. But then, is it really wrong? It's proven time and again that the sense of safety can make men lazy in a relationship. That's why some of them cheat. They're always seeking that sense of thrill. The taboo of it.

When we learnt that the neighbour is divorcing her husband because of adultery, Aunt Blair said that most cheaters who later become in an official relationship don't last long. The strong desire they had was only because they were in a forbidden relationship.

It's all about the chase.

There's no denying that the chase turned Aiden on. My struggle gave him a challenge he needed to crack. A game he had to win.

He did everything to make me bend to his will and once he had me, his flame turned to ashes.

He got me out of his system and now he's done.

I'm not going to cry.

As soon as the bell rings, I stuff my things into my backpack and hurry to the washroom, ignoring Silver's shrill laughter.

I need to wash my hands.

No one talks to me or shoots bullying remarks in my direction. Seems that whatever brief thing I had with Aiden will keep the school off my back.

Yet, I don't feel happy.

I don't feel... anything.

For two years, I always had Aiden's attention. In some twisted way or another. But now it's like I don't even exist.

I'm not going to cry.

Something invisible crawls on my hands, and they feel so dirty inside and out.

I barge into the washroom and thrust my hand under the tap. I scrub them over and over. Between my fingers. Underneath my nails. I rub my palms, the back of my hand and even my wrists. I don't stop until my skin is red and stinging.

I stand in the washroom alone, the sound of water fills the empty silence.

As I stare at my red hands, the first tear falls on the side of my palm.

The second follows.

Then the third.

I sniffle, trying to hold back the tears as I did since Saturday.

Only this time, I can't fight the tide.

So I let it loose.

I promise myself that this is the last time I cry for Aiden King.

THIRTY-THREE

For the rest of the day, I try to pretend that Aiden and Silver don't exist.

But the thing about pretending? It's all about putting a cool mask on the outside and burning on the inside.

Every time I see Silver's arm draped around Aiden's, I itch to break it. I want to pound her face into the floor until she no longer breathes.

That's another scary thought.

I've been having too many scary thoughts lately. I'm probably backpedalling. To what. I don't know. I'm not even supposed to think I'm backpedalling. That would mean I admit having a worse state of mind and I'm rearing back to that.

I really need to see Dr Khan.

With heavy feet, I head to the pitch. I'm really not in the mood to share a practice space with Aiden.

I contemplated cutting school, but that would mean I'm running away.

And after the washroom episode, I promised myself to never cry or run away anymore.

My gaze strays to the pitch where some of the football team players are stretching. Aiden stands at the sideline talking to Silver. It's like he's honey and she's a bee. She wouldn't stop hanging off his arm like a parasite.

But is she a parasite if he keeps smiling at her like that?

If he keeps flirting with her?

He wrecks everything in his path with a smile on his face. Including my heart.

I want to play tough, to think I'll wake up tomorrow and he'll be in the past. But I'd only be fooling myself.

So I hide in the corner like a creep, having a pity party with myself. We still have fifteen minutes until practice. I already changed into my track clothes, but I'm dreading going down there. I don't even have Kim to keep me company.

Screw Aiden and his barbie doll. I won't run away.

The moment I straighten myself, I notice a shadow lurking in the back. I startle with a small gasp.

Cole sits under a plum tree, reading a book—*Nausea* by Jean-Paul Sartre.

My cheeks tint with red at the thought that he's seen me act like a coward for the past five minutes.

He's dressed in Elites' jersey and shorts. His hair is slightly wet as if he ran it under a faucet.

Aside from Aiden, Cole has always been the most mysterious. He's not talkative at all. I can count the number of times I heard his voice. He's usually the audience of Ronan's animated speeches and the most adult-like out of the four horsemen. That's probably why he's Elites' captain.

Cole never showed me malice or interest. He just exists as if passing through the school is a breeze in his life.

He's popular, but he's not a manwhore like Xander and Ronan. He's just… serene.

Now that I study him closely, he's quite handsome with long chestnut hair and dark green eyes like the forest after the rain. If I weren't so biased, I'd say he's even more good-looking than Aiden. His beauty is calm compared to Aiden's dangerous one.

He throws me a glance over his book. I can't help but smile at the image. He's reading Jean-Paul Sartre while he's in his football uniform.

"Is my book funny?" he asks with no maliciousness.

"I never thought athletes were interested in existentialism theories."

He raises a thick eyebrow. "Aren't you an athlete, too?"

"*Touché.* I should've said football players."

"Because we're so dumb?" There's still no threat in his tone. If anything, it's filled with mild curiosity.

"I didn't mean that." My cheeks tint. I don't want to come off judgemental.

"Well, we can be." He points at his book. "So what do you think about existentialism?"

I'm taken aback. He didn't ask what I know about it, but what I think about it. So he's sure I read about it. But then again, I wouldn't have associated Nausea and Sartre to existentialism if I didn't at least know something about it.

"Hmm." I lean back against the stone wall. "I believe it's a negative and a nihilistic philosophy."

His posture quirks up as if he's a kid given his favourite toy. "So you don't believe that existence precedes essence?"

"Not per se. It can be true to some extent, but the whole theory is hyper-individualist. A person isn't an entity that can't be touched or manipulated." I tip my chin.

Challenge that, mister. Your ace striker is a class one manipulator.

Cole seems smart. Probably to Aiden's level of high intelligence, but like Aiden, he doesn't show it.

I can bet money that he knows about Aiden's true character. I suspect Xander knows, too.

They couldn't possibly have known Aiden for all these years and not detect that something is wrong.

His brow quirks as he closes the book and lets it fall to his lap. "What if the person's lack of existentialism causes them to be a target of manipulation?"

I approach him and sit beside him on the grass. "Then do you believe those who manipulate have a sense of essence?"

He gives an easy smile. "Perhaps they suffer from an existential crisis, too."

"In that case, and according to the theory, people who manipulate can be manipulated. It's an endless circle."

"It is." He shakes the book in front of me. "You read this, yes?"

I nod, but I don't mention that the main character, Antoine, bored me with his existential crisis. He seemed very psychologically unwell and needed some psychotherapy. It doesn't help that I was never a fan of Jean-Paul Sartre's theory.

"Have you ever thought why Antoine Roquentin kept questioning his existence?" Cole asks.

"Because he's an existentialism freak and a self-insertion from Sartre."

He chuckles, the sound easy. "That's one way to look at it, but maybe you should read it again and search for some hidden clues."

Before I can say anything, he drops the book in my lap. "Aiden gave it to me, so keep it in good shape."

Aiden gave it to him? I never thought he'd be interested in philosophy, let alone existentialist theories.

Cole and I spend the next fifteen minutes discussing Sartre's work and some of his philosopher contemporaries. It's a heated conversation since Cole and I disagree on almost everything, but it manages to keep my head off what's happening at the pitch.

We switch to music, and I laugh when Cole says that he likes Coldplay. "At least we agree on that."

"At least your taste in music is better than your taste in philosophy."

"Hey!" I bump my shoulder against his.

Smiling, he hops to his feet and offers me his hand. "Come on. It's time for me to practice like a dumb athlete."

"You hold a grudge, don't you?" I take his hand.

"Me? Never."

"Try again, *Captain*."

He chuckles and so do I. The sound drifts in the secluded area around us. If I knew Cole would be such a good sport, I would've befriended him earlier.

Or not.

Cole belongs to Aiden's small circle and I never looked twice at them before.

"Am I interrupting something?"

Aiden stands near the brick wall I was leaning against earlier, arms crossed over his chest.

My heart skips a beat, no matter how much I hate it.

But that's the thing about hearts, isn't it? They can't help beating despite the pain.

I look around him, expecting to find Silver hanging off his arm like some puppet.

She's not here.

Aiden's eyes narrow on where I'm clutching Cole's hand. If looks could kill, we would be on fire now.

I should let Cole go and ignore Aiden, but screw him. He had the bitch queen hang off his arm all day. What right does he have to glare at me as if I'm doing the wrong thing?

"Yes, you are, actually," I say in a light tone. "Cole and I were having a good time until you showed up."

Cole raises an eyebrow, but he doesn't say anything. In fact, his lips quirk in amusement.

"Let her go, Nash," Aiden grinds out, his breathing turning harsher.

I grip Cole's hand tighter. He doesn't attempt to leave, either way.

"Elsa…" Aiden's voice drifts in clear menace. "Let go of that hand or—"

"Or what? What will you do now? Make me watch while you fuck Silver?" *Shut up, damn you.* I'm giving him ideas.

Before he can reply, I lift my chin in false bravado. "I can do the same if you're into voyeurism."

Aiden is in my face in a split second. I flinch back as my heartbeat picks up speed. Aiden looms over me like doom and glares down at me with flaring nostrils that might as well breathe fire.

In my stupefaction, I don't even realise that Cole has slipped his hand from mine.

"Don't be late for practice, King. You need to make up for your mess last game." Cole offers me a warm smile and disappears around the corner.

Aiden advances into me. I try to keep my ground, but it's impossible with all the demons swirling in his eyes.

I gulp past the lump in my throat. With every step he takes forward, I step back.

My shoulder blades hit the tree, and I wince.

Aiden leans his forearm on the tree above my head, caging me in. "Are you done playing, sweetheart?"

THIRTY-FOUR

Done playing?

Is this all that it is to him?

Are my heart and my body a bloody game?

The fury from earlier sweeps over me. My posture stiffens, but I keep my tone level when I speak.

"Actually no, Aiden. I'm not done playing. I think I'll take Xander up on his offer and become his girlfriend—for real this time. Then, there's Cole. I didn't realise he's so interesting and smart. Even Ronan is so charming. Choices, choices."

"Are you done?" Aiden's jaw is tight, but he manages to control whatever temper is trying to blaze through.

"I'm not done. You don't believe me, do you? Do you think I'm bluffing? I'll prove it to you."

He grips my arm with brute force. "You're not going *anywhere.*"

"Watch me."

I push at his stupid broad shoulders. I should know better than to use physical strength against him, but at this moment, I'm so worked up I can't think straight. He keeps me pinned to the tree with an effortless hand around my arm.

"Let me the fuck go," I pant with frustration.

"Never."

He says the word with so much conviction. So much... authority.

I stop and stare at him with what must look like an 'are you shitting me' expression.

"You already moved on, so let me do the same." My voice breaks and I clear my throat. "What the hell do you want from me anymore?"

I resist the pressure building behind my eyes.

I'm not going to cry.

"Do you honestly believe it's even possible to move on from you, sweetheart?" The strange mixture of tenderness and anger causes my heart to jump.

"Everyone at school saw you move on with Silver just fine."

"I don't care about everyone at school. The show was only meant for you."

"For me?" The bite of anger returns again. "Did I miss some memo that you should be parading with another girl after we had sex for the first time? Not to mention that you abandoned me after said sex."

Aiden's lips quirk in a victorious smile. "There. That's the reaction I've been hoping for."

"What?" I snap.

"You wanted this."

"*I* wanted this? Your manipulation game is strong but it's not strong enough to make me believe I wanted you on another girl's arms!"

"You wanted to have a choice. A real one." The grey of his eyes hardens to gunmetal. "So I gave you a chance to choose me. Your reply is three days late, but I'll take it."

My lips move to say something, but nothing comes out. I'm speechless.

After a few seconds—or minutes—of staring at his wrongfully beautiful face, I say, "Your way of giving me a choice is thrusting Silver in my face?"

"An encouragement."

I laugh without humour. As usual, he always makes the

choices swing in his direction. "Why Silver? Why not any other girl?"

"She threatens you."

"What?"

"It's subconscious, but I noticed that she's the only one you glare at. Even when she doesn't get in your way."

"Wow. I'm really speechless. You never play fair, do you?"

"Oh, but I did. I gave you the choice that you were itching for. If it were up to me, I wouldn't have left your side."

The heavy weight that's been perching on my chest since Saturday eases like a silent wave.

I'm still angry as hell at him, but he was giving me what I wanted—even if his method sucks.

"If you sent me a text or called me over the weekend, I wouldn't have resorted to this method." Aiden continues, not appearing the least bit apologetic. If anything, his left eye twitches as if he's pissed off. "You know patience was never my thing."

"What would have you done next with Silver? Date her? Kiss her? Fuck her? Maybe in the opposite order."

"Silver means fuck to me and she knows it." He lets go of my arm to palm both my cheeks. "You're the one who keeps me up all night."

"Screw you, Aiden." My words are muffled when his lips brush against mine.

A lump clogs my throat and a moan fights to escape. I fight back tears but this time it's for an entirely different reason.

It's like my heart has resurrected after being stabbed to death.

It's scary how Aiden controls my mood. I lost my body and my better judgement to him, and now my happiness seems to be controlled by him, too.

"If you go near Silver again, it's over, Aiden," I whisper near his mouth.

That earns me a glare. Aiden dislikes being threatened, but I need to draw the line there. It's not really about jealousy or pos-sessiveness—although part of it is true. But mostly, it's about my self worth. As much as I hate to admit it, Silver threatens me and I'll never allow him to make me feel like I did this morning.

"Don't say the word 'over' when we didn't even start."

"Then don't go near Silver. I mean it, Aiden. I'll never forgive cheating."

"I like your possessiveness, sweetheart." He places a teasing kiss on the corner of my mouth. "But will you be able to get over me?"

"I'd rather break my heart in pieces and step on the remains than be with you."

He pulls back enough to study my face with an indecipherable expression. "Noted."

"I want to trust you. I really do. But until then, I can't be in a relationship with you."

He narrows his eyes, but quickly lets it go. "I'll prove that you can trust me."

"You can trust me, too. I'll never cheat on you."

His expression darkens as if the mere word offends him. "I know you won't."

"What will you do if I somehow cheat?" I'm treading into a dangerous territory, but curiosity gets the better of me.

"Kill the bastard." No hesitation.

"How about me?"

He cups my jaw with false tenderness. "That's the difference between you and me, sweetheart. You'd leave me in a heartbeat if I cheat, but I'll never leave you even if you cheat."

It's a hypothetical situation, but it strikes a chord within me. I feel an overwhelming need to kiss him. Devour him. Just pluck him away and hide him from the world where I'm the only one who can look at him, touch him, and talk to him.

I won't be sharing his smiles with Silver or anyone else.

He seals his lips against mine, biting my bottom lip into his mouth and pulls away too fast. "Now, say it."

"Say what?" I pant.

"Say that you choose me."

"Isn't it obvious?"

"Say the words, Elsa."

My arms wrap around his neck and I graze the hairs at the back of his neck. "It's crazy, but I choose you, Aiden."

His mouth claims mine as his fingers grab a handful of my hair, releasing it from the band. His hand snakes under my arse and I lift myself, wrapping my legs around his lithe waist. I'm lost in the moment. In him. Everything seems to be moving way too fast and in a direction I don't recognise.

But I'm done pretending he means nothing. I'm done fighting against myself and the pull he has on me.

My fingers thread into his hair as I open up to him. His other hand grips my hip, pulling me against his hard muscles. My breasts crush into his chest and suddenly, I hate our clothes. I hate my tracksuit and his jersey. I hate that my skin can't be glued to his.

The need to engrave myself in him hits me again.

It's a strange, sporadic urge that overwhelms me and refuses to let go.

I rub my stomach against his growing erection. The sense of time and space escapes me in a heartbeat. In a moment, I picture us in a room. There's no one but the two of us in that room. It's quiet except for our harsh breathing.

Footsteps pound beyond the room's door. I continue kissing Aiden, not wanting to break the spell.

Something nags at the back of my mind. My limbs start to tremble and my shoulder blades stiffen with black, deep fear.

"He's coming," I whisper against Aiden's mouth.

The school's backyard comes back into focus, and Xander's blonde hair peeks from behind the corner. "Coach is after your arse, King."

Aiden's dark attention stays on me.

It's like he knows that I didn't mean Xander or anyone here when I said 'He's coming.'

THIRTY-FIVE

During practice, Aiden throws me grins every chance he gets. My cheeks flame at the attention he draws towards me.

Even the girls on the track team—who rarely talk to me—nudge me a few times. They were never mean to me, but they never bothered with me before either.

Once practice is over, I linger back and glance one last look at the football pitch.

I don't need to search for Aiden since he's running in my direction.

He has such breathtaking athletic ease when he runs. His form is taut, graceful, and full of so much confidence. He reaches me in a few seconds, his jet black hair sticking to his forehead with sweat and his breathing controlled.

Almost everyone in my immediate surrounding grows silent as if they're watching the show.

I fidget, feeling uncomfortable with all the attention. It's different from bullying, but it's attention all the same.

Being under the spotlight causes my skin to prickle, but since I've gotten involved with Aiden, I should've known that he comes with attention plastered all over him.

I clear my throat. "Nice game."

He tilts his head to the side. "If you replied two days ago, I would've had an actual nice official game and wouldn't have Coach breathing down my neck."

Okay. He's still salty about that.

His fingers brush a strand of my hair back. My skin tingles and I want to lean into his hand so bad, but the audience stops me.

"Meet me in the car park," he says.

"Why?"

He pinches my cheek. "Stop with the questions and meet me there."

I nod.

"King," Coach Larson calls from behind Aiden. "Locker room meeting. Now."

"Yes, Coach," Aiden calls back but he never takes his eyes off me. The pull between us is crazy and addictive. Despite the audience surrounding us, I'm lost in his smoky eyes. It's like he's able to erase the world just like I can.

He's a compelling type of madness.

Ronan clasps Aiden's shoulder from behind, shattering the moment. "Yo, King! Let's go to the meeting or Coach will make us do push-ups."

Aiden throws him a glare. "Push-ups are better than the grave I've been digging for you."

"I'm hurt. You better pay for the psychological damage." Ronan's eyes flick in my direction. "Tame the beast, Ellie."

I smile. "I don't think I can."

"Sure you can." Ronan waggles his eyebrows. Aiden elbows him and he howls in pain.

"Our friendship just gained an expiration date, King. The only way to save it is by letting me drive your car."

"Friendship over."

I burst into laughter as Ronan's eyes widen comically. "How about just an hour?"

"Over, Astor."

"Okay, a loop?" He nods at me and clasps his arm around Aiden's shoulder, guiding him away.

"Outside." Aiden mouths to me as Ronan drags him, spouting a monologue about friendship before whore cars.

I'm still smiling when I feel someone watching me—or glaring at me. I turn sideways, but the track team girls seem to have dreamy eyes more than anything.

After searching my surroundings, I spot Adam. He leans against the railing leading to the football team's locker room, staring at me.

Silver stands beside him. While Adam's gaze is unreadable, hers is full of contempt.

"Nevermind Silver." Tara, a member of the track team, interlaces her arm with mine. "She's just bitter that King will never look at her the way he looks at you."

Tara and I walk into the locker room. Like Kim, Tara has been an elite since she was a child. I think her father is a Knight, too. I often forget about her aristocratic title because Tara is the modest type.

"Silver wishes she was you," Tara continues.

"What do you mean?"

"She's been gunning after King since Royal Elite Junior, but he never really showed interest in her. Then you come along and he openly shows you off. She feels threatened."

"She's been gunning after him how?" So much for swearing to never get into this drama.

"In a territorial kind of way?" Tara taps her lower lip, seeming deep in thought. "It's weird, you know. I don't think she's even attracted to him, but she's been working to score him, anyway. The rumour is that she has a secret boyfriend, but is using King as a cover-up. Maybe she's dating a thug."

Or maybe she's dating Aiden or sleeping with him and the whole secret boyfriend deal is a deflection method.

Nope. Not going there. I promised to try trusting Aiden not two hours ago.

Tara keeps talking about the multiple rumours that circled around the school since Royal Elite Junior until now. I never had so much contact with Tara because we both keep to ourselves. I never thought she's so much into gossip.

Apparently, I've been missing out on half of what's happening at RES. Like the fact that Mr James, the previous rugby coach was fired for a complaint of harassment against one of his players. I thought he was transferred willingly. Tara doesn't know the player because the school's board made sure to keep everything under wraps.

There's also the fact that King, the father not the son, will be personally overlooking the football team's schedule. Tara says that he has friends in big teams of the Premier League and will be sending scouts over. I wonder if Aiden will pursue Football professionally like his cousin.

We're in the shower with only a thin, blurry glass wall separating us when Tara blurts, "Can I ask you something?"

"Sure." I apply the shampoo over my head and massage my skull.

"Don't take this the wrong way, Elsa. I hear a lot of rumours and I just want to know which is true and which is false."

I laugh. "No. I'm not really 'Frozen' if that's what you're asking."

"You kind of are, though."

"What do you mean?"

"You don't even know ninety per cent of the stuff that happens at RES. You don't care about anyone other than Kim. Everyone thinks you're…"

"Stuck up?"

"I was going to say a recluse?" There's an awkward smile in her voice.

"It's okay. I don't mind what everyone thinks. I'm only here because it's the perfect way to get to Cambridge." I want to tell her that being selected as a target on the first day at school didn't really warm me up to the students here, but I keep that to myself.

"That makes sense." She sounds thoughtful again. "Then the rumour about you and King can't be true, I guess."

"What rumour?" Once I'm done rinsing my hair, I towel it and wrap another towel around my torso.

Tara and I get out of our stalls at the same time. Her wet chestnut hair falls to a sleek bob around her round face as she ties the towel around her body.

The other girls are at the back, talking about their plans for the rest of the afternoon.

Tara approaches me and whispers, "Some say that you and King are old acquaintances and you hurt him. That's why he hated you the moment he first saw you at RES."

My heart jolts and picks up speed. The rumour makes perfect sense. If I weren't one thousand per cent sure that I met him that day for the first time, I would've believed it, too.

"I didn't know anyone in RES the day I came here," I tell her.

"I thought so, too. That means the second rumour is more correct."

"And that is?"

She lifts a shoulder. "He only targeted you because you were the new girl."

"I'm sure that's the right version."

After more gossip from Tara while we change our clothes, we part ways near the teachers' office. She has to talk to the swim team's coach about her younger brother's application who's a sophomore.

I visibly shudder when I pass by the pool area. Deep water stiffens my shoulder blades with fear, especially if it's dark and I can't make out my own limbs.

After a few panic attacks when I was younger, Uncle and Aunt quit taking me to the beach altogether. They always eliminated anything of discomfort from my immediate vicinity. I'm beyond thankful for the lengths they've been going through to make sure I live a comfortable life.

Speaking of which, while I walk to the car park, I retrieve my phone and open our chat room. I shoot them a message that I'm not heading straight home.

Aunt's reply is immediate.

Aunt B: Where to?

Elsa: Out with Kim.

I bite my lower lip. After the tension this morning, I would rather lie to her about Aiden.

At least until I figure out where we stand.

Uncle J: Have fun, pumpkin.

Aunt B: Promise you won't eat any junk food.

Elsa: Promise.

I shoot a message to Kim that I'm catching a ride with Aiden.

Kim: Ehhh with King? Weren't you guys fighting this morning? Isn't the bitch queen his date for the day?

Elsa: Long story.

Kim: Face time later. I need details!

Elsa: Kay.

Kim: And this better not be a rip off from a Korean drama where the BFF is always in the dark.

I send her a laughing emoji and promise to talk to her later.

Once I'm outside, the humid air cools the skin of my face. I spot Aiden waiting by his car. His uniform is dishevelled at best like he wore it in a hurry and he's fussing with his shoelace.

That strange awareness starts a war, slashing and clawing at my abdomen as I walk towards him. My steps are fast and silent as if I'm floating through the air.

This pull is terrifying.

He's terrifying.

Still, there's no fighting how much I want him close. Now, I know how moth feel when they fly to flames. The flames are worth the burn.

I stumble to a halt a small distance away and stifle a gasp with the back of my hands.

As he ties his shoelace, his uniform's trousers' rides up, revealing his skin. A deep circular scar surrounds his right ankle. It seems as old and as faded as the scars on his back and the underside of his forearm.

What on earth happened to him?

Something light hits my shoulder. I jump up with a small yelp.

Cole comes into view. "Sorry, I didn't mean to startle you."

"No. I'm fine." I look around him to Aiden who's already straightened up and is heading in our direction.

Cole opens the outer pocket of my backpack and slips Jean-Paul Sartre's Nausea. "You forgot this."

I smile. "Didn't anyone tell you that you shouldn't open a girl's bag?"

His lips twitch. "I'll remember that next time."

"There'll be no next time." Aiden stands beside me, surrounds my waist with a strong hand and pulls me into the curve of his body.

"That depends on how you act from now on, King." Cole sounds half teasing, half-serious before he gives me a knowing look.

"I agree with that," I say.

"Tell me, Nash. Do you want your grave next to Knight's or Astor's?" Aiden's face is dead serious as he speaks.

"I prefer to not have a grave yet." Cole smiles at me.

"Then stop threatening what's mine."

"I will when you do."

My gaze bounces between Aiden and Cole. Unlike the war of gazes he's had with Xander the other time, Cole appears completely nonchalant. However, I can sense the tension in the air. It's like a cool sheen over my skin, threatening to explode any second.

This is odd. Aiden and Cole don't strike me as the fighting type. They have the most laid back relationship in the group.

Movement catches my attention. Silver stomps in our direction, her cheeks red and nostrils flaring.

I sigh. She'll ruin my mood if I face her.

"Take care of her," Aiden tells Cole in a calm tone as if they've dealt with this before.

"On it." Cole's cool expression disappears. His features tighten as he goes to intercept Silver.

I don't get to watch what's happening since Aiden guides me to the passenger seat of his car. I don't hear Silver and Cole, but I see her screaming at him. She doesn't spare Aiden a glance. Instead, she cuts me a glare before she starts pushing at Cole's chest.

He keeps her at arm's length, his expression still as tight as earlier. Silver continues struggling against him.

Cole leans in and says something in her ear. Just like that, Silver goes limp against him, eyes widened. He takes the chance to drag her out of the car park. Or maybe he's taking her to his or her car. I can't tell for sure since they're out of my field of vision.

"What was that all about?" I ask Aiden once he's seated in the driver's seat.

"Nothing important."

"Do you always have Cole take care of your girl problems?"

He gives me an 'are you serious' look. "No one can make Nash do anything he doesn't want to do."

"Not even you?"

"Not even me." He pauses. "Besides, Silver is his step-sister. He knows how to deal with her best."

"His… what?"

"His mother and her father are getting married."

Woah. I must be really out of it when it comes to school news. I knew Silver's parents were divorced, but I didn't know she was going to be Cole's step-sister. They have completely different personalities. I wonder how that will go.

The engine revs to life, and I clench my thighs at the vibrations. It's such a strange, thrilling sensation.

Aiden's lips pull in a mischievous grin. "You like that, don't you?"

"I don't."

"Sure thing, sweetheart," he says with a mocking edge.

Dickhead.

As we weave out of the car park, Aiden threads his fingers through mine, and places our intertwined hands on his hard thigh.

My breathing cracks at the amount of tenderness in his touch. It's almost… normal. His side profile oozes so much masculine beauty. Tingles start between my legs and the engine's vibrations don't help.

"Where are we going?" I ask to distract myself from ogling him.

"You'll see."

I narrow my eyes. "Where to, Aiden?"

"Not to a slaughterhouse. I won't go all serial killer on you."

I can't help but laugh. He winks, squeezing my fingers in his.

"By the way," He glances at me. "Why don't you come to Elites' games?"

"Eh… I don't go to school games."

He raises an eyebrow. "You only go to Premier League games, Miss Snob?"

"No. It's…" I want to say I don't like Elites, but that would be a lie. I hated them before, but now, I have no reason to.

"If you come to a game, I'll take you somewhere special."

"Where?"

"You'll have to agree first."

"Why do you even want me to come? Your Instagram stalkers aren't enough?"

His grin widens. "If you know about them, then you must've been stalking me, too."

My cheeks heat. "That's not true."

"Hmm. You're one of those silent stalkers, aren't you?" he continues in a contemplative tone. "You stalk all the time without liking or commenting as if you're a ghost."

"You're so full of yourself."

"Silent stalkers are the scariest." He throws me an amused gleam. "Do you fantasise about me, sweetheart?"

Yes. But screw him.

"Are you going to tell me where we're going?" I sulk.

"A place you'll love."

THIRTY-SIX

Turns out the place I'll love is Arsenal.

No shit. Freaking *Arsenal*.

And I'm not talking about watching practice like the rest of the fans. As soon as the players headed inside, Aiden guided me to the locker room. I stood there like a gaping idiot as I stared at my favourite players. Alexandre Lacazette. Maitland-Niles. Monreal. Levi King. Freaking *Ozil*.

Then I got out of my stupor and asked to take selfies with as many of them as possible—including Coach Emery.

I stare in a stupor at the picture while Aiden and I sit for an early dinner. We're in the same coffee shop-restaurant as the other time. There's some indistinct chatter coming from downstairs. It's quiet at the top level. Only the older gentleman from the other time sits near the window, reading a book, and sipping from his coffee.

My fingers flick over my phone. I can't believe I smiled like a normal human being and didn't actually lick the guys. Ozil even had an arm over my shoulder.

"Uncle will be sooo jealous when I show him these." I absentmindedly sip from my orange juice. "I'm so going to gloat about meeting my idols."

"Are you done?" Aiden doesn't sound amused. He's been in a pissy mood since he practically dragged me out of the locker room.

I peel my gaze from the phone to him. He removed his RES

DEVIANT KING | 295

jacket, remaining in the white T-shirt with his cuffs rolled to his elbows. The view of his strong forearms and the tattoos gets me every time. He's stuffing French fries in his mouth and glaring at my phone.

He doesn't seem impressed with my enthusiasm, but I smile at him anyway. Meeting Arsenal's players is such a geeky moment in my life. I didn't even think it was possible unless I hoard in front of the stadium for years and hope to catch a picture.

However, with the right connections and the King last name, anything can be possible. Aiden said Arsenal's president is a family friend. Of course, he is. Otherwise, Aiden wouldn't have been able to waltz me right into the team's locker room.

"Thanks for taking me there," I say. "It made my day. No, my year!"

He grunts in response and continues shoving French fries down his throat. "Stop staring at your phone and eat. You haven't touched your food."

"*Oookay*. You sound just like Aunt." I place my phone on the table and dive into my salad. "What are you so upset about?"

"Are you acting like you don't know?"

"Uh… not really? You seem to have your knickers in a twist since the locker room."

"Don't idolise other men in front of me. I don't like it."

A burst of laughter slips from my throat. "Are you jealous, mighty King?"

"Damn straight I'm jealous. I'm so possessive of you, it drives me fucking crazy."

I bite back a grin and try to stuff it with a forkful of salad. Is it so wrong that I love driving him crazy? I'm getting high on this feeling and like any junkie, I want more.

"Is that why you punched Xander and threatened Cole?"

He pauses eating, eyes squinting the slightest bit before he flashes me the devil's threatening smile. "Do you think it's fun to antagonise me?"

"I don't know what you're talking about."

"Is that why you pulled that show with Nash earlier?"

"Cole and I were discussing philosophical theories."

"Like?"

My head tilts. Cole said that Sartre's book, Nausea, belongs to Aiden.

I still don't think he's the type who'd be interested in philosophy.

"Existentialism," I say. "Ever heard of it?"

"Boring and illogical. Next?"

I play with my fork on the plate. If he thinks it's boring and illogical, he wouldn't have kept a copy of Nausea. I sure as hell returned mine to the library as soon as I was finished with it.

"Have you ever read any book by Jean-Paul Sartre?" I prompt.

"A few." He's quiet for a long time that I think he's done talking. "My mother had a thing for French philosophers."

What happened to her?

The question hovers at the tip of my tongue, but I doubt that he'll answer it, and I don't want to sound pushy, so I ask, "What else did she like?"

"Me." He smiles, seeming lost in his own thoughts. "I think I'm the only person she liked."

"How about your father?"

"Maybe at some point, but I never witnessed it. She dissociated from Jonathan as much as he dissociated from her. His work came first. His brother, Lev and I came second. She was always last."

My heart aches at an image of a young Aiden and his mum being ignored by his father for work. But at that time, he at least had his mother. Maybe his transformation started after he lost her. Which means that I'm right to assume Alicia King's death played a significant role in shaping his deviant personality.

"I understand what it means to have workaholic parents," I say sympathetically.

"Your real parents were workaholics?"

"I don't know." A slash of pain grips me whenever they're

mentioned. Maybe this is also how Aiden feels when he talks about his mother.

"What do you mean you don't know?"

"I told you, I don't remember my life prior to the fire. The only parents I remember are Aunt Blair and Uncle Jaxon."

A contemplative look looms over his features. It disappears so fast that I wouldn't have noticed it if I weren't watching him so intently. "I see."

"It sucks to have workaholic parents."

He lifts a shoulder. "Not really. Jonathan can be workaholic all he likes. I'm leaving for college anyway."

I chew on the salad before speaking. "Are you going to pursue football professionally?"

He laughs and it's the sexiest sound I've ever heard. "You truly think Jonathan King will allow his only son to be a football player?"

"But he let your cousin."

"On the condition that he simultaneously studies at a university."

"Oh."

"I like football, but it was never my endgame. It's a short career and is insignificant in the great scheme of things. Jonathan and I agree on that."

I go back to picking at my food. "Then what are your plans for college?"

"Oxford." He appears bored.

My fork stills against the plate. Invisible hands grip my chest. Why does knowing that we'll be on different sides of the country hurt so much?

I force a smile. "Wow. You really need to work hard for that."

"Why do you think I stay in the top five per cent?" He winks.

Sometimes, I forget that he's one of the top students in RES. "Does your father throw a word with the teachers?"

"My father doesn't need to throw any word. They'd do it on their own." He sips from his cola. "I don't need the push, though. I can get the grades."

"Really?" I sound as suspicious as I feel. "I don't see you study even during the finals."

He chuckles, eyes glinting with mischief. "You *are* stalking me."

"I'm just saying that those in the top ten per cent care more about their grades than you do."

"That's because you guys work hard instead of working smart. What will slaving for grades give you?"

"I don't know." I mock. "Good universities?"

"And then what? Elite jobs. An expensive house in an upper-class neighbourhood. German cars. Wife. Kids. The whole cliché. What after?"

He seems bored with the whole list, but then again, why wouldn't he? Since his birth, he already knows he'll have it all without making any effort. He was destined to be King Enterprises heir.

Someone else might've felt the pressure, but Aiden is the opposite. He lives for challenges, so the whole mapped out future must look so dull in his eyes.

"If it were up to you, what would you have done?" I ask.

He lifts his head abruptly as if he's been taken by surprise, then grins. "Kidnap you into my cave."

"I'm serious." I hit his leg underneath the table and take a sip of water to soothe my dry throat.

"I'm also serious. You're the only thing that breaks the endless vicious cycle."

I choke on the water and it splatters all around the table and my jacket.

Aiden laughs and offers me a napkin. "Jesus."

Instead of giving me the napkin, he reaches over and wipes my cheeks and around my mouth while I stare at him.

Somewhere in between, the napkin slips away and he grazes my cheeks with his fingers. Then he dips them down to my bottom lip, tracing them with the tip of his fingers as his smouldering gaze devours my mouth.

Each stroke is like a lightning bolt to my aching core. My thighs clench in a futile attempt to chase away the throb.

"Aiden…"

"Hmm, sweetheart?" His attention never leaves my lips.

"We're in public." My whisper is barely audible over the erratic beat of my heart.

"I'm not even kissing you," he says in a slightly husky tone. "I'm only wiping away the water ever so innocently."

Yeah, right.

I try to control my breathing and fail. "Nothing about you is innocent."

"But there's so much innocence about you, sweetheart." He leans in to whisper in hot sultry words. "And I'm tempted to tarnish it."

That should scare me, and maybe it would have a few weeks ago, but now, I can only feel myself falling harder and faster than anyone should. My nipples tighten and I'm so glad that the uniform's jacket is thick enough to conceal my reaction to him and his words.

Something flashes in my peripheral vision. My head snaps to the window, but there's no one there except for the man who's still reading from his book and sipping his coffee.

"What is it?" Aiden puts two fingers under my chin and turns me back to face him.

"I swear someone was watching us just now."

"I would've seen them. No one is out there."

"I must be imagining things." I stand up, still trying to fight the throb between my thighs. "I'm going to the washroom."

I leave before Aiden makes me sit on his lap or something crazier.

In the empty washroom, I remove my jacket and put it under the hand dryer.

I'm not even a minute in when the door to the washroom clicks opens.

I feel him before I see him.

Or maybe it's because of his distinctive clean scent mixed with his unique body odour.

The hand dryer's sound cuts off when I remove my jacket and face Aiden.

He leans against the closed door and reaches behind his back to lock it. The pitch-black look in his eyes starts a riot at the bottom of my stomach.

"What are you doing?" I whisper as if someone can hear us.

He abandons the door and strides towards me with sure, wide steps.

My heart flutters, and my nails dig into the jacket. "This is the ladies' —"

My words die in my throat when his lips crush to mine in an all-consuming kiss. It's hard and angsty and so passionate. The jacket slips from my hands and falls to the counter.

My back hits the wall with a thud. It's painful and delicious at the same time.

Aiden places both hands under my arse and lifts me against the wall. My legs wrap around his waist and my soft curves clash against his hard muscles like it always belonged there.

Like it's a blasphemy that we didn't do this before.

"Aiden…" I try to argue, but he wraps a hand around my throat and kisses me savagely, nipping at my bottom lip, and killing any protest I have.

Screw public places.

Screw everything.

"You don't idiolise other men in front of me and expect me to do nothing about it," he grunts, biting my lip. "You're lucky I didn't fuck you in front of them."

His tongue thrusts inside and I let him. My fingers thread into his hair and I let him consume me.

Own me.

Ruin me.

I don't care anymore as long as he makes me feel this consuming passion.

"You're fucking everything up," he says roughly before claiming my lips again while yanking my skirt up to my waist.

I try to help with his belt but it's awkward with this position. To my defence, I never had sex against the wall in a public washroom.

Aiden lets go of my throat. He yanks down both his trousers and his boxers with one hand and shoves my underwear down with the other.

I grind against his erection, chasing the throb between my shaking thighs. I wrap my arms around his neck, my movements turning frantic and uncoordinated.

"Fuck me, Aiden."

His face morphs in surprise before he curses. His features tighten with furious lust and something else I can't figure out.

"Fuck, Elsa." He slams inside me in one agonising go.

I shriek but he swallows the sound with his mouth against mine.

The harsh, unyielding strokes of his tongue match the maddening rhythm of his thrusts.

My limbs go into a puddle and my heart almost leaps out of my chest.

The threat of someone walking in on us doesn't water down my wild need for him. If anything, it makes it even more animalistic and out of control.

I don't last long. I *can't*.

When he wraps a hand around my throat and squeezes, I come hard. I bite Aiden's shoulder to muffle the hoarse scream.

Aiden grunts against my neck, sucking on the skin, as he spills inside me.

We're locked around each other against the washroom's wall. Our breaths come in and out in a frenzy and the air mingles with the scent of us.

I can't believe I just had sex in a public place.

I smile, a genuine happy smile.

I never felt so alive.

THIRTY-SEVEN

Weeks pass and with each passing day, I wander deeper into Aiden's maze.

It's not bad. It's just… surreal.

Everyone has demons. Aiden's are just darker and meaner.

It takes a lot to get used to his mindfuckery and manipulative streak. It takes a lot to see past the façade and into his true image.

For one, Aiden is the jealous type. When we sit for lunch, his teammates try to keep all contact to a minimum. All except for the three horsemen—especially Xander. I swear he doesn't have any sense of self-preservation.

The three of them are actually fun to hang out with. They're the only people around Aiden who aren't scared of him and who don't bow down to his royal decrees like the rest of RES.

Aiden carries my books as we get out of the library. A few students stop and murmur about us in the hallway, but I'm starting to get used to the attention.

His phone vibrates and since he has his hands filled with books, I sigh and retrieve it from his back pocket for him. "I can carry my own books, you know."

He arches a teasing eyebrow. "If you do, you won't touch me inappropriately at school like now."

"Stop it." I remove my hand from his trousers with heated cheeks. It's a jab at me because last week after practice, I snuck with him to a dark corner near the locker rooms. At that time, I only meant to kiss him. That kiss ended up with me against the wall and him pounding inside me and muffling my screams with a hand to my mouth.

My body tingles in remembrance. There's something about having sex with him. It's never enough.

His lips quirk in that infuriating smile. "What? You're thinking about it."

I shake my head and my eyes fall on the screen of his phone. What the…?

It's locked but since it's a text, I'm able to see it.

Jaxon: Thanks for the tickets, son. Go, Gunners.

It can be a different Jaxon who also loves Arsenal and is thanking Aiden for the tickets.

But it's very unlikely.

I stop at the corner of the hallway and thrust the phone in Aiden's face. "Since when are you communicating with Uncle behind my back?"

"You make it sound like some sort of a conspiracy."

"Are you telling me it isn't?"

"It isn't. He loves Arsenal, and I have backstage tickets."

I narrow my eyes. "Stop trying to take my family away."

"I'm only being a good sport so he'd approve of me."

Uncle approves of him all right. While Aunt is still sceptical and continues reminding me that my studies come first, Uncle is all over Aiden whenever he drives me home. He even invites him for dinners and breakfasts with us.

And since Aiden is opportunistic, he jumps all over any invitation he gets. If I'm not lying to myself, I'd admit that having him in my space is fun.

Kim says he's making an effort for me, and maybe she's right.

I'm just scared that if I let go completely, he'll swallow me whole.

That's why I haven't attempted to make what we have official.

We're exclusive, but we're not really dating in the conventional term.

"You're incurable," I huff.

Still holding the books, Aiden backs me up so my shoulder blades hit the wall. He lowers his head until his warm breath draws shivers on my skin. His voice is low and raspy when he says, "There's nothing I wouldn't do to have you, sweetheart."

"Nothing?"

"Absolutely nothing."

The thought should be scary, but I'm feeling anything but scared right now. I tiptoe and plant a chaste kiss on his cheek. Before he can deepen it, I duck and escape.

There's no way I'd let him kiss me in the school's hallways.

I'm giggling as I run down the hall. My head collides against a torso. I fall on my arse and pain explodes in my hipbone.

Ow.

Adam looks down at me with a glare. "Watch where you're going."

He throws one last malicious stare before he stalks off.

I stand up and dust off my skirt just in time for Aiden to catch up with me.

One look at me and his playful expression disappears. "What's wrong?"

"Nothing." If Aiden knows, he'll do something unpredictable and I really don't want any trouble now.

Not when both of us need a clean record to get into Cambridge and Oxford.

"By the way," he says. "You still haven't come to one of my games."

He keeps reminding me of that fact. It's silly, really, but I want to keep some things from him. Like not going to his games. Not following him back on Instagram—although I stalk it all the time.

I feel like those little things will keep me dependant.

I check my watch. "I have an appointment with my doctor."

He narrows his eyes. "I'll pick you up after practice."

I suppress a nervous smile and nod. Today, we're watching the Champions League game in his house with the guys.

Kim agreed to join us, and I hugged her until she called me a creep.

It's the first time I'm going to Aiden's house.

He's always eating at my house, sneaking into my room, and spending nights in my bed when Aunt and Uncle are caught up in work.

What's so hard about going to his palace-like house and meeting his father, the mighty Jonathan King?

Nothing... right?

THIRTY-EIGHT

Being back in Dr Khan's office after more than a year of interrupting my therapy is weird, to say the least.

The office is white without anything distinctive other than the wall-length library opposite us. The lack of paintings or objects is on purpose to not distract patients and to keep their minds as open as the white walls. Or at least that's what Dr Khan told me when I asked him a while back.

He's sitting on the brown, leather chair with a notepad in hand while I lie down on the recliner chair.

Dr Imran Khan—who I learnt is the same name of a Bollywood actor—is a small-built man in his mid-fifties. His salt-and-pepper hair is more salt than pepper now compared to when I first met him ten years ago.

His skin is tanned but is considered light compared to others with Pakistani heritage.

"I'm happy you decided to return, Elsa." His tone is welcoming and he looks genuinely happy to have me back on his recliner chair.

"Mr Quinn mentioned trouble with stress for exams." His kind but piercing brown eyes focus on me. "What do you think is the cause of that stress?"

"It's senior year and the pressure is real." It's not a lie, but it's not the reason I'm here either.

Dr Khan bites it. His eyes fill with what I call detached care.

I think that's what makes him perfect at his job. He has the ability to empathise but not let his patients' feelings rub off on him.

He jots down a note. Another thing about Dr Khan is his traditional methods. He doesn't use recordings much.

"Has there been anything triggering lately?" he asks.

"Yes." I shift against the leather and it squeaks in the deafening silence of the room. "I've been having nightmares about you hypnotising me, Dr Khan."

His pen pauses on the notepad and his shoulders tense. That's all the answer I need. It hasn't been a play of my imagination.

Dr Khan recovers fast. "Why do you think you had such a nightmare, Elsa?"

I sit up, the leather squeaking, and face him. "It's not a nightmare. It's the truth."

He opens his mouth to say something, but I hold up a hand.

"I'm not blaming you, Dr Khan. I know you have two thesis, one in psychotherapy and the other in hypnotherapy so it's not like you're doing anything illegal. I also know that Aunt and Uncle probably made you do it, but I need to know why."

He shuffles his notebook as if he's about to stand up. "Perhaps we should call your guardian and —"

"Soho Miller," I cut him off. "He's the reason why you don't practice hypnotherapy anymore. After you helped him restore his memories, he committed suicide."

Dr Khan's eyes fill with what resembles sadness, and I know I struck a chord. I did my research before coming here.

"I'm not Soho," I puff my chest. "I'm not suicidal either. I promise to stay alive if you promise to not have Aunt and Uncle involved in this. They're hiding something from me and I need to know why."

"Soho also said something similar," He sighs and the wrinkles around his eyes ease. "He begged me to know who he was before losing his memories. When he remembered he was behind the accident that killed his wife and children, he couldn't handle the truth and took his life."

"I'm not him. I can handle the truth." My tone turns pleading. "I just want to know what Aunt and Uncle called you for."

He slouches in his chair but keeps his posture uptight. "When your guardians first contacted me, you had violent episodes of screaming and falling in and out of consciousness."

I straighten, my hands turn clammy in my lap. "Like my nightmares?"

"Your nightmares are a manifestation of your subconscious. When you were a child, your consciousness was filled with nightmares. You were traumatised and in severe shock due to the fire."

"And?"

"And I used regression, a hypnosis method, to help resolve past traumas."

"Are you saying that Aunt and Uncle asked you to erase all my memories up to the fire?"

A sense of betrayal fills my chest at the thought of them doing something like that behind my back. They violated my mind. So what if they're my guardians? That doesn't give them the right to erase my past.

"Your aunt and uncle only called me to reduce the anxiety because they heard hypnosis helps." He appears nostalgic. "They were desperate, especially your aunt. She looked ready to do anything to chase away your pain."

"So what? Did you erase everything behind their backs?"

"No, Elsa." Dr Khan gives me a quizzical stare. "I didn't erase your memories. You did."

THIRTY-NINE

My head won't stop spinning after I exit Dr Khan's office. I still can't wrap my mind around the last thing he said.

I only put you in a stance to resolve your traumatic experience, but when you woke up, your memories were gone.

My child version's solution was to erase everything. Dr Khan said that sometimes when things are too much, the brain can resort to skipping over the traumatic parts. Suppressing memories becomes a vital need, not an option.

I was mentally and physically all over the place after the fire.

I entwine my fingers together as I walk down the hallway. Did I do the right thing?

How about Aunt and Uncle, then? They hid this truth from me for ten years. I doubt they would've told me anything if I didn't put two and two together.

I can't say I blame them, though. Since they swept me off from Birmingham, Aunt and Uncle did everything to protect me—to the point of overkill, sometimes.

Dr Khan said I needed to think carefully about restoring my memories. It's a one-way road. He didn't guarantee anything, but he can get me into a regression mode and help me access places in my subconscious that my consciousness isn't even aware of.

When I came here, I was so sure that I wanted my memories back. However, after the story about Dr Khan's other patient,

Soho Miller, I'm not sure anymore. What if, like him, I open Pandora's Box and discover things I'm not supposed to?

Besides, do I really want to relive my parents' death? I shudder at the thought.

My hands itch, and the urge to wash them swipes over me. With jerky fingers, I open the small pocket in my backpack and retrieve my hand sanitiser. I pour half the bottle in my palm and scrub all over until it's dried.

I release a breath when the itch slowly withers away.

Pocketing the hand sanitiser, I exit the building. I stumble to a halt on the pavement. Aiden's car is parked across the street and he's standing by the driver door talking to a familiar blonde-haired barbie doll.

Silver.

My nostrils flare and a violent rush shoots through my veins.

I stride across the street, trying not to break into a run.

Silver isn't known to lose her cool. She's pretty much the female version of Aiden. But right now, her hands fly all around her.

Aiden, on the other hand, appears bored. That should water down the fury bubbling through me, but it doesn't. The fact that he's even talking to her when he was supposed to pick me up sullies my mood. Did she come with him or something?

Facing Silver is really not what I want to do after the life changing talk I just had with Dr Khan, but if that's what she wants, that's what she'll get.

"You promised, King." She hisses.

"I said I'll think about it," he says.

"You don't get to escape this," she grinds her teeth.

"Escape what?" I stand right at her back.

She jumps up and Aiden whips his head towards me. It's like I've caught them off guard.

A frown etches between his eyebrows, but there's no trace of guilt.

But then again, Aiden doesn't do guilt.

"Make a noise, would you?" Silver cuts me a glare over her shoulder. "Creep."

What is she talking about? I'm pretty sure I made a sound when I approached them.

Right?

"What are you doing here?" I meet her haughty gaze with one of my own.

"I don't answer to you, bitch."

"Watch it, Queens," Aiden warns.

"Oh, so now that you're dipping your dick in her, I should watch it? Is that it?" She places a hand on her hip as she faces me. "How does it feel to have leftovers, Frozen?"

I've had enough of Silver and her bitchiness. I've had enough of everyone controlling my life or humiliating me while I choose to be the better person.

I. Have. Had. *Enough*.

Aiden steps forward, but I act first.

My hand shoots up and I grab a handful of Silver's hair. She shrieks as I tug her head back so I'm staring down at her.

The expression on my face must be scarier than the tug because Silver's lips clamp shut and her face contorts.

"If you throw one more snide remark my way, I'll fucking kill you. I'll cut you from limb to limb and bury you in the back garden." I smile. "And stay away from Aiden."

There's a need to hurt her. To stab her. To see her bleed —

Steel blood runs through your veins, Princess.

You're my masterpiece.

My legacy.

As if the words burn, I let Silver go with a shove.

She stumbles forward, massaging her scalp. "Crazy bitch."

"Leave, Queens." Aiden's voice is tight, but I'm not hearing him properly. Those haunting words keep playing at the back of my head.

Steel blood. Princess. Masterpiece. Legacy.

I'm too caught up in my own thoughts that I don't notice Silver charging at me.

Aiden steps between us, facing her. "*Leave.*"

"This isn't over." She wiggles a finger my way then turns to Aiden. "You, too, King. It's far from over."

Silver disappears around the corner or down the street, I'm not paying her attention.

"What happened just now?" Aiden stands in front of me and lifts my chin with his thumb and forefinger so I'm staring at his hooded grey eyes.

I'm scared he'll see the disorientation or whatever demon took over my body earlier. I legit wanted to hurt someone, and if I didn't have that flashback, I might have bashed Silver's head against the pavement.

That's scary.

I'm *not* like that.

Instead of thinking about my decimation, I direct my anger at Aiden. "What was she doing here? You're picking me up with your ex by your side?"

"I didn't come with her and she's not my ex."

"Yeah, right. Could've fooled me."

"I never dated Silver."

"So you just fucked her?"

He grits his teeth but doesn't say anything.

"Oh my God, you did." I think I'm going to throw up.

"It's complicated."

"There's nothing complicated about a dick in a vagina, Aiden. Either you stick it in there or you don't."

An old lady passing by gives me a look of dismay. Under different circumstances, I would've been embarrassed but right now, I'm too livid to care that I'm causing a scene.

Aiden backs me into his car and shoves me into the passenger seat before he takes the driver's seat.

The door slams behind him so hard, I would've winced if it weren't for the pent up, energy swirling around my head.

"I told you that if you have anything with Silver, we're done." I fight off the angry tears trying to push through.

"Even if we had anything, it was in the past."

Aiden's devil peeks his head through his metallic eyes. The fact that he's talking calmly makes me want to smash his head in.

"So you did have something."

"Yes, we did. I fucked her and I loved it so much that I dumped her." He rolls his eyes. "What's wrong with you today?"

"Why was she talking to you? What did she want?"

"Piss me off. And by your attitude, she succeeded."

I inhale a sharp breath. Maybe I'm being over the top. Damn it. Now that the haze is slowly dissipating, everything seems absurd. Aside from the fact that I loathe Silver. If I see her claws near Aiden again, I don't know what I'll do.

Looks like he's not the only caveman around.

Aiden's face is closed off and his left eye twitches. I open my mouth to say something but come out with nothing and close it again.

He doesn't spare me a glance as he starts the engine and weaves down the streets. This time, the vibrations don't give me the usual thrill. I hug the backpack to my chest as I stare at Aiden's solemn features.

The entire ride is spent in tomb silence. He doesn't hold my hand and place it on his thigh as he usually does and he doesn't glance at me.

He must be truly pissed off.

I spend all the way, trying to find the right words to say. I can't actually apologise since I didn't do anything wrong. But one thing for certain, I hate the tension between us. It reminds me of those awful days when we were on an invisible battlefield.

The Ferrari rolls in front of a mansion—no, a palace.

I forgot that we're watching the game at his house.

I reach a tentative hand to his that's still gripped around the steering wheel. "Aiden, I —"

A loud bang hits the roof of the car and Ronan sticks his head inside from Aiden's open windows. "Come on, bitches, the game starts soon."

He continues hitting the roof of the car with a ball. He really has the worst timing.

Aiden flings the door open and exits without a glance.

FORTY

The King's mansion falls on a large piece of land, it's impossible to see the end of it.

Three-storeys high, the house stretches horizontally like a palace. There are even two towers on each side and the entire structure appears old. I wouldn't be surprised if this was a noble's estate before. There must've been renovations, though, because all floors are filled with huge glass windows. Sometimes, glass takes more space than walls. It's like a glasshouse.

A fountain rests not far from the entrance. A sad angel ceramic statue pours water from a jar. A woman dressed like the Virgin Mary holds him with a tear sliding down her cheek.

What a strange image to have at the entrance of a house.

Aiden doesn't wait for me and disappears inside. Ronan, however, falls behind. At least someone has the decency to not leave me alone on my first visit here.

I pull my phone and text Kim.

Elsa: Are you here yet?

Kim: Coming. Just finishing up orgasming.

My lips hang open and I cast a glance at Ronan, hoping he didn't see.

A shit-eating grin greets me.

"Tell her to take all the time she needs." He waggles his eyebrows. "I'm available if she needs a hand."

"Eww."

"What?" He jokes. "If she's texting while finishing up her orgasm then she's not doing a good job. I can teach."

"Keep your teachings to your horde of admirers, Ronan."

"Just trying to be a good sport." He grins and I can see why the girls at RES melt for him faster than cheese on pizza. His ruffled handsome looks are primary reasons, but it's his charming nature and outgoing personality that makes him so desirable.

Ronan and Xander are more approachable than Aiden and Cole.

And more playful, too.

My phone vibrates again.

Kim: Shit! ORGANISING, not ORGASMING. Stupid autocorrect.

I laugh and thrust the text in Ronan's face. "Happy now?"

"No." He genuinely appears disappointed and I laugh harder. He opens the door for me. "My offer still stands, though."

"You're an animal."

We continue bickering on the way inside. A butler who appears as old as Bruce Wayne bows in greeting upon seeing us. He's wearing a butler outfit all complete with white gloves and a white napkin dangling from his arm.

I bow back while Ronan nods in acknowledgement. He doesn't seem the least bit fazed, but then again, he has butlers in his house, too.

These people are on a whole different level with all their butlers and mansion-sized houses. RES is only a stop in a long chain of places they'll rule in the future. Be it politics or economics or even sports, these guys have it in their DNA to be leaders.

Everything probably starts at school and builds up from there. After all, they're more inclined to do business or politics with someone they studied with. It's all about connections.

I was so stupid to think I could belong when I first joined RES. Outsiders like me will always be that. Outsiders.

But then again, I never wanted the connections they offer. RES was and will always be my stop for Cambridge.

Or at least it was until Aiden barged into my life at the beginning of this year.

All my cards are being shuffled without my permission.

My heart caves as I recall my quarrel with Aiden. I can't believe I allowed Silver to get under my skin.

I look over at Ronan as he guides me down endless halls while texting away at his phone. "Do you guys hang out here a lot?"

"Not really. We usually go to the Meet Up."

"The Meet Up?"

"Yeah. Our secret hideout."

Oh. I wonder why Aiden never mentioned it before.

"Then why are we here today?" I ask.

"We come over when Uncle Jonathan isn't around."

"Do you bring girls, too?"

"Just Astrid and Silver."

I come to a halt, my fingers digging into the straps of my backpack. So she's been coming to Aiden's house the entire time.

Of course, she does.

"Shit." Ronan lifts his head from his phone. "Silver doesn't come anymore, so forget I mentioned her, okay?"

"Why doesn't she come anymore?"

He shrugs. "King doesn't want her around."

That's supposed to make me feel better, but it doesn't. My pessimistic brain conjures a different type of theory. If Aiden threw her out after he got tired of using her, then he'll throw me out any time, too.

Ronan smiles. "We all grew up together. It sticks, you know."

I knew he meant to reassure me, but his words only tie the noose tighter around my heart.

If Aiden discarded his childhood friend, what's stopping him from throwing me out when he only knew me yesterday?

I'm being dramatic. After all, I'm the one who asked him to stay away from her.

"Margo!" Ronan all but yells.

My attention snaps back to the present. Ronan has led us into a spacious, sparkly kitchen. The decor is spotless grey and white like in those cooking TV shows. A petite woman stands behind the counter, closing the stove.

At Ronan's shout, she turns around and comes out from around the corner. She appears in her mid to late forties. Her brown hair is pulled into a bun and covered by a disposable cap. She's wearing a black skirt and white shirt all complete with an apron.

"You startled me, boy." She scolds in a motherly tone.

"Sorry." Ronan doesn't appear sorry at all.

"Who's this?" She asks as her kind blue eyes fall on me.

Ronan clasps an arm around my shoulder. "This is Elsa. You know, like the princess in Frozen."

I elbow him and he winces. "Ouch. What was that for?"

Margo smiles. "I'm Margot, you can call me Margo like the boys. It's rare to see a new face here."

Interesting. So Aiden limits access to his house. Except for Silver, of course.

What? I'm not salty about that.

Not at all.

Ronan waggles his eyebrows. "She's the one that got King all worked up."

I elbow him again and this time, he lets me go. "And will break my ribs. Damn, Ellie. I didn't know you were so strong. Are you open for threesomes?"

Margot is the one who hits him this time.

"On second thought, don't tell King I mentioned that." He looks around before whispering to Margot. "Are there listening devices here?"

"I wish there were." Margot has a bit of an Irish accent.

When she faces me, it's with a renewed type of interest. "I'm glad to finally meet you, Elsa. Do you want anything to drink or eat?"

"I'm fine, thanks."

"I do!" Ronan's eyes glint like a kid waiting for his Christmas present. "Have you prepared the chips?"

She motions at the counter behind her where there are a few bowls of homemade chips. "They're cooling."

"You're the best, Margo!" Ronan slaps a noisy kiss on her cheek.

"Don't you have your own cook?" She sounds resigned as if she asked this a thousand times.

"They're not as good as you." Ronan snatches a chip and must've been burnt because he winces and drops it back down. "My offer to come over still stands. We'll pay you double what King does."

"Stop trying to take Margo away." Comes Aiden's familiar voice before he strolls inside with Xander on his toll.

Aiden changed into black trousers and a plain grey T-shirt that brings out the smouldering colour of his eyes. It doesn't help that the cloth tightens around his chest muscles highlighting his agile, sculpted physique.

My cheeks heat no matter how much I try to control my reaction. Why does he have to be so hot?

Aiden spares me an unreadable glance before he focuses back on Ronan who still hasn't given up on the burning chips.

Did I mention that I hate the tension between us?

No. Not the tension. I hate that he ignores me.

I've been his main focus since the beginning of the year, it stings to be reduced to nothing.

"I made an offer first, Ro. Get in line." Xander tosses a ball in the air and catches it with his head.

"No balls in my kitchen. You broke the dishes the other time." Margo scolds.

Xander tucks the ball under his arm. He's also in casual jeans and a denim jacket. "It was a one time only, Margo, come on."

"Yeah, Margo." Ronan quips. "Don't be a dictator."

"You have no right to talk. You almost burnt my kitchen

over the weekend. I can't believe I take one day off and all hell breaks loose."

Ronan smiles sheepishly and Aiden says, "That's it. No one is allowed in Margot's kitchen anymore."

"That's my boy." She smiles warmly at him. That motherly feel returns in full force even more than the look she gave Ronan earlier.

When Aiden smiles back, I'm struck by how beautiful his genuine smile is. I look for signs that he's putting on a mask, but right here, in his home with the closest thing he has to family, he appears carefree.

"And no one is taking Margot away." He gives pointed glares to Xander and Ronan.

The latter huffs. "I won't stop trying."

Xander lifts a shoulder. "Me neither."

"Stop it, boys." Margo gets between them. Her petite size is almost comical compared to their ridiculous height. "Don't fight in front of Elsa. It's not every day Aiden brings his girlfriend."

Girlfriend.

I don't know why my cheeks heat at that word. Aiden and I never talked about what we call each other. We didn't even make it official yet.

I look over at Aiden, but he has that infuriating poker face on.

Xander wraps an arm around my shoulder and brings me to his side. He's so close that my nostrils fill with his expensive perfume. "She was my girlfriend first, weren't you, love?"

One moment, Xander is standing beside me, the next, he's shoved back and my shoulder is free of his arm. Aiden has him by the collar of his jacket and is dragging him away.

With a chip in hand, Ronan lowers his head to whisper in a teasing tone, "Don't say a word about the threesome suggestion. My life depends on it."

Still clutching Xander, Aiden grabs Ronan by the back of his nape.

"My chips!" Ronan hugs a bowl to his chest as Aiden drags them both away.

"Tell everyone I was a good person!" Ronan shouts over his shoulder at me. "I want this line on my tombstone, *He had a 7 inch dick and used it well.*"

Xander and I burst into laughter as they all disappear around the corner.

"Boys." Margo shakes her head and places the remaining bowls of chips on the tray.

"Let me help," I offer, setting my backpack on a stool.

"It's all right, sweetie. I can do it."

"Please let me. I do everything on my own at home." And I'm not used to people serving me.

"It's so rare to find reliable teens these days." She steps aside and motions at another tray.

After she adds a few other snacks and mayonnaise to the mix, we carry the trays out of the kitchen.

"Have you been living here for long?" I ask.

"I've been here since Aiden was born." A look of nostalgia covers her features. "He was my boy since then."

"You raised him?"

"I did," she says with pride.

"Then you knew his mother?" I'm being nosy, but I hope she doesn't mind.

"Poor woman died too soon."

I'm like a cat who caught a fish and would do anything to keep it. "Aiden doesn't talk much about her."

"There's nothing to talk about." Margo's warm tone turns biting. "Alicia was messed up and took all sorts of pills."

I don't miss the note of dismay in Margo's tone as if she either hates Alicia or hates what she did. It's probably the latter since Alicia's suicide must've wounded Aiden and Margo seems to care about his wellbeing.

I'm about to probe some more and ask if it was suicide or an accident, but Margo stops. "I forgot the salt."

"I'll go back with you."

"No, go ahead. The game is about to start and the boys would flip without their chips." She points down the hall. "The theatre room is around the corner."

Of course they have a theatre room. Why did I think we'd watch the game in the lounge area like normal people?

When Margo trudges back from where we came from, I sigh and continue my path. I stop down the hall. Margo forgot to mention whether I should turn left or right. There are equally long hallways on both sides.

Footsteps sound down the hall. Maybe the butler or one of the boys returned and I can ask them.

As the footsteps approach, they're more measured and confident like what I'd imagine a prime minister or a president's footsteps to sound like.

A tall man appears from the right. He's wearing a tailored navy blue suit that screams wealth and status. It's not until I meet his gaze that I'm stuck staring at the older version of Aiden.

Jonathan King.

I saw him on TV and in newspapers and a few times at school, but this is the first time I'm this close to him.

He has the same jet black hair as Aiden, although Jonathan is more styled and streaked with a few white strands. His jaw is more defined than Aiden's. His eyes appear a darker grey than his son's. If I thought Aiden's gaze is intimidating, then his father's is a killer.

His attention falls on me with pure aggressiveness.

FORTY-ONE

My grip tightens on the tray so I don't drop it.

If I weren't so sure that Jonathan King wouldn't kill me with so many witnesses in the house, I would've bolted towards the door.

How can someone show such aggressiveness on a first meeting?

He cools down fast. A welcoming expression takes over his silver fox features.

"Hello," he says in a smooth posh accent and offers me a tight-lipped smile along with his large hand.

If I didn't sense the earlier aggression in my soul and felt it in my bones, I would've thought it was all in my head.

"Hello." I hold the tray with one hand. The heavy weight falls on my arm and palm.

The moment I slip my hand in his, he squeezes so hard that I wince.

Uncle Jaxon taught me to always give firm handshakes. He said that first impressions matter the most and in the business world, status and deals can be decided upon handshakes.

As a rule, Uncle never deals with anyone who has weak or soft handshakes. Even Aunt's handshake is as firm as Uncle's. As a result, my handshakes are as strong as theirs.

However, the onslaught of a near-aggressive handshake from Jonathan catches me completely by surprise. Maybe his handshake is as strong as his business tycoon status. Or maybe this aggression is only directed towards me.

Either way, I don't give weak handshakes.

I meet Jonathan King's cold eyes and squeeze back as hard as my strength allows. My other hand screams with pain at holding all the tray's weight, but there's no way I'm bailing out first.

Something like contempt flashes on Jonathan's blank face. At this moment, he looks so much like Aiden, it's uncanny. Now, I know where the heir got his personality.

Jonathan King and his son are the type of people who crush while staring at their opponents in the eyes.

To say I'm not intimidated by the sheer power Jonathan exudes without talking would be a lie. However, I won't cower away.

He can break my bones and I'll still squeeze with the intact bones I have left.

"Dad."

Aiden's detached voice comes from the side. I was lost in my silent war with Jonathan that I didn't sense his presence.

That's a first.

Jonathan's sharp gaze slides from me to Aiden without breaking the handshake. I stare incredulously at the battle that erupts between Father and son.

Aiden is a carbon copy of the older King. It's like a battle royale between a larger-than-life power and his younger self.

The king and his heir.

I'm not sure who's winning or if there needs to be a winner, but the tension hangs in the air like a thick sheen of smoke.

Suffocating.

Mysterious.

Enthralling.

"Have fun with your party, Son."

Just like that, Jonathan lets me go as smoothly and as predatory as a panther.

"Will do."

Jonathan smiles like a refined, aristocratic gentleman. Not

too welcoming, but also not repulsive. It's conserved with a hint of the darkness that coats Aiden like a second skin.

The dark demons are in their damn genes.

After giving me another once over, Jonathan starts towards the entrance with domineering strides.

I face Aiden, thinking he's watching his father like I just did.

Instead, Aiden's full concentration is on the tray in my shaking hand. He snatches and carries it in his grasp without uttering a word or sparing me a glance.

He strides in the direction Margo and I were heading to.

I massage the hand that Jonathan nearly broke and fall in step with Aiden.

"What was that all about?" I ask.

Silence.

"Aiden?"

More silence, but his strides turn wider.

Did I mention how much it sucks to be on his bad side? Who thought someone like Aiden would use the silent treatment?

I jog and stand in front of him with both my arms flung wide.

He halts and cuts me a glare so harsh, it's like he's slicing me open with knives. His knuckles tighten around the tray.

"W-what is it?"

This side of him always puts me on high alert. Aiden isn't the type who parades his emotions so freely. The fact that he seems close to combusting means something disastrous is bound to happen.

"Say something." I push when he remains silent yet again.

"Stay *away* from my father." He enunciates every word in a near growl.

"I didn't approach him, I —"

"I don't give a fuck about what you did or didn't do. You don't speak to Jonathan. You don't shake hands with him, and you certainly don't fucking talk to him. When you see him, you turn and walk in the opposite direction. Is that clear?"

My head spins. "Why?"

"Because I fucking said so."

"I'm sorry, *your majesty*, but I don't do things because you fucking said so."

"Elsa..." He growls, deep and low.

"Tell me why."

"This is one of the times where you just say yes and don't argue with me."

"Or what?"

His metallic eyes turn calculative. "Or I'll get Reed drunk and let Knight take her home."

"You... wouldn't."

"Watch me." He brushes past me into a room.

My heart skips a beat.

I just provoked the ugly, monstrous side of Aiden. The side who doesn't care who he hurts as long as he gets what he wants.

For him, Kim is just a means to an end—which is me. He used her before and will use her again to prove he can make me agree to whatever he wishes.

He knows how much Kim means to me and that I won't hesitate to protect her.

What he doesn't know is that two can play this game.

This time, Aiden isn't going to win.

FORTY-TWO

I should've known that this night will be a disaster the moment Cole and Kim walked into the theatre room together.

Or when Xander's jaw ticked.

Or when Aiden watched the scene with cold calculation.

We all sit facing the huge TV that occupies the entire wall. Hell, it's the same size as cinemas' screens. The leather sofas can easily swallow a person. There's even a place to put hamburgers, chips, and beer.

Kim and I settle for soda. I ignore the fact that Aiden snatches the regular coke and thrusts a diet coke in my hands. I told him before that diet coke is only lower on calories but isn't healthy. However, I let it go this time.

If there's anything I learnt from being with Aiden, then it's to pick my battles.

Right now, the most important battle is to know what the hell he has planned for Kim.

When I tried to slide in beside her, Aiden dragged me and sat me between his parted thighs.

He's all around me and surrounding me. His chest hovers inches away from my back, but I can taste his scent mixed with the after-shower gel. Every breath I take is filled with his overpowering presence. He seeps under my skin and settles in my core with a harsh wave of lust. Aiden isn't even touching me, but he doesn't need to. It's like he owned me since the first touch.

The air ripples with the promise of his skin on mine. I clench my thighs together and focus on the screen.

Today, Arsenal plays the most important games of the season in the European Champions League. If I were with Uncle, we'd be hotblooded Gunners cheering our hearts out like Xander and Ronan.

They jump like rabbits on crack, shouting and even kicking imaginary balls. They even speak in thick cockney accents that posh folks shouldn't even have heard of. It must be due to mingling with other football fans.

I wonder if Aiden can speak cockney, too.

The theatre room fills with fan cheers, the commentators' enthusiasm and Xander and Ronan's fanatic madness.

Cole and Aiden are the calm types of audience. Cole says some *ooh* and *aah's*, but he never moves from his position.

Kim sits beside me and Aiden with Cole on her other side, drinking her second—or third—beer.

She might be an Elites' fan, but she doesn't care much for the Premier League.

While Ronan and Xander shout, curse, and throw chips and snacks everywhere, Kim watches them with keen interest like they're the game.

In a way, they make an entertaining show. When Arsenal is on the run, they kick balls with them. They throw imaginary free kicks and bump shoulders when something good happens.

I'm laughing by the time they sing along fan chants in an off-tune. Kim laughs, too, with her eyes half drooping. When she finishes her beer, Aiden pushes another one into her hand and she accepts it with a sloppy smile.

I cut him a glare. "Are you trying to get her drunk?"

His cold gaze remains on the screen, but he doesn't appear all that interested in the game. "She's already there."

"Aiden." My voice lowers as I half-turn so my back rests against his bent thigh. "What are you doing?"

His metallic gaze slides to me in a slow, predatory way.

Just like that, Aiden's loathsome, psycho side comes out to play. Just because I overlook his nature sometimes doesn't mean it disappears.

"Do you agree to what I said earlier?"

"Not until you tell me why." I thin my lips in a line to avoid lashing out on him and causing a scene.

"Wrong answer." And just like that, his attention shifts back to the game.

I push away from him, but he traps my elbow in a deathly grip, forbidding my escape.

With a frustrated sigh, I scoot closer to Kim as much as his clutch allows.

Her navy blue striped dress reaches the middle of her thighs and is bunched at the bottom. A flush covers her cheeks and her pupils dilate. She's definitely at the drunk stage.

I try to snatch her beer away. God knows what Aiden has put in it. I want to think that he wouldn't hurt Kim and that he's not the type to drug women, but he's a psycho demon who doesn't stop until he gets what he wants.

Kim isn't a person to him. She's just a means to an end.

She pulls her beer closer to her chest and pouts as if I wanted to take her favourite toy.

"Kim. Come on, you drunk enough."

"Nah-uh," she slurs. "I'm totally sober, Ellie."

For the next few minutes, I try and fail miserably in breaking her up with her beer.

Aiden watches with that emotionless coldness that I want to slap off his face.

I don't know how he figured out how Kim becomes wild when she's drunk, but he's using it for his advantage.

The first half of the game ends with nil to nil. Xander and Ronan finally sit down. Ronan devours chips like a starved soldier at war while Xander throws hard glances in Kim's direction.

When the European Anthem plays, she staggers on unsteady

feet and sings her heart out with it. In slurred German. I knew she has German classes, but I didn't know she's this fluent.

Ronan puts a hand on his heart and places the bowl of chips up as if it's a cup and sings along. In gibberish.

Cole chuckles "Well, what the hell."

He stands so Kim is between him and Ronan and sings Ode de Joy in a more perfect German than Kim's—though it's probably because he's not dead drunk like her.

"Don't kill my vibe, Captain!" Ronan throws a chip at him. "Sing in the gibberish version we all know."

I laugh both at his silliness and at Kim's easy smile and slurred words. It's worth it if she's having a good time.

I attempt to stand and join them, but Aiden grabs my arm and stares at a solemn-faced Xander. "Hey, Knight. Maybe you should take Reed home before her parents worry."

"No!" I shout at the same time as the song cuts off.

All eyes turn to me as if I'm the maniac who just suggested that Xander, Kim's archenemy, should drop her home.

My cheeks heat as I cut Aiden a harsh glare, he would've been flamed or even embarrassed if he were anywhere near a human being status.

I jerk to my feet and pull him outside of the room. I'm surprised he follows without a word.

"Don't move, Kim," I tell her and address Xander. "And don't touch her."

Cole nods in my direction as if in assurance. I don't know why I trust him, but I do.

Ronan seems oblivious to the whole mess, busy stuffing his mouth with chips and snacks.

Once we're outside, I slam the door shut and walk into Aiden's space. "Stop using Kim to force me into doing things."

"And if I say no?" He's cool, so cool, it makes my temper hit the roof.

"Kim is my best friend."

"I know that."

"Then how can you suggest to send her home with her tormentor? What if he hurts her? Are you going to take responsibility for that?"

"I don't take responsibility for other people's shit. Besides, if Knight wanted to hurt her, he would've done that years ago, not now."

"That's not the point!"

"Then what is?"

"If you want my trust, you can't use my best friend's wellbeing to threaten me. That'll make me trust you less not more."

"If you agreed, I wouldn't have used this method. Stay away from Jonathan and I'll stay away from Reed. It's an easy bargain."

The fact that he insists on that makes me more curious about King Enterprises' tycoon. However, I'm not curious to the point of risking Kim's wellbeing.

Aiden knows he got me where it hurts.

"Fine!" I slam my shoulder against his arm as I go back inside, seething with pent-up anger.

I clutch Kim's elbow, halting her drinking competition with Ronan. "We're leaving."

"Naww," she whines. "Look, Ron is teaching me how to take shots."

"*Ron?*" Xander scoffs, his shoulders crowding with tension.

"Come on, Kim." I drag her, but she might as well have turned into stone.

"I'm staying." She squirms free and goes back to Ronan as if he's holding baby Jesus instead of a bottle of beer.

My attempts are futile no matter how much I try. It's impossible to control Kim when she's drunk.

Aiden smirks at me from his sitting position beside Cole.

Dickhead.

During the second half, Kim is cheering with Ronan non-stop.

"Why do you say Gunners?" she asks him.

"Because it's Arsenal, babe!"

That earns him a smack at the nape from Xander.

Ignoring Aiden's attempts to get me to sit between his legs, I join Kim, Ronan, and Xander. After two beers, I loosen enough to cheer for the team. The game is too exciting and fast-paced not to enjoy it.

When Arsenal scores, the four of us pull each other in a group hug. Cole cheers from the background, and a strong hand grabs me by the collar of my shirt. I wiggle Aiden off and continue celebrating.

I'm so mad at him right now. The least he can do is to not ruin the game for me.

There are still fifteen minutes in the game when Kim collapses on one of the chairs, snoring softly. I move her to a comfortable position and return to watch the rest of the game.

Ronan, Xander and I argue about the substitute players that came in the second half.

The game ends one to nil. We could've done better but we're on the way to the championship.

I celebrate with Ronan and Xan and even Cole who joined us near the end by singing 'We are the champions'.

A phone rings. Kim's.

I fish into her pocket. Her mum.

Shit.

She'll ground Kim if she returns home in this state. I dig my teeth in my bottom lip as I contemplate a solution.

"Spend the night." Aiden quips from behind me. I startle and that only makes him push into my back more.

"What? No." It comes out more surprised rather than cold.

"Just spend the night with Reed." He sighs heavily. "Don't make everything so difficult."

My options are limited. I can ask Aiden to drive us the small distance to Kim's house and have her grounded. He can drive us to my home and put Kim in a bad light in front of Aunt and Uncle.

"Fine, but I'm locking the door."

I take the phone outside where there isn't noise and answer Kim's mum. I tell her Kim is spending the night with me and that she's already fast asleep. She agrees without questions. Then I call Uncle and after geeking about Arsenal's win, I tell him I'm spending the night at Kim's.

Weird. It doesn't feel bad to lie to Aunt and Uncle anymore.

When I return inside to where the guys—except for Aiden— are celebrating, my spine jerks upright. He's watching me with an unreadable gleam that resembles the first day we met.

I'm definitely locking the door tonight.

FORTY-THREE

Xander helps me in getting Kim to the guest room. I tried to stop him, but he wasn't hearing my protests.

As soon as he placed her on the bed, I kicked him out and turned the key.

After removing her shoes, I tuck Kim in and cover her with a sheet. She's mumbling something that sounds like Ode to Joy by the time I shimmy out of my uniform and bra. I remain in boy shorts and my sleeveless T-shirt.

I lie next to Kim.

Exhaustion rears on my nerves endings, but for the life of me, I can't fall asleep. The bed is comfy and the pillow seems to be filled with feathers. The guest room is as sterile as a hotel room. All white and prim with nothing personal in sight.

As I stare at the ceiling, all I keep thinking about is the chaos that happened today. Dr Khan then Silver then Jonathan King.

Aiden had to be the cherry on top by deciding to be a jerk.

I didn't miss how he stood by the side of the door while I kicked Xander out.

I puff a frustrated breath and screw my lids shut.

Half an hour later, I still can't sleep. I skim through Instagram and get bored soon after. I push the covers away and slip on a bathrobe before getting out.

The house is eerily calm as I make my way to the kitchen. The boys must've all left and Aiden is fast asleep.

On the counter, I find chips and whipped cream and even

some untouched Hamburgers. I sit down on the stool and devour them all. The rich taste fills my mouth.

Aunt would kill me for this, but it's been forever since I had my last junk meal. Maybe years? Uncle used to take me for a random junk meal occasionally—and in secret, but after my heart acted up in middle school, he stopped the habit altogether.

Half of me feels like a sinner, but the other half just enjoys this rare meal. Once done, I clean up the kitchen and head back to the room.

Then, a crazy idea comes to mind. I want to see where Aiden sleeps. It's stupid after all what he's done, but it's not fair that he saw my room but I didn't see his.

I go downstairs where I saw him head earlier and suppress a yelp whenever an automatic soft light goes on. It's impossible to sneak about in this house.

A sound of splashing water comes from my right and I follow it like a curious kitten. I round the corner and stop in front of double glass doors.

On the other side, water glints under a closed dome. The indoor pool is completely dark aside from the soft white lights coming from within the water.

Aiden sits on the steps, half into the water and half above it. He's not swimming or attempting to. He just sits there, his naked back rippling with tension and his arrow tattoos pointing at his sides.

The mere sight of water increases my breathing. My hands turn clammy and the itch to scrub them overwhelms me.

You can do this.

With one last deep breath, I open the door and slip inside.

Aiden's head cocks to the side in my direction. His wet inky hair falls in a perfectly imperfect mess across his forehead. Droplets of water draw a path along the fine hairs of his chest and the rippled abs and to underneath his black boxer briefs. I find myself following them as if I'm enchanted.

I'm supposed to be mad at him, damn it.

"I was coming to get you."

I halt a safe distance away from the water. "I locked the door."

"Do you think a locked door will keep me away from what's mine, sweetheart?"

"I'm mad at you. If I want you to stay out, you'll stay out."

"Sure thing." He doesn't seem to believe a word I say. "Now, remove that robe and come join me."

"No way!" My shout borders on hysterical as I fist my hand into the robe.

He tilts his head further. "Saying 'no' doesn't have to be your knee-jerk reaction to everything I ask."

"It's not that." I motion vaguely at the pool. The bottom isn't even visible. "Deep water scares me."

His smokey gaze roams over me for a second as if he's contemplating the information. "I'm on the steps. You won't drown."

"Still no." I clutch the railings. "Besides, did you miss the part where I'm mad at you?"

"I'm mad at you, too. We can be mad at each other while you're sitting on my lap."

While my body is tempted by his offer, my gaze strays to the pool then away again. There's no way I'm getting into the water. Hell, I can't even look at it for more than a second without feeling something crawling along my skin.

"You can come willingly or I'll drag you."

I huff and turn to leave.

"Don't run or I'll feel the need to chase and conquer, sweetheart."

A part of me wants to do just that and see his reaction, but for today, I'm a coward. And he's right, we're both mad at each other and I hate it.

I hate that we're not close when this is my first visit to his house.

I open the robe and hang it on the railing, remaining in a sleeveless white T-shirt and boy shorts. My steps are cautious as I approach the pool where Aiden awaits me with a furrowed brow.

"How about we go to your room?" I ask as a last resort.

"Next time."

Once I'm within reach, Aiden clasps his hand around my wrist and tugs me down. I yelp as I splash in the water to my middle. I land on his lap facing deep, dark water.

My heart slams in my chest, wanting out. Needing out. I feel the colour drain from my face as I continue staring at the water.

This isn't real. It isn't real.

"Hey," Aiden's hands snake along my neck. I turn around so my knees are on each side of his thighs on the steps and my chest is flush against his. I wrap my arms around his neck and hide my face in the crook of his shoulders, breathing heavily into his skin.

"Talk to me," Aiden's fingers dig into my hair and he undoes my bun, letting my hair fall to my shoulders.

"I hate it." My voice trembles. "I hate so much water."

"Why?"

"I don't know. I wish I knew."

"Then let's talk about something else."

I open my eyes the slightest bit, my breathing still ragged. "Like what?"

"Like how you celebrated with the guys earlier when I was sitting right there."

I chuckle. "Are you being jealous right now?"

"I'm stating facts."

"Right." I jab his shoulders. "Besides, I didn't agree to be your girlfriend yet."

His arms tighten around my waist in a vice-like grip. "Titles don't matter, the only thing that matters is that you're mine. Stop acting like you aren't."

"And you stop making me distrust you." I palm his cheeks. "I want to trust you, Aiden, I really do, so help me out."

With me on top of him, he plunges in the water. I shriek when I'm drowned to my neck.

"Damn it, Aiden. This isn't the way to help me trust you."

"Shhh." he soothes as my limbs shake. "Trust me."

I hold onto him with all my might because if I don't, I'll be left to the merciless water.

"Aiden…" I warn.

"Just imagine that it's only us here."

"I can't." The water is about to swallow me. Those hands will keep me down. I won't be able to breathe or —

Aiden's lips press against mine in a slow, dominant kiss. His fingers thread into my hair as he continues his relentless exploration.

Fear is the least of my worries as he trails his lips to the hollow of my throat then to my transparent rosy nipple through the soaked white cloth. He bites down on the hard tip, and I moan, my head tipping back.

He divides his attention between my two breasts; sucking, biting, and teasing.

His free hand pulls my boy shorts down until he finds my aching pussy. My head falls on his shoulder where the water barely reaches his collarbone.

His fingers find my folds and he rubs up and down before thrusting inside me with two fingers at the same time.

"Oh, God," I breathe into him.

"Relax," he rasps into my ear, working me faster.

I mentally order my body to loosen the tension.

Then, Aiden is kissing me again and it's like an aphrodisiac. I thread my fingers into the back of his wet hair as I kiss him back with complete abandon.

A different tension builds inside me and I let go. I cave into Aiden and come in a wordless cry.

But he's not done.

No.

He backs me against the edge of the pool. My back hits the cold tiles and he wraps my legs around his waist as he thrusts inside me.

I gasp, holding onto his shoulders. He kisses me wildly and with untamed frenzy as he pounds into me. My arse hits the tiles with each of his merciless thrusts. The water intensifies the friction at one second and takes it away the next. It's like a game.

"Aiden…" My nails dig into the rippling muscles of his back.

"What is it, sweetheart?" he grunts against my mouth.

"I… I…"

He wraps his hand around my throat, and something inside me cracks.

I come at the same time as his thrusts turn wild. He pulls almost completely out of me and then pushes back in.

When he softens inside me, I hide my face in his neck, tears rimming my eyes.

Aiden just took a scary place and turned it into a happy place.

I palm his cheeks and kiss him as he carries me out with my legs wrapped around his waist.

FORTY-FOUR

For weeks, the six of us watched football together. Even Kim has become a regular in our nights at the King's mansion. Sometimes, Levi and Astrid would join—when Levi doesn't have a game.

Aiden still didn't take me to the 'Meet Up' but he promised to.

During all the time we spent at Aiden's place, we bonded over football—the only thing we all love.

I learnt how goofy Ronan actually is. How passionate Xander can be and how cool, but enthusiastic Cole is.

And Aiden.

Damn Aiden.

Since that night in the pool, he's been taking each of my phobias and turning them into an erotic bliss. Once, he snuck into my room, turned off my night lamp and jumped me in bed. I was so wet and came within seconds.

Another time, he took me hard and merciless against a table in the basement near his indoor pool. I couldn't think about how closed off the space was or how I'd suffocate to death inside it. All I could feel was the shattering pleasure as he rammed into me from behind.

We had sex in the pool so many times, I lost count.

While all that pleasure washed away the fear, it was only temporary.

I still wouldn't set foot near a pool, a basement, or the dark if Aiden isn't holding my hand or carrying me in his arms.

That strangely sounds like trust.

Do I trust Aiden?

I want to. God, I really want to extinguish whatever little distrust I have for him. It doesn't help that he always resorts to his manipulative ways whenever he wants something.

Aiden will never stop snatching what he wants just because he can.

When Jamie, a rugby player, asked if we can tag along for an assignment, I agreed.

Aiden, being his usual jerk, told me to say no.

When I didn't agree, he just walked away. A day later, Jamie apologised that he won't be able to do the project with me.

Later, I heard that Jamie's rugby gear was ruined and his place in the team was also under jeopardy for alcohol addiction.

It didn't take a genius to know who was the reason behind it. When I faced Aiden about it, he said, "The sorry fuck shouldn't have looked in the direction of what's mine. Besides, he needed a wake-up call to play rugby without polluting his liver."

"What are you? Rugby police?" I asked.

His eyes darkened in that way that made my thighs clench together in both dread and anticipation. "Now you prefer rugby over football?"

"I'm a Football girl, but that's not the point. Stop being a jerk to everyone."

"I'm not a jerk to everyone. I'm a jerk to who threatens what's mine."

He even posted a pic of my back view as I snuggled in his lap during a game night with the caption 'Football girl'.

After that incident, and a few others where Aiden and his pack of wolves shut out anyone who breathes in my direction, it's like I'm being hated all over again.

Only now, it's for a different reason. They hate seeing me

with Aiden and the rest of the football crew. The queen of haters is Silver, but she's been keeping her claws hidden.

I don't like the smugness she has on her face whenever she brushes past me and throws one of her 'peasant' taunts.

After school, I'm bummed that Aiden has practice and won't be able to drive me home.

Since Aunt and Uncle work today, I was planning on him staying the night and forcing him to watch a crime thriller with me. I don't know when I moved on from pleading with him to leave to where I want him to spend the nights.

Everything is a process with Aiden. It's not easy to look past the surface, but when I do, I can clearly see the little gestures. Like the way he always puts me on top when we sleep. How he prepares breakfast when I wake up. How he runs long hot baths for me. Even his crude night and morning texts can be sweet sometimes.

He's slowly but surely crumbling any wall I've been keeping around my fragile heart.

I even followed him back the other day on Instagram.

Truth is, I never had a choice about whether or not I should let him in. Aiden barged right in and carved his comfy place in my chest.

The thought of plucking him out brings a taste of bitterness and horror.

On my way to the car park to meet Kim, my phone rings. I grin like an idiot when Aiden's name flashes alongside that picture of our first kiss in Ronan's house. He changed it for me, but I didn't remove it.

"Aren't you supposed to be in practice?" I ask.

"The keyword being 'supposed'. Coach will kill me if he finds me talking on the phone."

"Then go. I don't want you killed."

"It's worth it if I get to hear your voice."

I dig my teeth into my bottom lip to stop myself from grinning like an idiot.

"Where are you?" he asks, his voice dropping a range.

"Heading home with Kim."

"Don't let her stay the night. I'm coming to stake my claim after practice."

"Didn't you stake your claim already?" Still smiling, I walk slower than needed, kicking imaginary rocks.

"Not even close, sweetheart. I need to stake my claim some more just in case. I don't like feeling threatened."

"Oh, the mighty Aiden King feels threatened?"

"If you keep insisting on having the guys watch the games with us, damn straight I feel threatened."

I chuckle and press the back of my hand against my mouth. "They're your friends."

"Disposable if they threaten what's mine." He sounds dead serious when he says it. "If one of those fuckers put their hands on you again, I'll break it and their legs so they can kiss their last football season goodbye."

God. He's an anomaly.

Sometimes, I feel like Cole, Ronan and especially Xander poke his possessive side just to see him act out. They're used to the calculative, albeit calm version of Aiden. His carefully tucked monstrous version is frightening, but they want to see it anyway.

"King!" Someone shouts in the background.

"It's Coach." Aiden releases a sound between a mumble and a groan.

"Don't get killed."

"Not when I have a claim to stake." He chuckles. "See you later, sweetheart."

"See you," I say back but he's already hung up.

I'm still smiling to myself as if I lost my mind—which wouldn't be wrong considering that I have feelings for Aiden.

It's screwed up and wrong, but it's true.

I walk to the car park, trying to convince myself that I won't cave and wait until after his practice, or even watch from the wirings like some of the fangirls.

It's not that I'm above being a fangirl, but I need to study before I lose not only my heart, body and soul to Aiden but also my future.

"You promised, Uncle."

My feet come to a screeching halt at Silver's agitated voice. I hide behind the corner leading to the car park and peek my head.

Silver stands near a shiny black Mercedes with... Jonathan King?

His broad, tall frame towers over her. He's wearing a three-piece black suit all complete with diamond studs. Silver looks pristine as usual in her pressed school uniform and designer shoes.

"Keep your voice down," Jonathan says in a firm, authoritative tone.

"You said she'll be gone. You said Aiden will dump that little bitch Elsa in a heartbeat. Obviously, he hasn't. If anything, he's doting on her more than ever."

My nails dig into the stone as I register the load of information. Aiden told his father he'll dump me?

"Silver, Silver. Didn't your father teach you the tactic of luring before attacking? A prey is ought to fall harder when she trusts she's not in danger, not the other way around. That's what Aiden has been doing all this time. Luring the prey. Now that she trusts him, her fall will crush her apart."

My breathing hitches and the itch starts beneath my skin. I grip the straps of my backpack and turn to leave, not wanting to hear anything else.

They're lying.

They're both lying.

"How can you be so sure, Uncle?" Silver asks.

I come to a halt despite myself, my fingers trembling around the strap of my backpack.

"Elsa's parents killed his mother. The only reason Aiden has ever looked in that monster's direction is to make her pay for her parents' sin."

Jonathan and Silver continue talking, but I'm not hearing a thing. My feet carry me in the opposite direction, but I'm not seeing a thing.

The colour has drained from my cheeks and my heart slams against my ribs, wanting out.

Out.

Out!

I trip and fall, but I stand back up again. Something burns in my knees but it's nothing compared to the itching burn beneath my skin.

It's like I'm igniting from the inside without fuel or even fire.

I trip again, but this time, a hand clutches my arm and steadies me. I push whoever grabbed me away. They're asking something, but I can't hear anything over the loud buzz in my ears.

My unfocused gaze stays ahead, I'm already in the school, walking God knows where.

I need to go to the pitch and ask Aiden to tell me that what I just heard is a lie.

That his father is mistaken. That my parents didn't kill his mother.

That he didn't approach me for revenge.

I will destroy you. He told upon our first meeting.

No. No. No…

My feet falter as I find myself at the edge of the pool. Everyone but the football and rugby teams have left for the day so it's empty and dark except for the blue water.

What the hell am I doing here?

I turn to leave, but a strong hand pushes me. I fall, shrieking.

The sound is drowned when I'm swallowed whole into the water.

Everything turns black.

TO BE CONTINUED …
The story continues in *Steel Princess*.

WHAT'S NEXT?

Thank you so much for reading *Deviant King*! If you liked it, please leave a review.
Your support means the world to me.

If you're thirsty for more discussions with other readers of the series, you can join the Facebook group, *Rina Kent's Spoilers Room*.

Next up is the continuation of Aiden and Elsa's story in *Steel Princess*.

The princess isn't supposed to dethrone the king.

Elsa

He said he'll destroy me, and he did.
I might have lost the battle, but the war is far from over.
They say it starts with one move to dethrone the king.
No one mentioned he'll yank me with him on the way down.

Aiden

If Steel's little princess wants a war, then war it is.
There's only one rule: my rules or none at all.
By all means, show me what you got, sweetheart.

ALSO BY RINA KENT

For more books by the author and a reading order, please visit:
www.rinakent.com/books

ABOUT THE AUTHOR

Rina Kent is an international bestselling author of everything enemies to lovers romance.

Darkness is her playground, suspense is her best friend, and twists are her brain's food. However, she likes to think she's a romantic at heart in some way, so don't kill her hopes just yet.

Her heroes are anti-heroes and villains because she was always the weirdo who fell in love with the guys no one roots for. Her books are sprinkled with a touch of mystery, a healthy dose of angst, a pinch of violence, and lots of intense passion.

Rina spends her private days in a peaceful town in North Africa daydreaming about the next plot idea or laughing like an evil mastermind when those ideas come together.

Find Rina Below:
Website: www.rinakent.com
Neswsletter: www.subscribepage.com/rinakent
BookBub: www.bookbub.com/profile/rina-kent
Amazon: www.amazon.com/Rina-Kent/e/B07MM54G22
Goodreads: www.goodreads.com/author/show/18697906.
Rina_Kent
Instagram: www.instagram.com/author_rina
Facebook: www.facebook.com/rinaakent
Reader Group: www.facebook.com/groups/rinakent.club
Pinterest: www.pinterest.co.uk/AuthorRina/boards
Tiktok: www.tiktok.com/@rina.kent
Twitter: twitter.com/AuthorRina